RESTORATION

THE RISE OF RESURGENCE

RESTORATION

THE RISE OF RESURGENCE

BOOK II

JONATHAN,
YOU WERE RIGHT!
THE STORY REALLY IS
ABOUT CHARACTER
DEVELOPMENT!!!

Joshua W. Nelson

Copyright © 2017 by Joshua W. Nelson

All rights reserved. No part of this book may be used or reproduced in any manner whatsoever including Internet usage, without written permission of the author.

This is a work of fiction. The names, characters, places, or events used in this book are the product of the author's imagination or used fictitiously. Any resemblance to actual people, alive or deceased, events or locales is completely coincidental.

Book design by Maureen Cutajar
www.gopublished.com

ISBN: 978-1521477519

Special Thanks to the Friends who gave me the Inspiration for Dan, Jason, and Wayne. This one is for you.

INTRO

AltCon Headquarters – Boardroom

Terrence Jolston stood at the head of the boardroom table as the various members of the board of directors began to file into the room. Terrence was usually the last to arrive at these meetings, but today he arrived 15 minutes early. Each move of this chess game needed to be played perfectly to instill the right amount of fear and subservience in the members of the Board. Terrence's part in this game could not be questioned.

As the first members arrived, each glanced in Terrence's direction but said nothing as they took their customary places around the table. Placed before each chair were two separate hand-held displays. They were currently blank and would only connect to Terrence's main display at his command. Again, timing was key in how the information was doled out.

These men and women, while each brilliant in their own right, were chosen by the Old Man for their lack of backbone. They were not the type to question orders, nor were they the type to show initiative. At least, this was what the Old Man thought about them. The one exception, the former head of the board, had overstepped his bounds, and this was why Terrence now stood in front of the assembled "elite" of AltCon.

Terrence imagined he would need to start off the conversation and lead the members of the Board along his prearranged path. Therefore, it was a bit of a shock to Terrence when one of the Board members actually spoke up.

"Where is the head of the board?"

Wearing a sharp pantsuit, one of the more unassuming members sat with a ramrod straight back near the front of the table. Terrence couldn't remember her name, and he wasn't inclined to try. None of the board members had ever showed more than the slightest bit of initiative.

"He arrived just a short while ago," Terrence answered. "Please take your seats and the meeting will begin shortly."

What Terrence hadn't said—but what they would all learn in but a few minutes—was that Terrence was now that very head. The woman had unwittingly played into his plan, and Terrence didn't think he could have crafted the situation better if he had orchestrated it himself.

As each member sat in their seats Terrence waited patiently. He watched them as they waited. Some fidgeted. Others attempted to act unworried, but their eyes betrayed them, moving around the room in a searching pattern but not knowing what to look for. No one knew why they were there, and so no one was truly relaxed. The great reveal that he had in store would happen all at once in order to achieve the greatest effect.

Once the fractious group of snivelers were all in place and waiting long enough, Terrence activated the first of the two hand-held devices sitting in front of them all. What they saw was the same article Terrence had seen in the Old Man's office the previous day, only in a digital format. Terrence didn't bother with any preamble before he activated the screens, and he allowed each member to fully absorb the information in front of them. There were audible gasps, and one of the men started sobbing.

It was the same woman who asked the earlier question who spoke first. Terrence didn't need any strong willed characters on this board—ones who would challenge him from the outset of his reign—and decided he would simply replace her if she spoke out another time.

"What the hell is this? You said the head of the board arrived a short while ago. Is this supposed to be some kind of sick joke?"

"I did not misspeak," Terrence responded. "The Head of the Board did arrive just minutes ago. Only it is not the man in those pictures."

"Are you saying that you are..."

At that moment, Terrence activated the second screen in front of each individual. Instead of an article detailing the death of the head of the board, this display detailed the appointment of Terrence, however on a temporary basis, to the Head position. The order was signed by the Old Man himself. His word was not to be questioned.

Sure, Terrence could have simply had the Old Man's orders replace the article on that first screen, but the visual impact wouldn't have been as strong. Terrence wanted them looking back and forth between both screens. The psychological effect would be greater as their minds filled in the blanks. The imagination can produce horrors more frightening than the truth, after all.

Another useful idiot finally found their ability to speak and voiced their confusion. "I don't understand this. This document claims you are taking the position due to the former Head's unethical conduct. Yet the other is..."

"Last night I was called into the Old Man's office," Terrence began before the man could voice the obvious association between the two pieces of information on their screens. Yes, Terrence wanted them to make the logical leap that the Head's actions "could" have led to his death, but he couldn't confirm it since the Old Man never said as much to Terrence either. "It appears the former Head of this Board requisitioned assets in the Resurgence Beta to implement his own trial of the subjects. Where we had previously tested the loyalty and susceptibility of the subjects—under strict protocols and using vigorous oversight—the former head thought with only greed. At every turn, he disregarded the timeline set down and approved by the Old Man. He attempted to turn the beta toward his own vision of milking subscribers and users of our technology. His final act of treason was to implement a protocol forcing the test subjects to buy AltCon stock."

"Was that the reason for the small rise in value I noted this morning?" asked another. Terrence couldn't make out the man's face as his eyes were glued to the screen showing the former Head's body under a sheet. That was exactly the effect he wanted this little show to have.

"Yes, it likely was," Terrence replied.

The man finally looked up from the screen, but continued to avoid eye contact with Terrence, "Well then how could that be a bad thing? It benefitted the company."

"Because the modified protocols implemented forced the subjects. It drove them. We have painstakingly designed the parameters to avoid this very scenario. We cajole, we manipulate, we coerce. We do not, under any circumstances, force our subjects. It is paramount to the success of this project that our subjects believe that everything they are doing is based on their own decisions.

"The Old Man was not pleased when he discovered this treachery. He called for a thorough review to determine who was culpable. The former Head was greedy, but not at all concerned about covering his tracks and his involvement was easily discovered. After that, he ordered a review of all of the board members.," Terrence said as he glanced around the room.

Someone blurted out, "None of us had any idea!"

Terrence saw it was the man who had been sobbing only moments earlier, and who had finally made eye contact. Self-preservation is a powerful force, after all.

"We are aware," Terrence said coldly. "If any of you had been involved, you would not be sitting in this room now. You would have been removed from your position."

Terrence paused for a moment there, allowing that statement to soak in. That one word, "removed," was given an almost imperceptible inflection, leading them to at first assume that they would end up like the former head: a corpse on the sidewalk. The product of a "failed robbery."

"You would have been fired," Terrence finally added.

Although there were a few sighs that could be heard around the room, the majority of eyes strayed to the display with the story of the former Head's demise. Terrence didn't think many of them believed his words concerning how their "termination" would unravel. The fear that Terrence wanted to instill in the remaining board members had been achieved. It was time to implement the new system.

"Your previous goals—milking every cent of profit for this company—are over. The only goal this company now has is to see Resurgence come to fruition. For that purpose, all tests on subjects will be dictated by the Compliance Department. You will be briefed on the successes and failures, but you will no longer take part in the process and decision making on what the tests will entail."

These were not men and women who took to being sidelined easily, and Terrence could see a range of objections about to form. Before any could voice their umbrage with the new guidelines, Terrence put it to rest.

"Review the documents in front of you. This comes from the Old Man himself and is not open for debate. I am informing you, as is proper, because of your standing in this company. But that is all this is: a consideration to your position."

Terrence watched for a few moments while he allowed everything to soak in. Some wanted to object, but they wisely held their tongues. In the end, everyone remained silent. Terrence wouldn't show it, but he had an immense feeling of pride at that moment. The goal—to put these fools on notice—was a success in his eyes.

"There will be no further incidents while I sit at the head of this table. There will be no repeats of the wanton disregard for policy. Things will be done according to how I dictate them. In that way, we can assure there are no further situations that need to be rectified."

With that, Terrence grabbed his belongings from off the table and began to walk out of the boardroom. Just before turning to leave, Terrence shut off the display outlining the Old Man's directions for Terrence to take over. Only the report from the day's paper, detailing the former Head's death, was left on.

Every pair of eyes was staring at that article as Terrence left the room.

CHAPTER 1

October 9th, 2043

I barely slept last night. And even when I did, I tossed and turned restlessly. Whether I was awake or asleep, I kept going over my conversation with the AI, the Wanderer as he called himself. The ramifications of what he told me were just too much to process all at once. This started as a great opportunity to make some money while beta testing a new game, and had changed dramatically over the course of twenty-four hours. The Wanderer told me his suspicions that the company, through the game, used Resurgence as a platform to undertake some nefarious deed. The problem was the Wanderer didn't know what that "deed" was, and had very little information that could help him unravel the mystery. And, of course, he was a computer program that really couldn't be seen by the company to have any part in trying to uncover what, if anything, they were up to.

Not being able to sleep, I logged back into Resurgence hours before my teammates were scheduled to join me. The most basic of reminders that this world had changed for me, the ever present "error," greeted me just before I entered the game and the hyperspace-esque lines appeared. I no longer noticed any deviation between where my character logged out and logged in, but I now knew that the "error" was the Wanderer's way of manipulating my character.

I walked aimlessly through the streets of the big city, rewinding each part of the story I had heard just the day before. I kept hoping that there would be something in the past two months that would make it all click for me, and that I could say without a doubt that everything the Wanderer said made sense. But there was nothing I could recall that made me think AltCon was doing something dastardly or fiendish.

Yes, it was unheard of for a company to offer a group of people a stipend to test their beta. But that alone was not enough to convince me that all of us were just lab rats in some nefarious plot. After all, AltCon was putting their whole company on the line with the introduction of the Virtual Reality Augmentation Containers (VRACs, also known as simply RACs) and the launch of Resurgence. If the game took off, and the RAC became the new standard for virtual interface, AltCon would reap huge rewards. It only made sense that they would look at this beta differently than they had for any of their other games.

But I kept going back to the story of Robert Shoal, his death, and how his former girlfriend Katherine O'Malley played into it all. On one side, I had the words of a biased AI that Shoal was murdered by AltCon to cover up their unknown plans. And if that was all I had to go on, I might think the machines had taken over. Katherine changed all that for me. She was the flesh and blood interviewer that sat across from me and began my journey into the beta. I only spent a short amount of time with her, but that was a woman that definitely had a good head on her shoulders, and certainly not someone who was suffering from any type of paranoia. Yes, our time together was short, but first impressions tell you a lot about a person, and I've learned to trust my instincts.

My instincts told me that if Katherine was involved with the Wanderer, she truly believed something happened to her boyfriend, Shoal. I could also try and track her down outside the game, just to see if the Wanderer was being truthful about removing her identity and hiding her, but I didn't see how that would help me and could needlessly endanger Katherine. In the end, I knew I had to accept what I was told as truth, and go forward with that as my premise.

And to be honest, I spent more time than was likely healthy recounting the whole process for joining the beta. I hadn't put much thought into the tests and exercises my teammates and I went through in the months prior to starting the game. From the outset, the whole thing was weird. I had never heard of a company giving a Myers Briggs test before joining their beta, or what effect my INTJ result had on the decision, if any. Nor did I ever hear of a six-month evaluation phase before confirmation would be given. I overlooked it all because I was getting paid, and at the time we were enjoying the whole thing. Hell, I still enjoyed the game.

I'll likely never know why they wanted us to play with toys, replicating that silly Lego castle and trying to build it exactly as it was laid out. It was a team building exercise, that was easy to determine. But what if there was a deeper reason for all of the hoops we jumped through? What if AltCon was looking for specific types of people to examine for their plot?

It was obvious that the AI had been influencing the game for me from the day I logged in. With the alterations to my character, giving me a Chance modifier that guaranteed success when it came to loot, the Wanderer had certainly given me an unfair advantage. That wasn't the only thing, though. The additional benefits that came from my specialized Rogue training had already paid substantial dividends, and as I progressed they would certainly provide even greater opportunities. But the fact that the Wanderer, a near-sentient AI, was controlling all of this never even crossed my mind. The "error" every time I logged in, the inflated Chance, and the inaccuracies of my log-in and log-out points, were just not enough clues for me to figure it all out.

I took a look at my character yet again, gauging whether all of the Wanderer's efforts had made me an unstoppable force, or just a player slightly better off than the normal gamer:

Alex:	**Rogue**	**Level 20**			
				Resistance:	
Str:	22 (+7)	Atk:	490	Fire:	30

Cst:	24 (+19)	Hps:	4300	Water:	30
Agi:	10 (+23)	Mana:	0	Air:	30
Dex:	45 (+31)	Armor:	80	Earth:	45
Wsd:	6 (+6)	Movement:	90	Holy:	30
Int:	1 (+6)			Dark:	30
Chn:	190 (+7)			Poison:	30
				Disease:	30

Armor:	Commonality:	Weight:	Armor:	Bonus:
Worn Leather Jerkin	Common	8	20	N/A
Worn Leather Leggings	Common	7	15	N/A
Worn Leather Boots	Common	5	10	N/A
Worn Leather Helmet	Common	4	10	N/A
Worn Leather Bracer	Common	2.5	5 X 2	N/A
Worn Leather Shoulders	Common	5	10	N/A
Worn Leather Gloves	Common	2.5	5	N/A
Simple Ring of Might	Common	0.1	10	+1 Str/Cst, +1 Bash

Bloody Rabbit Foot	Rare: Binds on Acquisition	0.1	N/A	+1 Chance
Force Multiplier Ring All Classes	Epic Min Level: 15 Binds on Acquisition	0.1	N/A	+15 Dexterity +15 Agility Unstoppable: All of Character's stats 4X for 5 minutes (Once/24hrs)

Weapon:	Commonality	Weight:	Atk Mod:	Spd:	Bonus:
Dagger of Jagged Rock	Rare (Magic)	1.0	+10	0.3	+15 Earth +10 Dexterity +10 Cst Effect: Lacerations of Rock: Lowers Targets Armor 40 percent for 10 Seconds.

Specialty:	Level:	Modifier
Blacksuit	95	+10 to Conceal and Stealth
Disembowel	N/A	X4 Backstab Damage on successful Disembowel. Must be in Blacksuit to conduct Disembowel.

Skill:	Level:	Modifier:
Dagger	100	+10 Atk
Conceal	95	(+10)
Stealth	95	(+10)
Backstab	100	N/A
Dual Wield	0	+0 Atk
Double Attack	0	N/A

Title:	Bonus:
Bunny Slayer of Port Town	+1 to all Skills +1 to all resistances
The Bandit Conquerors of Port Town	+5 to all Skills +20 to all resistances

My armor was nothing special. That was the first thing I noticed. Sure, I had two magic items, and the Force Multiplier ring was supposed to be removed from the game because it was too powerful. Even then, though, my stats were not that outrageous. In fact, the three other guys that made up our team of four – Dan, Jason, and Wayne – all had better stats than me. That was the point of creating a team rather than focusing on boosting my own stats or those of any one individual. We were supposed to complement each other and we never put our own greed before the needs of the group. On multiple occasions, any one of us could have rightfully asked for an item that we would have sold or traded for something else. In my opinion, our "need over greed" philosophy was one of the most important reasons why we were the top group in the beta. In fact, the only stats I had that were likely far outside the normal player, aside from my Chance, were my resistances. Even that was thanks to our titles, not our gear.

Reviewing all of this made me feel comfortable that our gear alone wouldn't bring unwanted attention to my group. It certainly didn't make me, or my group, an unstoppable force.

With nothing else to do, I decided to practice my Conceal/Stealth to max it out. Now that we had all reached Level 20, we would be able to reach the maximum potential for the Skills we already had. The first on my list, as it would be for any Rogue, was my bread and butter; Conceal and Stealth. I couldn't begin to count the number of times the combination of those two Skills, which lent me my ability to move around in an Invisible status, had saved my hide in the game.

While I ran around with my Conceal/Stealth activated, I thought about the Rogue class I had been playing for the last several months. The choice was made in part because we needed someone who could be our Damage Dealer (DD), and that ended up being me. Looking back, I couldn't imagine playing anything else. Jason was our Cleric, and therefore our Healer, Wayne was one of the best Tanks I had ever seen with his Warrior, and Dan had used the abilities of his Ranger to master the role of Crowd Control (CC). These were the four necessities in any team; Tank, Healer, CC, and DD. If your Tank couldn't maintain the anger, or aggro, of the thing you were killing, while your CC kept the rest of the beasts away from the group doing the killing, you were going to be fucked. The guy healing and the guy doing damage is self-explanatory.

I shook my head a bit when I thought about the words in my lexicon that had become a part of my normal life, but meant nothing in the real world. Explaining the anger of something as "aggro," or a beast you were fighting as a "mob" because it was a mobile object and no one wanted to say that many syllables.

You could be sure if they weren't going to fully say mob, they certainly weren't going to take the time to say something like Non-Player Character either. Yet another that got shortened down to an acronym—NPC. Simply stated, scientists, military members, and gamers love their acronyms. The only difference is the rest of the world tended to recognize, accept, and use the ones the scientists and military came up with.

I focused back on the task at hand and went about increasing my Skill. In order to increase my Conceal and my Stealth, I simply needed to run around with the two Skills "activated." For other Skills, like proficiency with my dagger, I would need to actively stab things. Since I only needed to run around, I decided to spend some more time mapping out the Capitol, which had a name that I needed to learn. Once my Conceal/Stealth was maxed, I planned on finding the exact location where the quest NPC the Wanderer told me about would spawn. That was another word no one but a gamer would use—spawn. I would have to ask the guys if they thought it was weird that we used terms like "spawn point" to explain where something suddenly appeared, like a quest NPC. Or "bind point" to explain where players would appear after they died in the game.

It was easy to figure out where to go in Port Town. Its size was comparatively just a small district within a metropolis this size, and I didn't want us to waste more time than was necessary within the city. The guys didn't know it yet, but soon enough we would be trying to complete two quest chains at the same time. Time was not going to be on our side if we wanted to continue our history of being the first to accomplish tasks in the game.

Secondly, I wanted to find the merchants within the Capitol so I could begin pricing out upgrades to our armor. We were pretty broke at this point with all of the new skills and spells we purchased, but if I was sure of one thing, it was that we were going to need upgrades to deal with these new quests.

I hoped that the armor for Jason and Wayne would be cheaper from the Dwarves. The whole point of negotiating with the King Under the Mountain wasn't for the East Range Mountain Clan to get a steady income, although that was a plus. No, the point was to increase the relations between my team and the dwarves, and in turn hopefully get some good quests and better prices on armor. Having a status of "friend" should lead to cheaper prices. Likewise, if I could get the Dwarves to "ally," at least if Resurgence worked like every other MMORPG, we would get the best quests and deals possible; however, even at "friend," the prices were still likely to be quite high since dwarves were famous for creating magnificent plate armor.

Plate armor was what Jason and Wayne needed, but it wasn't going to do Dan and I a lick of good. I doubted the Dwarves even bothered with the lighter armor that my Ranger friend and I would wear. And, if they did sell it, it wouldn't be Dwarven-made, so not even worth looking at.

My mind flitted from thinking about armor and focused back to the special quest chain from the Wanderer. The hardest part was going to be manipulating the guys into traveling to where the quest giver would appear. According to the Wanderer, this NPC was only going to spawn for five minutes and then disappear. And the location for the NPC was in the middle of the woods, far enough away from the Capitol that I had not come up with a single reason why my group and I would be in that forest at that particular time. If I could have spoken with the Wanderer before he put all of this in motion, I would have told him to put the spawn around when we usually logged on, and then blame being in the woods on my log-in error. But at the time when the NPC was supposed to spawn, we would have already been inside the game for hours.

I continued to search out the merchants and map the city while I wracked my brain over what plan I could use to get us into those woods. Each one I thought of never got past the first questions the guys would ask. Why? Why are we going there when we have a quest to start and new content to see? It was going to have to be good, or none of them would be up for it.

Undisclosed Location

Sitting at the large table, bedecked in a Hawaiian t-shirt and knee length shorts, was Daniel Hamson. When one thinks of a covert operative, they normally think of tuxedos, fancy parties, and expensive cars. They wouldn't normally pick out a person like Mr. Hamson, and that is one reason he had been successful in infiltrating AltCon on behalf of the Department of Defense.

Another reason was Mr. Hamson's amazing memory. Who knows if anyone has ever had a true "photographic memory," but Mr. Hamson possessed the closest thing The General had ever seen. If you had to label it, Mr. Hamson would be called someone with hyperthymesia, or "superior autobiographical memory." It made recalling what Mr. Hamson did, saw, and heard as simple as speaking.

Sitting next to Daniel at the large table was Colonel Thompson, his handler of sorts, and the two were discussing the next steps for Resurgence. The previous handler was sitting in the arctic temperatures of North Dakota after fumbling the most basic of details concerning Mr. Hamson's cover and backstory. He hadn't liked Mr. Hamson from the beginning, and certainly didn't appreciate being mocked at every turn by the man in the swim trunks.

It likely never dawned on him that Daniel had saved his career for quite some time as well. By not reporting all of the mistakes made, that very same soldier was able to go on in his comfy job. It was rare that the General looked forward to signing resignation papers for someone who was under his command, but this was the exception.

Thompson, on the other hand, was a good fit for Mr. Hamson. He was a quiet man, thoughtful, and a master tactician, which was offset perfectly by the fact that Mr. Hamson rarely shut up.

"It's time we start thinking about next steps, Mr. Hamson."

"I couldn't agree more, General. Colonel Thompson and I were just reviewing a number of ideas we came up with," Daniel said. Colonel Thompson simply lifted his eyebrows.

"Ok. I came up with the ideas. And did all of the talking. And the changing. And the new ideas. But Colonel Thompson is a really great listener and can say a lot with an eyebrow raise."

The General shook his head and looked at Thompson with a touch of pity.

"This is actually a perfect time to be talking about next steps, General. My group has entered the next phase if you will, for the game. The story line should follow the same basic arc, but we will be getting all different types of quests, going to new areas, interacting with new people and computer models, and meeting the players that started at the Citadel," Dan said while practically bouncing around in his chair while waving his hands all around. "I'm really excited."

"Mr. Hamson, you understand this isn't a game," the General said. Realizing the words he just chose, the General quickly continued before Dan showed off his juvenile wit. "We are dealing with matters that could impact the entire U.S. economy. This needs to be taken seriously."

"Absolutely. And I am sir. Really, I am. But it's still pretty cool."

"Cool or not, I want your thoughts on where you think we should go from here."

"Follow the arc of the quests. Keep grinding through the levels, but also start looking for more anomalies within the game that could be exploited by us. At this point, all we have is vague data suggesting something nefarious. We don't have any clue as to the how or the who, other than the corporation of AltCon itself."

Dan thought back to the latest scheme enacted by AltCon, forcing the players to buy their stock and encouraging others to do the same. He still had the headache from the hatchet job they had done on his brain. Dan really wanted to find out who was responsible for putting all of this in place and have some serious words with him or her. Or let the group's Tank, Wayne, do it. On the scale of small to massive, Wayne was far closer to the massive end than Dan was. As a professional bouncer Wayne likely knew exactly how to make others feel pain. Yeah, definitely let Wayne do it.

"This is exactly what I was thinking as well, Mr. Hamson. However, we've reached the limits on many of the authorities I have under the charter from the DoD. From this point forward, I am going to need greater support than just what we have in this facility. Tomorrow I am flying to Washington to get that support. If I am successful, and I have every reason to believe I will be, we should have the full backing of most, if not all, of the US Government."

"Nice! You want me to go with you?"

The General cringed inwardly thinking of Daniel Hamson conversing with the stuffed shirts and bureaucrats he was traveling to meet, but outwardly he smiled. "No, Mr. Hamson, your place is in the game. That is where you bring the most skill to this endeavor. Politics is my game, even if I've been playing longer than I care to admit. This is a job for me. If someone would have told me that being a general would have more to do with politics than leading militaries, I probably would have stopped at colonel."

Colonel Thompson chuckled at that and looked to Dan. "How long till you need to be in the game?"

"I should leave now. I have no idea what today holds, but I am sure Alex will come up with something good. The guy is an amazing leader, General. You really should consider hiring him when this is all over."

"Just be mindful, Mr. Hamson, that Alex seems to be one of these anomalies you spoke of earlier. Watch him closely."

"I won't leave his side, sir!"

The Colonel raised his eyebrows again at Dan, obviously challenging his last comment.

"Except to go to the tavern. But that's recon. It's my job!"

The General walked out of the room as Dan continued to argue the merits of tavern work and the pillow talk from the "ladies."

The General knew the meeting in Washington would determine the course of the operation. Given the impact virtual reality had on humanity's day-to-day life, possibly on the fate of the world economies themselves.

I had been sitting in the square next to Sir Arthur Chadwick for a good ten minutes when my first teammate logged in. I had grown tired of calling the city "the Capitol" over and over again in my mind, and determined to find out what the actual name was. As Sir Arthur was the main point of contact in the city, responsible for giving out all of the quests for the story arc, I figured he would know the name.

"Yerkich," Sir Arthur said while waving his arm across the square, "is the ancient name of our city. The square we stand in is where the city's namesake, King Yerkich the Conqueror, brought every clan and tribe together under one flag. His flag."

Sir Arthur looked around the square one last time before finishing, "today, only this gathering point remains of that original city, and is called Yerkich Square by the locals. Otherwise, both aristocrat and commoner call this Kich's Keep or just the Keep.

Shortly after finishing my conversation with Sir Arthur, Dan logged in. Dan saw me after a few moments, walked over with a fist bump, and then sat down next to me.

"Been on long?" he asked.

"A couple of hours actually. I couldn't sleep, man. I've been too excited about the whole thing and decided to jump online and get started mapping out the market places. Getting upgraded gear is going to be high on our list of priorities."

"Tell me about it. I was looking at my gear before I logged out yesterday, and we really need to get better stuff," Dan said.

"Our rare items are great. But the non-magic stuff is barely keeping us alive. I'm sure that the mobs here are going to be much harder than what we found in the forests around Port Town."

"Well, my thoughts," Wayne said as he approached from behind us, "is that we test our mettle against the mobs in the surrounding area before we accept the quest. This area should be a 'starting area' for the Capitol anyhow."

I almost jumped too fast to agree with Wayne. Here I had spent an hour wracking my brain to come up with a way to convince the guys to stick around to the woods, and Wayne gave it to me with no prompting. I formed a plan immediately.

"I like Wayne's idea. And good to see you, brother."

Wayne nodded in my direction with a big smile.

I relayed what I had learned from Sir Arthur about the name of the city and continued to support Wayne's ideas. "We really should see how Wayne handles tanking these mobs out in the surrounding area and how Jason will be able to handle healing. It will also give us a chance to see how the experience differs here in Yerkich from the mobs around Port Town."

"No argument from me," said Dan. "All we need now is to wait for Jason to log in. Anyone know if he was going to be on late for any reason?"

"I'm here," Jason said as he came around the corner of one of the buildings. "Did I miss anything?"

Dan gave Jason the stink eye for a moment before saying, "Where you been there, brother Baron? Last time you went sneaking around town we found out you were itching to be royalty. I don't want to imagine what you could be up to now."

"I was looking to see if there was any way to put a bounty out on loudmouth wood elves. No such luck."

"Wayne suggested we tour the area checking out the mobs outside of the city, which as it turns out is called Yerkich, according to Sir Arthur. On top of that, the locals apparently call the area where the more well to do live, Kich's Keep," I said.

"Getting back on track, though, we are hoping to see how our abilities stack up against the strength of the mobs, and naturally we will need your healing. Dan and I agreed. You good with that?"

As our only High-Elf, the Race in Resurgence that would best describe what you would expect of the aristocracy, Jason was well placed to carry the title of Baron. He had received it as part of a quest, but he wore it with pride. I called it pride anyhow; Dan called it a stick up his butt. "Yup, sounds good to me. The quest isn't going anywhere."

I had mapped out exactly where the quest NPC was supposed to spawn earlier that day and led the group in that general direction. I knew from my exploration that there were plenty of mobs in that area that would give us experience. I also noted that the area where the NPC would spawn was absent of mobs for a large enough area that we could use it as a base to pull mobs.

As a group, we headed out toward the woods that surrounded Yerkich.

"Two Healthy Bears incoming!"

We had learned quickly that the mobs in this area were definitely harder than the ones we fought in Port Town. Not just a higher level, either. They were doing a significantly larger amount of damage than the level would indicate. I believed this was due to our armor.

Dan successfully kited one of the beasts around the area while Wayne and I ripped into the other bear. Kiting is a bit of an art form; when you are doing it right, it reminds you of the simple beauty one sees from a masterpiece of the great Renaissance era. When you fuck it up, it looks like the shit your four-year-old brother smears on the walls and for some reason your parents praise. If Dan couldn't keep the extra mobs chasing after him, while also reducing the mobs' movement speed through his spells, we would all end up looking like smeared shit.

I had my own problems from the get go as well. One of my signature Rogue attacks, Backstab, was doing some serious damage. I always led with this attack since it did twice the damage, and even more with a critical strike, if I activated it from Conceal/Stealth. With that much damage, the mobs aggro'ed me immediately and I almost got sent to my spawn point. I learned quickly to hold off a bit before jumping into the fight.

That experience reminded all of us that we had forgot a vital step upon arriving at Yerkich. Immediately after finishing that fight we all ran back to Kich's Keep and reset our spawn point to the city. Having died out here would have led to a two-day journey on foot from Port Town and back to the Capitol.

The Healthy Bears were dropping Fine Quality Skins that could be used for making large backpacks. One of the most sacred tenants of online role playing games is to always carry as many bags as you can. The ability of a group to accumulate wealth is almost always tied to the number of items they can carry to sell at a future time. We had previously crossed paths with a player that had begun the Crafting skill of making backpacks. I had already reached out to the player and he said he would be interested in the skins. He admitted he probably wouldn't be successful on many of his initial attempts to make them, given their high level, but he promised he would give us the ones where he did succeed. And we would get them for free, where other players would expect to pay handsomely for this upgrade. Why? Because the Fine Skins were going to raise his skill level in record time, ensuring that his reputation from the last time we made this deal stayed intact.

I kept glancing at the in-game clock to make sure we weren't in the middle of some crazy pull when the NPC spawned, but there was no way I could just call for a break and sit around. Not unless I really wanted to arouse the suspicion of my friends.

As our killing continued, my skills in Dual Wield and Double Attack continued to increase. This was making my damage output soar.

Wayne was also increasing his Double Attack, but the difference in our damage was obvious for all to see. As the time neared for the NPC to spawn, I decided to take a risky chance that could cost us the quest entirely.

The first part of the plan required me to not only be Invisible with my Conceal/Stealth, but to activate my Blacksuit as well. If you asked any Rogue, they would tell you that Conceal/Stealth was the greatest skill they had. It made them Invisible to 95 percent of the mobs in the game. Due to the interference of the Wanderer, I was the only Rogue in the game with a Blacksuit. By gathering the "shadows" around me, I was able to make myself Invisible to 99.9 percent of the mobs. The Blacksuit was also the first key component in executing my Disembowel strike.

Dan pulled two more mobs, very much the norm for us at this point, and I immediately led with my Backstab while in my Blacksuit. My plan worked and I successfully executed my Disembowel. I still didn't know the percentage, but on occasion my Backstab, while I had my Blacksuit on, would turn into a Disembowel. Where the Backstab did twice the damage, a Disembowel did four times the damage. And if I landed a critical strike, where the mob had less resistance and therefore took more damage, I could guarantee our Tank would never take aggro from me.

Without missing a beat, the bear turned on me and started raking me with its claws. I started to see my hit points fall dramatically, but I wanted to really sell the next part so I kept attacking, keeping the aggro, the mobs' utter hatred, on me.

"Dammit, Alex, stop stabbing it!" Jason yelled as he started casting a healing spell on me.

"Sorry!" I yelled back and after two more seconds stopped attacking. At this point, there was no way the Bear was going to stop attacking me.

"Shit!" I yelled as I watched my hit points continue to fall and activated the Force Multiplier ring in order to "save myself." If I hadn't timed it perfectly, I would have died. There was no way I would have gotten back in time to trigger the NPC.

Immediately the number of my hit points jumped dramatically, and my Agility was such that I was able to dodge many of the attacks from the Bear. More importantly, the NPC would spawn in three minutes: enough time to finish both mobs. Healing me and Wayne after the Bears died would mean Jason had to rest to regain mana, but Jason was not happy—and rightfully so.

"What the hell, Alex? You almost got sent back to the city! Why didn't you stop attacking, for god's sake?"

"I'm sorry, guys! My head wasn't in it. I was thinking about what we should start doing next, and I just went on autopilot! I got hit for so much health that I just froze up. I promise it won't happen again."

I don't know if they bought it, but it kept the group in place for the time it would take for Jason to regain his mana. If my rough assessment was right, it should be enough time for the NPC to spawn while my ring was still active and I wouldn't have to move from the spot we were sitting at. I was happy with how the gamble turned out, but my teammates weren't.

"Seriously, man. I don't know what would have happened if you lost so much experience that you dropped below Level 20. Would you even be allowed back to the Keep?" Wayne asked.

"Shit. That's a really good question. For once, not one that I am inclined to test with one of my experiments." I resisted calling my three friends a bunch of babies when I saw them cringe at the word "experiment." I had barely killed anyone in all the time I had tried to map out the inner workings of Resurgence. Sure, Wayne got beaten up by some bunnies and some goblins, and I had the rest of our group running around in circles, but it was for science! And by science, I mean my curiosity. "I said 'no experiments,' Dan, so stop giving me the side-eye!"

The guys calmed down a bit after that, and Jason was sitting on the ground to regenerate his mana faster. I had no idea where exactly the NPC would spawn, so I was looking around at our surroundings without trying to look like I was looking for anything in particular. I must have looked like a moron.

"Dammit! Mob spawned right on me!" Dan yelled out to the group. I stood up from the ground and ran to where Dan was standing.

"It's not a mob! Look, it isn't aggroing at all," I yelled before Dan could be true to his Ranger Class and shot the NPC full of holes.

"What the hell is it then?" Jason asked as he approached Dan's location. "Is it an NPC? What would it be doing out here?" Wayne was right next to his healer, intent to keep him safe.

"Holy hell! She's beautiful," Wayne said when he got in front of the NPC, whose name we could now see was Lady Tessa.

"If you forget about the Pink Tutu Affair Wayne, I promise I won't tell Jenny you just said that," Dan threw out.

"Forget it, chump. The Affair never dies," Wayne said while fist bumping Jason.

There were few memories in Resurgence that could immediately bring a smile to my face, but the "Pink Tutu Affair" was definitely one of them. Why Dan ever thought that telling every person he knew, in every bar, that not only had he saved Wayne's life, but that Wayne was wearing a frilly pink tutu while it happened, I still have no idea. The next day, Wayne received dozens of messages commenting on his tutu and asking what type of Warrior needs a Ranger to save his hide. Dan has been trying to get Wayne to forget about it ever since.

Dan also wasn't ashamed to bring Wayne's girlfriend into play to get what he wanted, either. Jenny, or Serenity in the game, was a member of our larger team. Her, Gary (Sayhey), Kaitlin (Anastasia), and Tim (Slovak) made up the second part of our eight-person team. Jenny and Wayne started dating soon after the beta started for us. Dan wanted desperately to date Kaitlin. Or even have her acknowledge him. No one was trying to date Gary and Tim.

"Why the hell are you fist bumping Allidonus?" Dan asked. And there was the other thing that always made me laugh on the inside. Dan had more names for Jason, or Allister in the game, than I could count. Dan used to use real words that began with "Alli" or "Ali." He had exhausted those options long ago and now just made up words as he went, like "Allidonus." It probably wouldn't be so bad for Jason if he went by his regular name; but he insisted he play in character as much as possible and everyone had to call him Allister. Wayne and I never minded. Dan didn't either, as it just added to his own enjoyment with what wordplay he could incorporate that day.

"That's my Tank. I always got his back," Jason replied.

"Focus here, guys," I said, breaking up the banter, but enjoying the interaction all the same.

"Says the guy who just five minutes ago admitted to not paying attention because he was cyber sexing some hottie," Dan added.

"I wasn't cyber sexing anyone!"

"It's cool, bro. I won't tell anyone else. As long as she has a friend for TheClaw."

I ignored Dan, a task that seriously got easier the more days we spent together. It had become surprisingly easier when the aforementioned party decided that his in-game name would be "TheClaw," and spoke about himself in third-person.

I made my way toward Lady Tessa. I knew this was the NPC that the Wanderer told me about, and I knew she wouldn't be around for long.

I took a good look at the NPC and was amazed at the quality of the character. Robert Shoal really went all out when he designed this one. All the characters and NPCs in Resurgence looked lifelike, but you didn't realize the quality of that likeness until you saw Lady Tessa.

"She looks more than real. If that makes any sense," Dan said.

"In your own twisted way, Dan, that's probably the smartest thing you've said in days."

I kept staring at Lady Tessa and took in all the details. She was an elf, which was clear from the pointy ears, and likely a high elf, given the air that she seemed to carry herself. It was like with Jason, the way his character looked; the high cheek bones, the piercing eyes, it led the viewer to immediately think, "High Born."

Her skin was flawless. The color was a white so perfect it would rival the greatest pearls in comparison. Her eyes were the darkest forest green I had ever seen. Her hair blew in a breeze that was only affecting her, as I watched her golden strands wave through the air. She wore a gossamer gown and it clung to her curves and accentuated every part of her form. There was no doubting this was a woman and she was a picture of radiance.

I could have stood there and stared at her for hours, but I had to trigger the quest or this would all be for naught.

"Good day, Fair Lady," I said.

"You would not think it so good if you knew my story, adventurer," Lady Tessa replied.

"Bingo! Quest NPC! Hot damn on toast, we are the luckiest bastards this side of Port Town!" Dan exclaimed.

"Well, Alex is. We just keep you around to make our IQs look better," Jason said.

"Thanks, Baron. That's nice of you to say!"

"He means yours is so low it makes ours look high," Wayne replied while laughing.

"Oh. Damn. I really should have seen that one coming."

I ignored the banter of my friends and continued on with getting the quest.

"What is your story, Lady Tessa?"

"It is not a happy tale, I fear. Do you really want to burden yourself with my sad affairs?"

"Please tell me your story," I said again. I could now see the guys were all ears.

Lady Tessa paused for a moment, and I thought I hadn't said the right phrase to keep the quest script going. I really should have asked the Wanderer for the right combination of words. Just then Lady Tessa looked up to the sky, as if she were recalling a memory, and sighed mournfully before she began to speak.

"Years ago, who could really say how long now, mine was an honorable and well respected family. We were the only family of our kind. Scholars who traveled the world in search of knowledge.

"Now you may be thinking, 'There are entire institutions of learning for this specific purpose,' and you would be right. But where those institutions are filled with men and women whose knowledge came at the hands of a tome or a lectern, my family's knowledge came from the end of a sword. Where they were book scholars, my family was filled with warriors. In fact, our family was renowned for our acumen both on the field of combat as well as in the library. Sometimes the closest kept secrets are held by the foulest of creatures, and a warrior is needed to secure such booty.

"With our profession, the members of my family ranged far and wide, and our house never grew large. My father had no brothers and only one sister, and she died in a tragic accident before she was betrothed. At the time my story starts, all that was left of my house were my four brothers, my father, and myself. That is if you still wish to hear it."

"Damn this is good. Say the words, Alex," Jason said.

"Lady Tessa, we implore you. Tell us your story."

At that prompt, Lady Tessa turned and regarded each of my groupmates, looking into their eyes for a brief second, before finally locking those beautiful green orbs on me. She nodded her head once and then began anew.

"My father, Lord Lancaster, was regarded as the greatest warrior scholar my family had ever produced. There was almost no place he wouldn't go in this land to find secrets hidden from this world. The King called on his services often, and our family was welcome in court more than any other.

"But it was on one of his own forays into the wilds that the demise of my house began." Tessa turned away for a moment, letting out a heavy sigh, and then looked to muster the courage to go on. "My father had heard rumor of a tome of history trapped away on the outskirts of the great swamps of the east. There, so rumor had it, a mage of great age and experience had begun the life of a hermit and shunned the outside world. His library was said to be the most expansive in the world barring that of Yerkich itself. But none could approach him as the swamp itself answered to his call.

"My father, never one to back down from a challenge, set off to confront the mage. His return to us showed he had won, but had been soundly thrashed along the way. His armor was in ruin, and much of his belongings were lost in the swamp. But he returned with what my family valued more than anything else. Knowledge.

"That knowledge, however, was to be our downfall." Tessa paused at that point and walked away from the group. Not far from her spawn point she stopped and sat on a section of fallen tree. The roots, ripped from the ground by a force of wind no doubt, could be seen in her background. It was a study in contrast. The most beautiful creature I had ever laid eyes on sitting upon a piece of wood, mangled from its descent. The similarities to the fall of Lady Tessa's house were not lost on me and I silently gave Robert Shoal a salute for his efforts in crafting this quest. Once seated, Tessa began again.

"The hermit, as my father learned, had fled the land, fearing for his life with the information he possessed. It was not a rare tome on magic, no spell that would change the landscape of battles, but a simple journal. In fact, it contained words more powerful than some mere incantation, for they spelled out a story wherein the history of our King's succession was cast into question.

"My father, being the loyal subject he was, as well as personal friend to the King himself, immediately informed his Majesty of what he had found. My father believed the journal to be a fake, and that the King should know of its existence in case any other such falsehoods ever came to light.

"Father didn't think it at all odd when the King asked who else knew of the journal. Without realizing the error he was making, my father informed his Majesty that only his children knew of his quest and what he had found.

Lady Tessa dropped her face into her hands and shook her head back and forth. When she finally lifted her eyes back toward ours, we could all see the tears flowing down to her chin. She closed her eyes tightly, took a deep breath, and with resolve she began again.

"Telling my brothers and I of the encounter, my father recalled in minute detail the look on the King's face the fateful night of that conversation. Father had turned away to refill his glass as he informed his Majesty on the details, and when he looked back he saw an ocean of sadness looking back. It would still be several moments before the King would attempt a facade of happiness for my family's efforts to retrieve any and all knowledge for the kingdom, and told my father to forget this book. That smile never touched his Grace's eyes, though, and my father knew an ill omen when he saw one. Two days later, my family received our summons.

"Each of my brothers, like my father, was a warrior scholar. Their skill levels differed, but each was highly regarded for their abilities. As a rule, however, our house never sent more than two of the family on a mission. This wasn't always the case, but none of my brothers had taken wives, and as such they had no heirs to their positions or property. Until such time that more males were sired father would not risk losing more than two men at a time. Women, such as myself, handled the politics of our house and not the sword.

"The summons called for each of my brothers and my father to report to His Majesty the next morning. Here the King erred and gave some clue as to why the summons was sent. Each of my brothers was being sent on a quest to retrieve a piece of lost lore, and my father was to be given the hardest task of all: to secure a tome from the clutches of a dragon. More importantly, the King claimed these tasks to be of the gravest nature that could only be trusted to my family. And none other. Each would be traveling alone.

"Once my father and brothers returned, a family meeting was called in the great room of our home," Tessa said and then stood up to walk back toward the area where we originally found her and then continued for several more seconds toward Yerkich.

"There," she said while pointing toward the city, "my father recalled that look of sadness and believed that not only was the King aware of the journal, but his orders suggested it was real.

"That night, my father removed the journal with the information. You see, he told the King of its existence, but never told the King that he actually kept the tome. All the King knew was that my father shared the information with my brothers and I. That is why his Majesty believed killing off my family would also kill off his lie.

"My father divided the journal between him and my four brothers. They were to carry it with them as they traveled into what became their ultimate demise. I was not to have knowledge of the eventual resting place of the journal and was instead to be spirited away in the night.

"I protested, but my father begged me to keep their secret, saying that if the family didn't return, one day it would be my responsibility to find those who could travel the lands and collect those lost journal pieces and to exact vengeance for my family. Are you such adventurers?"

For a long time, none of us said a word, though Wayne summed it all up after just a few heartbeats.

"Wow."

Wow was right. This looked to be a most epic quest chain.

"So, are we in, guys?" I asked my friends. I received three nods in the affirmative.

"We are those adventurers, Lady Tessa."

After a few heartbeats Lady Tessa looked up toward the heavens and mouthed "Thank you."

The guys started waving their hands at me, wanting me to press on Lady Tessa to get her to give us more information, but I wanted to let the script play out on its own. The Lady walked around a little more and then set her feet to the ground. With a nod, and a straightening of her shoulders, she turned back toward the group.

"If you are honest in your claim, and if I am prepared to set you on this most dangerous of journeys, then you will need a place to start. There was a housekeeper that lived on our estate for longer than any of us children, and considering elves live for hundreds of years, you can imagine her age. And while we lived there, it was truly her home. She was much like a second mother to all of us. Her name is Madeline, though we just called her Old Lady Madsie. She still resides within Kich's Keep, and the King and his men are none the wiser as to her identity. When I fled Yerkich, I gave her my youngest brother's diary. In it, he wrote of the quest that he was being sent on. I could never bear to read it and have no knowledge as to the location where my brother was sent.

"But that diary will point you in the right direction. My youngest brother was not much higher in skill than you four likely are, but I know he did not return from the quest he was given. So the beast that slayed him must have been formidable. I pray that should you find his remains, you will find answers to help you find the rest of the journal. When you approach Old Lady Madsie, tell her 'Lady Tessa says she wants more of the happy juice.' This was a phrase I used as a child and it remained a running joke for decades between us. That phrase will let her know that I sent you. This is all I can tell you for now, but I hope finding the pages of the journal will assist you in your efforts. Go with the grace of the gods."

A glow surrounded us, and we were all given the quest. I quickly examined the details to ensure we didn't miss anything like additional players for a mini-raid, a mistake we had made in the past when we were given the Bandit raid from Port Town, and that I did not in any way want to repeat. As I looked at my mates, I confirmed that we had all received the quest "Restoration of House Lancaster – Part I," and that the details provided by Lady Tessa were echoed in the quest's description. The reward for completing this quest was listed as "Unknown." With the Wanderer's conversation in my head, I had visions of the most epic of loot befalling us.

I looked at my map and there was an icon inside Kich's Keep that corresponded to the quest we just received. This was likely the location where we would find this Old Lady Madsie.

We nodded our heads at Lady Tessa again and began to make our way out of the forest. Before we had made it more than several meters, Lady Tessa called out to us.

"If it isn't too much to ask..." she said, and then paused.

Before I could react, Wayne approached Lady Tessa and, in the kindest words, said, "If there is anything we can do, Lady, you need only ask."

I didn't think she would respond to Wayne, as he wasn't the group leader. To my surprise, she looked up into Wayne's eyes. After holding him there for a second, Lady Tessa said, "If you find my brother, please, give him a proper burial."

Wayne took one knee to the ground and said, "On my honor as a warrior, I, Naugha Hyde, will see your brother buried properly, or I will die trying." Nobody sold the warrior like our boy Wayne.

Lady Tessa reached her hand out to Wayne and placed it on his forehead. After several seconds, her hand began to glow with a golden hue, and Wayne's body was covered in light. Despite not being touched by Lady Tessa, the same happened to everyone in the group.

With looks of astonishment on our faces, Lady Tessa once more addressed us, "My father was a warrior, as were my brothers. I am something else. I am the last member of my family. I am the Lady Lancaster. As such, it is within my rights to offer a boon to any I deem worthy." She then helped Wayne to his feet.

"Thank you for your sincere words Naugha. You spoke truth in your oath. Go with the blessing of my station."

With that, we started walking out of the forest to an area where we could summon our horses. As we walked, I looked at my character, and there was a new subset of information. Under "Titles" there was a new heading: "Gifts." According to my character screen, I now had the "Gift of the Lady Lancaster," which gave a +5 to all stats and resistances. I let out a mighty whoop that caught all of my companions off guard.

I explained to them what I found, and they all checked their characters as well. To a man, we had all received the "Gift" from Lady Tessa.

The Wanderer hadn't lied. His intervention was already paying dividends.

CHAPTER 2

We traveled in silence for the next several minutes. I didn't want to be the first to discuss the quest, but I knew everyone was thinking about it. Wayne would remain stoic, as was normal for him except when he was in battle. Jason was likely having a hell of a conversation, only internally. And Dan, well no one ever really knew what was going on in Dan's head.

When we arrived at the entrance to the Capitol we banished our mounts and began walking through the gates. Since no one had said anything, I began to head in the direction of the marker on my map. I figured we might as well get the first part of this quest over, but Jason stopped us with a signal.

"I don't think we should start this new quest yet, guys."

"Seriously?" Dan asked. "Why not, man? This thing sounds awesome."

"Well, we know it isn't a timed quest, so we have all the time in the world to start it. We also know from what the NPC told us that the level will likely be very difficult. We've already seen what a bear in these woods can do to us. I'm not one for just running out and getting ourselves killed. Besides, we have something else to consider."

"When the bar opens?"

Jason just shook his head at Dan. "No. We have another quest to get from Sir Arthur."

"That's right!" Wayne exclaimed. "We could be looking at two very diverging quests that we need to do." Wayne thought about it some more and then nodded his head toward Jason. "I'm with Allister. I think we need to wait on starting this quest until we have at least spoken with Sir Arthur. Maybe we get lucky and the two are in the same direction, but even I don't think we are that lucky."

"Alex is, but I doubt his luck will have anything to do with this." Dan said, looking at me a little suspiciously.

In response to the back and forth, I shrugged my shoulders and said, "I'll follow wherever you guys decide to go. I'm not sold on starting Lady Tessa's quest straight away either."

With that response, Dan nodded his head and agreed with Jason and Wayne. With our new destination, we traveled through the interior of the city, mapping out the different stores and locales as we traveled. And by mapping out, I mean I kept shouting out, "Dan, remember that place!"

It wasn't long before we were back in the city square and approaching Sir Arthur. Despite my earlier comments, mostly to get Dan to stop looking at me with suspicion, I wasn't totally sold on this idea. I did agree with Jason's assessment, however. Our gear was rather weak and we would probably get slaughtered if we headed out straight away for the special quest.

Once I was in front of Sir Arthur, I said the words to trigger the NPC's dialogue. "We are ready to answer the call."

Sir Arthur regarded my group with an air of confidence and stated, "Ah, brave travelers! You have come at an opportune time. The King is in desperate need for fighters of your caliber to assist in the struggle against the Children of Loust. The front lines have taken a beating, and we are struggling to hold our positions."

"I'm not going to be cannon fodder, Alex," Dan said. "If that is the next quest, I'm done with this thing."

Jason and Wayne nodded their heads, but I kept my thoughts to myself. I didn't want to say anything in front of Sir Arthur that might come across as accepting the quest.

However, Sir Arthur wasn't done speaking. "To compound the problem, the main route to the front lines has been disrupted by a clan of trolls that continuously destroys the bridges we have built to cross the Danning River. As you know, trolls consider bridges their domain, as the tolls they extract from them are their main source of income. The King does not recognize their claim and has repeatedly stated his refusal to pay a toll in his own lands. Many thought the trolls would attempt to back up their demands with a fight. Instead, these crafty buggers have destroyed each bridge we build, trying to force the King's hand.

"Our Kingdom needs those men on that front line. Will you assist in eradicating the troll menace that is plaguing our military's progress?"

It was Wayne who spoke up this time with excitement. "Now that we can do!"

Everyone was in agreement. I responded to Sir Arthur with, "We will eradicate the troll menace."

Our characters were surrounded by the golden glow of yet another quest, and we received "The Troll Menace" information in our logs, including the amount of gold and experience for the reward. A quick look confirmed that this was neither a raid quest nor on a timer. We had the freedom to choose our next move.

And since we had no idea what lay before us in either the Troll mission, or Lady Tessa's quest, we had some serious discussion ahead of us. While I wanted to jump in head first to Lady Tessa's, and Wayne likely wanted to immediately go kick some Troll ass, we were in this for the long run and couldn't take the next steps lightly.

Our armor was terribly weak. This had become evident when we were fighting the bears in the forest that were only one or two levels higher than us. Our damage output was fine, but if we couldn't keep our people alive, no amount of damage per second ratio, or DPS, was going to make a difference.

Our real problem, though, was money. We didn't really have much. I checked our funds again and saw we were just over 50 gold. The skills and spells we had purchased upon arriving here had tapped us out. We needed a money tree, like the area where we previously found the undead and every corpse gave up almost a full gold. That option was out, though, as we had already cued our teammates to that area. We couldn't take their loots while they were still farming it.

Of course, where we ended up getting our funds was contingent on how expensive our gear would be. The first step was finding out how much money we needed to raise.

"Ok, guys, I have a plan," I said.

Wayne took an involuntary step back. I laughed at his reaction.

"A plan, Wayne, not an experiment. Nobody is going to die."

"You scare me, Alex. Just saying."

"We need new armor. Everyone is in agreement there?"

They all nodded their heads.

"Then I think the first step is to determine just how much we will need in order to upgrade Dan and I from the merchants here in the Keep."

"Why just you guys?" Jason asked.

"Because Allister, in order to get your and Wayne's gear, we need to take a trip to see our friends and our kin," I said with a smile.

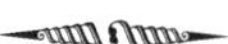

"It's bloody robbery is what it is!" Dan exclaimed.

Dan was not the least bit happy at what we found while investigating the prices for our new armor. The stuff we were currently wearing was Worn Leather equipment. The next level above ours was Common Leather. It wasn't a large jump between the Worn and the Common. Not wanting to waste money on a minimal upgrade, we searched out the next level above the Common gear. What we found was Fine Leather Armor. It must have been really fine, because the price was insane.

"Seriously though, that is a crazy jump from Worn to Fine armor. Twenty gold for each of the smaller pieces, 40 gold for the leggings, and 50 gold for the top? That's a whole lot of platinum for you and me to get new gear. And we haven't even looked for Wayne and Allitater."

"Allitater?" Jason asked.

"I ran out of words. I'm just making things up now."

"How about just calling me Allister?"

Dan looked at Jason like he had never met the man before and was in total confusion as to how this man knew him. Jason sighed noisily.

"The Plate stuff is probably going to be even more expensive than our Leather, Dan. So just get ready for that."

On a suggestion from Jason, we checked out the prices for the Plate in the Capitol. And it definitely was more expensive than our Leather. But we had no clue what kind of discount we would get for our friendly disposition with the dwarves. We just hoped it would be way less than what the merchants were trying to pass off.

The first stop, however, had to be to our kin from the East Range Mountain Dwarf Clan. Dan needed more arrowheads for his upgraded arrows, and he wanted to harvest some more wood from the Elder Elven tree located close to our kin's mine—the one we had liberated of Orckin for the Dwarves.

I was also keen to begin a dialogue with our friend Tibble, the head of the Clan and the dwarf Wayne first encountered that started this whole endeavor with the dwarves. I was hoping to talk about possible profit sharing on the Fermium Ore that the Dwarves were extracting. I wasn't clear on the price that Fermium was going for, but based on the extra damage Dan was getting from his new arrows, I imagined the metal would sell very well. It wasn't a money tree, but it could be a steady stream of income for us. I just had to keep Wayne from losing his shit when I brought the topic up. We were all fond of the Dwarves, but the giant barbarian looked at all of them as little brothers who needed his protection. Even from us. And my conniving ways especially.

Finally, none of us actually knew how to get to the dwarves that resided under the mountain. We needed to lean on Tibble and our kin for a guide to the area.

We were about a half mile away from the mine when I saw an arrow fly through the air. It wasn't headed in our direction, but going back toward the mine. Attached to the arrow was a green streamer. Everyone else made note of the arrow and I leaned over to Wayne, "Your idea?"

"Nope. They came up with this one on their own. I am wondering where they got the idea though."

We continued to ride toward the mine and were greeted by a number of dwarves when we arrived. Tibble was in front of everyone with a big smile.

"Our kin!" he yelled.

"Huzzah!" answered all of the Dwarves surrounding him.

Wayne dismounted from his summoned horse, and Tibble immediately approached and clasped his wrists to his own. "I did not think I would be seeing ya lads for many a fortnight when I heard ya was heading to Kich's Keep. It is not a short distance from here. And I know there be adventures a plenty for a Warrior like you, Naugha!"

"Any time is too long when we are away from our brothers, Tibble. But this trip was born out of necessity. There are indeed great adventures to be had and beasts fierce with which to contend. But we find that our armor is not on par with the dangers we will face," I said as I approached Tibble. The language read like a script, but I was playing the character of the leader, and I wanted to get our needs out quickly so as not to waste time on celebrations and the like. Besides, we hadn't brought any beer with us.

"Aye, Alex, I had heard much of the same from those Dwarves who have braved them lands. It may be that you can find what you need with our brothers under the mountain. At least for Naugha here and the Blessed One."

Tibble and the other Dwarves referred to Jason as the "Blessed One" ever since they learned of his Legendary shoulders, crafted by the greatest dwarf Smith to ever live, Grumblewat TwoHammers.

"We ain't much for stitchin' and the like. If it can't be made with fire and a hammer, you ain't going to find a dwarf making it!" Tibble exclaimed.

"There is truth to your words, Tibble. We will look to the merchants in the Keep for our leather gear, just like we wouldn't look anywhere but the dwarves for our plate. Despite being friends to the Dwarves, however, not a one of us knows how to make that journey."

Tibble laughed deep from his belly. "Of course ye don't! Your first journey to our home will be by the hands of an East Range Mountain Dwarf, this I promise ya!"

I looked around and saw Dan was engaging with Tibble's best smith, Thaddeus, about his arrows. A group of dwarves were playing with Dan's pet dire wolf, Broham. Jason was happily showing another group of dwarves the legendary shoulders of Grumblewat. Wayne was hovering nearby, listening to the exchange I was having with Tibble, likely making sure I didn't try to fleece our friends. If it weren't for the times they had seen me done this very thing to other players, I would have called him a damn untrusting warrior, what with their oaths and honor.

I looked over at Wayne and got him engaged in the conversation, asking about the arrow we had seen on the way in.

"Right. That was something new, Tibble. I can guess at what it means, but tell me so I can see if I was right," Wayne said.

"Ahh, the green arrow ya saw. That mean there be friendlies approaching. "

"So you have three different colors. Friendly, Unknown, and Enemy?" Wayne asked.

"Five lad. The three you said, but two more also. Green for friendly, yellow for unknown, yellow with black stripe for unknown on horse, red for unfriendly, and red with black stripe for unfriendly on horse. This way we have different contingencies for preparing a defense."

"That's brilliant, Tibble! I want to meet the East Range Dwarf who came up with that! I'll personally train him!"

Tibble chuckled at Wayne, "That would be a she lad. I took Alex's advice and hired a healer from the King's own. It ain't been cheap, but none of our hunting parties have fallen with her around. And she has fought in more campaigns than any member of this clan," he said while laughing again.

"She commented on this tactic used by the King when he sets up camp, and we took it immediately. As you can see, we find it useful. She has told us about a fair number of other defenses she wants us to build once we have the funds. I would appreciate if ya would talk with her about them, Naugha. We are taking ya directions seriously about defending this mine and improving our abilities. This be just a small part of it, I am sure."

"Have you had anyone encroach on your mine?" I asked, focusing in on the part where the tactic was beneficial for alerting the Clan before visitors arrived.

"*Our* mine, Alex. You be a part of this Clan too lad. And only the random adventurers like yourselves. When they see a group of armored dwarves with battle axes though, they run the other way they do!"

A group of Dwarves must have been listening in on our conversation, because there was a loud "Huzzah" just as Tibble finished speaking.

"Where is this awesome battle cleric you spoke of, Tibble? I want to meet her!" Wayne said.

"Behind ya, lad. Your brother Allister is trying to convince her she doesn't need to kneel in his presence."

We three looked over, and indeed Tibble was right. The female Dwarf was kneeling in front of Jason. And Jason was begging her to stand up. Those damn Shoulders again.

Wayne walked over to Jason, hoping to save him, and I got back to the discussion with Tibble.

As I turned back around, Tibble had a knowing smirk on his face. "Ye ready to talk business now, lad, what with Naugha no longer here."

I laughed for a bit saying, "Is it that obvious?"

"Well, I know Naugha looks after us dwarves."

"It's fair. Naugha has seen me work wonders in the markets, and so he thinks I'm always going to do the same wherever I go."

Tibble nodded and said, "In all me life, Alex, I've seen the likes of Mithral only a number of times. Once I was able to lay me hands on a breastplate made of the fine material, and then only for the briefest moment. But never in my days did I think I would hold a piece of the raw ore in me hands and call it me own. That's because of you, lad. I know you will always do right by your kin, as you already have."

Tibble and I walked toward the mouth of the cave and I asked for a status update on the mining efforts and on the leveling of the dwarves.

"Both have been steady, lad. We haven't delved deep into the mine, and yet still we are finding thick veins of the Fermium. Decent quality as well. The lads are also improving their skills at an even pace, both in mining and fighting. We can handle all of the creatures around this mine with little effort, but even now we would have fallen to the Orckin. I remind the boys of that, and so they keep working."

I was happy to hear about the leveling progress of our brothers, but my attention was on the Fermium that Tibble mentioned.

"I know you are using some of the Fermium here to make arrowheads, but have you tried your hand at any additional items?"

"Aye. Thaddeus has been working away at a number of battle axes made of the Fermium ore, but he hasn't been terribly successful. We hate to use the Medium Quality ore for this, but if we used Low Quality, it is almost certain that Thaddeus would create a product no better than the axes we have now. It wouldn't be worth the effort."

"What happens to the axe when he fails? Can any of the materials be saved?"

"Aye, if we use the Medium Quality ore and Thad fails, we can usually recover the ore at Low Quality. We then sell that ore. Everything else we need to make the axes is lost, though."

"And if successful, how well do the axes sell?"

"Have no idea, lad! We been using 'em!"

I saw the wisdom in that and didn't question the decision. The better gear the dwarves had, the more they could defend the mine. And the better these boys would be when we decided to conquer the second level of this mine. That was definitely going to happen eventually.

"Have you successfully mined any High Quality Fermium?"

"Aye again, although not much. We've been selling that straight away to finance the mine, improve the defenses, and improve the forge. Not to mention the materials needed at the forge to make the goods. And I can't be forgettin' the lovely Sharla. She be costin' us a pretty penny."

I sighed inwardly. I didn't think I would be able to get much out of Tibble cash-wise, but it sounded like they were running the mine at about even. I said as much.

"Oh no, lad, not at all. We be getting lots of Low Quality ore, and we sell that Under the Mountain. The more advanced smiths can take a number of Low Quality and combine them to make 'em Medium Quality. And it is in high demand. There ain't many veins producing like we are!"

"I realize not much time passed between our bargain with the King, but did he come through with any Mithral? I am guessing yes based on your earlier statement."

"He did indeed, lad. Low, Medium, and a piece of High Quality ore. We are following the same plan as with the Fermium. Sell the Low Quality, save the Medium for forging, and the High Quality is being saved for when we can hire a Master Smith to craft us an item with it."

I thought over this plan and found I didn't like it. Thaddeus was doomed to fail on every single Smithing try he made with the Mithral, even when he maxed out his skill with the Fermium. I needed to test a theory, but if my thoughts were correct, I should be able to convince Tibble to change his selling strategy.

"The Mithral. Does the same hold true about high level smiths being able to combine pieces of Medium Quality to make Higher Quality?"

"Master Smiths only, and there are few of them. Only one or two that work outside of the King's personal forge."

"If you could supply these Smiths with Medium Quality Mithral, how well would they pay?"

Tibble started smiling and said, "The King guards the Mithral closely and controls any flow outside his personal forge. Them Masters are hard pressed to even get a piece of Medium Quality, let alone the High Quality. They would pay out the nose me boy."

"Second question. What happens, Tibble, when you fail with a Low Quality ore?"

"Ya lose the ore entirely. And of course all of the parts to make the item."

"But how quickly would Thaddeus go up in skill if he was working with Low Quality Mithral ore? Enough to offset the cost and in turn improve to the point where he was producing successful pieces of High Quality Fermium?"

Tibble thought about this for a few moments and then nodded his head in the affirmative. "Aye, he would progress quickly. I didn't consider using this method to raise his skill with Mithral in order ta work the Fermium. I see why Naugha worries about ya," Tibble finished while laughing.

"Good thing I am always thinking about how to benefit my friends and my kin first then," I said while smiling.

"So what do ya suggest then?"

"Continue in the same method with the Fermium until Thaddeus feels he can be successful on one of every three combinations with the High Quality. But in order to get there, he needs to start working the Mithral, even though we know he will fail every time.

"Sell the Low Quality and the High Quality Fermium, until he has mastered the Medium Quality. Then sell the Low and Medium and work only with the High. Even when he fails a High Quality attempt, you will still get a Medium Quality ore as a byproduct, yes?"

"Yes."

"For the Mithral, save the High Quality as you planned, let Thaddeus work the Low Quality, and sell the Medium Quality."

Tibble began running the numbers in his head and, after a few moments, realized he would be making a profit. But he needed to control the flow of ore out of the mine.

"Last thing. In order to make sure you don't flood the market and drop the price of Fermium, you need to control how much you are releasing. Have you been doing that?"

"No, lad. That is a common practice by us dwarves, but we haven't produced so much that we are in danger of reaching that level. But I already planned to put such a thing in place."

"Good! Then I have nothing more."

Tibble shook his head at me. "We be kin, lad. I know better. You boys are going to the Mountain to look for armor for Naugha and the Blessed One. That ain't going to be cheap. How much you need?"

I smiled at Tibble and placed my hand on his large shoulder. "Thank you, brother, but we can't be taking from our kin, or our mine, when we have just started. We will find another way to raise the money.

"However, I would suggest a system to reward the members of the Clan. A system where each member of the Clan receives a percentage of the profits from the mine. It will embolden them to work harder. Or in this case, encourage them to continue working hard!"

Tibble thought for several moments on this recommendation and then nodded. "Ain't never been done before, but I like this idea too,

Alex. Gives everyone a real stake in the mine. Not just for the Clan but for their future dreams. I'll put it in place."

"Then all that is left is to find a guide to the Mountain once TheClaw has received his arrow heads, Naugha reviews the defenses, and Allister convinces Sharla to stop bowing and kneeling in front of him."

We both laughed as we left the mine and saw, in fact, that Jason was now kneeling in front of Sharla begging her to stand, with her trying to kneel lower to remain below him. The two continued to get lower to the ground and looked like they would lay on the ground before they would give up by the time we were in front of them.

October 10th, 2043

I was contemplating what choices we had in front of us while Jason continued to complain about the treatment he received from Sharla. We had spent the evening at the East Range Mountain Clan mine, and Sharla never left his side the entire time. Even when he logged back in, she was right there waiting for him.

Jason was very embarrassed by the whole situation and begged our guide, Brindle, to please get the East Range Dwarves to please stop referring to him as "Blessed One."

"Ha!" Brindle said while shaking his head. "Ain't no chance them dwarves is gonna stop that!"

"Can you at least get Sharla to stop kneeling in front of me?"

Brindle shook his head seriously. "Nope. She scares me. Scares all of us."

Wayne laughed but sympathized with his friend, "It could be worse, brother."

"Oh really? How?"

"Basically anything having to do with Dan."

That got all of us laughing. Even Dan.

"Ok, you have a point. I still don't like it," Jason conceded.

While the guys were going back and forth, I kept thinking about our dilemma. My plan had failed entirely, and now we were far away from the Capitol. Far away from any of the mobs that could give us experience and loot. We still had no idea how we were going to raise any money. I was very frustrated.

"I hate to interrupt the fun, but bringing us back to business, anyone have a clue how we are going to make any money. I'm seriously out of ideas," I said.

"Haven't really thought about it, Alex. You handle the money things," Wayne said.

"I know. And that's what has me pissed. I can't come up with any ideas."

"Well, how have we done it in the past?" Jason asked.

I thought about that for a moment. Each time we have needed money, we have come across an area or a dungeon that has set us up. We haven't been hard pressed for cash like we are now, at least not for a while. Even if we hadn't set up the dwarves with all of their gear, we might have enough to outfit Dan or myself, but we still wouldn't have enough for everyone.

"Things have just fallen in our laps, I guess. The undead. The dungeons. The Simple Ring of Might. How quickly we were able to collect the Venom Sacks on our very first quest. I guess we've just been really lucky."

"That's an understatement," mumbled Dan.

"We can't rely on that, though. That's obvious now. We need to come up with a way to make some money regularly, at least until the mine starts producing."

Wayne and Brindle, who were talking tanking strategies, perked up at the mention of the mine. "What does the mine have to do with anything?"

"I made some recommendations to Tibble on selling and whatnot. He saw the value in them. One of them was to begin giving a percentage to every member of the clan from the profits. A small percentage. But it will grow as the mine becomes more profitable."

"You made him give us a percentage?" Wayne asked angrily, almost yelling.

"Calm down there, big guy. It's for everyone. Ask Brindle what he thinks."

Wayne looked over at Brindle and saw the young dwarf was shaking his head. Wayne immediately thought he was angry. But then Brindle spoke. "Really Alex? For everyone?"

I nodded my head.

"That's...that's never been done. We all get a small salary, and we all hope to branch out on our own one day, but that is hard to do. This would make it possible to do... to do so much. Thank you, Alex. Thank you!"

Brindle approached me and gripped my forearm, with me doing so in kind.

"You had something you wanted to say, Wayne?"

"I hate it when you're right all the time. Sorry."

I laughed it off and patted the giant warrior on his upper back. I couldn't reach his shoulder. "I'll always do right by the Clan, brother. So stop worrying about that."

Wayne looked very embarrassed, but I waved him off. "Back to the matter at hand. Money."

"I could sell arrows," Dan said. "Or at least the shafts. I'm not going to share my Fermium arrowheads."

"Would those sell well, just the shafts?" Jason asked.

"For a bundle of 100 Birch, I could probably get 10 gold."

"Not bad. How long would that take to craft?"

"Two hours."

"Two hours out of leveling, when I'm sure we are going to need to increase our levels to do any of the next quests without dying," I said.

"Yeah. And any more than that and I would lose my mind. I could always make the Elven Elder shafts and clean up in no time."

"First off, too late on the mind. Second, not a chance. I don't want anyone knowing about those arrows and looking for our tree." In order to replenish his stock of arrows, Dan had spent a couple of hours collecting more of the Elven Elder wood while we were at the mine.

"I could be a Cleric for Hire," Jason added.

"That's really a thing?" I asked.

"Yeah. Some groups look for an extra healer who stays out of the group, periodically healing and buffing, like when I give Naugha magical protection or magically increase our resistances to disease, poison, and the like. It allows the group a shorter down-time between pulls, but the extra healer doesn't get experience. The going rate is about 10 gold an hour for a cleric with my level and skills."

"Again, it stops you from leveling. I don't like it."

"Me either," said Jason, "but I'm looking for solutions."

"I know, man. Thanks."

"Wayne? Any ideas?"

"I kill stuff," Wayne said.

"Noted."

I looked around at the guys for anything else, but they were all deep in thought. Even Brindle, which made me smile.

"Keep thinking, guys. No idea too crazy," I said. Then I added, "That doesn't count for Dan."

Dan was reaching out to say something just as I made that last statement and put his hand down. There's no telling what I just saved us from.

CHAPTER 3

We continued walking for a couple more hours. I was happy that Resurgence had a map function, because there was no way I would have been able to find this location again without a guide. Dan probably could, if he had been paying attention, but it was doubtful he was. Like me, he was probably relying on his map to pinpoint our destination.

Looking out into the distance, I didn't realize that Brindle had stopped next to a cliff face and a copse of trees. I stopped walking and looked back at Brindle with a question.

"We're here."

I looked around again and could not see a cave opening, or a door, or anything that would indicate we had arrived at our location.

"I don't want to question you, but I'm having a hard time imagining that this is the entrance to the Mountain."

"Aye, Alex. 'Tis not the main entrance. This be for dwarves and their kin. Tibble wanted ya to know this one and the main. When ya leave, one of the dwarves from the clan who still reside in the mountain will take ya back through the grand gates and on your way back to Kich's Keep."

Brindle then got very serious. "I don't need to be tellin' ya, this ain't a location most folks know. Only a handful of non-dwarves ever seen this way. Our clan trusts ya like family, but others may not. Keep it to yourselves unless asked."

Brindle then walked over to a spot on the side of the mountain and put his hand against the rock. I saw a flash of light when his palm rested against the stone.

"Do like I just did. Note the spot. Hand against the rock and the Mountain will recognize ya as kin."

Dan was the first to approach, and he looked around the area extensively before pointing to the specific spot to touch. I knew Dan was committing it all to memory. Brindle nodded, and Dan placed his hand on the cliff. The same bright light was seen as with Brindle. Brindle let out a loud sigh.

"Wasn't sure it was going to work, huh?" I asked.

Brindle laughed and nodded his head. "Aye, brother. I was there when the King Under the Mountain accepted ya as kin, but I didn't know if the Mountain would as well."

"Wait. The mountain is alive?" Wayne asked.

"Not like ya be thinking, Naugha. Ya can't tank it!" Brindle said with a mighty laugh. Wayne chuckled as well.

"But the Mountain be the home of dwarves for a thousand or more years. We don't know the relationship between the King and our Mountain, but every king has said they ascend and feel as one with her. Beyond me tiny warrior brain. I'm just glad she recognizes ya."

Jason and Wayne went next, with me approaching last. Ever since I learned the Wanderer had muddled with my in-game code, I worried about what effect it could have on game play. If this didn't work, I would have a lot of explaining to do.

Thankfully, I was met with the same light, and we all now had access to the Mountain. But I still didn't see a door.

Without another word, Brindle walked toward the rock face. And then right through it. Not missing a beat, we all followed suit and found ourselves inside a tunnel.

I had no doubt that if I hadn't been granted permission to enter, that rock face would have not been forgiving, and I would have lost a few hit points smacking my noggin against the stone.

We hadn't been in the tunnel for five minutes when a young dwarf came running up to us, out of breath. "The King...Under the Mountain...he requests your presence in the throne room," he said, clearly panting.

"You run all the way here, lad?" Brindle asked. The young dwarf nodded.

"That's not a short run. Take a moment to rest and then you can lead us back," Brindle stated.

The dwarf thanked Brindle, accepted a drink of water from his pouch, and stood for a few moments with his hands on his knees. He was very young—still without a beard—and didn't seem to need much time before he was ready to lead us on to the throne room.

"Is this a bad thing, Brindle?" I asked.

Brindle shrugged his shoulders and said, "Don't know. Never met the King meself."

The young dwarf spoke up, "Lord Steelhammer called everyone to the throne room when you arrived, but he didn't seem upset."

I thanked the dwarf and we continued on in silence for the next several minutes until we reached the vast cavern that acted as the throne room for the King Under the Mountain. A large door blocked the entrance, made of stout wood, and I had no doubt it would take a sizeable army to get through that door. Two guards, one on each side of the door, stood at attention as we approached.

Sometimes I wished Resurgence had more than just the five colors to delineate the level of the mob and the danger it poses to the player. Green was an adversary of little difficulty, three or more levels below the player. White was one level below or at the same level, while Blue represented a mob one or two levels above the player, and Yellow three or four levels. Anything more than that and the mob was Red. But that didn't tell you if the mob was 5 levels or 15 levels above, and made it pretty difficult to gauge the risk versus reward of trying an attack.

For example, each of the guards at the door was red to me, but my money was on 15 levels and not five, and so I knew they could likely take out my whole group without breaking a sweat. The dwarven guard placed his hand against the door, and a bright light shone. After that, the guard easily pushed the door open and announced our arrival.

"The East Range Mountain Dwarf Clan!"

There was no mention of "and guests," so I took that to mean we were accepted as part of the clan. The guards ignored us almost entirely until Wayne began to pass the threshold. Both guards looked at Wayne and gave a single nod in recognition. Warriors did stuff like that.

King Under the Mountain, Lord Steelhammer, was not sitting on his throne. In fact, I couldn't even see a chair that would qualify as a throne. Instead, Lord Steelhammer was walking toward my group with a big smile on his face. I felt a tension in my shoulders ease that I didn't even realize was there. Dealing with unknown, powerful NPCs could go wrong quickly, and it seems my paranoia manifested without me realizing it.

"Boys, make no mistake. I ain't be joking when I tell ya to hide your Mithral around this one!" the King said as he approached and clasped wrists with me.

"That joke will never get old, Lord Steelhammer," I said.

"What joke? You negotiated a Dwarf out of Mithral! That ain't something that be happening every day, lad. You be famous already!"

I laughed and regarded the other dwarves. All had smiles on their faces and looked anxious to meet us newcomers.

"What took ya so long to get here? Figgered you and your boys would be 'round before now. Not out causin' trouble I hope. And how be the tree?"

"What tree?" I replied.

"Good lad. Keep that one as close as you would the secret entrance ya came through."

"On our word."

"Good enough for me! Now, what brings ya boys down to the Mountain?"

I explained to the King our needs for better armor, and how we knew we would find no better steel for Wayne and Jason than here among the Dwarves. Further, I told him that this was a preliminary look, as we hadn't the funds yet to purchase the high quality products the Dwarves produced. The King nodded his head in understanding.

"You're welcome here amongst us, me boy. Feel free to look around at yer leisure. I'll have one of me kin go around with ya, so you don't get lost."

"Afraid I'll run off with more Mithral?" I asked jokingly.

"Bah! You ain't be the thievin' type. You used them sweet words to fleece me good!" the King responded in kind, adding his own laughter.

Another dwarf approached the King and said, "Me Lord."

"Aye, I had not forgotten, Perry" the King said as he looked at me. "This here be one of our Master Smiths, Perry Firehands. He has asked if he can look at the shoulders of the Blessed One."

Jason groaned behind me, and I smiled a bit. Lord Steelhammer took Jason's reaction to be a negative response and asked if he had offended the cleric.

"It's not that, Lord Steelhammer. I just wish people would stop calling me Blessed One. Some take it a little too seriously."

The King gave me a sidelong glance with a raised eyebrow.

"Sharla," I responded.

All of the dwarves in hearing distance started laughing mightily. The King was the first to respond. "You're lucky that one didn't demand to come with ya! She didn't tell you her story did she?"

Jason shook his head and said, "She almost did force her way to come with us. Tibble had to remind her three times of her contract before she would relent!"

"Aye, sounds about right. She be a distant relation to Grumblewat. She considers any piece of his armor to be a dwarven treasure and would likely put herself in any danger to protect 'em."

"Can we just stop with the 'Blessed One' stuff for now? Please."

The King nodded his head and every dwarf in the room did the same. Jason gave a sigh of appreciation.

"How can I help the Master Smith?"

"He would like to look at them shoulders, if ya don't be minding. Just examining a work of Grumblewat's can tell a lot to a Smith of his level."

"Of course, Lord Steelhammer."

Master Smith Perry approached Jason and began looking at the shoulders closely. He took out a pair of spectacles with varying colors of lenses and started flipping through the color spectrum while examining the armor. Jason stood still for the examination, and after ten minutes, Perry spoke to our cleric. Jason looked over at the smith quizzically.

"Everything ok, Allister?" I asked.

"Yeah. But I got a personal quest from Perry here. Basically, it says that if I get more armor like this, let him examine it. Reward is experience. See any problems with it?"

I thought for a moment. After considering the situation, I looked at the King. "I see no issues with it, as long as Allister can let any other Master Smith or below examine them at his leisure."

"Ha! Told you Perry! This one will see through any loophole! Not to worry Alex, there are no restrictions on what the Bless—dammit, I mean Allister does with his items."

Jason nodded, accepted the quest, and let out a "whoop!" when he got a nice amount of experience from Perry "If I receive any more pieces of Grumblewat's armor, I will be sure to find you, Master Smith. As long as Sharla doesn't find me first!" Laughter could be heard throughout the mountain.

We spent almost two hours walking through the marketplace of the Mountain. Almost everything one could find at a regular market was there, including leather armor for me and Dan. As we suspected, however, the armor was more expensive and of a lower quality than what we could find in the Keep. The same could not be said for the plate armor.

There was so much plate, and so many merchants selling it, we were overwhelmed at first. Even I didn't know where to start.

And Wayne... Well, Wayne was like a kid in a candy shop—if that kid had no adult supervision and the shop had a sign saying "Free

Candy All Day, Every Day!" He looked at everything wide-eyed, and on multiple occasions I almost had to slap his hand away and tell him "no touching!" Dan and Jason soaked up the experience and enjoyed themselves. It did take me a few minutes to convince Dan that, despite the fact that we weren't buying anything for him, he still couldn't go off to the tavern and get blitzed. It was an overall excellent experience, though, and another new thing for us in Resurgence. I had to remind myself that my friends were in this for the game, and these moments meant the most for them. For me, this was a means to an end, a tool toward finding the code, even if I still didn't understand entirely.

What I understood quite well by now, though, was that our upgrades were not going to be cheap. Even the armor without stat bonuses or magical properties was expensive. With our discount for having a friendly disposition to the dwarves, each suit of full armor of a Fine quality would run 5 platinum. High Quality was 10 platinum each. It wouldn't cost us quite that much since both Wayne and Jason had items they wouldn't be replacing, but it was still going to cost a fortune. It wasn't that long ago that we worked our asses just to raise a single platinum piece each for our horses.

The only purchase we made ended up being for me. I had been using a crap dagger in my off-hand to help me level my Dual Wield and up my DPS. We decided to replace it with a Shiny Dagger that had a better attack modifier and only cost us five gold. Given my earlier faux pas with the bear, I was reminded that I needed to be focused on my attack strategy now more than ever. If they only knew.

I talked to as many NPCs as I could. I was hoping to find an NPC quest giver that in turn could lead to us raising some money. Unfortunately, they were all regular NPCs and had nothing but their wares or hellos to offer. Things just weren't going our way.

"Maybe we could go at the second level of the mine," Brindle said as we kept walking through the market.

I looked over at him with a questioning look on my face. Brindle stopped and stared up at me, stating, "Well you said you wanted ideas."

I nodded, thankful that even Brindle was trying to come up with ways for us to make some cash. I knew the second level of the mine was going to be out of our league, though, and said as much. I also thanked Brindle for his recommendation.

"Ya don't think with our new armor and skills we could take it?" he asked.

"Sorry, but I'm guessing that dungeon is going to be way out of our league. I could have checked when we were there last, but based on my experience, we would get slaughtered."

"If there be Fermium on that top level, I can't imagine what be below it. Would have to be something better. Maybe even Mithral."

"Or maybe nothing at all," I countered. "And it wouldn't be worth getting ourselves killed. I don't want to see Naugha sacrificing himself again."

That quieted Brindle. The dwarves still remembered the selfless sacrifice that Wayne had made so that none of them would die when we took the mine. For the dwarves, Wayne gave his life so that no more from the Clan would die. For that, they named Wayne and the rest of us "kin" to the Clan.

Brindle nodded, and kept on. I didn't want to dissuade the young dwarf, though.

"It was an excellent idea, brother. And we will tackle that second level. Just not yet. Keep improving on the battlefield, and you can be sure we will explore that region soon enough."

Dan had been mostly quiet during our travels through the Mountain, so it was a bit of a surprise when he spoke up suddenly.

"Range and grind," Dan said.

"What?"

"I've been thinking it over a lot. And I don't see any option for us. We are going to have to range out and grind through. It sucks, but that's part of the game. If we just stay in one place, there is no way we will make enough to improve our armor. We need to range out farther from the Keep and start grinding through mobs.

"And we haven't really explored the city either. Could be some quest NPCs that we haven't found that give experience and cash for mundane tasks, like collecting venom sacks. I think our best chances will be there, not here in this area."

Jason and Wayne nodded in agreement. I had come to a similar conclusion. The trip to the Mountain hadn't been a total loss, though. We had found a secret entrance to the home of the dwarves, I had established a system for the East Range Mountain Clan to make more profit, and we had a solid understanding of the type of money we would need to raise our armor class. But now it was time to go.

"Brindle, we thank you greatly for all of your assistance, but it's time for us to get back to the Keep. You said there was a member of the Clan here that could lead us back toward the crossing to the city?"

"Aye, he should be around the main gate, waiting for us. Will be sad to see ya lads go, though."

"Don't worry. We'll be seeing each other soon enough, I am sure."

The trip to the main gate only took a matter of ten to fifteen minutes, with an additional twenty minutes to find our guide. Dwarves and even a few non-dwarves crowded the area in front of the gate. That was the first we had seen anyone other than dwarves, but these too were NPCs. I took the time to speak with them, hoping they were quest givers, but such was not the case. Each was a merchant selling wares that were not produced commonly by the dwarves, but none were selling armor.

Our guide, Cog, was stoic but ready to get us on our way. I assured the dwarf that once we were in a location we were familiar with, he could return home. Cog seemed happy with that news and led us out of the Mountain.

We could have traveled much quicker with our horses, but since Cog did not have a mount, we were forced to walk. I checked with Dan when we exited the Mountain, but he was unfamiliar with the terrain. We directed Cog to begin leading us toward the closest main road, and he readily agreed.

During our walk, Cog thanked us for all of the work we had done for the Clan. He noted that the prosperity of the Clan had never been higher, and he was constantly busy selling the wares coming out of our mine. I told him about the new arrangement made with Tibble, and much like Brindle, this gave him pause.

"This is for the whole Clan, or just those working the mine?" Cog asked suspiciously.

"The whole Clan, brother, whether in the Mountain or in the mine. All will reap the reward."

"I don't know how the King will take that, but I can tell you all of the East Range boys is going to be as happy as TheClaw in a tavern on half off night!"

Jason spit out the water he was drinking and looked at Cog, "What? What did you just say?"

Dan piped up immediately, "My legend is known far and wide, Allinator!"

Wayne and I were laughing uncontrollably, and Jason walked off in a huff. As we were settling down I saw Dan hand Cog a few coins and heard him whisper, "Perfect. Absolutely perfect."

We continued on for another hour, with Dan steadily pestering Jason to recognize his greatness. Jason kept repeating that Dan was not a legend, and never would be. I don't know when Dan had orchestrated the interaction with Cog, but I was fully ready to give TheClaw his recognition. It was beautifully executed.

We soon came upon the road and recognized where we were. We thanked Cog for his assistance and bid him safe travels back to the Mountain.

"If ever you come back through our way, be sure to look me up. I like this one," Cog said while pointing at Dan.

"Heaven help us, he has a fan!" Jason exclaimed after Cog had departed and we had summoned our mounts.

"It was bound to happen, Allister. The mentally ill have always gravitated toward each other, and there had to be a few unstable NPCs in the game. Sad he is a part of our Clan." Wayne said.

"Not cool, man! You are totally not getting the first edition of 'TheClaw official Fan Club' buttons I'm having made up. Allistilla will, though. I know he is my number one fan."

"That title belongs to Broham, and only because you bribe him with food," Jason replied.

"I'm totally up for bribery. Name your price, cleric."

Jason seemed to think about that for a moment then shook his head. "If I didn't know you were filthy rich, I wouldn't have even considered that thought. But for a brief moment there, it was tempting," Jason said while laughing.

The road we were traveling took us through the checkpoint we originally crossed to arrive at the Capitol. Soon enough, we were back in the area around the city and stopped to consider our next moves.

"If we want to range and grind, we can do so from out here or head back to the Keep and start from there. Any preference?" Wayne asked.

"Dan made a good point earlier when he said we still needed to see if we can find some NPC quest givers in the Capitol. That city is huge, and I doubt we really saw much of it," Jason said.

"See, he is already recognizing my greatness."

"From now on I'm just going to stay quiet," Jason replied.

"Nah, we'll put a ball gag in Dan's mouth before we let that happen. Or something similar. He might like that," I said.

"Not necessary," Dan said. We all nodded our thanks. "Besides," he added, "rubber tastes horrible."

We all looked toward him. Wayne finally broke the silence saying, "Seriously man, I don't know if you are kidding half the time."

"Me neither, brother. Me neither."

Dan's suggestion panned out and we found a number of NPCs that were providing low level quests. Well, low level for the Keeps region. In most cases, they required us to turn in a number of items to the NPC, and in kind we would receive experience and cash. For example, those Fine Quality skins we had already mailed to our friend in Port Town would have fulfilled one of these quests. We decided as a group to forego that particular quest, as we wanted backpacks for our group desperately. It wasn't much of a decision either as it required 20 skins—five from each of us—to complete the quest, and it also took five skins to make one backpack. I had no doubt that as we progressed in the game, that extra carrying capacity was going to be necessary, and we could find other ways to grind.

Other quests required items from different animals, while some just required a kill count. One of the latter specifically required us to kill 100 undead mobs. Naturally, we gravitated toward that quest because of our past experience grinding undead with Wayne's hammer and Jason's Banish Undead spells. Activating the quest as our primary, however, did not show where those undead were located. In the end, we received six different quests and we would have to accomplish them through normal game play. Things were looking up, and I liked this idea of ranging out more and more. Not that we had much of a choice.

"Well, Dan, this was your idea, and a good one at that," Jason said. "So it's your choice. What direction do you want to go first?"

Dan didn't comment on Jason's recognition of his good idea. Instead, he took an arrow from his quiver, threw it in the air with a spin, and let it land on the ground. Once he saw what direction the arrow head was pointing, he picked it back up and put it in his quiver. Then he pointed and said, "that way."

"Very scientific of you, Dan," Wayne said.

"You know how it goes, 'When you have no idea where you want to go, let luck lead your way.' Or something like that."

"Should have let Alex do the twirling, then."

"Damn! I didn't even think of that!"

With our direction laid out, we headed away from the Keep and got ready for a long, drawn out session of grinding for experience and, hopefully, cash.

Washington D.C.

The General entered a spacious office, and was led by an administrative assistant to a large wooden desk adorned with framed photos of family and notable people of power in Washington.

The woman behind the desk, rising to welcome the General, was Melanie Grissten, Director of the Federal Bureau of Investigations. Grissten had held the position for the last three years, and was well respected by law enforcement and within the Beltway.

On top of that, Director Grissten was no pushover, having defended her people and organization numerous times on The Hill and in the White House. This was one meeting the General had definitely not been looking forward to having, even if his earlier meeting at the White House with the President's National Security Advisor had led him to believe it was unavoidable.

"Good morning, General. Please have a seat. Would you like anything? Coffee? Water?"

"Coffee would be great." The General watched as Grissten nodded toward her assistant and then sat behind her desk.

He took a moment to soak in the various awards that rested on the walls, and the pictures of Director Grissten's children on the desk. The General noted there were more pictures of her family than awards on the walls, a trait he found admirable.

"How is the family, Director? The kids look to be getting big," the General said, nodding toward a photo with Grissten and her three children.

"A handful." Grissten's exasperated sigh did little to conceal her obvious pride in and devotion to her family. "Both of the boys are playing sports, and Emily is competing for a programming scholarship for college next fall. If ever there were a separation between brains and brawn, it would be those three."

The assistant returned at that moment with the General's coffee and left after verifying that Director Grissten wanted her calls held until after the meeting had ended.

With the door closed, Grissten brought out a manila folder and set it on her desk.

"A little outside your lane on this one, don't you think, General?"

The General couldn't help the smile that formed on his face. One of the reasons he admired and respected Melanie Grissten was her no frills approach to getting the job done.

"You didn't even let me get through my coffee this time."

The Director smiled in kind, as she knew what the General meant. "This is serious business. We can chat over coffee after, that is, if we are still talking."

The General put his game face back on before answering. "My oath is clear, Director. I am to defend this country against all enemies, foreign and domestic. This falls in my lane, and the White House agrees."

"Well, I wasn't at that meeting, now was I? I wonder how it would have gone if I had been."

"It would have gone the same. My unit is already established within the network. This is not a time to be changing drivers."

"You suspect AltCon of tampering with the minds of players—a serious criminal offense—and you want me to do nothing about it?" The Director quipped, tapping on the manila folder.

Within those pages was the framework, set up by the General, to get FBI assistance on the operation. In a support role only. The General needed more information about AltCon than his resources could uncover, and the FBI was the top game in town. The FBI, however, worked to investigate, arrest, indict, and convict. All of their efforts went toward those goals. In this instance, the General was telling them to stop after the first step. Investigate only. It's why he wasn't looking forward to this meeting. It's like telling a soldier to advance on the enemy, but then don't fire, even when fired upon.

"I don't want you to 'do nothing.' I need the thing your Bureau does better than any other law enforcement agency in the world: unraveling the mystery. I have small pieces, Director, but there is definitely more going on here." The General pointed at the folder. "You've read the report?"

"I have. That is why I don't understand your request. Let me subpoena a few of the players and take brain scans. That should show the same results as your inside man."

"Wouldn't be enough." Fortunately, the General had already predicted this suggestion. "We were lucky to have a historic brain scan—that DoD was in complete possession and control of—prior to taking the second one you see there. So our findings are not in question. Even if you could find a player who was willing to give a historic brain scan, there is no telling how that would hold up in court.

"Not to mention, who knows what the players would end up saying to their AltCon reps. Our guy has the training necessary to do the work and avoid suspicion." The General thought he might have been selling Dan a little too hard at this point, but it wasn't that big of a stretch considering how he altered his backstory as needed. "Grabbing random players could severely tip our hand and bring the operation to a grinding halt."

"Isn't the goal of the operation to stop AltCon from tampering with the players' minds?" The Director asked, already knowing the answer to her question. "We're putting people at risk to get the whale, and we both know it." The General understood she wanted that part said out loud.

"You know that just stopping them isn't the ultimate goal," The general replied gruffly. "We want to stop AltCon entirely, and to do that we need to know why they are messing with these peoples' heads."

The Director of the FBI sat back in her chair and stared at the General for several long moments. Director Grissten would assist the DoD. That was not in question. The file on her desk was from the White House, and it had given her the most general of instructions to "support the General" in his operation. What the Director was deciding now was just how that support would manifest.

"Alright. You're playing it straight with me. That's the most I could ask for. Figured you would, but I had to be sure. What do you need if you don't want us to build a case for the mind tampering?" Grissten asked while taking out an old-school notepad to write on.

The General nodded his head in thanks. "Information," he replied. "Information on AltCon, their leadership, and any dramatic changes within the last six months to a year. I don't have to tell you that discretion is key here."

"You do realize you are talking about one of the largest companies in America, right? It's not like I can just call down to the boys in

'AltCon Division' and have them bring up a file. I'll have to assign some Agents. And you don't need to tell me about discretion, General. I know what's at stake here."

"I know that." The General made sure Grissten understood he had complete faith in her stewardship of the FBI. "And I'm not talking about a full work-up of AltCon's history. Whatever they are doing would have to be decided at the highest levels. That's who I want to know about."

"Ok, that we can do. I can tell you right now that the CEO and President of AltCon, whom everyone just calls 'The Old Man,' is a bit of a recluse. Getting information on him won't be easy."

"I understand," the General said.

"Anything else?"

"Robert Shoal. He was the lead designer for the game's artificial intelligence. He died in circumstances that my office believes to be suspicious. I would like you to look into that as well."

"Can't just say, 'We think someone killed him' like normal people do?"

"I want your team to look at it without any preconceived notions."

The Director finished taking notes and raised an eyebrow at the General.

"That's it. I know it isn't much, but I will share fully with your office on this one, Director. I was not kidding when I told the President's advisor that I believed this to be a great threat to our country."

"Good to know. We'll keep you informed as well." The Director stood up from behind her desk and briefly rolled some of the tension out of her shoulders while looking out the window. "Now let's go get some coffee, General. And you can start calling me Mel now. You know, since I'm not going to tear your head off."

CHAPTER 4

October 14th, 2043
AltCon Tech Room

"Mr. Jolston, sir."

Terrance Jolston looked up from the hand-held device he was holding and nodded toward the technician walking his way.

"Sir, you previously asked us to keep an eye on Subject 271, the player who noted a bug not previously seen in the game."

"Yes, I remember the player. Is there an update?"

"The player continues to do well in the game, sir. His group received two titles: Bunny Slayer and Bandit Conqueror. His group was also the first to reach Level 20 and enter Kich's Keep."

"Items?"

"Mostly merchant bought and not terribly high. He has a nice dagger though, especially for a Rogue. He also has a summoned horse, although those have become more common in the game in the last few weeks."

"He was the one with the Rabbit's foot, right?"

The technician nodded his head. "That's the one, Mr. Jolston."

"Have there been any more reported problems with the log-in and log-out?"

"None, sir."

Looking over at the technician this time, Jolston asked, "And do you see anything odd about the character?"

"Nothing, sir. Seems like a good player, the kind we wanted."

Jolston appeared satisfied with this answer. As an afterthought, Jolston asked, "Out of curiosity, what is his Chance at?"

The technician reviewed his notes again and said, "Base 19. With bonuses, 26."

Jolston had insisted on linking many of the games mechanics to Chance. Most didn't know that. Only those in the technical department knew the secret, and they would never let it out. No one wanted to anger him.

"And is there anyone with a Chance score close to that?"

"I believe so, sir," the tech said while reviewing the pad in his hand. "There is a Level 18 Dark Elf at the Citadel with a Chance of 17, but no bonuses. No one else comes close."

"Well there you go. No surprise he is doing so well. I'll be interested to see how he progresses. Keep me informed."

"Yes, sir. I will make routine inquiries."

I'm a moron. Like a newbie, I had spent the last three days running around the area with Dan, Jason, and Wayne killing anything and everything we came across. The whole time that damn quest given to me by the Wanderer weighed on my mind, and I knew we had to get it started.

The Wanderer. I'm such an idiot.

We wasted days running around when I had, literally, the greatest resource in the game at my disposal. A veritable WikiResurgence was over in the Underground.

We had collected tons of quest turn-in items, gained our Level 21, and had various pieces to sell. That was reason enough to go back to the Keep, where maybe I could start using the gray matter between my ears.

After turning in our quests and receiving some experience and cash, the group had a total of 2 Platinum to their name. This was enough to buy armor for me or Dan but nowhere near enough to take care of either Jason or Wayne. The turn-in quests were repeatable, so we refreshed those and then decided to take a few hours to ourselves.

Wayne believed Jenny and her group would be arriving at the Keep this morning, and he wanted us to be here to greet them when they arrived. I agreed wholeheartedly. Dan, naturally, wanted to scope out the multiple taverns in the city while Jason, aiming for something higher than baron, was off to see if there was a similar title quest in the Capitol. We all thought "Baron" was a good fit and told him so.

I told the guys I was off to scout out merchants. I headed toward the Underground, where I hoped to find the Wanderer. I had questions for him.

As I was heading down the last alleyway, Stan turned the corner, walking right towards me.

Stan was my first teacher and mentor in the game for using the unique Rogue Skills that the Wanderer told me only I had. He also seemed like more than just your regular NPC with depth and emotion. When I thought of him, I thought of how patient he had been. That isn't an attribute one would normally ascribe to an NPC. It shouldn't be any shock that when I saw my old mentor, I was all smiles.

"Sta—I mean Dhalean! How are you?" I yelled out as I approached him.

"Could ya possibly yell any louder boy? I don't think the guards at the castle heard ya," Stan rebuked, though he had a big smile on his face.

"Sorry. I'm really happy to see you is all."

"Me too, boy. And this ain't happenstance. I had someone at the gate watching for ya. I was coming to find ya, so this makes me life a bit easier."

"Find me for what? I was just on my way to the Underground to see our friend," I informed him.

"Well, as it turns out, it's time for your next bit of training."

"Oh. That's awesome! What are you going to teach me?"

"Not I, lad. Him," Stan said while pointing over toward a corner where a very handsome man was coming out of the shadows. He was human and dressed in the finest clothes I had ever seen. It wasn't armor at all, just frills and lace. He was also carrying two very ornate daggers that shined in the little sun that sneaked into the alleyway. He was an NPC, and his name read "Waseem Harami."

I turned back toward Stan and asked, "What can he teach me that you can't?"

Stan just stood there patiently. When I turned back to look at the newcomer again, he was right next to me, just inside my personal space and a little too close for comfort. I took a step back and greeted him properly. "Alex," I said while putting my hand out to shake. "It's nice to meet you."

The Rogue reached out with his own hand and then handed me my coin purse.

"What the hell?" I asked.

"I'm going to teach you how to be a thief. It is the second art of being a rogue. You already know how to sneak around, so says Dhalean, but it's obvious you don't know about protecting yourself from a cutpurse. I'll teach you to perform the task and avoid letting anyone else do it to you. Well, except for me. I am a master after all."

"A master of gibber gabber," Stan said under his breath.

"Now, if you will follow me, I will begin your instruction," Waseem said.

"It's going to have to wait. I'm on my way to talk to the Wanderer. But I'll meet you back here when I'm prepared to begin, or at the Stinky Pit if that is more convenient. Or wherever you deem appropriate."

"The Stinky Pit will work fine, but I'm afraid we need to start now."

"Sorry, can't. Gotta go see the Wanderer. Bye," I said as I was walking the last few steps toward the Underground.

Waseem never turned to follow me as he said, "Poor lad, it is not any young scamp who can walk through to the Underground and request a...hey, where did he go?"

Stan laughed as he walked away saying, "pompous git."

The Wanderer was sitting behind the same desk when I entered his room. He looked to be expecting me.

"Alex. I've been following your progress, and I must say I am a bit perplexed. I saw that you activated the quest I set for you, and the main game quest, but you have not done more than that. Nor have you completed any of the other major quests in the game. You've been spending your time doing meaningless tasks for pittances. Please explain this."

"Hello to you, too. It's that very reason that I am here. We activated the quests for both the main storyline and Lady Tessa, but we came to a very stark realization. We won't be able to tackle these objectives, not with the gear we have."

"I gave you this quest for the very reason of improving your gear. What is the problem?"

"You've seen my character. Hell, all of our characters. Our gear sucks. Yeah, we have some cool rare items, but we are still wearing low-level armor. We spent too much on the dwarves, and that hasn't turned into a steady income, at least not yet. We went to see the Dwarves to fix that issue and to check on improving our gear. When we saw the prices, we couldn't afford any of them," I admitted.

"I told you, I can't place items on mobs that aren't already there. It would alert the people in AltCon," the Wanderer reminded me.

"I don't need you to mess with the game any more than you already have. What I need is information. Somewhere around here has to be mobs that drop money, or perhaps there's a side quest we aren't seeing. If I could find a cash cow, we could be on the road in no time. You literally run this game, so don't worry about gear, just locations."

The Wanderer closed his eyes for a moment and then nodded. "You are right, Alex. With your current equipment allocation, you would likely fall in combat to either the Trolls or the first part of Lady Tessa's quest. You succeeded so quickly through the first part of the game that I did not factor in the level of your items. Your strategies were executed masterfully, and that led you here quicker than I anticipated."

"Thanks. I do appreciate it, but even I have to admit that strategy can only take you so far. I can't overcome insurmountable odds. So I need to even out those odds a bit. Makes sense?"

"It does. As I am sure you have noted, there are many types of creatures in Resurgence. Around the Keep you will find fauna, humanoid, and undead. Farther out there are flora that attack as well, but you won't encounter them for some time. The animals provide little to no money, but their loot is the basis for all crafting skills. The humanoids are likely to drop items more frequently. The undead rarely have items other than spells, but they provide greater amounts of money. As you progress through the game, you will find that the items from animals will likely lead to a greater profit, but that is not the case now. Due to the average level of players and their respective Crafting skills, none could use the high-level animal items successfully, so they probably wouldn't pay a fair price for them. Therefore, I suggest humanoid or undead. What is your preference?"

Since I knew Jason could add his damage to the mix and we could earn money quickly, undead was my first thought. But then it occurred to me: what if we didn't need to earn money?

"You know all the loot tables. Are there any of the mobs that drop the kind of armor that we are looking for? Fine Leather or High Quality Plate?"

The Wanderer shook his head. "Not at your level, no. You could improve to Common Leather from a camp of Horned Goblins to the west of Yerkich, but there aren't any good options beyond that for leather and very few for plate."

"Undead it is then."

"Alex, if you are concerned with these quests and how to complete them, why not just have me show you the best strategy for each?"

"Believe me, that was one of the first things I thought of when I realized I should ask you about places we should go to get gear or money. But the more I thought about it, the less I liked the idea."

"Would this not make your mission to find the code quicker?"

"See, that's the thing. I don't think that it would. In fact, figuring out these quests and making my way through the storyline is likely to be more beneficial. I will be taking note of everything going on and not just rushing from one quest to the next. The more I pay attention to the details, the likelier it is that I will figure out this code problem."

"I can see your logic, but I worry that the obstacles you can't overcome will slow down your progress."

"I'll try it my way at first. If I run into a problem that is too much for me and the team, I will let you know. I don't want to be stagnant at one particular quest or objective, either. Deal?"

"I leave it in your capable hands. I've sent you the locations of the undead."

The Wanderer updated my map, and I thanked him profusely. "This will be a great help, and hopefully I won't have to come down here much more to get this information or any other. Any time I come around here, I am sure I am putting you at risk."

"I am shielded here, but constant travel to see me could raise questions."

"Understood. Thanks again."

"Before you leave, Alex," the Wanderer said as he stood and came around the desk. "Someone in AltCon recently accessed your character."

"Why? What were they looking for?"

"I don't know, exactly. What I do know is that there is an order on your account to review periodically. It is likely due to the bug report you sent in when you first began the game, due to your log-out and log-in position being out of sync. This was not a bug the company had planted within the game, so they are monitoring it. And to that extent, you."

"Is that going to be a problem?"

"For you, no. I have been able to mask all of the improvements in your character through the 'error' you noted on your log-ins. The same error occurs when you log-out, although you do not see that one. In essence, I am showing you as a character without certain skills, items, or the 'Gift' from Lady Tessa."

"So we're good?"

"In regards to your character, yes, but I cannot do the same for those in your group. If AltCon were to look at the others, they would see the Gift and it could be their undoing. I will look for ways to hide theirs as well, but I wanted you to be aware."

"Nothing we can do about that now. I appreciate the update, and please do whatever you can. I know you have every stake in this working."

Since I had a few hours to kill, at least until Jenny and her group arrived, I decided to hit up the Stinky Pit and contact Waseem. I was intrigued with the idea of becoming a thief. The Blacksuit skill had already saved me numerous times, and I knew the power of these additional skillsets.

Waseem was sitting at a table in the corner, sulking over a mug of ale, when I came in. He didn't look up when I approached the table, but he did note, "I thought you were supposed to be a sneak. I could hear you from outside the tavern."

"Well, I wasn't trying to sneak, now was I?" I replied defensively, while standing in front of the table.

"First rule of thieving, always be aware of your surroundings. You turn your Blacksuit on and off, but if you want to know if someone is going to steal your purse, you need to be more aware."

At that moment, another of the inn's patrons walked over to our table and plopped my coin purse on the wood. "He didn't notice a thing," the man said as he walked off.

"Damnit! Again with stealing my coins? Now I see why they have a bank here!"

"Wouldn't that be a fun place to rob," Waseem said with a twinkle in his eye.

I calmed down and took the seat across from Waseem. "Ok, I get it. I suck at the thief stuff. No argument from me there. So what do I need to do?"

"Dhalean tells me you have gotten very good with the shadows at sneaking around. Says you are a natural. If that is the case, this first part won't be hard for ya."

"I'm not up to Dhalean's level, but I'm not bad."

"Hell man, ain't none of us up to Dhalean's level! That little bastard routinely sneaks into the Kings' throne room and just hangs out. And the throne room has more protections than the bank! Little runt will never try to rob it with me though."

I could tell he had a rivalry with Stan but was showing respect for his skills, so I let the comments pass.

"So what do the shadows have to do with being a thief?" I said, changing the subject.

"Everything and nothing. Such is the nature of shadows."

"Wow. Overdramatic much?"

Waseem laughed long and hard at that. "Ok, I like you. So let's get started. First lesson is to understand how the shadows work in this skill. Before, you grabbed the shadows and wrapped them around you to create a skin of sorts that hides you from view. In overcoming a cutpurse or a pickpocket, you grab the shadows, but you don't wrap yourself up. You basically cocoon them around you."

"But that's what I do when I make my Blacksuit. How is this different?"

Waseem nodded his head. "Right, but you grab a lot of shadows to do that. In this case, the smallest amount is all you need. You aren't becoming unseen. You are just creating a barrier against your skin. To the casual observer, you won't look any different."

I nodded in understanding. "And what will happen if I am successful?"

"I prefer for you to succeed and then tell me what you felt."

I stood up and grabbed the smallest amount of shadow around me, then I tried to spread it out over my body, like I would my Blacksuit. I felt like there was a thin layer of cotton laying against my body.

"Ok, now what?"

"Stand in the middle of the room. These four boys are going to walk around you, behind you, in front of you, basically every direction. Your eyes won't be able to see them at all times. Don't worry about it. Use your shadows, not your eyes."

I did as Waseem said and stood in the middle of the room. I stared straight ahead and unfocused my vision. I tried to feel what was happening around me. The four men started circling me like the sharks they were. They were talking to each other, making lewd remarks, and trying to draw my attention. I drowned them all out.

And then I felt it. The slightest push against my side. Another came from my back. One of them stumbled in front of me and I felt the same thing from my belt area. In total I counted five attempts.

Waseem called a halt to the exercise and asked each man to approach him separately. They leaned over and whispered in his ear. When the last one finished giving his secret, Waseem asked me how many times I had been "robbed."

"I counted five attempts. Two from the back, one from my left and right side, and one from the front. That one almost had to pay me for the goods."

The four laughed at that, and Waseem joined them with a chuckle. "Very good. But there were six attempts," he said while placing my coin purse on the table yet again.

"Damn, who did the sixth one?"

"I did," Waseem said. "I'm going to teach you how I did it and how to defend from it, but you are already well on your way to learning the art of Awareness. Practice keeping that layer of shadows around you at all times. Over time, it will become second nature."

I walked over to the table and grabbed my coin purse. Waseem put his hand on my forearm and looked in my eyes. "That was the best first attempt I've ever seen. You have a great future in front of you. Come back to me when you are ready for the next lesson."

With that, I left the Stinky Pit and made my way back toward the city square. I made sure to wrap a thin shadow around me before I made a single step.

The guys were waiting in the city square when I arrived, and they were talking to Wayne.

"She's going to be here any moment," Wayne said and then saw me approaching. "Oh, Alex! There you are. Jenny is coming! I want all of us to give them a big welcome."

"Of course, man. Totally. Dan, what's the closest tavern?"

"Three blocks away. The Wilted Willy."

Wayne laughed and Jason shook his head. Jason said, "There is no way that's the name!"

"It's the Wilted Willow, but I like mine better."

"Me too, TC. I'm totally going with the Willy," I said.

"Encouraging him doesn't help anyone," Jason sighed but smiled along with the rest of us.

"Sounds perfect. Let's head there as soon as they arrive and congratulate them like they did for us. There won't be any other players, but we should get them a drink for sure."

Wayne nodded his head in thanks and then turned as our teammates approached the city square. Wayne took off toward Jenny and embraced her in a Barbarian-sized hug. Gary, Kaitlin, and Tim approached the rest of us. We exchanged regular hugs and bro-hugs: you know, where you are hugging but you are hitting at the same time. Dan tried to go in for a second hug with Kaitlin, but she slapped his arm and laughed him away.

We led the four over to the tavern, with Dan emphasizing the catchy name he had given it. Kaitlin smiled and said, "Naturally you would associate with a place called the Wilted Willy, Dan."

Jason, never one to miss an opportunity like this, gave Kaitlin a high-five and said, "Yeah Dan, tell us about how much you love the Wilted Willy."

Dan turned on Jason immediately and yelled, "Not fair! You hated the name five minutes ago!"

"That was before I saw the wisdom in our Druid's words."

Our laughter could be heard from far away, and the NPCs were looking at us strangely as we walked down the road. One particular NPC brushed past me, and I felt a push against my Awareness. I immediately grabbed his wrist. He turned and said, "Waseem says hi," slipping his wrist from my grip and disappearing down a side alley.

Wayne noticed my attention on the alley and asked, "Everything ok, Alex?"

Kaitlin's pet, Rocky, was nipping at Wayne's heels as he always did whenever Wayne was around. Wayne kept leaning down to scratch behind Rocky's ear and grumbled about having aggro. Wayne had a really soft spot for that wolf.

"All is good, brother. Just thought I saw something. Let's get to the Willy. I could use a drink." I suspected I would be having many similar encounters in the future.

We passed mugs around and told our teammates about our time in the city so far. They were excited to hear about the quest we had received and stated they would go out to the same area and try to trigger it. At 14, Tim's Chance wasn't bad, but I knew that wouldn't be enough to trigger Lady Tessa. Of course, I couldn't tell them that.

I hoped that parts of the quest would be mini-raids, like ones we had done in the past, and I told our teammates that we would want their help if it came to that. They naturally agreed and said they would extend the same offer to us.

As it turned out, our teammates had pretty much the same gear that we did. They had made more money and did not have to spend cash on the Dwarves like we did. They had three casters to our two, and Kaitlin and Tim were pure casters like Jason. Those spells were not cheap at all. Not to mention Jenny also had to pay for new skills like Dan, Wayne, and I did. Overall, we were sitting on about the same amount of cash, but we had been grinding for days to get there. Our teammates would be reaping the rewards from our exploration, and that was ok with me.

I knew that our teammates would end up taking advantage of the undead when we had finished with them, but my competitive streak wanted us to keep the knowledge secret as long as possible.

With Wayne in a serious relationship with Jenny, I expected that to be all of five minutes.

In my mind, I started coming up with a rotation where we could do 4-8 hour stretches at the undead, and then rotate out with our teammates. Their improvement in level was a benefit to us as well.

Kaitlin gave us a rundown on what had occurred at Port Town since we departed. Apparently, there were three other groups who were approaching Level 20 and would soon be joining us in the Keep. All the talk was on a particular group who had no love amongst the players in Port Town.

"They're a bunch of Kill Stealers, Alex," Kaitlin said. "They have made it their tactic to take other's people's mobs and steal the experience. We've made complaints to the administrators, but they've said that the group isn't doing anything wrong. If the game mechanics allow for it, then it can't be challenged. If they had found some kind of exploit that allowed them to do it, then that would be something different."

"Why don't they just kill their own mobs?" I asked.

"Because they're morons. They don't have a brain between them, and that's obvious by the makeup of their group. Not a single main healer. They have a Warrior, a Brawler, a Rogue, and a Paladin. Only the Paladin can heal. They can dish out massive amounts of damage, but they have to sit for long periods of time before they can attack again," Tim explained.

"Yup. So they wait till a group has taken a mob down about twenty percent. Then they establish aggro, jump in, and attack the mob. They end up out-damaging the rightful group and steal their kill. And since the mob doesn't turn on them to aggro until near the end, they lose very little hit points," Gary added.

"They try that stuff with you guys?" Dan asked.

"Yeah. They tried it once," Jenny said with a big smile on her face while looking over at Gary.

Dan couldn't hold the smile off his face, "Oh man, what did you pull?"

"Well, I decided that if they liked killing mobs so much, I would bring them some. I then collected 10 different mobs and took 20 minutes to bring them over to these bastards. I might have forgotten to yell incoming. The only one that survived was their Brawler who was able to Play Dead. He had many a nasty thing to say to me as we both lay there on the ground until the mobs returned to their spawn points," Gary finished while laughing loudly.

I informed our teammates that the Keep was the start of Player vs. Player combat, and that we would need to be careful of this group when they eventually made it this far. If anyone was going to be a bunch of Player Killers, or PKs, it was going to be these guys.

We sat there in the Willy for a couple of hours, drinking, joking, and just enjoying each other's company. None of these people knew that they had been chosen specifically to complete a quest that was bigger than all of us—a quest that had already claimed at least one life. The knowledge weighed heavy on me, but I was determined to not let it get me down. The best thing I could do for my group, and my teammates, was get them all prepared for the inevitable showdown. I only wish I knew where, and when, that was going to be.

FBI Headquarters

The Director for the FBI sat in her office with a heap of paperwork in front of her. Of all the jobs that came with being the Director, Melanie Grissten hated the bureaucracy parts most, even though she knew it should have been expected. The root word of bureaucracy is bureau, after all.

As Director Grissten began to review another file for her approval, her secretary knocked on the door and poked his head in. "Director, Special Agents Bolden and Colvin are here to see you."

"Please send them in, Alan."

Grissten removed the files from her desk and prepared herself mentally for this next meeting. She had tasked Bolden and Colvin with the General's request. Despite having a team of Special Agents already assigned to ongoing investigations on AltCon, Grissten wanted fresh eyes on this project. She hoped to avoid any bleed-over from already preconceived opinions on the company.

"Welcome. Please have a seat and let me know what you have. Alan, I am not to be disturbed unless the call is from the White House or a no-kidding emergency."

Alan nodded his head and shut the door behind him. Alan knew a no-kidding emergency was considered a "direct threat to national security or assassination/death of a senior government official." Grissten didn't expect to be interrupted with those directions.

Annabelle Bolden was lead for this ad hoc team, and she began opening her briefcase as soon as she sat down. She pulled out a thin file and set it upon the closed briefcase, now sitting across her knees.

"Before we get started, did you or Agent Colvin have any problems with the folks in Corporate Concerns?"

"Nothing more than what you would expect, Madame Director. They wanted to know why they weren't responsible for the project and naturally wanted to know what assignment we were working on. Once I told them this was a directive given to us straight from the Director, they complied without further comment. They provided us access to all of their information and have no idea that we are focusing on only the top-tier individuals in the company."

"So nothing I need to deal with in the future to make sure you can complete your task without problems?"

"No, Madame Director, that won't be necessary. Your name holds the weight we needed to get things done without problems."

"Well at least I am good for that!"

Just as Bolden and Colvin looked to say something, Grissten held up her hand and interrupted, "Not fishing for compliments. Let's get to what you found."

"Given the task, we split this up between us. Nico is handling the research on the AltCon higher-ups, and I've been looking into the President/CEO Galvin Schneider, whom everyone calls 'The Old Man.'

"I'll lead off, since the information I have found is not much different than what was found in our archived collection of reports. Schneider started AltCon 40 years ago producing your run-of-the-mill videogames. Prior to that, Schneider worked in his family business, an investment firm started in the early 1900's. Schneider came on the videogame scene with lots of money to his name."

"Nothing nefarious about how his family made their money?"

"Not at all. The Schneider family was squeaky clean."

"Continue."

"Schneider got in on the ground floor of virtual reality. When the company went public, they were already experimenting with limited VR. Many of the advancements in the realm of VR were funded, researched, and developed by AltCon."

"Has anyone figured out what AltCon even stands for?"

"No, but the consensus is 'Alternative Consciousness.' At least, that is what the folks down in Corporate Concerns told us."

"Sounds about right. Sorry for the interruption. Continue please."

"Not a problem, ma'am. With the advancements in VR, Schneider began exporting his company and his products. As was the case here in the United States, many countries had problems at first with VR. Schneider began a campaign to increase the awareness of VR's benefits, and he also started supporting the individuals who shared his vision.

"Before you ask, all of this was done above board. Schneider never donated directly to a foreign government. Instead, he donated money to think tanks and non-governmental organizations that supported either VR or the politicians in their respective countries who did.

"I don't need to tell you about the impact that VR has had on our society. In the 20's, it took off to such a degree that our populace was turned on its head. There have been more laws regulating VR in the last ten years than there have been for any other particular product. At the forefront of all of it was Schneider. The power of his company, and by extension Mr. Schneider, grew exponentially. He is now considered one of the most powerful men in the world, given his extensive outreach and donations over the years. On top of all of that, those same politicians he supported in the early years of VR are now leading their own countries, and they all owe a debt to Schneider.

"He has never married and has no children. He has no apparent heir. He is rather reclusive and hasn't done a public interview in years. He is rarely, if at all, spotted in public. He seems to live in the high rise that houses his business. And despite all of my research, no one knows what his overall ambitions or his endgame may be."

"That's pretty light, Agent Bolden."

"Don't I know it. The man is a ghost. He is rated as the second richest man in the world, but with all of his connections, some would say *he* is the richest man alive. Yet no one knows anything about him. Or if they do, they aren't saying anything. Keep in mind, we aren't able to interview any of those top-tier employees that Nico will discuss in greater detail."

"Let's move on to them. Please, Agent Colvin, what do you have."

Nicodemus Colvin grabbed his files and opened the top manila folder labeled "Board of Directors." From within the folder, he removed a newspaper clipping and several pages of handwritten notes.

"Before we go into too much detail about the different board members, of which there is little information of value, I wanted to highlight the one topic of interest that occurred recently. The former Director of the Board, Thomas Bradshaw, was recently the victim of a robbery gone wrong. According to the police, two unidentified men robbed Mr. Bradshaw, likely at knifepoint. During the course of the robbery, where the initial autopsy reported defensive wounds, Mr. Bradshaw received a number of knife wounds to his upper torso. This is the newspaper article of the incident."

Director Grissten took the article and read the details twice. It read just as Agent Colvin described, minus the autopsy report.

"You noted that the initial autopsy report showed defensive wounds. Was there a secondary autopsy?"

"Not an official report, Director. I was able to get a look at the report and pictures of the body. If I was writing a report, it would surely be different.

"There were no "defensive wounds," per say, like the report indicates. Bradshaw had two or three wounds on the inside of his hands but nothing that would indicate he fought back. More likely, he was putting his hands up and begging for his life.

"Secondly, there are numerous wounds on the upper torso, but almost all are superficial. Only one of the wounds penetrated farther than one inch. That wound just happened to be the one that penetrated and punctured Bradshaw's heart.

"Finally, the police have no witnesses and no suspects. After two days, the case was moved to their "unsolved files." No further work is being done on the case as far as I can tell."

"Murdered?"

"Impossible to say, ma'am, but it certainly looks like more than a robbery gone wrong. Although, given my other interests in this case, I am probably biased. Still, it led me to the next part of my report.

"The day after Bradshaw's untimely demise, Schneider appointed a new Director to the Board—Terrence Jolston, the head of AltCon's Emerging Technologies department. Jolston is acting as both the head of AltCon's current beta testing for their new game and now the Board of Directors. This is highly unusual, and it led me to look deeper into Jolston's background.

"Jolston started with the company approximately 20 years ago. Initially working in the coding and programming sections of the company, he rose to prominence due to his excellent work. While working on one of AltCon's previous MMORPGs, Jolston uncovered a catastrophic flaw in the game's coding. The game was due for launch two weeks before Jolston's discovery, and his work saved the company millions of dollars in potential hacks by issuing emergency patches. The Old Man took notice.

"In order to thank him personally, Schneider requested a face-to-face meeting with Jolston. During the meeting, Schneider learned that Jolston was recruited by the company after Jolston showed an affinity for coding.

"It's just like every feel-good story you have ever heard or seen. Jolston came from a depressed neighborhood and had little chance of affording a university education. Because of AltCon, Jolston not only went to university but was also awarded a position within the company after graduation. Not long after he started, his mother became ill. Because of AltCon's healthcare provisions, Jolston was able to get his mother the treatment she needed.

"In short, Jolston is a 100-percent company man. If Schneider wanted a yes man in that position, there would be no better choice than Jolston."

"So Jolston does not have any of the qualifications necessary to run a Board at the level of AltCon?"

"Jolston doesn't have the qualifications to lead any board, anywhere. It's obvious to me and Bolden that Schneider chose him to be more of a mouthpiece than an actual manager of the Board."

"What else is he working on?"

"The final stages of the beta for their newest game, Resurgence. He was also responsible for the design and release of the first fully immersive virtual reality platform—the VRAC, which stands for Virtual Reality Augmentation Container. All of our research indicates the game will work solely with the VRAC, and that AltCon plans to release them at a discount for game use. Plans seem to be in the works to modify all of their former games with the VRAC technology, and their long-term plans are to revolutionize the VR market with their technology. Imagine anytime you want to enter into a VR conference, finding yourself doing so in full immersion. It has the potential to touch all aspects of life and make AltCon even more profitable than it is now."

Director Grissten sat back in her chair and thought about the information she had learned. Honestly, she hadn't learned much. She could have gotten any of this information from her Corporate Concerns division. She hoped her hand-picked duo would have more to offer.

"It's not much, although the part about Bradshaw's death does raise questions that need to be answered. What's your next step?"

Bolden reached into her briefcase and withdrew a single piece of paper.

"We would like to request the assistance of Ryan Grimes from Forensic Accounting."

Grissten read the request and saw that it was highly general. Per the request, Bolden and Colvin did not intend to disclose the overall purpose of their assignment. This suited Grissten, and she signed the request.

Grimes was the best Forensic Accountant the Bureau had, and it was the exact kind of outside-the-box thinking she was looking for from Bolden. "Where will you focus Grimes?"

"We are looking for outliers, so I plan to have him look at connections to the main headquarters, but not directly within their scope. AltCon is multi-national, with several international branches. Unfortunately, our ability to collect information on these international entities is limited. We can only investigate—and without a warrant, at a very superficial level—those actions that occur while entering or leaving the US. For example, bank transactions and the like.

"My belief is that if there was something nefarious, AltCon would want to keep it close enough that it could be dismantled quickly and with direction from HQ in real time. In today's age, that can happen from almost anywhere, but human intuition is to keep these set-ups physically close as well."

"Keep me apprised as to what Grimes finds. Follow the rabbit down whatever hole it takes you."

CHAPTER 5

October 15, 2043

The time had come for us to range out again and begin our grinding. We still needed to make enough money to pay for upgrades all around, as I didn't want to settle for only half best before we challenged the Trolls or Lady Tessa's first quest.

Once we got to the front gate, I decided to take advantage of an earlier comment made by Jason and asked if I could "twirl the arrow" this morning; essentially, I was asking to choose which way we went. There was no argument from anyone.

I took Dan's arrow and manipulated it to land in the general direction of the Undead location I had highlighted on my map.

"Let's start heading in that direction. We kill everything that gets in our way," I said. Looking at Dan I added, "keep your eyes on the map, Dan. We never know what might be out here."

"I always do, my sneaky friend. So far it's been a whole lot of trees!" Dan said as he headed out ahead of us to look for his first pull. At this point, the mobs near the Keep were all Green to us, so we wouldn't get a single point of experience from them. However, if we saw one that would complete a quest requirement, we killed it without a second thought.

The forest here was dense, so we were unable to use our mounts for travel. This made for slow going, but we quickly left the easier mobs behind and started finding Blues that could give us experience. The occasional White was mixed in there. The experience wasn't as good, but we often needed the items they could drop for our quests.

I kept watching my map, making sure we weren't deviating from the path I had set for us to find the Undead. By my estimation, we would come upon the area in the next thirty minutes. Dan could potentially see it in the next twenty minutes or so.

After killing another mob, Dan ranged out ahead of us and finally yelled the words I was waiting to hear.

"Jackpot, boys!"

I hurried toward Dan, along with Jason and Wayne, as quickly as I could. Dan was standing near a clearing and was pointing in the direction of the marker on my map. We had arrived.

"Suck it, Allibong! The legend of TheClaw lives on. Look at what I found! No one ranges like this Ranger."

Jason approached the clearing, and a large smile began to spread on his face. With an almost reverent whisper, I heard him say, "Undead."

Jason turned toward us and said, "Amazing. I'll admit it. You are truly amazing."

Dan began to gather his steam and looked to be ready to start an epic soliloquy, when Jason turned to me and said, "I mean it, Alex. You are, without a doubt, amazing."

"Of course I am Allib... wait, what? Alex? Why Alex!?" Dan exclaimed.

"Duh. He threw the arrow. Don't try to take too much credit for walking in a straight line."

"But... but... I found it!"

"Indeed you did, Dan," Jason said. "And I will spread the legend of the Ranger who walks in a straight line through the woods to everyone who will listen."

Dan walked off in a huff, muttering, "I totally would have found it eventually."

I patted Dan on the shoulder as he passed. "No doubt, TC. No doubt at all. Now let me go see what you've uncovered."

I activated my Conceal/Stealth and started toward the Undead area. After a few steps, I paused and gathered the shadows around me to add my Blacksuit to the mix. I had no idea what was in front of me, and I didn't want to take the chance that there could be a mob that would see through the standard Conceal/Stealth.

A broken-down outpost was in front of me—not terribly large in appearance, but packed full of mobs. I easily ran through the structure and selected each mob to gauge its level and likely difficulty. The good news was that all of the mobs were at least Blue. There were also two Yellows. Those would need to be pulled last.

There was no boss, though. This was just a location that players could farm Undead. This was exactly what I was looking for. A cash cow.

After fifteen minutes or so, I arrived back at the edge of the clearing to tell the guys what I had found. Wayne was the first to approach me and said, "Jenny is so super stoked, bro. This is an awesome find!"

I looked over at Jason and asked, "How long?"

"You lost this one, brother. Pay up. He made it past five minutes."

"Damn. Who won?"

"Dan. I had seven minutes. He had nine. Wayne made it an amazing ten minutes."

Wayne was looking back and forth between us with a look of befuddlement. "What the hell are you guys talking about? Dan won what?"

Dan moseyed up and said, "How long it would take you to contact Jenny and tell her when we finally found an awesome spot to farm. Alex totally had the odds on you being 100 percent whipped. But I had faith you could hold out, brother!"

"Ten minutes is a hold out?" Wayne asked, looking annoyed.

"I had nine, brosef. You did us all proud."

Wayne laughed at that and addressed the group, "You guys aren't mad I told her without asking you right?"

"Nah, we planned to share whatever we found anyhow. We just figured it would be fun to see how long it would take you to tell the missus," Dan said.

I relayed what I had found, and the guys were slightly disappointed there was no boss to fight. I reminded them we had two very good quests waiting for us, and what we needed now was money, not a risky encounter where we could get killed fighting a Red mob.

After explaining how packed the mobs were, Dan started to go around the outpost and gauge the best spots to pull from. I had no intention of interrupting Dan's methods, as he had shown himself to be more than capable at his job. I gave Dan the info that it seemed all of the mobs were stationary and no roamers. He thanked me for the update and said that would make pulling infinitely easier.

After ten minutes, Dan pulled the first group of two Blue mobs, and we got ready to begin the slaughter.

After doing two rotations of the Undead, we learned that their respawn time was one hour. A round of killing took us about 45 minutes with a plus/minus 5 minutes, considering how many Yellows spawned. Our first pull there were two, but the second round had four. More importantly, there were 47 mobs total. We netted close to 45 Gold on the first round and almost as much on the second round. Several days here and we would easily be able to buy all of our gear. This is what I was talking about!

During our second round of pulls, Jenny and her group arrived at the clearing. They wanted to see what the mobs were like. I hoped they would go out and range for a few days like we did, but I couldn't get angry that they wanted to see this spot for themselves.

Jenny reported that the mobs were more Yellow than Blue for them, and they had stars in their eyes, thinking of the cash and experience that was in front of them.

Wanting to benefit both our group and our teammates, we decided that we would limit our time at the Undead to five hours. It would take us close to 30 minutes to arrive from Kich's Keep and another 30 minutes to return. The area wasn't safe for logging out, and we decided as a group that we would travel back to the Keep at the end of our time. Well, everyone but Wayne.

Just like with "Clerics for Hire," there was a "Tank for Hire" as well.

In that case, the Tank would do their role outside of the group, and the rest would reap the benefits as they would out-damage the Tank. The Tank got paid by the hour. I have no idea what Wayne was going to get paid in, but I heard Dan whisper something so inappropriate that it even made me blush.

With the weight of finding the Undead and securing our ability to outfit our group off my shoulders, I had another task that needed attention: figuring out who, or what, was the embodiment of the code that the Wanderer had told me about. That was the other reason I so readily agreed to five-hour rotations between our two groups. Sure, Wayne needed rest, but I also had work that had been sitting on the back burner for too long.

Letting that rest in the back of my mind until I had a chance to think on it more, we got back to making money. We had two more hours before Jenny and our friends would take over. The plan was to grind at this spot until we had raised enough to outfit Jason and Wayne, the two who needed the better gear the most. If the guys were up for it, we would stay for a couple more days to gather enough to gear up me and Dan. At my current estimate, this would take us about a week. Plenty of time to gather information on the Wanderer's dilemma as well.

I was frustrated. I had been striking out more often than a straight man at a lesbian bar. Not a single NPC I spoke with was able to provide me any insight as to what could be the mob or item that was the placeholder for the code.

I started by asking the NPCs if they were aware of any mob that seemed impossible to kill. Each one responded in the positive, but then went on to list whatever mob was linked to a quest they would give. This was great for learning there were more NPCs that had quests, but they were listing various fauna and undead. I knew we could tackle any of these mobs, so I knew it wasn't any of them.

Another group of players had reached Level 20 and had arrived in the Keep. I saw them standing in the square, talking with Sir Arthur and accessing the quest to "The Troll Menace." Their gear was about on par with ours, but they lacked the rarer items we sported as a team. These guys would need to level up quite a bit before taking on the Trolls.

Once I saw them finish acquiring the quest, I approached the group. I walked toward the leader, the one who had been speaking with Sir Arthur, and said hello.

"Look at this boys, it's one of the legends!" a character named Itsy said, smiling.

"Oh, stop all that. We just got lucky is all. In the grand scheme of things, the fact that all of us are getting to Kich's Keep this quickly tells me you guys know what you're doing," I said. "I'm Alex. Nice to meet you guys."

Itsy shook my outstretched hand and introduced his teammates. "Thanks for the compliment, Alex. It's much appreciated. How are things around here?"

"Lots of good mobs as soon as you get out of the gates. It's like a starter zone for Level 20s. I'll send you a couple of markers for your map. These guys are the NPC quest givers for the items that the mobs drop outside the gates."

Itsy looked over at his teammates, who also looked a bit befuddled. "What do you want for the information?" Itsy asked a little suspiciously.

I laughed at that and said, "Nothing, man. It's a game, and we should all get the fullest experience out of it. The more people at the higher levels, the more we will learn what's out there. Besides, as we get higher in levels, you know there will have to be raids and the like. No reason not to make good relations now," I said with a wink.

"Well, friendship is a price I don't mind paying!" Itsy exclaimed while shaking my hand again.

I started walking in the direction of the NPC quest givers along with Itsy while the rest of his group started walking around the city. I knew that if our teammates had ever run into an impossible mob, they would have told us. But here I had another player, and maybe he knew something we didn't.

"Sometimes I felt the designers went a little overboard with the level of the mob's difficulty, especially since it was just a starter area.

Seriously, there were times that I couldn't believe we pulled out some of the victories. That damn Bunny down in the sewers was a perfect example," I said, trying to get the conversation going.

"Yeah, man. That Bunny was no joke. But compared to the Boar we fought, that Bunny was nothing!"

"Hard mob?"

"Impossible mob."

Oh, how my ears perked up at that!

"You guys couldn't take it down?"

"It was crazy. We started engaging, thinking we would get some big loot out of it, since it was a Red, but it was in the middle of this clearing so we knew we could kite it if nothing else. We were throwing everything at the War Boar, but its hit points didn't seem to go down at all."

My first reaction of excitement began to wane. I knew exactly what Itsy and his crew had found. Next, Itsy was going to tell me about more mobs, of equal level, coming after him and his group, and likely them getting wiped.

"So you guys tried to kite it or not?"

"Didn't even get the chance to. Before we could get a good rotation set up, one of the other guys must have aggroed another mob. Where first there was just the Boar, we suddenly had a massive Wolf coming down on us. Also Red."

Yup, they had found Stan's place. I knew from my talks with Stan that there was no way they could take those mobs without first killing the Elder Elven tree. I didn't think any of them could be the mob I was looking for, since there was a known way to kill them.

"You guys wipe?"

"Nah. We ran and the mobs boomeranged. Believe me, I wasn't tempted to try that encounter again. Maybe after we gain some more levels, you know?"

I nodded my head in agreement but knew that without the location of the tree, no amount of levels was going to help these guys.

"You guys try the Trolls yet?" Itsy asked me.

"Not yet. We're trying to level up and get better gear. What we had was barely enough to get us to the Keep. I don't think it will be enough to take on a bunch of Trolls, though. So basically we're grinding through it. You guys thinking of taking a shot at them soon?"

"Yeah, I think we will. If for no other reason than I want to get one of those title that you guys have!"

"Well, let me suggest one thing."

"What's that?"

"Get some experience first. We didn't die out there, but none of us know what would happen if we died straight away and lost enough experience to get us below Level 20. Would we be denied access to the city?" I offered.

"Man, you are right. That isn't something I would want to try out either!"

"Other piece of advice: don't forget to change your bind point to the Capitol. I almost bit it once and none of us had changed our location. That would have been a very long run from Port Town!"

"Dude, I forgot about that too. Been a while since any of us died. Didn't even cross my mind."

"Same with us."

"Really appreciate the help, Alex. You guys ever need another party for something, look me up. Mind if I add you to my friends list?" Itsy asked me.

"Not at all, and I'll do the same. Good luck with the Trolls. We won't be going after them for a week or so. If you want to try to take them before then, I wouldn't be mad at all to see more players with titles!"

"You guys are alright in my book. Lots of talk out there that you are the team to beat, so you can imagine that most think y'all are a bit stuck up. Glad to see that isn't the case at all. Good luck to ya!" Itsy said as he went off to the different NPCs to get his quests.

I hadn't learned anything that I didn't already know about the mobs out there, but I did make a new associate in the game. Sometimes that can be more helpful than the best gear. No matter what else I learned, I was going to call this a solid day.

There were still quite a few NPCs that I hadn't spoken with, so I began to make my rounds again. While I was walking down one particular street, an NPC yelled out, "Hey Rogue! Want to make some extra cash?"

I turned to look at the guy and see if he was talking to me. He had a beaming smile on his face, and I started to approach him. After a few steps, he held up his hand and said, "Sorry, never mind. I thought you were a higher Level."

It was at that moment that another person grabbed my wrist. I turned, ready to engage in a fight. Although it is generally not allowed to fight within the city grounds, I still didn't know all the rules for PvP in Resurgence. When I turned, however, I didn't see another player but an NPC. And the little bastard was holding my coin purse.

"Misdirection is the first thing they teach us in Thief academy."

"I hate all of you so much right now."

"Oh, and Waseem says 'hi.' You should probably go and visit him at the Pit."

With that, the little urchin vanished. I looked around for a bit, knowing that I could ask the NPCs the same questions I had been asking for an hour, or I could go learn more Rogue skills. It had been a while since I had visited the pompous Thief, and it was obvious my skills had taken a hit because of it.

There was no one but Waseem in the Pit when I arrived, but I had learned long ago that looks can be very deceiving when it came to Rogues. I had brought up my Awareness before I entered the Pit and tried to concentrate on my surroundings without alerting anyone I was doing so.

Waseem looked up from the table and smiled at me, waving toward the seat in front of him: the one that would put my back to the room. I wasn't about to fall for that one again.

Instead of joining Waseem at his table, I took the one next to him, and put my back to the wall. Waseem started laughing loudly and waved at the area in front of him. I couldn't be sure, but I thought I saw a number of shimmers in the air where I assumed Rogues were standing using their Conceal/Stealth.

"You learned that one rather quickly. Although I did hear that you got took on the street earlier. That was quite a disappointment."

"I'll admit it; I wasn't on my game. Let my Awareness slip. It was a good lesson, and I won't let it happen again."

"We shall see. Next time, I'm going to tell the thief that grabs your purse that he can keep any one of the coins in there. I imagine that could be Gold in your case."

I wanted to call Waseem a dick, but there wasn't a better way for me to learn than to have a negative condition set to cement the lesson.

"I won't argue with that. You're the teacher, and it will keep me on my toes."

"Good. It's time to start your next lesson, if you are ready."

"Let's get to it. I still want to know how you were able to get my purse the other day when I felt all the other attempts."

Time flew by as we went over different exercises to heighten my Awareness. Even with blatant attempts at distraction, I was still able to maintain my shadow shroud, as I had begun to call it. The only times I failed, out of hundreds of attempts, was when Waseem made the grabs.

After his fifth successful steal, I finally relented and told him I had no idea how he was accomplishing it. It seemed this was what Waseem was waiting for, and he nodded his head.

"Sometimes you find people who are better than you. When you do, try like hell to beat them. But if you can't, admit it to yourself, suck in your pride, and ask that person for help. The world is full of people who get more joy from seeing others succeed than they do from their own successes."

"And that's you?"

"What? Hell no! In general, I couldn't give two shits if someone succeeds or not," Waseem said with a devilish grin. "But I'm your teacher, so I'm sure I'll get some kind of joy from watching this." Dude was a bit of a sociopath, if that was possible in a game.

Waseem then started to explain to me how to manipulate shadows to interrupt another's Awareness. In essence, Waseem was opening a hole through my shroud with his own shadows. To my Awareness, the shroud was never broken, as his shadows overlapped with mine. It was awesome to think of, but it wasn't something I was able to accomplish despite my dozen tries. When it came to being Aware of the intrusion, I was only right three times out of ten.

"Take a break, Alex. As it turns out, there are only three or four Thieves that can even do this, and I'm the only one in Kich's Keep at the moment. Keep practicing, but don't worry about me keeping any of your money when I steal your purse."

"About that, when am I going to learn how to steal things? I know it's important to protect myself from others, but isn't it the point of being a Thief to steal stuff?"

"That it is. And I'm certainly willing to let you try," Waseem said. "Tiny Tommy, come over here and stand in the middle of the room. No hiding."

One of the Rogues who had been trying to pick my pocket over the last hour stood in the middle of the room. He had a long cloak that covered most of his body. Naturally it was black. Other than the color, it was similar to many of the cloaks I had seen other NPCs wear around town.

"Now, I want you to hide yourself. Use your regular Conceal. Don't put your Blacksuit on just yet. That is a whole different level of Thievery that you aren't ready for yet."

I did as Waseem said, and he continued to look at me as I moved around the room. Waseem obviously had a See Invisible skill or item, and he was able to track me around the room. He told Tiny Tommy to remove any spells or items that would allow him to see me.

"Ok. Next step is simple. Steal Tommy's purse."

Over the next fifteen minutes, I unsuccessfully tried to relieve Tommy of his money. Every time I started to reach toward his coin purse, he slapped at my Invisible hand. It was more frustrating than having Waseem continuously succeed at robbing me.

"How did he do?" Waseem asked.

"For a first timer, really good. Almost got me twice. He's got nimble fingers that one."

Thinking that I had failed miserably, it was a boon to my spirit to hear that I had done well. I wondered if the ability to steal was directly tied to my Dexterity. If so, I should be successful, since I had a high Dexterity and lots of bonuses.

"Good. I can definitely work with that. Time for your next lesson, and then we call this quits. Come see me tomorrow and we will continue your training.

"The problem you are facing is that you are trying to grab Tommy's purse. You aren't trying to Lift it. There is a huge difference. For now, I want you to practice with this ice cube. Using only your thumb and middle finger, I want you to practice lifting this ice cube out of the cup. You can't touch any of the other ice cubes, or the glass. A chime will go off when you fail. Keep at it for an hour."

I walked over to the table next to Waseem and saw a glass that hadn't been there before. It was a large, round glass, almost like a bowl. There were multiple ice cubes in the glass, and the one that was my target was slightly discolored.

"See you tomorrow, Alex," Waseem said as he exited the Stinky Pit.

I turned back to the glass and reached in for the cube. Within two seconds, I heard the chime as I touched another one of the cubes. This was going to be a pain.

After two hours—and way past the time I planned to stay online—I had noticed some marked improvement. I started having better luck with the cube and could get the ice out of the glass three times out of five. But after the first hour, I had to deal with a new obstacle: my fingers had gone numb from the ice.

I could have quit then, but I decided to think of it like I was wearing gloves. I tried to depend on the feelings lower in my fingers, where they hadn't become numb, to gauge the pressure I had on the cube and my eyes to deal with the obstacles of the other cubes and the glass. I had no doubt that at some point Waseem would have me do this blindfolded, but that was a worry for another day.

After another hour, I was back to the point where I could succeed three times out of five, and that with my numb fingers. I was looking forward to the next day when I could try it again with regular feeling in my hands.

Before I logged off, I took a look at my skills and saw two new ones that I hadn't noticed before. Awareness and Lift were now permanent skills I had, just like with Blacksuit. Practice would make these go up and hopefully give me more bonuses down the line.

With a feeling of happiness, I headed out of the Pit and made my way back to the square. The guys planned to meet back there the next day so we could continue our rampage through the Undead.

Waseem and Stan stepped out of the shadows just after Alex left the Stinky Pit. Stan had a smile on his face as he looked over at the Thief.

"Told you. That one knows how to work."

"I doubted you for sure, my little friend, but I no longer have any reservations about training him. Most would have stopped once their fingers grew numb, but he took it as a challenge. I have no doubt he will become accomplished as a Thief."

"That he will. But be certain of this, Thief: you try and pull him inta one of dem harebrained schemes of yours to rob the Bank, and I will put me dagger in yer appendix. Not even joking."

Waseem gave a deep and throaty laugh as he looked down at Stan. "I make absolutely no promises! He may very well welcome the challenge when I'm done with him!"

Stan shook his head as he headed out of the Pit. "Damn nuisance. Gonna be the death of me."

Unknown Facility

"Thank you for the update, Mr. Hamson. Keep at it and let me know the moment you learn anything new."

The General watched as a despondent Dan walked out of the conference room. It had been two weeks since the last piece of new information had come from Dan's investigations. The General could tell it was putting stress on the eccentric technician, but there wasn't much he could do about that.

Ten minutes after Dan departed the conference room, an aid entered the conference room where the General was still sitting. "Sir, the next one is here."

"Send her in, Lieutenant."

The General knew you did not win wars by relying on only one stream of information. Because of this, he had begun implementing a secondary operation soon after placing Dan within Resurgence.

Emily Renart walked into the room and took a seat at the end of the conference table. "Good afternoon, General."

"Good afternoon to you, Emily. Thank you for coming in. Please report."

With the focus of the General's investigation geared toward the game, the General wanted to cover both aspects of the situation. With Dan, the General had an in-game mole who could report on the activities within that environment. With Emily, the General had infiltrated the other side of Resurgence; Emily was working in AltCon's IT section of Emerging Products.

Admittedly, the General would rather have had someone working directly on the beta itself, or as a systems administrator in the Emerging Products office. On such short notice, the best the General could do was an IT specialist in the section.

Emily came from the very same IT office as Dan but was not nearly as eccentric as Mr. Hamson. Of course, if that had not been the case, the General would have had to take a serious look at that office's hiring practices.

Emily had begun working for the General's specialty office several years earlier and was the perfect match for someone who could transfer from one job to another with little concern. She was in her mid 20's, single, and had no direct family. She was also eager to take on the challenge of infiltrating AltCon after learning of the General's suspicions concerning Robert Shoal's untimely demise.

More importantly to the General, Emily came from a family with a long history of service to their country. Her father did three deployments in Iraq during the second Gulf War, her uncle served in Afghanistan, and her Grandfather served in Vietnam. Emily went the route of formal education, but she only applied to one place after her graduation: the Department of Defense.

"I've been working on a timeline of RAC work orders handled by the IT office. I've been performing my routine duties and then ostensibly going through back work orders to determine if any of the requests were not completed. I found a number of items that had been languishing, awaiting completion, and finished those projects. This did lead to a bit of scrutiny by IT management."

"Anything that could affect your placement?"

"No, sir. The managers were impressed with my initiative and gave me the green light to continue investigating any previous orders that went unfulfilled. In essence, I was given permission to do exactly what I wanted to do on the sly.

"As you can imagine, there were a number of work orders submitted just prior to the beta's commencement. Routine checks and the likes. Outside of routine requests, there has been nothing of note since the launch of the beta."

"So, another dead end."

"Since the beginning of the beta, yes. But when I looked back further, I found something interesting. There were numerous requests of the same nature almost six months prior. These requests matched the types received by Emerging Products' IT section before the beta was released."

"What is your assessment, Emily?"

"Based on the number of requests, I believe there was another set of RACs that AltCon used for an indeterminate amount of time. Given the volume of work orders, the number of RACs were likely close to the same number being used in the current beta.

"Another anomaly was a set of work orders I had not seen previously. With these requests, the Emerging Products office ordered diagnostics one would expect when the RACs were to be taken out of service. The time difference between the initial requests and the out-of-service requests was close to five months."

"Is there any way to determine if AltCon has tried something similar with this beta?"

Emily sat back in her chair and thought through the question. Along with the routine work orders, she had noted orders for diagnostic checks on all the RACs transplanted from AltCon headquarters to the homes of the beta testers. She had seen nothing similar during the period she referenced earlier. If there had been another beta, it had to have occurred within the building. Emily explained this to the General.

"Would there be any reflections, IT-wise, if this were the case?"

What many people never realize is that with so much of the world going digital, you could map out the timeline and lifestyle of users and companies by IT logs alone. There was so much data, however, that doing so required a path to follow. Otherwise, it was like looking through hundreds of haystacks for that one single needle.

Secondly, whatever Emily needed to do had to be consistent with her position. The General had explained, time and again, she was not to be overly ambitious in her investigations.

"Access, General. If individuals were being tested within AltCon, it stands to reason they would need access to certain areas of the facilities. Those would require work orders. If these were AltCon employees, they likely wanted access to their own work near their RACs. That would require more computers and multiple access requests," Emily said as she thought around the problem.

"And your thoughts?"

"Yes. Yes, I believe I can, and within the framework of my position."

"Good. Thank you, Emily. I look forward to your next report."

CHAPTER 6

October 18th, 2043

We finished up our fourth day with the Undead, and we were stacking up the funds quickly. One more day and we would have enough to outfit Jason and Wayne in all new gear. We had also gained another level while we were fighting the Undead, and everyone was at Level 22. The mobs were all Blue to us now, but we were there for the cash, not the experience. I thought it might be helpful to ask the Wanderer where we could find an experience rich area, but I was also cognizant that every time I saw him, I put him in danger. I think.

Jenny and her crew also gained a level and were collecting cash each day. Since all of the gear we planned to buy from the Dwarves was tradeable, we had agreed to purchase a full set for Jenny as well. Although it could have been we were told by Wayne that we would be doing this. I don't remember the details exactly.

Finally, both Broham and Rocky were getting solid level increases, and both were now at Level 13. They still only had one attack, Bite, but they were getting to a point where they were doing some serious damage. Broham was never in fear of pulling aggro off of Dan when he was kiting, but Kaitlin had to be careful with Rocky. If she tried to hold a mob in place through one of her spells, there was a chance it could turn on Rocky if she hadn't done enough damage.

Not to mention, these were no longer little puppies. Broham was starting to look like a regular-sized, two-year-old wolf. They still weren't up to Dire size, but I was sure that they would continue to grow as they were fed and leveled.

When we weren't actively engaging the Undead, we all did our own thing. Wayne continued to help Jenny and her crew, Tanking for them. Dan would travel back to the Elder Elven tree to collect wood for his arrows. And Jason had decided to take up being a Cleric for Hire to make a little extra cash for himself. When we played as a group, that money primarily went toward whatever the group needed. In Jason's case, though, he was able to keep all the money he earned for himself. I had no idea what he planned to buy with it.

I spent all of my down time at the Pit. I had spent the first day after learning the Lift skill to ask more of the NPCs about impossible to beat mobs but kept getting the same response. None of what they told me had any relation to what I was looking for. Instead of wasting more time, I decided to focus on my two new Rogue abilities: Awareness and Lift.

I usually spent three hours at the Pit with Waseem, fine tuning my Awareness ability and improving my Lift techniques. I had improved at trying to overlap my shadows with those of Waseem's, the first step I would need to master before I could move through the shadow itself.

After Waseem felt that I was able to lift an ice cube with my thumb and middle finger with ample success, he made me do the same thing with my thumb and all the other fingers. Then he made me try other combinations, like my ring finger and index finger.

Waseem also made me do the lessons with both hands. My dominant right hand had little difficulty adapting, but my left hand was as sloppy as shit.

No matter how good I got with any combination of both hands, however, my Lift score never went above "1."

It was all done when I finally "mastered" the ring finger-pinky pinch to Waseem's satisfaction. If you don't think this is difficult, go drop a piece of ice in a glass and use just those two fingers to lift it out of the glass. And don't forget, it needs to be a little melted and it can't touch the glass in anyway. I'm sure I'd hear your curses all the way in this virtual world.

As I was getting ready to reset the cube in the glass, Waseem came over and had me stop what I was doing. I figured the next task would have me lifting the ice cube with my toes, but I was in for a pound at this point.

"Great work, Alex. You've got the lifts down well. I'm going to have you try again on Tiny Tommy and see how you manage."

Just like before, Tommy stood in the middle of the room, and I activated my Conceal/Stealth. Tommy wore the same cloak, and I slowly maneuvered around him as I tried to reach in to get his coin purse. The first two attempts were met by a slap on the hand, but the third was successful. I then realized that Tommy had multiple coin purses on his body and I had to try and get as many as I could.

The fifth and sixth were also successes. I had to stop myself from jumping up and down right there and then. In total, I removed him of his coin purse seven times out of the ten.

When I finally dropped my Conceal/Stealth, I had a huge smile on my face, as did Tommy. Once I stopped hiding, Tommy knew I had finished my run and he was just as happy as I was that he hadn't caught me more than he did. With a quick run of his hands down his cloak, Tommy looked over at Waseem and said, "He got seven. I didn't feel a bloody thing."

"Damn good work, Alex!" Waseem said as he shook my hand. At this point I didn't take anything for granted and kept my Awareness up all the time, but even more so when Waseem was around.

"You can call it a day, Tommy. I appreciate your help." He flipped a small coin purse to Tommy who thanked Waseem profusely. Tommy backed out of the Pit, and I found myself alone with my teacher.

"What you just learned is what all the street urchins learn. You took to it pretty quickly, though. It takes the kids, who usually have smaller and nimbler hands, at least a month to learn what you did in a few days.

"But now comes the fun part. I asked Tommy to leave because he doesn't have the same tools we do. Tommy can hide with the best of them, and he can out-pickpocket almost any kid on my crew. Since he doesn't have a feeling for the shadows, though, he wouldn't understand how they play into your next lesson."

"I was wondering when the shadows would come into play. It doesn't seem like hardcore thievery if we aren't cheating more than a little, after all."

"And there you go. Hit it right on the head. We already plan to be conniving bastards, so why not take it to the next level? And that next level is where you will go from being a good cutpurse to being a Thief."

I sat on top of one of the tables and got ready to listen to whatever Waseem had to say.

"You use your shadows right now to trigger your Blacksuit, correct?" I nodded my head at Waseem. "So you constantly have a layers of shadows around you whenever you travel around in this manner. Those shadows become the key for a Thief."

"How?"

Waseem paused for a moment, then nodded. "I'm going to back up a bit here. You use your shadows to raise your Awareness. It allows you to know when someone enters into your space, right?"

I nodded my head in the affirmative.

"If they have the ability to heighten sensitivity, couldn't it be the case that they could deaden an area as well?"

I nodded my head again. "That makes more sense to me than the fact that we use them for sensing things. You think of shadows as darkness, so deadening someone's senses through them is perfectly logical."

"A Lift, with shadows, doesn't just pluck the pretty prize from the target; it ensures the target can't feel it, because the shadows numb that area, much like your fingers were numb after so long with the ice cube. It can be the difference between a successful Lift and a failure. In some cases, like if someone has wards and spells on them, it's the only way you could ever attempt to steal from them. The most difficult thefts I ever attempted would have been impossible without the gifts of the Rogue. And actually accomplishing the theft would have been impossible without these skill and others that only a true Rogue can wield. Now it's time you learned how it's done."

October 21st, 2043

Three more days at the Undead and we had enough cash to outfit the whole group. I was so damn happy to be done with the week of constant grinding. My only solace came from my time with Waseem practicing my Lifts. After several hours, even that became tedious. The upside was, my Lift skill was increasing, and I was now at a Level 31. The higher my Lift skill, the less chance my target would detect my theft, even with magic to aid them.

In order to increase past my current level, I would need to start stealing from someone other than Waseem. The skill topped out at 31 if you were only increasing from your instructor.

It would have been a nice break to travel back to the Dwarves and meet with our friends and Dwarven kin, but time was wasting in starting these quests. After Wayne collected the necessary funds from Jenny to buy her new armor, we sent Jason to the Dwarves on his horse. Jason had the same friendliness to the Dwarves that we all did, but Jason could simply Gate back to the Keep after he made the purchases. He would be overweight with all that plate in his bags, but he wouldn't have to worry about any negative effects. As soon as the transaction was made, Jason would return to the square near Sir Arthur.

Dan decided to spend his time at The Willy while Jason went on his run. With all the harvesting of the Elven Elder tree he had been doing, Dan had seriously neglected his duties at the Tavern—keeping them in business through his drinking.

Jenny and her group stayed at the Undead to gain another level, and Wayne decided to stay with his girlfriend and help them out. They offered to split some of the money with us, what with Wayne helping so much, but Wayne wouldn't hear of it. I was all for saying yes. Wayne is bigger, so he won.

I was passing the time by robbing the NPCs at Yerkich Square. There was no other way to explain what I was doing. In order to raise my Lift score, I needed to successfully abscond with someone else's purse. I could have done so with my teammates, but then I would have had to explain where I got the skill. It was while I wandered around the square taking from various NPCs that I encountered a new phenomenon.

I had wrapped myself in the shadows of my Blacksuit and was skulking down a boulevard when I spotted what looked like a tasty mark. He was dressed in the latest fashion and had more money in clothes than I had in the bank. His money pouch was practically begging to be taken from his waist. I made my approach as Waseem had taught me and was about to make my grab when a red tinge enveloped the NPC. As any gamer knows, Red is bad. Red is always bad. You run from Red. In this case, I slowly backed away from the NPC and started jogging back the way I came as soon as I felt it was safe. I then immediately went to the Pit to find Waseem.

Molly greeted me when I walked in and told me neither Waseem or Stan—or Dhalean as he was known in the Capitol—was about. I asked her if she could get a message to Waseem and waited until he arrived.

Twenty minutes later, Waseem breezed into the Pit and asked what had me so spooked. I relayed to him the story of my Lift attempt, including the guy's description, and he got a big smile on his face.

"Thank the gods you didn't actually try to steal from the Constable! I definitely would have gotten my ass handed to me by Dhalean if you had tried that! No matter what, he would have found a reason to blame me."

"Wait. That guy dressed in who knows how many Platinum worth of clothes was the Constable? How much money does that guy get for a salary?"

"A pittance, I'm sure," Waseem answered. "But he's as corrupt as they come, and every gang pays him to operate in Kich's Keep. What I wouldn't give to rob that fool."

"Why haven't you?"

"Two-man job. At least. And Dhalean never wants to help. You interested?"

Internally I screamed at the quest being offered to me, but knew I couldn't take it. In order to be of any use, I would need to devote myself full time to increasing my Lift skill. I just didn't have time for that.

"Gotta know your limitations, and I know I'm not ready for that. I'll tell you when I think I am, and we can go at that bastard together."

Waseem smiled, showing all his perfect teeth. "Better than I've ever gotten Dhalean to commit to. It'll do for now."

After Jason returned, Dan and I took all the extra money we had and purchased our own full sets of armor. We were finally ready to tackle some quests after that long grind.

I opened my inventory and took a quick look at my new gear:

Item:	Commonality:	Weight:	Armor:	Bonus:
Fine Leather Jerkin	Common	5	35	N/A
Fine Leather Leggings	Common	4	30	N/A
Fine Leather Boots	Common	2	25	N/A
Fine Leather Helmet	Common	1.5	25	N/A
Fine Leather Bracer	Common	1 x 2	15 X 2	N/A

Fine Leather Shoulders	Common	2	20	N/A
Fine Leather Gloves	Common	1	15	N/A
Simple Ring of Might	Common	0.1	10	+1 Str/Cst, +1 Bash
Force Multiplier	Epic Binds on Acquisition	0.1	N/A	+15 Dexterity +15 Agility Unstoppable: All of Character's skills 4X for 5 minutes (Once/24hrs)

With all of the new gear, I went from having 80 Armor to 190. Dan had a similar raise in his gear, although he refused to abandon the Furry Britches until he could replace them with another set of Rare or better leggings. All of us knew he really just wanted the novelty of the name and the attention they gathered. Dan had rocked those Britches with style to this point, so none of us could argue.

Wayne had been at 142 Armor with his Dark Breastplate and Dented Plate armor. According to him, his Armor was now over 300, as was Jason's total. And for the first time, I wasn't the first one to suggest an experiment!

"It will be totally good for us to see how much damage we take! Keep your regular gear on, all the old shit, and let's go get smashed by a mob!" Dan said to the group. I couldn't find any fault with his thinking and immediately started to the forest just outside the gate.

No one was worried about dying, since all the mobs in this area were Green to us. This was the safest experiment we had ever done. I still had a thing or two to teach Dan.

The results were immediate. All of us cycled through getting aggro and letting the mob hit us for a few rounds, and then did the same with our new gear. The damage was less than half between our new and old gear.

With everyone happy with the results of our experiment, it was time to decide on our next step; whether we took the storyline quest or Lady Tessa's quest. I was leaning toward the second, since I knew the rewards would be far better than any other.

Before I could voice my opinion, Jason took the reins of leadership. I had told the guys from the beginning that I was, at the best of times, a reluctant leader. I was happy to see another take some initiative.

"I've been thinking about this for a while," Jason started. "I think we should do the storyline quest from Sir Arthur first."

Neither Dan or Wayne looked ready to agree, as I knew Wayne liked the mysterious Lady Tessa and her requests for Wayne to honor her fallen family, but Jason continued on without waiting for a response.

"Now hear me out. This will make more sense after I am finished."

All of us nodded at Jason to continue.

"The quest from Sir Arthur was available as soon as we arrived here at Level 20. Before, when we got quests from Sir Kenyon, they were always in line with our level. So, in theory, we should have been able to do the storyline quest straight away."

This was sound logic that I could find no fault with.

"But we know," Jason continued "that the guys that got here after us weren't able to pass the quest, and they are out in the forest now trying to grind like we just were. The reason was just as we suspected: our gear was not good enough to go up against the Trolls when we got here, even though we do have our titles and a few more pieces of epic loot than they did.

"Still, in almost every fight we had before we reached the Keep, we survived by the skin of our teeth. Sometimes we lost people. I bet others had to get more levels before they could have completed the same.

"My guess is that AltCon has these quests geared to what players will *likely* have when they reach levels as the game progresses. In other words, months down the line when people can equip themselves with better gear at lower levels through the market and whatnot."

I had to admit to myself that I hadn't thought of this at all. Of course AltCon would want to make the quests challenging. Jason was right. As the game progressed people would be able to outfit their characters in the gear we were now wearing at much lower levels. Players would start crafting the armor and selling them at less than the merchant price. As supply increased, the price would go down significantly. Jason was definitely on to something here, and I nodded for him to continue.

"I don't think there is any rush on the Lady Tessa quest. We should definitely go talk to this Old Lady Madsie before we head out, but I doubt there will be any timer on the quest since it has been 'years' since the brothers and her father departed. I just want to see if the quest will take us in the same direction as the Trolls. If it doesn't, we do the Trolls first, then do Lady Tessa's quest. Our gear should now be around where AltCon expects players will be when they hit Level 20 when the game has gone live for some time."

I still wanted to start with Lady Tessa's mission, but when I looked at Dan and Wayne, they were nodding their heads vigorously in Jason's direction. I was outvoted.

"Let's go see this old lady then."

As soon as we made Lady Tessa's quest the active mission in our quest log, a location sprang up on our maps. The icon that represented Old Lady Madsie was located in the nicer parts of town, far away from the seedy underbelly that led to the Underground.

Dan led the way, and after several minutes of walking, we were approaching a building with a small porch jutting out from its entrance. Sitting in an old chair, pruning a potted plant, was Old Lady Madsie. As we approached the NPC, Madsie turned her head toward us, and then slowly started lowering her right hand toward her side.

With Dan in the lead, he was able to see what was happening easier than we could, and his outburst took us by surprise.

"Woah! She totally just pulled a blade! Wayne, she could totally be your mom!"

"My mom would beat your ass three ways from Sunday, Dan."

"That's what I just said!" Dan exclaimed. "Alex, I think you should take the lead on this one."

"Look at our mighty Ranger, boys. He's totally afraid of an old woman," I said.

"You laugh now, but get jolted with a Taser and you won't be making so many jokes," Dan replied. "Try to do one nice thing for an old lady, and as soon as you grab her arm to help her across the road, 50,000 volts in the neck."

"Well that explains the twitching."

"Screw you, Allidouche! I do not twitch!" Dan exclaimed. Then he looked over at Wayne and whispered, "Dude, do I twitch?"

"A little."

"Fuuuuuuck."

As the banter continued between my group, I approached Madsie and said the quest line, "Lady Tessa says she wants more of the happy juice."

Madsie slowly lowered her right hand back to her side. Dan was right, and I could see the glint of a blade as she rested the dagger near her leg. She then looked at each of us as we approached her porch and shook her head gently.

"I thought after all these years that Tessa would have given up on this foolishness, found a husband, and settled down to a quiet life. She lost all her family save me that day, and I can't begin to think what would happen to her if the King ever found out she was still alive. Did she look well?"

Wayne stepped up to the old woman and said, "She did. The hurt was obvious in her eyes, but she was determined to see her family's honor saved."

"Bah! Honor! That and a few coppers will get you a drink at the Tavern. This is a foolish quest for you men and will likely cost you your lives. Not a one of those boys returned. Not a one! Do you really think you can succeed where the greatest warrior scholars in this land failed?"

Wayne took an involuntary step back at the anger that roiled off of Old Lady Madsie. Honor being an important trait in the Warrior class, Wayne looked none too happy at the old woman's words. He rose up to his full 6'10" and approached the woman again. As he reached the porch, he leaned in so he could be closer to the woman and look her in the eye. Putting all of his command into an angry whisper, Wayne responded, "Each of those 'boys,' as you called them, were sent on a suicide run. Their bodies are likely lying in a heap somewhere without a soul around to give them a proper burial and send them to the gods. Now you tell me, Madsie, does laying the dead to rest sound like a fool's errand to you?"

Madsie leaned in even closer and said, "Don't give me that poppycock! If all you were doing was burying the dead, that would be one thing. But you fool adventurers will try to take on the same beasties that killed each and every one of them. And die for your efforts!

"But I made a promise to Tessa that I would aid the ones who came spouting that silly phrase. Since you won't take my advice and just run the other way, here is what you need to begin your own 'suicide run' as you called it."

Lady Madsie handed me a parchment with a rough sketching of a map. The location of the Capitol was obvious, and from there I was able to determine the direction the first brother must have taken to arrive at his assigned task. Unfortunately, it was not in the same direction as the Trolls. Where we would need to head due east to reach the Trolls, Lady Tessa's quest had us heading north-by-northeast, toward the mountains.

Once the sketch was in my inventory, I expected a section of my Map to start glowing. It would be impossible to see what was in that area since none of us had traveled there previously. All I could see on the map was a large black splotch between the Keep and where the quest would eventually lead us. I figured we would need to get closer before our Map would give any indication as to where the quest area was located.

"Thank you for your help. We will not bother you anymore."

The old lady continued to stare at us without answering. I figured this was the end of the quest dialogue and we should just head out to

Sir Arthur, but when we started to turn away, Madsie gave us one more comment as a parting gift.

"That fool boy that made that sketch was too smart for his own good. Was always writing things down, even when he shouldn't. Find Tristan's satchel and you will likely find more about where the rest of the boys and their father was headed.

"And if you do somehow return, please come tell this old lady what ya found. I may seem like a grumpy old hag, but I loved those boys like they were my own sons."

"It will be the first thing we do when we return," Wayne replied. I was happy he didn't swear an oath as well, as I still didn't know how those oaths could affect the game. Oh well, another thing to ask the Wanderer.

According to the map, it would take us most of a day just to travel to the damaged bridge, and none of us were against the idea of trying to find some new mobs along the way to gain experience and discover new content. The fauna so far around the Keep had consisted of the usual bears and wolves, but I was hopeful that this new direction would give us an opportunity to encounter a new type of mob. The usual grinding against the same mobs did wear out on a player after time, but I had to remember that we were still low level and that this was just a beta. The mobs we found would be your run-of-the-mill type. If it weren't for the horrible truth of AltCon, I would be excited just thinking about the expansions that would come out for this game.

Choosing to start our travels the next day, everyone logged off with a renewed vigor. No more grinding. We were excited as we thought about demolishing this next quest.

October 22nd, 2043

With that renewed air of excitement, the guys ran around before we headed out, stocking up on supplies like food and drink and treats for Broham. It was still necessary for Dan to feed Broham to keep him as a pet, and Dan always kept a large supply of snacks on his person for the wolf. Between that and arrows, Dan had little room in his bags for loot we got from the mobs we killed.

We had been grinding pretty hard and working long hours between our numerous side jobs. Dan was constantly having to travel back to the Elder Elven tree to gather supplies, and Jason had been working non-stop as a Cleric for other groups. Wayne had no problem leaving Jenny and her group to their tasks now that they had leveled up a bit and gotten some of the new gear, and with my initial training done with Waseem, the previous evening was the first time we had all logged off relatively on time.

"Everyone well rested and ready to do this?"

"Yeah, Alex," Jason said, "I slept like a baby last night."

"That sucks, bro. I'm sorry."

"What the hell are you talking about, Dan? 'Sleeping like a baby' is a good thing."

"Homey, do you even think about the things you say?"

"Homey?" Wayne asked.

"I'm feeling kind of gangsta, with us going on this quest!"

"You are many things, Dan, but gangsta will never, ever, be one of them," Wayne said.

"Forget gangsta. Dan, did you really just ask me if I think before I say things? Is the irony of that statement totally and completely lost on you? Do I need to bring Kaitlin into this?"

"Not cool, Allihater! And obviously sleeping like a baby is a bad thing. Unless you like the idea of waking up every two hours, screaming your head off, and nine times out of ten covered in your own shit. Sorry, dude, but that is not how I want to sleep!"

"It means resting peacefully!"

"But that's not what happens! Now me, I want to sleep like a coma patient. Talk about uninterrupted sleep!"

"Still covered in your own shit," Wayne pointed out.

"Damn. Good point. I'll think about this some more and come up with a better analogy. But of all the things one could sleep like, it most certainly would never be a baby!"

"Hate to break up this exchange, but we are getting far enough away from the Keep now that we can probably find some mobs. You want to go range out a bit, Dan?" I asked.

"Sure thing. I'll stay pretty close to the road, though, in case you guys need me," Dan responded. "Or in case the Baron there says anything more that needs my clarification."

As soon as Dan cleared the tree line I looked over at Jason and asked, "So, slept like a coma patient last night, did ya?"

"Sure, just minus the colostomy bag," he said while laughing.

While traveling the road, we rode our horses. When we sent Dan off to range, we dismounted and walked while he checked out the area. After several minutes, Dan informed us he wasn't seeing anything out in the forest but Green mobs and nothing new to us. I told him to return to the group and we would continue along the main road for a bit longer before we sent him out again.

When our group traveled together, there was usually fun and witty banter going back and forth between myself and the guys. Usually it was Dan getting on Jason's last good nerve, but we all knew by now that he secretly enjoyed it. For the first time in as long as I could remember, we were traveling in relative quiet. It had been a while since I took in the beauty of my surroundings and appreciated the artistry of the game for what it was.

As I had seen before, the level of detail was extraordinary. The road we traveled was just packed earth with a few well-worn ruts where wagons had traveled the same lane. Those ruts were located on the right and left side of the road, leaving a fairly large area for horses to travel down the middle without the worry of turning a leg. On the sides of the roads were ditches for what I thought must be water during the rainy season. It wasn't the level of detail that surprised me, but the fact that they were there. So much thought put into just a simple road. The grasslands and the forest blended perfectly with the edges of the road. There were no sudden changes of vegetation to dirt. Painstaking detail was put into every part of the game to make it seem more real. And because of the realness of the game, we often went right past it without noticing. If there had been those places where the "game" aspect was obvious, it would have led us to pay more attention to the nature of our surroundings. The reality of the world made us feel like we were walking through a normal environment.

The sky didn't fool you, though. The sky was too blue. You can't walk through the cities of our world and see such a vibrant blue. Pollution had stopped that from happening anymore. However, that same pollution made for the most beautiful sunsets in the real world. In Resurgence they were pretty dull. Clouds and birds passed overhead while we continued down the road, and I wondered if we would ever encounter any avian mobs. I bet those would be a beast to take down. Pun intended.

The one thing I never tired of, however, was the quality of the air. Nowhere on Earth that I had ever been could claim an air so clean and smelling so fresh. I imagine AltCon had to send someone to the tops of the Himalayas to get an air sample they could use in the game. I often found myself—and other gamers—inhaling deeply when away from the towns. They too were likely enjoying the air around us.

"Contact in front of us."

And just like that, our peaceful travels came to an end with Dan's announcement.

"Dismount. What have we got, TC?"

"Looks like other players, Alex. but with the PvP rules in effect now that we are past Level 20, I think we should be on our toes."

"I'll take point," Wayne said.

The new group of players would soon come close enough to make out, and I was reminded of the story Kaitlin told us about the group who stole the kills of others. I would be keeping an eye out to make sure these people weren't all damage dealers.

To everyone's surprise, these guys weren't from Port Town at all. They were from the Citadel, which was obvious from their Dark races. There were two Dark Elves, a Halfling, and an Ogre. The Ogre looked to be their Tank, and the Elves were likely casters, given their robes. I wasn't too clear on the Halfling, but I figured he had to be their healer.

"Holy shit, guys! It's the legends!" the Halfling said as he approached us.

Wayne immediately stepped into the path of the Halfling, whose name was Tyke, with his hand resting on his formidable War Hammer. Tyke stopped quickly and held out his hands toward Wayne.

"Woah, man! We aren't PKs!"

"And I'm supposed to know that how?"

"PKs get a red border around their names. I thought everyone knew that."

Despite not wanting to ever say it out loud, I wanted to maintain an air of formality as I said, "TheClaw, is he right?"

To Dan's credit, he didn't so much as brag once that I used his ridiculous name. "Checking, Alex."

After only several seconds, Dan confirmed what Tyke said and apologized for not noting that bit of information before.

"No worries. It's not like you can remember everything."

"But... but..."

I looked over at Dan with a stern visage and repeated, "You can't remember everything. So no big deal."

He finally started picking up what I was putting down and nodded his head. Dan's memory was an asset I never wanted anyone outside of our team to know.

"Sorry about that, guys. You've actually done us a favor by tuning us in to that little fact. So thanks for that."

"You hear that, guys? We helped the legends!" Tyke said while looking back at his group and laughing. "I guess the rumors of your unbeatable abilities aren't so true after all."

There was no malice in his words, just playful banter.

"TC there gets beat all the time. Although he tells us he has to pay extra for that."

"Ok, Allister. I see. You want to play with the big boys now."

Jason's timing was perfect, and any lingering stress of the situation washed away with everyone's laughter.

"You guys out grinding or heading to do the Trolls?" the Ogre asked.

"The Trolls. You guys beat 'em yet?"

"Nope," said the Halfling while shaking his head. "We are heading back from there now. But best of luck to you guys."

"Any hints you want to throw our way?"

One of the Dark Elves started laughing, "Oh no. We want you to experience that for yourselves. Although, if you do beat them, we may be asking you guys for advice!"

"Well then, let's hope we have something to tell after we get there," I said as we parted ways.

As Tyke and his group were walking away, I could hear them still speaking. The Ogre, who had a voice that matched his large body, said, "Those guys don't seem like dicks at all."

I was shaking my head at the same time Dan reacted to the Ogre's words. "Why do people keep thinking we are going to be a bunch of ass clowns? How serious can anyone take us when I'm wearing pants that came from a damn rabbit?"

"Relax, Dan. This is always the case when people think you are at the top of the food chain," Wayne tried to explain. "They hate. Like you do because Allister is wittier than you. And just like with that, you have to learn to accept the truth."

"Allibater is a lot of things, *mon frère*, and most of those are way better than what I got, but no fucking way is he wittier than TheClaw."

This was too good to pass up and I just had to get involved. "What are the best jokes ever, Dan?"

"Fart jokes, bro. They're always funny."

"And there you go proving Wayne right. Case closed."

"You know you guys just don't have the depth to appreciate TheClaw's humor."

"Indeed, Dan. We have not yet sunk to that level," Jason added, while giving Dan one of his signature looks.

"Damn. That was good."

We didn't encounter any further players or mobs before hitting the location of the soldiers' camp. There looked to be two thousand soldiers and all the accoutrements that go along with that many people. Horses were tied to posts, tents were laid out in an orderly fashion, and every ten tents or so had a fire pit for cooking and keeping warm. What I gauged were the officers' tents were larger and in better shape, but no one was living in grandeur. The camp had been set up along the river, and in the distance, I could see the bridge the Trolls kept destroying. It wasn't a full-on demolition, but the damage was sufficient enough that the King's men would never be able to cross their supplies over.

The flashing quest icon on our maps was not leading us to the Trolls but rather a grouping of tents that belonged to officers. Standing in front of the tent that was our destination were two sentries in chainmail. Full plate would have been far too exhausting on a sentry standing guard, but even the chainmail looked to be extremely uncomfortable. And if there is anything I've learned in my short time on the planet, it's that uncomfortable people don't like people who aren't as uncomfortable as them.

"State your business!" The sentry on our left said while leaning the pike in his hand a tad bit forward toward our direction.

"We have been sent by Sir Arthur to assist in your problem."

"Finally. Those latrines have been needing a good cleaning for a week now!"

"Maybe a little more clarity there, Alex."

"Thanks, Dan. I wouldn't have figured that out without you," I responded. "We are here to eradicate the Trolls."

The sentry on our right looked over at his companion, back to us, and then back to his companion. Then, without a word, he began laughing hard.

"Oh sure. No doubt you four will be able to take out that tiny little problem. It isn't like we sent twenty men in there to kill those beasts. You remember what they said when they came back?" the sentry asked to his companion.

"They didn't ever come back."

"Oh, that's right. They didn't." The laughter was gone and he was all business now. "If you lads want to go over there and get killed, that's your business. But don't say we didn't warn ya. Twenty of ours couldn't stop those animals. Don't seem like you will have any luck, either."

"We appreciate your warning, but we have our orders."

"Sure enough you do. Go on in and talk to Captain Treeswain. He'll tell ya what ya need to know."

Without another word, the four of us entered the tent and saw the lone occupant standing over a map of the area. It was highly detailed, and I nodded at Dan to get close to it and give it a gander. In the meantime, I approached the man I suspected was the Captain and repeated the quest phrase again.

While Dan reviewed the map, the Captain explained the situation, to include far more details than we needed about the impact the bridge's destruction had had on morale and the efforts of the war. After several minutes of trying to move the Captain along to giving us the quest location, I finally broke down and asked, "Where are the Trolls?"

"Fine. I never do meet any of you adventurers who appreciate the grand scale of warfare and all the strategic objectives one needs to consider to achieve victory."

The Captain then walked over to the map and pointed at a location on the other side of the river from where we were. Immediately a quest icon showed up on our maps labeling the location of the Trolls. "Best of luck to you. We need to get that bridge fixed, and none of my soldiers will go near that place again."

We left the tent and walked to the outskirts of the camp before I asked Dan where we should cross.

"If that map in there was accurate, and I have to believe it is, we have to go about a half hour south of our location to find the best place to cross."

"You know shit flows downstream right?" Wayne asked.

"I thought that was downhill," I said.

"In this case, both. Any chance we can cross somewhere north of the camp?"

"I am afraid not, my Barbarian brother. The river just continues to get wider as we travel north. South with the shit is our only option."

"South it is. And if it isn't terribly deep in that part of the river, we can probably ride our horses across."

Thankfully, we didn't encounter any problems on the way to the crossing point, although the tree line along the river was too dense for us to ride our horses to the spot. If we could find a suitable area of open ground, we could summon a horse, although we would likely have to do this one at a time. I had yet to see an area outside of the camp where we could have summoned all four at the same time.

After a few minutes of searching, we found a spot that worked. Dan volunteered to go first, but I overruled him since I could Invis and he couldn't. The horses didn't have a problem with going through the river, but their movement speed was cut down to only 10 percent of normal. This was likely a game mechanic that stopped players from using the rivers and mounts to escape being attacked. At 10 percent of normal speed, the horse was moving at a speed slower than I could move while on land. Once everyone was across, I planned to see what happened when I tried to walk through the river, and if it would affect my movement speed as well. But that would be after everyone was across and we were north of the shit factory that was the soldier's camp.

Once everyone was across and Dan reported there were no mobs in the area, we unsummoned the horses and made our way north to the Troll camp. We would have loved to stay on the horses, but just like on the west side of the river, the tree line on this side was too dense for that.

I kept our pace at a leisurely trot. We had no knowledge of the area, and Dan needed to move slower than normal to make sure we weren't running into a pack of mobs.

We encountered a couple of Green mobs between our crossing point and the Troll's location, but we dispatched one quickly and avoided the other. Otherwise, there were no further obstacles in our path.

Upon arriving at the locator on our maps, we saw a large cave opening. Apparently when Trolls weren't living under bridges, they were living in caves—and damn big ones, as the mouth of this cave was easily 15 feet high.

"Well, boys, there's our quest. Let's buff up, get full mana, and go wreck shit."

The guys nodded in my direction and went to work. After a short time, we were ready to go.

As a team, we entered the cave-home of the Trolls.

And then we were annihilated.

CHAPTER 7

October 22nd, 2043

Maybe all that talk of "legends" had gone to our heads. Maybe we were a step off of our game. Either way, we went into the cave of the Trolls and got our backsides handed to us due to our own stupidity. I didn't go first and scout the area. A total and complete newb mistake and that cost us experience and time.

We rushed into the cave entrance expecting it to resemble every dungeon we had ever encountered. You go through the entrance and make your way through who knows how many mobs until you reach the end. Only this "dungeon" didn't follow the rules of the other dungeons we had faced. Instead of the immediate area surrounding the entrance being a safe zone, it was a complete and total ambush. Five Trolls were located immediately within the entrance, and walking into the cave set off some sort of door trap that blocked the entire 15-foot entrance and kept us from just running away. Then all five of them rushed our group.

The mobs were all Blue. Normally, Blues are our bread and butter and we can do two at a time. Sometimes we can do three. We can't do five.

Wayne immediately went to Jason's side and got aggro on the two mobs approaching our Cleric. Unfortunately, Dan drew the aggro of two other mobs, and I got aggro on the last one. With Dan receiving a beat-down from two separate mobs, he was unable to launch a snare and try to kite the mobs around. I was unable to shake the mob on me, and Jason was busy trying to keep Wayne alive.

As soon as the two Blues destroyed Dan—and Broham soon after—they rushed Jason. I never saw what happened next, since I was killed in quick order. It doesn't take a genius, though, to figure out what happens when five mobs take on two players.

I thought about using my Force Multiplier Ring, but I wanted to save that for the boss mob and a chance for better loot. I only get to use it once every 24 hours, after all. And honestly, the Ring would have done nothing but prolong the death that was going to come our way. As I have noted repeatedly, we were stronger than the average player, but we were in no way unstoppable.

"That was so much suck, I don't even have words to explain it."

"For one of those rare occasions, I am in complete agreement with Dan," Jason said.

"Damn. We totally thought you guys would be able to take the entrance."

I turned around and saw Tyke and his group of Dark aligned players resting near the fountain.

"Think you could have given us a heads up?"

"Hell nah," Tyke said, a little too enthusiastically for my taste. "Where's the fun in that?"

It had been a long time since we had all been in nothing but our starting clothes. Clothes that have no armor. Basically, we were walking around in our birthday suits when it came to defense. Despite that, Wayne still looked very formidable as he approached the little Halfling. Jason stepped in front of Wayne as the Ogre Warrior, Lug, stepped in front of Tyke.

"Relax, Naugha. We can't be mad at these guys. We got our asses beat because of our own stupid actions."

"Don't take it so hard, Naugha. We tried that entrance three times and were killed each time. It's a beast of a way to start a quest challenge."

Wayne calmed down a bit as Lug kept talking. Like anyone that ever played an MMORPG, Wayne hated to lose experience. More than that, Wayne hated losing, period.

"Sorry. I'm not the friendliest after getting beat down."

"You'll have plenty of time to calm down and hit your Zen. It takes forever to walk back to that camp. Trust me on this one. I've had to do it three times now."

The thought of wasting a day walking back to the camp was enough to bring everyone's moods down yet another notch.

I hoped by talking a bit about our strategy, we could get some more information out of Tyke and his group. "I guess we can try pulling them out of the cave to take one at a time."

"Won't work," said one of their casters. "We tried doing the exact same thing, and the mobs will only come to the entrance of the cave and stop there."

"Why not nuke them while they are stuck at the entrance?"

"Oh, we tried that! After about ten seconds, they boomerang back to their starting position and go back to full health."

"I bet it was awesome the first time they just stood there and took your shots!"

"Yeah. We totally thought we found a loophole for those ten seconds."

"You guys figure it out, we would love to know how. That entrance is going to be impossible until we come up with a strategy that works," Tyke said.

"I fear a lot of experimentation waits in our futures, Tyke. If we come up with anything, we will let you guys know. Thanks for the info on the entrance thing."

At the mention of experimentation, I saw Wayne wince. I was glad to see I could still instill a small bit of fear into our Warrior.

After saying our goodbyes to Tyke and his group, we started the long trek back to the Troll cave.

"Getting our bodies won't be a problem, at least. I'll go in there and drag them out. And with Allister's new spell, we will get half of our experience back."

"I'm more worried about the fact that we could very well have to do this all over again tomorrow. Those guys said they had lost three times already."

"Have no fear, Allister. I have a plan."

"Alex, every time you have 'a plan,' I worry for my mental health."

"I would say 'this time will be different,' but I doubt any of you would believe me."

"Not a chance, sadist," Jason said with a grin on his face.

"You'll see. Let's go get our bodies and then log out for the night. If we stay to the road, we shouldn't have any problems with mobs. Getting across the river is going to suck, though. Guess it's time to level up our swimming."

Everyone was quiet for a while. But since we had several hours to travel, Wayne eventually broke the monotony of walking along the road.

"Jenny and I want you guys to come over for dinner sometime soon."

"Will Kaitlin be there?"

"Yes, Dan, Kaitlin is being invited as well."

"I'll be there!"

"You realize she's likely asking the exact same question and deciding on not going because of your invite," Jason chimed in.

"Not true, Allisister. Kaitlin loves TheClaw with all her soul."

"Guess her soul hasn't bothered to tell the rest of her that yet."

"You'll see. TheClaw is going to come with the thunder."

"You're totally welcome to come Dan, as long as 'the thunder' isn't the name of some inappropriate phallic symbol."

"That's 'The Lightning,' *hombre*! The thunder is just my normal awesomeness."

"Good. Keep The Lightning at home," Wayne said and then turned toward me and Jason. "How about you guys?"

Jason replied first. "I'd love to, Naugha. Can I bring my husband as well? James hears about you guys all the time, and I would love for him to meet you guys. He doesn't believe Dan could possibly be a real person."

"The awesomeness, right?"

"Only if that word suddenly became synonymous with ridiculousness."

"Of course James is welcome. Gary and Tim are going to bring their significant others as well. You can bring anyone you like as well, Alex, if you want to come."

"Oh, I'll definitely be there, Wayne. I'll be coming alone, but that's ok. Someone will need to be there to comfort Dan when Kaitlin shuts him down. Again."

We spent the rest of the walk hammering out when we would all meet up, what everyone should bring, and convincing Dan that this was not an opportunity for all of us to try and cosplay our characters from the game. Dan was adamant that it was totally appropriate and noted he had already had a set of Furry Bunny Britches made for just such an occasion. In the end, Wayne won out by citing the age-old truism of 'my house, my rules,' against which even Dan could not argue.

In true TheClaw fashion, Dan immediately began talking about the next gathering, but at his place. There was even mention of a unicorn ice sculpture that rained booze from its horn. This kept up all the way to the soldiers' camp.

We avoided Captain Treeswain's tent and made our way to the southern portion of the camp. Since we had traveled this area already, Dan was able to see for a good distance if there were any mobs in the area. Our trek to our previous crossing point went off without a hitch, as did our re-crossing of the river.

In fact, we were quite lucky in that we were able to avoid any of the mobs that would have crossed our path, although we did have to backtrack on a couple of occasions. I stayed in my Conceal/Stealth for the journey, just in case something bad did happen.

Upon arriving at the cave entrance, I waited for the guys to get a bit further ahead of me and then cloaked myself in shadows. With my Blacksuit engaged, I had no fear that I would be detected by the Trolls.

I had no clue if just entering the cave would set off the trap, but there was no way for me to know without trying. I should have asked

Tyke and his crew what they did with their bodies. Oh well. Nothing ventured, nothing gained.

I never had to find out though, as from the entrance of the cave I could "drag" the bodies of my group. When everything went south, we had tried to run out of the cave. That action put our bodies right next to the entrance when we died. From just outside the cave I grabbed the bodies and brought them over to Jason.

Jason had full mana but only his base Wisdom to supply it. Jason's gear gave him more potential mana but did not immediately fill up his mana pool. The shoulders did reduce the amount of mana Jason needed to use, but even with that, the spell to return 50 percent of our experience took about 1/3 of Jason's mana. After Wayne and Dan were finished, Jason sat and regenerated until he reached full mana. Fifteen minutes later, Jason and I were both returned and the experience loss looked marginal. Thankfully, we hadn't lost enough to negate our levels. I wanted all of us to log out with full health and full mana, so Jason got to work healing all of us up. After that, Dan and Jason sat until their mana returned and we were ready for the next day's adventure. Dan took that break to ask Wayne three more times if Kaitlin said she was coming to the party or not. Wayne enjoyed dragging Dan along without an appropriate answer.

October 23rd, 2043

Everyone was ready for my "plan" once we were all logged in. I had been thinking about how to approach the problem all night, and I felt secure in my thinking. The first step would be figuring out where the mobs were located and whether Dan would be able to get a solid shot off at them with his bow. If Dan couldn't get a shot off from outside the cave, this plan was dead in the water before we even started.

I activated my Conceal/Stealth and made my way toward the cave. As I entered for the second time in Conceal/Stealth, I was thankful to see the trap did not activate. The Trolls were arranged in a pentagram-type layout within the circular cave, with the entrance at the base of the star and a troll at the top of it. The cave was large, which hampered Dan's ability to get a shot off, but it was ideal for kiting mobs. Once I determined that the mobs were still Blue, I returned to just outside the cave where my group was waiting.

"Dan, I want you to get up to the edge of the cave but not inside it. I will go inside and target one of the mobs on the far side. I want you to approach the edge and shoot that mob with one of your arrows when I say the word."

After getting the nod from Dan, I went back in and targeted the mob that was to the left of the center positioned mob. With that Troll targeted, I returned to just outside the cave and told Dan to take his shot while engaging the mob I had targeted. As I hoped, Dan's shot landed, and the Troll came right up to the edge of the cave.

As soon as Dan's shot was launched, I started the timer. Tyke's group was slightly off, and the mob remained at the entrance to the cave for exactly 12 seconds. Excellent.

"Alex, we know that isn't going to work. As soon as we get the guy up to the edge, he is going to boomerang back to his starting location and return to full health," Wayne said.

"That would be the case if we were going to try and take them at the edge. Even we don't have the DPS to finish them off that quickly. So we are going to implement a three-part attack.

"We need to get all our buffs going and then wait until we have full mana. Dan, no Broham for this pull."

"No worries there, dude. Once Broham is killed, I can't bring him back for 24 hours. It sucks, but those are the game mechanics."

"That will work for now. Once everyone is buffed up and whatnot, I will go through what will go down."

It only took five minutes before everyone was ready and eagerly looking my way for the solution to our problem.

"I'm going to enter the cave and target the first mob. It's going to be the same one you just shot Dan."

Our Ranger nodded his head in my direction.

"Immediately after you take the shot, I will switch to a different target. This will be the guy to the right of the center Troll. As soon as you fire, switch targets and take the second shot. That will bring two of the Trolls to our position here in front of the cave."

I looked over at Jason and gave our Cleric his instructions. "Jason, hit Dan with the protection buff you normally give to Wayne. He is going to need it.

"As soon as both of those guys are at the front of the cave, hit each of them with Snare. As soon as the second one lands, call it, and all of us will enter the cave, activating the trap. You are going to get hit at the beginning, but with the protection buff you should be ok. Run into the cave, away from the Trolls at the entrance and target the guy directly across from us. All you will have to do is switch to my target. I'll have it ready to go."

I looked around to make sure all of the guys were tracking. So far they were following my logic. More importantly, none of them were questioning my plan.

"As soon as you get to the middle, hit the third guy with a Snare and then start running them around the outside of the cave. Kite those bastards for all you're worth. Don't worry about hitting them with any arrows. Just keep your Snare fresh.

"Wayne, as soon as you enter the cave, go to the left and Taunt the Troll there. Then, run to the guy on the right and give him a good Kick to his balls. Then take both of them into the center of the cave, and you and I will bring him down to nothing. After that, we take the second mob, and so forth. We should be able to clean up like this. Any suggestions?"

"Just one. Instead of taking them into the center, how about I take them just outside of the kite range but close enough that I can Taunt one of the kited ones while it passes. This way I can build aggro while we are fighting the other two and pull the third off of Dan with more ease."

"As long as you can maintain aggro on the two that will be on you so that Allister doesn't get a beat-down, I'm good with it."

"I got it. The day I can't maintain my aggro is the day I hang up my War Hammer and switch to a Bard."

"While I would love to see an almost 7-foot Bard, I think I would prefer just fucking up these Trolls. Let's make it happen."

I remembered the adage "No plan survives contact with the enemy," but I was pleased to see this didn't hold true to our second foray into the Trolls' cave. I could go into excruciating detail about how each part of the operation played out, but suffice it to say, there were no hitches in our scheme. The Trolls had a moderate amount of hit points and a crazy amount of regeneration, but we were able to whittle them down in due order. With our weapons and our increased levels, our damage-dealing abilities were above average. This was enough to win the day.

It was only five mobs, Blues at that, but you would have thought we had received the most epic of loot when we downed the fifth Troll. Everyone was cheering and patting each other on the back. Speaking of loot, there was none—just a few pieces of Gold, but we didn't care in the least.

Following our victory, I showed the guys our path. During my initial investigation of the cave, I had found the passageway that led from the entrance and deeper into the complex. As soon as everyone was healed up and had full mana, I activated my Invis and started making my way into the tunnel. I wasn't going to make the same mistake twice. After two steps into the tunnel and away from my friends, I activated my Blacksuit and progressed deeper.

What I found was more in line with the traditional "dungeon" set-up for Resurgence. There were a number of tunnels and several mobs, but nothing looked like it was going to cause another ambush. To be on the safe side, I planned to have Dan shoot each one from a distance and make them run toward us. If one got stuck, we would know it was hitting the edge of an ambush.

I didn't travel too far, since I didn't have a comprehensive map of the cave network. Thankfully, this "dungeon" actually had the map available. Otherwise, I wouldn't have been able to travel as far as I had.

The relief on the faces of the guys was clear when I told them I hadn't found anything that looked like more ambushes. I gave them my thoughts on engagement, and they agreed. Once we were all buffed up and full of mana again, I made my way back down the same hallway.

We pulled singles and doubles and did not find another ambush. By and large, the Trolls weren't difficult; they just took a long time.

I was starting to think we might just sail through the rest of the dungeon and call it a day. I expected the dungeon boss to be tough, sure, but not anything we couldn't handle.

As we crept down the tunnels, my map started showing me that I would be coming upon a large room. Large rooms were good. Dan could kite in large rooms with no problems.

Not about to make the same mistake again, I made sure my Blacksuit was activated, and slid my way in.

"You have got to be shitting me!"

All my happiness went right down the drain as I took a long look around the room, trying to count all the damn trolls.

"Well that doesn't sound promising."

"No, Dan, not promising at all. Give me a minute, guys. I have to count up all the mobs in here."

"What the hell do you mean 'count?' You see three mobs, you say three mobs."

I didn't bother to answer Dan. Once I gave them the final number, it would be obvious what I meant by count.

The room was large, alright. It had to be. When I stopped counting, the total was 10 Blue mobs and one Red. No problem guessing what the Red one was. The way the room was laid out, all of the mobs were on the far side of the room, packed together, directly across from the entrance. There were no mobs to either side of the entrance. The only other things of note were several fire pits laid out within the room. At first glance, they looked like cooking fires, as there were a number of bones splayed out around the fires.

Apparently, even Trolls want to cook meat before they eat it, at least when it came to eating bipeds. There were all kinds of easily identifiable bones from various humanoid species.

I relayed what I found and told the guys to slowly move up to my position just outside of the large room. I wanted them all to get a good look at what I was seeing and figure out if anyone else could come up with a way to tackle this room.

After one quick look, Dan let us know there was no way he could pull singles—or even doubles—in this place. They were way too packed together. If he tried to pull just one or two, he would likely get the whole group.

I couldn't see any way around just going at them straight on. That was obviously not the answer. There was a riddle here, and I was sure it would involve the fire pits. Everyone knows that Trolls hate fire, since it is the only thing that can stop their regeneration. While they may use it to stay warm or even cook food, they will try to avoid it at all costs. The problem was, I couldn't possibly see how we could light the fires before we were overtaken by all the mobs.

"Anyone else notice that we had our maps this whole time?" Jason asked suddenly.

I nodded along with the rest of my team. Having the map meant that if someone was outside of the cave, they would still likely get experience from a kill. That didn't really help us here.

"Ok. Give me a second and let me try something," Jason said as he went back further into the tunnel.

After only a couple of seconds, Jason gave out a long sigh. "Oh well, it was worth a try. I thought we might be able to summon our horses if we were still connected to the map. But I am getting the message that you may not summon a horse within this area. It's the same message I get when we are in a dungeon."

"It was worth a try, Allister."

Wayne kept looking back and forth between the cooking pits and finally said, "It's obvious, I think, that we need to use fire against them. So far we haven't had to worry about their massive regeneration rates. But you can almost be certain that the boss's hit point regen is going to be astronomical. Can we start those fire pits from here?"

"I don't have any fire arrows or anything like that," Dan contributed.

"We all have fire-making tinder boxes, but we would need to be right on top of the fires to get them started and it isn't like we have practiced this skill all that much. It's impossible to say how long it could take," I added.

"Dan, does your direct damage spell have a fire element?"

"Afraid not, Allister."

The fact that Dan called Jason by his in-game name, not some variation, was evidence of how serious everyone was looking at the problem.

"The thing I don't like the most here, Alex, is that we have no idea how the mobs are going to react. If one of us runs into the room and over to one of the corners, will the whole pack follow that one person? Or will they auto-aggro the next person who comes in?"

"Yeah, even I don't want to try one of my experiments here. What does the manual say about starting fires?"

"Give me a second to look it up."

The rest of us continued to look inside the large room trying to gauge the best way forward. While Dan scoured the manual for anything about lighting fires with our tinder boxes, I reestablished my Invisible status and crept back into the room. This time, I headed over to the fire pits themselves and got a better look.

There was room between and around each of them. It was unclear how large the fire would get or if we could safely run around the outsides of them without taking damage.

"Well, this looks to be all you, Alex. The skill calls for a check against the player's Dexterity. On top of that, there is a certain amount of luck—meaning Chance—of the player lighting the fire."

"Ok. That actually makes sense."

I took one more look around the room and ran around the fire pits at full speed. I had no idea how the mobs would react to what I wanted to try, but I didn't see any choice for us.

"Just to be sure everyone knows, this plan sucks."

"I can't believe he finally admitted it."

"Shut up, Dan. My plans are almost always awesome."

"The plan, Alex?"

"Right. As you can all see, there are six fire pits, running in a line, with a good size gap in the middle. Let's label them 1 through 6. So you have, from left to right, fire pits 1-3, then the gap, then 4-6. My plan is to set myself up all the way over by pit 1. At my signal, Wayne will enter. I'm pretty sure that will aggro the mobs.

"As soon as he enters, he will start running toward me. I'm hoping that while the mobs are running toward him, I will have time to light this fire. Everyone following so far?"

This wasn't rocket science, so I wasn't surprised to see everyone's look for me to get on with it.

"Right. So as Wayne gets to me, he runs around the far side of the fire pit and then heads toward pit 6. As soon as I have pit 1 lit, I will run toward 6 myself. The idea is to slow down the advance of the Trolls and make them run a longer way around the room. That should give me time to light the fire and for Wayne to perform the same maneuver."

"There are a whole lot of 'ifs' in there, Alex."

"I know, Allister, but what other choice do we have? You can't heal Wayne at any point or the aggro will switch to you, and then we will have some mobs running toward you and others toward Wayne. The only way this works is if we can funnel them through that gap."

All eyes turned back to the layout of the large room and how the fire pits were set up.

"You know, if the fires get large enough, that might actually work. Only one would be able to get through that gap at a time."

"That's my hope, Wayne."

"So what happens on the last pit?"

"Instead of running around to pit 1 or 6, you will run right past pit 4. This one won't be lit. They will, hopefully, follow you through and into the area they are all standing at now. However, once they cross that threshold, I will light pit 4. You then sprint for pit 1 or 6, and they will be forced to come out of the opening gap."

"Hmmm. Doesn't look like I would make it back in time to engage the first mob that then turns to come out of that gap."

"You won't. We'll have to engage them before you get there and can take over."

"I'm not too keen on sacrificing any of us, man. There are too many mobs for us to lose a 1/4 of our strength before even taking one of them down."

"You're right, Wayne. That's why Dan will engage the first one that comes out of the gap, stopping the flow. As soon as he starts to engage, he will do nothing but cast self-heal on himself. Allister will only shoot off a quick heal if Dan gets down to 40 percent before you can get there. Naturally, as soon as you arrive, Dan will disengage while you throw a Taunt, Kick, and Bash into his mob. Dan will stand there and take his beating until the mob turns off him and engages you.

"Once that happens, you turn the mob at a slight angle so I can get shots off without getting hit with counter damage. Dan will back away and focus on shooting arrows at the mobs. Hold off on that first mob for a bit once Wayne has aggro. We don't want to reset aggro.

"If it does happen, for whatever reason, just Snare and kite. It will take us a lot longer to finish these guys off, but that's the only choice we have."

"What if the Boss is the first one through the gap?"

"With special abilities likely to go off as it loses hit points? Then we probably die."

"Aren't you just powered by optimism?"

It turns out there's a reason they say that most plans don't survive first contact. I realized this as I watched my well laid out plan go utterly and horribly tits-up immediately after Wayne entered the room.

The plan was sound—except for the part where I didn't factor in my likelihood to aggro half the mobs in the room when I dropped my Invis, which is exactly what happened.

As soon as Wayne saw half the mobs change their trajectory, he surprisingly followed my call to run back into the hallway with Dan and Jason. Unfortunately, as soon as Wayne crossed the threshold, it was impossible for him to run back into the tunnel. We met our end bunched up at the entrance, with all the mobs beating on us mercilessly. All but the boss. He stayed stationary through the whole thing and didn't show aggro on me or Wayne. I made sure to check as Wayne and I watched our hit points dwindle to nothing. That was good to know.

Thankfully Jason could cast that wonderful holy spell of his, regaining 50 percent of our lost experience. More importantly, though, the spell would return us to our bodies, meaning we wouldn't have to run back from Kich's Keep again.

Wayne and I gave Jason permission to drag our bodies back into the cave tunnel, and within minutes we were fully geared up again, just minus some experience.

If this was going to happen, it was going to require all of us to enter the cave at the same time. Well, all of us minus me in my Blacksuit. I could enter early without triggering the trap, but as soon as I let it fall, I would be caught in the large room.

"So, new plan."

"Yeah. You were right."

"About what, Dan?"

"That plan sucked."

I couldn't help laughing. Dan was right. The plan did suck. It ended up getting both Wayne and I killed, and we didn't take down a single mob. And if they thought that plan was bad, they really weren't going to like the next one.

"This is going to be a do-or-die moment, guys. With the traps set up the way they are, we will either win or all of us will die. I don't see any way around that."

"Do you guys remember when Alex had really good plans? Maybe we should pick a new leader."

"Shut it, Dan. We would still be stuck at the entrance if he hadn't come up with that shit earlier," Jason said, defending me.

"It's all good, Allister. Feel free to give us your grand strategy, oh wise Ranger."

Dan sat down against the rock face of the tunnel and looked to be thinking. "Let them die of old age?"

"Right. Anyone else have any thoughts?"

"Alex, if you've got something cooking, let's hear it. We knew we would be playing this one by ear as we went along."

I looked around to get everyone's consent. Despite his acting, Dan was nodding along with Jason at Wayne's comments.

"You've taken a couple of shots from these mobs, right Allister?"

"Sure have. They hit pretty good, but nothing I couldn't get away from if I had to stun and move back."

"Think you could take more than just a couple?"

"I wouldn't want to try and tank, but I think with my buffs I could last for a bit."

"Then here is what we will do."

Over the course of the next several minutes, I modified the same plan, only this time my three teammates would all enter at the same time. I would, again, be placed near the fire pit that I had marked as 1.

The difference this time around was that Wayne would pull four of the Blues to him, Dan would do the same, and Jason would take two himself. Dan would be able to get off two solid Snares before the mobs had a chance to get to him, and then he would run away enough that only two out of the four would get a chance to beat on him.

Dan would fire an arrow at each of the two he did not Snare to maintain aggro. Jason would take a swing at each of his two to do the same. Wayne would Taunt one, Kick another, Bash the third, and swing his war hammer in a normal attack at the fourth. Wayne assured me that he could cycle through each of the mobs easily enough. I already knew Dan had practice in doing similar things while trying to engage different mobs. I was also confident that Jason would be able to get the aggro on his two mobs.

Dan's mobs would be the most difficult to deal with. The others would all be running after my teammates at a set pace, though two of Dan's mobs would be running while snared. That could either hurt us or help us, depending on whether someone crossed their paths and they changed aggro.

If I could get the fires started quickly, and they were of a significant enough size to do what we wanted, we could win the day. There were still a lot of "ifs" in this scenario. But I remembered something about fortune favoring the bold.

On my mark, my teammates put their faith in my plan and entered the room as one. Immediately, the ten Blue mobs started running toward the tunnel entrance and my fellow adventurers. I had to hold off on dropping my Invis until all of the mobs had taken aggro, or this wouldn't work.

Wayne stayed in the middle, while Dan and Jason fanned out to the left and right respectively. Dan immediately cast Snare on one, and then another mob. When both turned toward Dan, along with several others, Dan fired off two arrows. Wayne then went forward and ran through his cycle of Taunt, Kick, Bash, and attack. Jason followed closely behind Wayne and performed his two attacks as well. So far, the plan was working as designed.

All that was left was for me to light a fire. I only hoped it worked.

Each attempt took only a second, but the first two attempts were failures. I was looking in the direction of my teammates as I attempted to light the fire, and I could see they were approaching my position at a rapid rate.

In this case, third time was the charm. With the successful strike against my tinder box, the fire ignited and then instantly took shape into a large fire. I didn't wait to see if my plan would work and stuck to what I was supposed to be doing. As soon as the fire took and grew, I ran across the room toward pit 6 and immediately began striking my tinder box again.

This time it only took me two attempts to get the fire going strong. According to my own plan, I now had to run back and forth, igniting pits 2, 5, 3, and 4, in that order. I spared a quick glance at the health bars of my teammates. While they were all partially depleted, none of them looked to be in any danger.

Wayne was shouting directions concerning where to run while I lit the fires. I was down to the last pit, number 4, as I saw Wayne run past me. Dan and Jason followed suit soon after. In order for this to work—if it was going to work—I had to wait until they dragged all the mobs back "behind" the fire pit line. As soon as Jason ran past, I struck my tinder box.

And nothing happened.

I struck again, with the same result.

Hoping that the third time was the charm yet again, I put the tinder box near the fire and struck again.

Nothing.

Each of the guys were yelling various obscenities, either at me or in my general direction, while I shot forth with every four-letter expletive I knew.

Apparently, the fourth time can be the charm as well.

As soon as the fire was roaring, the guys sprinted toward the gap. I dared to look at their health bars, and I became very worried. Jason's health was at 30 percent, Dan's was at 35 percent, and Wayne's was at 45 percent. I was the only one with a full health bar.

"As soon as you guys get past me, I will engage the first mob while Allister gets Wayne healed up. Dan, you focus on healing Allister."

With our funnel of fire in place, the Trolls did exactly what we wanted. And while it took longer than anyone would like, we eventually killed one Troll after another.

During that time, the fires started going out, and I had to disengage and restart a pit. The Trolls stayed bunched up near the gap between fire pits, still trying to attack either Dan, Jason, or Wayne, depending on whom had initially established aggro during the tour around the room. None of the Trolls disengaged, but I certainly didn't want to take that chance.

As we started on the last Blue Troll, I kept wondering what the Red would have in store for us. He was easily twice as large as the rest of the Trolls and had a wicked-looking club in his hands. He hadn't so much as twitched since we entered the room. The only benefit of it taking so long to take down the Trolls, with their crazy hit point regeneration, was that Dan and Jason both had a healthy amount of mana. Jason's mana took priority for heals, but you never knew when one of these bosses would spawn extra minions and we would need Dan to kite some mobs around the room.

"Allister, Dan, you guys good on mana, or do you want Wayne to draw this one out a bit more?"

"I'm almost full, brodonkakonk. All I've been doing is shooting arrows."

"I'm at 80 percent, Alex, and I rebuffed everyone just a few minutes ago. I'm ready for the boss whenever."

"Ok. Let's burn this guy down and hope Dan never says any variation of ba-donk-a-donk ever again."

"Amen to that."

With only a few percentage points left on the Troll, we made short work of him. As soon as the Troll fell, the Boss looked around and then started trotting in our direction.

"Do we want to move him more to the center of the room, Alex?"

"Yeah, this way we don't have any problem with Dan and I getting behind him to do our damage."

Wayne slowly backed up while keeping the rest of us behind him. In this way, Wayne could ensure that he would take the first swing at the Boss and, in turn, establish primary aggro.

Which is exactly how things played out. In fact, it was textbook maneuvering. After several moments had passed, we were all in position with Wayne fully establishing his aggro on the Boss.

Only nothing was happening.

Yes, I could see that I was doing damage, and I knew Wayne's hammer was proc'ing and doing plenty of damage as well. While I couldn't see what kind of output Dan was providing, I had no problem seeing his arrows fly true.

But the health bar on the boss only flickered slightly, and then was back at 100 percent.

It was after this happened two more times that we realized what was happening. The Boss' regeneration was unfathomably high; he was regaining hit points faster than we could take them down.

We were already throwing everything we had at this guy.

The only thing I had left in my arsenal was to use the Force Multiplier Ring, and I didn't want to shoot that off until we were close to finishing the Boss. Even with the extra bonuses, I didn't think we would be able to negate the Boss' regeneration fast enough to take him down in five minutes. The only thing that had ever been able to really negate a Troll's regeneration ability was fire.

Fire.

I turned around and saw that three of the six fires had gone down. I wouldn't have to wait long until the other three would go out as well.

And the unlit fire pits gave me an idea.

"Wayne! Move the Boss over to pit 1!"

Wayne started maneuvering the Boss toward the pit that I had earlier designated as pit 1. The fire in that pit had gone out already. Pits 3, 4, and 5 were still lit, based on how I originally started the fires. Pit 5 would go out soon.

As soon as the Boss was standing over the unlit pit, I stopped attacking and knelt with my tinder box. After the second spark, the pit lit up!

And the Boss immediately went from 100 percent, to 84 percent!

The Boss' next action was to destroy the fire pit, making it unusable. His second action was to start destroying me. I guess I pulled all the aggro since I was the one that started the fire.

My hit points started going south quickly, but Jason saved me with a well-timed heal. After only a short time—that felt like an eternity while getting pummeled—Wayne reestablished aggro on the Boss.

Wayne already knew what I had planned. Without any prompting from me, Wayne began to maneuver the Boss over to pit 6. We would follow the same path as earlier and move the Boss around the room. The reason for this was clear to my teammates. I wanted to have the last two pits be right next to each other, 3 and 4, with still enough room to maneuver around them.

"I'm going to hold off on my aggro building Skills until after you light the fire, Alex."

"Copy. Just let me know when you are ready."

Several seconds later, Wayne said go.

I lit the second fire on the first attempt. And just like before, the Boss dropped another 16 percent. His hit points went to 68 percent, which also activated his first special skill. Naturally, the Boss had a special surprise for us once he had lost 25 percent of his hit points.

While the Boss destroyed the fire, Wayne hit him with all three aggro building Skills. That didn't stop him from unleashing his special attack, but it did take the attention off of me.

The Boss hit us all with Troll Stun. In essence, he performed a whirlwind with his big-ass club, and we were all hit with a massive

Stun. We couldn't attack or move. While we were immobile, the Boss' hit points started going back up, although slower than before. When the stun finally broke, the Boss had regained five percent of his hit points and was at 73 percent. He had also beat on Wayne quite a bit, requiring time for Jason to heal more than normal and then regain some of his mana.

Pits 2 and 5 went off without a hitch, and the Boss followed the same pattern. He destroyed each fire and then beat on me until Wayne could pull back the aggro. When he dropped below 50 percent, three more Blue Trolls spawned and came at us.

Dan was about to enact our normal strategy for extra mobs and Snare two of them in order to kite them around the room. Before he got his spell going, I yelled for him to wait. If the fire had such an effect on the Boss, I hypothesized that it would have a devastating impact on the Blue Trolls.

"Wayne grab 'em! Hold 'em for now!" I yelled and then explained myself. "This could go really bad, really fast. He's at 40 percent and the next fire pit will take him down to below 25 percent. But if we focus our attention on these Blues, we won't be doing enough damage to stop the regen on the Boss. Let's use the fire pit on the Blues as well."

No one disagreed, and Wayne maneuvered the pack over pit 3. I hoped my intuition was on point, because if these Blues didn't die straight away, these four mobs were going to plaster me into the ground.

Wayne yelled that all of his Skills were ready. Without waiting another beat, I lit the fire.

The resulting fireball was glorious. As before, when the fire ignited it scorched the Boss and brought him down to 23 percent. But the fire also lit up the three Blues as I had hoped. Before the Boss could take out the fire, the Blues destroyed it themselves. But the extra flames of the Blues compounded the effects on the Boss, and his hit points went down to 20 percent.

I made a mental note that if we had tried to use the fire itself to kill the initial 10 Blues, there would have not been enough pits to take out the Boss. Unless the pits respawned, which I had no clue about. Trying to tackle a dungeon the first time always led to more questions than answers.

The three Blues went down quickly, and I didn't take much damage from them. The fire itself took out much of their hit points, and the extra damage from the combined fires of the three mobs standing on top of each other did the rest. All that was left was to light the last fire and beat down the boss.

However, this was going to be easier said than done. The Boss' last special skill was an AoE debuff that specifically targeted our Attack. Our resistances were no help, and we were all affected by the spell. The debuff took off 50 from our Attack. While not a huge amount, the Boss' regeneration now had a chance of negating any damage we did.

Once Wayne had all of his aggro gaining Skills refreshed, I lit the last of the fire pits and watched the Boss drop from 20 percent to 3.

Three measly percent. That was all that separated us from completing this quest. But with our Attack lowered, we were making barely any headway. I could see the Boss wasn't regenerating past his current level, but he was still dealing out plenty of damage.

Our main concern now was mana—specifically Jason's mana—as he had to continuously heal Wayne. I thought about using the Force Multiplier, but what if it didn't add enough to take down the mob in five minutes? That would be a waste for sure.

After five more minutes, the Boss went from 3 percent to 2.

"His hit points moved!" Wayne yelled out.

"Mana, Allister?"

"I've got 55 percent. At this rate, it will be close, but I think we can make it!"

"Then let's keep lighting him up!"

If Jason didn't have those wonderful Shoulders, we probably would have run out of mana. The reduction in mana cost was saving our hides in this one.

In the end, it didn't take some fancy strategy or some grand surprise attack to bring the Boss to zero. All we had to do was keep beating on his ass mercilessly like any good MMORPG.

Another 10 minutes into it, and it looked like the Boss was about done. I took that moment to activate my ring. With my new Strength and Dexterity, I was able to land successive Backstabs on the Boss with insane damage. Before he could turn and acquire aggro on me from the damage, the Boss fell to the ground.

"Hell yeah!" Dan screamed, pumping his fist in the air and then turning to give Jason a high-five. I patted Wayne on the back as I passed him, heading toward the Boss and our loot.

"Great job tanking, Wayne. I'd have been minced meat a number of times if you hadn't grabbed aggro."

"Hell, man, we wouldn't even be here if you hadn't figured this stuff out. Get our loot, Chance Master, and we can slap each other on the back later."

I approached the boss and looted the corpse. He had two very solid items. One was going to Wayne immediately, and the other would be up for consideration.

Item:	Commonality	Weight:	Armor:	Bonus:
Troll Hide Leggings: Large Races Only	Rare: Binds on Acquisition	7.0	55	+15 Strength +15 Constitution Effect: 50 Percent increase in regeneration of Hit Points.

"Nice, Naugha!" Allister said, while giving Wayne a fist-bump. Dan was also nodding his head. This was the first time we had seen an item that was specific to the size of a race. The large races were Barbarians, Trolls, and Ogres. Since this was for large races only, there was no question who would get them.

"Awesome. Thanks, guys," Wayne said as he approached the corpse. As soon as he looted the leggings, his plate armor vanished and was replaced by the new armor. It looked like leather, only scaly and a very dark grey that matched the skin of the Troll Boss.

"Kinda sucks that we just spent all of that cash on the Fine Plate

Armor Greaves, though. We won't get half back from a merchant for what we paid for them. And Jenny has her set of armor already."

"I don't know about you guys, but I was thinking about selling Wayne's leggings to Lug. Those guys don't know it, but their information was key in us getting through the entrance. I am sure we can get most of our money back, since Lug doesn't have our discount with the Dwarves. And we will make friends with those guys by helping them out. Never know when you are going to need more players."

Everyone agreed, and I made a mental note to contact Tyke as soon we left the dungeon.

With that piece of business finished, I showed everyone the second item.

Item:	Commonality	Weight:	Armor:	Bonus:
Amulet of Troll Resistances	Rare (Magic) Binds on Acquisition	1.0	20	+15 to all Resistances

"Hot damn! That is usable by anyone?"

"Yeah, Dan. It doesn't have any restrictions, other than it binds on acquisition. We could all use it, so I say we roll."

"I'm out, guys. I already got the leggings."

"I'm ok with it if you want to roll, Wayne," I said. Dan and Jason nodded their heads in agreement.

"Thanks, but I got loot, so I'm not going to hog. You guys roll."

As before, we rolled random numbers between 1 and 100.

If we could do backflips in the game—and with the mechanics in Resurgence we probably could—I would have thought Dan would do a whole floor routine with the amount he was jumping around after winning the roll.

Jason came a close second, and I was a distant, distant third.

I gave the room another good search before we headed back toward the cave entrance and called this quest a victory. All we needed to do was tell Captain Treeswain he could now use his bridge.

We decided to practice our swimming some more and crossed north of the camp and the bridge. The Skill went up slowly while we made our way across the river, and I saw that our movement speed was reduced to almost nothing while we were in the water. It took us a good while to cross the river, but I had finally got to try out my experiment with swimming without the horse. We definitely wanted to try and avoid running away from any mobs through water, especially if they had ranged attacks like bows or spells. We would have been sitting ducks.

Captain Treeswain was full of thanks when we presented ourselves to complete the quest. He went on for quite some time about how the use of the bridge would in turn lead to a turning of the battle between the Kingdom and the Children of Loust. None of us really cared. We just wanted our reward and hoped for another title.

The title was not to be had, however. Completion of this quest did give us a nice chunk of experience, with Dan and Jason almost hitting Level 23 after taking out the mobs and the Boss in the Troll quest. We also received 100 Gold each. I was sure that the cash would come in handy at some point. Wayne and I were still behind our friends in experience after having died to the ten Blue mobs in the dungeon, but we were creeping up on leveling as well.

Captain Treeswain told us to talk with Sir Arthur in Yerkich Square to see if there were any further tasks to be tackled by willing adventurers.

We had already planned to head back to the Keep as it was, as we had a few items from our grind through the dungeon to sell. Nothing of note, but it would likely get us 20 or 30 more Gold. Since we were heading to the city, I sent a message ahead to Tyke, and told him to meet us next to the quest giver.

"So you guys did it?" Tyke asked as we approached their group in the square.

"Woah! What are those pants Naugha?" Lug asked before I could answer Tyke.

"Check 'em out, Lug," Wayne said as he showed his new armor to the Ogre.

As we were traveling back to the Keep, I had asked Wayne what the price of Fine Plate Pants went for at the merchants. According to Wayne, they were selling them for 70 Gold. We had paid 50 Gold to the Dwarves. The discount for being friends with the Dwarves had paid off.

If we sold the armor to the merchants, we would have received 40 Gold. Since I knew what the going rate was, I planned to sell the greaves to Lug for exactly what we paid for them.

"Hey, Lug. If you have 50 Gold on ya, we can sell you Naugha's old armor. The merchants sell it for 70 Gold, so it will be a steal for ya."

"Damn. I've only got 30 Gold on me. But let me go check something really quick."

Lug lumbered off. After five minutes, he came running back with a noticeable difference: he was no longer wearing pants. That isn't to say he was naked from the waist down, but he was wearing only the starter "britches" that had 0 armor rating.

"My old armor sold for 25 Gold, so here is the 50 Gold for the upgrade, Alex."

I saw 50 Gold pop up in my inventory window that allowed me to execute trades with other players. Wayne had given me his Fine Plate earlier, and with the money in front of me, I completed the trade.

As soon as he had the new Armor, Lug equipped his new gear. He had a big ol' toothy Ogre grin on his face as he looked at his new leggings.

"These are awesome, bro! Thanks for the hook-up."

"It's not that we don't appreciate it, but why the kindness, Alex?"

"Well, Tyke, you may not realize it, but you gave us the clue we needed to get through the entrance."

"Seriously? How did you do it?!?"

Tyke, Lug, and the two Dark Elf casters leaned in as I explained to them how we used what they said. Giving this information to Tyke felt like the right thing to do since they inadvertently spawned the idea in my head. And again, I was all about making friends in the game.

"What about the final boss?" one of the casters asked.

"I'm going to let you guys give that one a try. Just remember, like with the entrance, controlling the mobs is key. If you guys have serious problems with the Boss after a couple of tries, give me a holler. I'll see what I can do. Hell, we died at the entrance and the Boss fight as well. But figuring it out was a lot of fun."

"Man, you guys are alright! You ever need help with a fight, you give us a call!" Lug exclaimed.

"With the way this game is going, I wouldn't be surprised if that doesn't come sooner than you think."

FBI Forensics Center (Basement)

Special Agents Annabelle Bolden and Nicodemus Colvin sat in the office of Forensic Accounting specialist Ryan Grimes. The office could be the centerpiece specimen of a hoarding documentary. Everywhere that Special Agents Bolden and Colvin looked, there were piles of papers stacked almost to the ceiling. At first, it looked like the Agents would be forced to stand throughout their meeting, as neither could see so much as a chair in the room. Grimes came from behind his desk and, in what looked like a very practiced set of motions, uncovered two chairs that looked rarely used for sitting.

Grimes certainly did not embody the look of your classic FBI Agent. Where Bolden and Colvin went for function with a hint of class, Grimes went with comfort. And only comfort. He wore blue jeans and a faded t-shirt with a death metal band on the front that looked like it said Deceased. His shoes were Vans, and he did nothing to hide his tattoos. Not that he could have, as he had a number of tattoos on his arms, hands and fingers, and a large tattoo over the left side of his neck.

"I'd say forgive the mess, but I don't really care. I've got too much data and not enough space to place it all. It may look like chaos to you, but there is a very defined filing system throughout. So please, don't touch anything and mess it up."

"It's your office, Agent Grimes. My name is Special Agent Annabelle Bolden and this is Special Agent Nicodemus Colvin. We are here assisting with an investigation from Director Grissten," Bolden said, handing over a note written out to Grimes by the Director.

Grimes took the note and set it to the side. He did not so much as look at the envelope twice, let alone open it. "How can I be of service?"

"Did you want to look at the letter?" Colvin asked.

"You would have to be mighty ballsy to claim you were here from the Director herself if you actually weren't. And in that case, I would probably help you for being so crazy. Otherwise, that letter is simply going to ask for me to do whatever you need. Again, because of that request, I'm going to help you. So like I said, how can I be of service?"

Bolden attempted to place her briefcase next to her chair, but she had to switch it to the other side due to a huge stack of papers in the way. "Have you ever thought of going digital with this? I would think it would make it easier to find things."

"There is truth in the hard copy that can't be changed or altered. I'm not a trusting man when it comes to all the digital necessity we have in our life. You do things your way, and I do them mine. And now this is the third time I am asking. What do you want?"

Colvin could see Annabelle was about to lose her top and stepped in. "Sorry about that, Agent Grimes. It's obvious your system works, as your reputation and track record indicates."

Grimes nodded his head at Colvin to continue.

"Have you heard of the company, AltCon?"

"Screw those guys!"

Bolden and Colvin looked over at each other for a moment. Grimes had a visceral reaction when they asked about AltCon, and they were both hoping this wasn't going to put a stop to their using his expertise in their investigation. "Obviously you know them. Did you work for them at some point?"

"No, but I wanted to. Kind of. It's complicated."

"You should probably explain before we go into any more details."

Grimes took a deep breath and said, "Look. I can tell that the two of you aren't going to understand how something like this would make me upset. But understand that, for me, this was the opportunity of a lifetime, and AltCon passed me up on it. So, yeah, I'm pissed."

"Ok. What was the opportunity?"

"The douches didn't sign me on to be a part of their beta for their new MMORPG, Resurgence! This thing is the next level of awesomeness, and they never even bothered to call me back after I put in my application."

What the Agents didn't know, of course, was that the very fact that Grimes was a part of the FBI was why he was not considered for the beta.

"I see," said Agent Bolden. "Would you have any problem running some things to ground for us? We need an unbiased assessment here."

"Yeah. I may be pissed, but it won't interfere with my job. What are you looking to uncover?"

"Abnormalities. I've heard that is how you unravel the mysteries here. You look for things that don't fit."

"That's the truth. We have a totally different way of looking at evidence. You guys look for fibers, DNA, blood samples, and the like. Something that ties a person directly to a crime. I look for breadcrumbs that can get you to those crimes.

"I remember one case in particular that will explain what I mean. There was a person that was suspected of nefarious activities while taking business trips for his company. The problem was, he was constantly taking trips for the company, and the Bureau didn't have the resources to monitor this guy every time he traveled. So they called me in."

"And you found something with credit cards or something?" Colvin asked.

Grimes gave Colvin a look that said what he thought of the question.

"Seriously? Credit cards? That's something any of you guys could figure out. If the guy was making mistakes like that, they wouldn't have needed to contact me.

"This guy was careful. Like, really careful. But in the end, it was his own personal accounting that did him in. And do you know what I found? The abnormality?"

"I'm not even going to try and guess and get my hand slapped again," Colvin said with a smile.

Grimes smiled back and replied, "Good call. It was tips. Gratuity.

"Every trip, this guy would get per diem for meals. But part of that per diem required for him to provide receipts for meals purchased. And he was meticulous about adding the amount he tipped. Now, he never went over his per diem, but I noticed that there were regularly times he tipped 30-40 percent. The rest of the time it was your standard 15-20. The agents that went out to interview the wait staff at these restaurants had the same look of incredulousness that you have right now."

Bolden blushed a bit at Grimes' words, but she just didn't see how tips would make a difference.

"It's fine, Agent Bolden. I'm used to that look. It lasts right up until the first time someone lands a big victory because of my work.

"Anyhow, when the Agents interviewed the various wait staff, they all remembered our guy. Because he tipped big. And he always paid with a hundred-dollar bill.

"That got the team to thinking that he was using money from a payoff he was getting at these meals. When I reviewed the records, I saw that they happened every 5-6 weeks. So when the time came around, Agents followed the man on his trip and put 24-7 monitoring on him. Sure enough, they caught him in the act of selling company secrets to the Chinese government. He received a fat envelope at the exchange, and in that envelope were all hundred-dollar bills."

"All because of an abnormality in accounting."

"Exactly, Agent Colvin. Exactly."

Bolden thought for a bit about how to address her request to Grimes. She came to him because she had heard that his methods led to results. And based on his story, she saw how he could benefit their investigation.

"Agent Grimes, you are aware that AltCon is not just a large company. It's a multinational behemoth. Due to our lack of a warrant at this time, the only avenues we have for investigating are through public channels. And on top of that, I can't really go into what exactly the investigation is looking at. I imagine that small tidbit is included in the Director's letter."

"Ok. That will limit a lot of what I can do. I will only be able to look at things in the US, obviously. That is, unless other countries have their records open to the public, which some do."

Bolden nodded her head at Grimes and continued. "Focus on the US piece for now. I would suggest, for reasons I can't really get into, that you start from the center and move outward. Their Headquarters first, then circle out."

"Any additional data you can give me? Something to narrow it down?"

"I wish that we could, but in reality, we are on our own fact-finding mission as well," Colvin admitted. "Our hope is that with your experience, you will see something that is glaringly obvious to you but that we would have just looked right past."

"Ooh, Agent Bolden, keep this one around. He definitely does the sweet talk better than you."

If it weren't for the honest smile on Grimes' face, Colvin may have been offended.

"I'll look into it immediately. I will try to have something for you in a couple of weeks. As you can see, I like hardcopy when I can get it, and that sometimes takes a while to be processed and delivered."

"We will be in your debt, Agent Grimes."

"Just call me Ry. And if AltCon has something coming to them, I've got no problem with helping. Teach them not to put me in their beta!"

CHAPTER 8

October 24th, 2043

After seeing off Tyke and his group, we decided to call it a night. None of us wanted to mess with Sir Arthur and trigger another quest right away, especially since we agreed that our next quest would be the first in Lady Tessa's chain.

I was studying the map, as we knew it, when the rest of the team began logging on. During our travels to the soldier camp, we had noted a number of smaller roads that branched off to the north and south of the main road. These could be clearly seen on my map, and I am sure Dan's was even more detailed. I planned on taking one of these northern routes toward our next quest.

Once everyone was logged on, I asked Dan to look at what had been uncovered on his map with all of our travels, and if anything jumped out to him that could assist us in getting to our next location. Since Dan's innate combo of Ranger and Wood Elf gave him the ability to uncover more of his map as he traveled, I was hoping for any clues that could help.

"Not from our travels, no. But that really detailed map in the Captain's office did have some interesting markers up in the northern reaches. It looks to be mostly forest before it breaks off into tundra.

His map was focused more on what lay along the river, but I could tell there were mountains the further north you went."

"Did the river snake toward our quest area?"

"Nope. The river stayed mostly north/south from the camp. It did meander a bit, this way and that, but in general it kept to a straight north/south."

"So then we are still looking at taking one of these roads that shoots off from the main King's Road."

"Looks like it, yeah."

"Allister, Wayne, any thoughts?"

"We don't have enough info at this point, so I think we just need to hop on our horses and start making our way to one of these roads and give it a shot."

"Yeah, Alex. I agree with Allister on this one."

We restocked supplies. Dan was able to summon Broham, so he needed to make sure he had plenty of treats for however long we would be out. Dan also took an insanely long amount of time telling Broham how sorry he was for getting him killed. Seeing Dan speak at length to a wolf should have been comical, but it looked normal for Dan.

Once we were outside the Keep's walls, we summoned our horses and began the trek back along the King's Road and toward the soldier's camp. It wasn't but 30 minutes before we came across the first road that branched off to the north.

We debated whether I should dismount and stealth my way along the route or let Dan ride along the road to check the lay of the land. With Dan's horse, he could escape quickly if he needed to, and Broham would have no problem keeping up. The Dire Wolf was as fast as the horse and would likely be faster once it reached maturity.

Although, being Dan's pet, it was hard to think of anything associated with him having the word "mature" attached to it.

Dan took off along the road and returned after only 15 minutes. The road continued for a short way and then ended at a lake. Dan saw numerous lower level mobs but nothing that indicated another road that branched off from the one he traveled.

Twice more we sent Dan along a road only to have him return and report something similar. The only things of note along the third road were several Blue and White mobs Dan could see on his map.

The fourth road is when we finally hit pay dirt for our route. Dan took off along the road as he had before, but after thirty minutes he had not returned. I started to get worried, not that Dan had been attacked, but that he may have just stopped somewhere to do a crossword or something.

"Bingo, boys! Ride on up. We are going to need Alex on this one I think."

We looked at each other for a second and then spurred our horses onto the road and headed toward Dan's direction. The road was nowhere near as well maintained as the King's Road, and we had to ride single file due to the narrow nature of the path. The realism of the game was evident here as well, as Wayne repeatedly had to duck to avoid low hanging branches that were creeping out over the road. We only knew this because Wayne took a branch to the noggin not five minutes after we started the ride.

"Think you could have told me about the branches, Dan?" Wayne yelled after he got thwacked in the face.

"What branches? They never bothered me."

"That's because you are a midget!"

"Well, one of us is in stature, and one of us is in mind. I believe I will keep my status, good sir!"

Wayne looked over at Jason and said, "Did he just call me a 'mental midget?'"

"Don't ever tell him I said so, but he gets mad points for that one!"

Once we arrived at Dan's location, I saw why Dan wanted my assistance. There was a small outpost of some kind along the side of the road. From my map, I could see there was a small tributary that ran through the area, likely feeding the river we had crossed previously. Upon closer inspection, the outpost could be some type of logging town, if it were only bigger. It also looked to be empty.

"I'll Conceal/Stealth and check it out. Did you see any mobs in the area, Dan?"

"No, sir! But I didn't get much further than this before I stopped. Anything like this could be a trouble spot. I thought better of bringing 20 mobs to you guys."

"When did he start using his brain? This is getting scary," I heard Jason whisper behind me, answered by Wayne's giggles.

I quickly dismounted and unsummoned my horse and made my way into the forest that bordered the small road we were on. Once in the woods, I brought my Blacksuit up and ran toward the outpost.

In Resurgence, the foliage could affect the movement speed of players. We didn't encounter it much in the areas around Port Town or around the Keep. Those areas were heavily traveled by players and did not have a chance to become "wild." But out here, off a secluded road, I noted my movement was cut down to 75 percent of normal. Not a problem with my Blacksuit, but it would make running away from any mobs more difficult, especially since I doubted their movement speeds would be penalized in kind.

Once I entered the outpost, I realized my earlier assumptions were correct, and I saw what looked to me like a small saw mill. The small waterway was moving swiftly through the mill, and the area seemed to be only mildly under kempt. It looked to be a fully functional mill, just with no people.

I traveled further into the outpost. A number of the buildings had windows, and I decided to look inside one as I passed by. Turns out the outpost wasn't empty at all. There were a number of residents within the first building I investigated, and they all looked to be cowering in fear. I checked out the other two buildings with windows and saw a similar scene. These people were afraid of something.

I ran along the road, back to my companions, and told them what I had uncovered. After discussing it for several moments, we decided to ride into the outpost at a slow gait so as not to freak out the residents. I smelled a quest, after all.

The road widened gradually as we approached the outpost. We could have gone through it and continued on our way, but there didn't seem to be any way around it with horses. One would need to take to the forest. With the road widening, we spread out and arrived at the open entrance to the outpost four abreast.

A small fence identified the borders of the outpost. We stopped just inside that fence line. Now in full sight of anyone that may be looking, we held our hands out, away from our weapons. “Is there anywhere here that a traveler can restock on supplies?”

We were met without answer. I waited a few more seconds before calling out again, “We have no ill will toward the residents here. We are only looking to restock our supplies and continue our journey northward.”

Several seconds later, a man rounded the corner of one of the buildings and walked toward us. He stopped a good distance away from our group and asked, “What business could you have up there? Better to head back the way you came. There is nothing worth traveling up there for.”

“It’s a personal matter, sir. We would like to ensure we have enough supplies for our journey and the appropriate supplies for the environment.”

The man, who had the single name of Geller, continued to look at us for another several seconds before responding. “It may be we can help you, although we may need your help as well.”

The residents came out of the buildings, and they were all men. I learned that this outpost was part of a larger network of mills along the offshoots that fed the Danning River. The men at the outpost worked in rotations, spending two weeks at a mill before going back to their village.

The trouble at Trasdor Mill, which I learned was the name of our current location, began three days prior. The current team arrived for their two-week rotation and were set upon by creatures on the second night of their stay. None of them could say what attacked, but the unknown assailant, or assailants, had killed one of the men savagely. According to Geller, the dead man’s chest had been ripped apart, with wicked-looking claw marks indicating some kind of savage beast.

“And there was howling!” Another of the mill men added.

"Yes, there was howling as well. Scared us all something fierce. We aren't the type to scare easy, either."

These were men that worked hard, and their physiques showed it. I wouldn't want to go one-on-one with any of them in a fist fight.

"So here's the deal. You boys are traveling to the Northern Reaches, but you will freeze before you get anywhere near whatever your goal is. You need traveling cloaks for sure.

"You help us with this problem, and we will make sure you have the cloaks. And I will throw in a Standard Map of the North as well."

All of the mill men were staring at us with anxious looks. Wayne would have helped them regardless, because that is how he liked to play the game. I was torn between riding back to the Keep to get what we needed gear-wise and accepting the quest. Dan and Jason looked indifferent.

"What are you waiting for, Alex? Say the words."

"Honestly, I'm wondering if we shouldn't just go back to Kich's Keep and get the gear. Who knows how long this could take? And we still aren't sure we are even on the right road to get us where we want to go. We can't take every quest, Wayne."

"That map could help us quite a bit though, Alex." When Jason was slogging through his AltCon Cartography quest, he did the absolute bare minimum to complete his tasks. Jason had no desire to be a map maker. He had learned, though, that Maps came in five different qualities: Incomprehensible, Poor, Standard, Excellent, and Perfect. A map could save us a tremendous amount of time, and so I had to agree with Wayne. The map did make this worth it.

"Fine. We will help with your problem."

As had happened numerous times before, our bodies were surrounded with the glow of a quest. Our habit now was to always review the quest to see what restrictions it may have and if there was a timer. We would not soon forget thinking we were ready to tackle a quest, only to find out it required eight players and not four.

"Well that's something new. We may get through this faster than we thought," Dan said to the group.

I looked at my quest as well and saw what Dan meant. According to the quest log, this particular task was labeled differently than any other we had encountered. Previously, we were always of a lower level than the mobs we were fighting, so the mark of “Simple” had never been attached to any of our jobs.

“Well that just made the quest awesome. It’s not like we are doing this for experience, anyhow. If we can finish it quickly, it will totally be worth the time.”

“I’ve got a marker on my map, Alex. Let’s head out there and take down whatever beasts did this.”

“Lead the way, Dan,” I said and then looked over at spokesman Geller, “We’ll be back soon. Have everything ready when we return.”

“Be careful. Whatever ripped apart our man’s chest was no easy prey.”

I left the building we were all sitting in and headed toward the guys. “Looks like we’re on foot from here. That marker is right in the middle of the forest.”

“I’ll take point, Alex. When we get closer to the mark, you can do your Invisy thing.”

Without a word needed, our group fell into their natural roles and headed out to the area on our maps.

“Does it seem weird to you guys that we just happened to run into a quest giver that would get us a map and gear we need?”

“Usually I would be the first to agree with you, Allitosis. Our luck—that is to say Alex’s luck—usually flies in the face of reason, but this one makes sense when you think about it.

“If we had ventured off to the north by cutting through the forest, a route that would have been quicker as the bird flies, we would have never received the quest. Instead, we stayed to the main road and then took a smaller but well defined road to head North. I would venture it’s set up that way for this very reason. And dollars to donuts says the cloak we get does nothing but protect from cold. It will have no other stats,” Dan said, finishing with, “And we are having donuts at my party. Just saying the word is making me salivate.”

“Disgusting image, Dan. Thank you.”

“Welcome, Allitosis.”

The rest of the conversation between our group consisted of Dan and Jason arguing on whether you had to say “as the crow flies” or if

Dan's more generic "bird" worked equally as well. Jason won when he rightly identified that not all birds fly, and therefore a more specific bird had to be included. Dan started using "sparrow" just to rile our favorite cleric.

It turned out that Rabid Wolves had attacked the outpost, and they were all Green to my group. Based on our level, I gathered this put them at Level 20. With our Levels, gear, and Skills, we killed all of the Wolves. I wish there was something greater to say, but this was a "simple" quest, after all. The decimation of the Rabid pack took a matter of an hour, and with travel time, we were done and back at the outpost in just over two hours.

"We have killed the Rabid Wolves."

"Well done! I didn't think you would be able to after what they did to our friend. As agreed, here are your cloaks and your Map to the North."

I opened the map, and it was just as I suspected. The major roads and some of the surrounding areas were now laid out in our personal maps, but for the most part, the area to the North was still hidden behind the grey fog. At least we could now see the roads that would take us toward our quest area.

Dan was right about the cloaks as well. Their only buff was "Protection from Environment: Cold."

It never hurts to try and get as much information out of an NPC as possible, so I asked spokesman Geller if he had seen any other travelers like us in these parts.

"No. There haven't been any travelers like yourselves in this area for years."

"Well I imagine you will be seeing many more in the coming weeks who will have need of your cloaks. One more question, have you seen any travelers that are not like us?" The fact that he said "travelers like yourselves" made me think there was more to it.

Turns out I was right. "Not since that Lancaster boy came through here all them years back. He never did return back this way, though. Hope he didn't die in the ice."

"Was that Tristan Lancaster?"

"Aye, it was. He came through here on some errand north of here. Stopped to talk with the men that were working here at the time. The Lancaster family is well known in these parts, although we haven't seen much of them these last few years. Never know where their searches will take them, so they could be anywhere."

Activating Lady Tessa's quest likely activated this dialogue as well. Since I knew Jenny and her group couldn't get Tessa's quest, I would have to tell them to come through here to get a map and the cold weather gear and—since they already knew about Lady Tessa's quest—have them use the same words to see what Geller would say. Not that it mattered in the end, but it would sate my curiosity.

I tried to get more information out of Geller, but that was the extent of his information. Keeping to my routine of asking NPCs about unbeatable mobs, I queried Geller on that as well. According to Geller, the only unbeatable mobs he knew of were the ones we just tackled. Another dead end there for the Wanderer's task.

With nothing more for us to do at the outpost, we saddled back up on our mounts and headed north toward the area that held Lady Tessa's first quest.

The road we traveled took us over a small bridge that spanned the Danning River's inlet. As we approached the bridge, I wondered if we would encounter a Troll demanding a toll for our passage. The bridge was just a bridge, however, and we traversed it without incident.

The overhanging branches continued to be a problem for Wayne's height. He was constantly ducking as we made our way along the trail. Other than Wayne's grumbling, we had no further problems until we cleared the forest and entered the tundra of the north.

The trees grew sparser as we traveled until there was only a smattering of saplings here and there. The open landscape gave us our first views of the extended north land, and it was a hostile environment, to be certain. The ground was craggy, with jutting shale fragments in one area, only to be replaced with boulders and smaller rocks in another.

We were starting to see pockets of ice and snow this far north, although the southern regions of the tundra where we were had mostly dry ground. The quest marker on our maps had us continuing north, though.

Due to the openness of the environment, we could see for quite a distance. The area that housed our quest looked to be largely icy in its makeup. And of course, plenty of mobs stood between us and our desired location.

Dan began to count off several Blue mobs that he could see from his vantage point at the head of our small horse train. As we had seen previously, these were predominantly wildlife in nature, though this far north we were seeing a variety that we had not encountered before. Dan called out a pack of Snow Leopards and Snow Lynxes. They appeared to be traveling in groups of three to four. Dan believed he could see more mobs farther along our desired route, but he couldn't get an accurate gauge on their levels.

Dan scoped out the area, looking for the best way to pull, while we found a spot that looked like a safe area to fight. Dan planned to pull the mobs we could see for now, and then we would move up and continue our journey. Move and fight. Move and fight.

It took a lot longer before Dan felt comfortable pulling the Snow mobs, as their patterns for moving were different than that of the forest mobs we had encountered before. For starters, they moved as a pack, very rarely separating from each other. Gary could probably pull one or two with his Play Dead Skill. Dan didn't think he could avoid pulling three at the same time, and I really didn't like that we would step into this fight with no knowledge of the mobs. Or that our bind point was back in the city. But as any gamer will tell you, it's hard to pass up an opportunity to get experience and play new content. There was never any doubt we were going to try these mobs.

"Well, that didn't work. Three Snow Leopards incoming."

"Keep trying whatever you can think of. In the meantime, kite one and we will deal with the other two."

Wayne grabbed aggro on two of the Snow Leopards while Dan and Broham ran the third around the small area. Wayne and Jason were talking about the new regeneration that came with the Troll leggings and how it would affect Jason's healing.

"With these lower level mobs, I think we will save a good bit of mana. They aren't hitting all that hard, so I'm guessing they are only one level above us. They definitely hit fast, though."

"They would tear us up in a pack. That's why they travel in groups. Just the two on you, no problem. But if there were four, we would probably be looking at our bind points," Jason commented.

I waited the usual amount of time and began adding my damage to the fight. The Snow Leopards were going down fast. Or maybe it just seemed that way after the marathon exchanges we had with the Trolls and their insane regeneration.

After a short while, the Snow Leopards were dead, including the one Dan was kiting. I was happy, to say the least, that we could take the mobs in this region and continue on our way. I hoped that it was a good indication of our potential to handle the boss from Lady Tessa's quest as well.

The rest of the day followed this same routine. We fought our way forward toward the area that housed our quest. Over the course of several hours, we fought more Leopards and Lynxes as well as a small pack of Wolverines.

Those little buggers tore through us like mad. They also had a huge resistance to Dan's Snare and would not be kited. Jason went through 3/4 of his mana just trying to keep Wayne alive from the five mobs that swarmed him. Dan and Broham tackled the sixth without kiting. The only person who didn't take any damage was yours truly, as I kept myself low on the aggro table. Even Jason took quite a beating as he was healing Wayne and Dan, taking aggro away on a couple of occasions.

It took us the entire day to grind through the area and arrive at the beginning of the quest. In front of us stood a crevice running through the sheer ice wall that covered the northern area from east to west. Without our quest indicator, it would have been very difficult to find this spot, let alone the crack in the wall.

We stayed just outside of the crevice for a good 15 minutes and did not see any mobs that wandered near our spot. I figured this was as good a place as any to log off for the night.

Another bright spot, we had achieved Level 23 while we were grinding through the mobs on the way to the quest area and we made sure to allocate our 5 points to our Stats before we called it a night. The next day would find us in yet another dungeon and another new experience in Resurgence.

October 25th, 2043

No one was going to make the same mistake as last time. Before any of my friends would get within 30 meters of the crevice, I was being pushed forward and told to scout out the area. Like the good Rogue that I am, I engaged my Conceal/Stealth and made my way into the crack in the ice. As was my routine, I quickly donned my Blacksuit as well and wound my way through the ice toward the dungeon. Based on my experiences so far in Resurgence, I was fairly certain I would start seeing some sort of tunnels soon.

And as I turned the next corner, I was reminded that I knew very little about this game.

Before me was a massive courtyard. The courtyard was around 100 meters long and 50 meters wide. It was devoid of life but had the feel of the walking gardens one might find in the tourist spots of Paris. Where one might find a garden of some sort, I was looking at beautiful and intricate ice sculptures. They were set up along a path, each with its own viewing area. From where I was, I could see the first sculpture was in the image of the very Snow Lynxes we had killed the day before.

The sun, which shone freely into the courtyard, highlighted the detail and intricacies of the Lynx. If I hadn't known it was ice, I would have thought it was ready to attack the first person to come by.

And yes, since this was Resurgence, I figured there was a pretty good chance that would happen, ice or not.

I only took a moment to admire the ice Lynx, however, because in front of me was a sight to behold. A massive wall of ice, with a building carved directly into the facade, stood on the far side of the courtyard.

Gigantic columns, windows, doors, words in an unknown language, and more sculptures like the ones in the courtyard were carved directly from the ice. I would have gauged the wall, and therefore the building, to be around four stories tall.

I had seen pictures of something similar in the real world: a city, Petra, carved directly out of the walls of a canyon in Jordan. Sand and wind, part of Mother Nature's unstoppable tools of erosion, had worn down those mysterious buildings, but the courtyard and the building were set in such a way that little to no wind was present, resulting in very little erosion.

Despite this, the age of the structure was evident. This was an old, old established building. Architecture wasn't something I majored in at school, but I didn't need any formal education to tell you what I saw in front of me was ancient. It was the same as when I entered Notre Dame in Paris years before. The building itself let me know that it had been there for a long time. But not by speaking. Jesus, I sound weird.

I relayed to the team that it would take me a few extra minutes to scout, but I kept the layout a surprise. I wanted them to have that same initial reaction that I did. I ran around the perimeter of the courtyard and through the middle but did not see any mobs. I also inspected the area next to the front of the ice building but again found nothing of interest. Finally, I ventured through the three-meter tall doorway that led deeper into the ice. I didn't venture far, maybe twenty meters. Again, there was nothing to discover, but the hallway continued on for quite a distance.

"Alright, guys. Move on up through the crack in the ice. I'll meet you at a good stopping point. So far I haven't seen any signs of mobs or the body of Tristan Lancaster."

After receiving acknowledgement from the guys, I went back to the ice tunnel near the entrance of the courtyard. We still didn't know if entering that courtyard would set off a trap, so I met the guys at the last turn before the courtyard began. And yeah, I wanted to see the looks on their faces.

"Go slowly around this corner. There is the potential for a trap to go off not too far ahead. I want us to take this slowly."

As soon as all three made the turn, they had the same open-mouthed expression that I did. It was like looking at a kid who was seeing snow for the first time as it comes down in flurries—all wide-eyed and trying to see it all at the same time. Just like mine did, all of their eyes eventually landed on the building carved into the ice, and they were mesmerized by its beauty.

"I keep waiting for the statues to start moving," Dan said as he looked on.

"I know. I kept waiting for them to move forward and attack while I scouted the place."

"Attack? Nah, man. I'm waiting for them to start twirling and jumping like when I saw Disney on Ice! That show was awesome."

"Dude! I totally did that when I was a kid, too! Good memories, man. How old were you?" Wayne said as he put his fist out for a bump from Dan.

Dan held his hand out, meeting Wayne's knuckles with his own and said, "Tuesday."

"Of course you did."

"Don't knock it, bubba. If you thought it was awesome as a kid, it's even better as an adult. You know. Leotards."

"And Dan just ruined my childhood. Again. Thanks for that."

"Any time, Alligastor," Dan said as he performed a bow in Jason's direction. "Now let's go see what this place has in store for us."

We crossed the threshold as a group. It would have looked humorous to anyone seeing us from the outside. It was like Dorothy walking down the yellow-brick road with the four of us in a line and walking in step. I started giggling as I pictured Dan as the Scarecrow and Jason as the Tin-Man.

And then I stopped. That would have made Wayne the Lion and left me as the chick in ruby red heels. I'm pretty sure I look horrible in heels. At least, that's what I was told the one Halloween I went as a woman. A story for another time.

After about ten meters into the courtyard, the first mobs made themselves known. It wasn't the ice sculptures, as we had first thought, but apparitions that rose from the ground and started making their way toward us. We stopped in our tracks as soon as we saw the mobs. Dan, Jason, and I took a few steps back, letting Wayne grab aggro on the two mobs per our usual style of playing.

The mobs, Ghostly Wraiths, were Blue to us, meaning decent experience. This was the first time we had seen any mobs that appeared in a ghost-like form, so we had no idea what types of attacks would work best on them. Trial and error was in store.

Wayne started by throwing an attack and Taunt at one mob while hitting the second with his Bash and Kick. No one worried about Wayne's ability to manage aggro at this point.

"Not doing much damage here, Alex," Wayne said.

Dan and I joined in the fight against Wayne's primary mob, and I realized what he meant after only a few swings of my daggers. We were doing a significantly lower amount of damage than what was normal for us.

"How hard are they hitting?"

"It's not much, although they do have a wicked little proc. My Vitality is going down way faster than it normally would. I almost don't bother monitoring these days, not with my Stats as high as they are."

"How bad is it?"

"Normally I would be down one or maybe two percent on Vitality at this point. After their procs, I am down ten percent."

I didn't have to remind anyone in the group just how bad it would be if Wayne lost his Vitality. All of his Stats would drop and he would do a whole lot less damage in the fight. That could really screw with our aggro management.

We kept going at the two mobs, and Wayne kept shouting out his Vitality percentage. We would probably win the fight between the two mobs, but this was going to take a long time if we had to rest after every two mobs for Wayne to regain what he had lost. Jason's heals did nothing for replacing Wayne's Vitality.

The first mob was almost finished, with Wayne's vitality sitting at 65 percent. Once the first mob died, there would be a reduction in the amount of procs hitting Wayne, with only one mob remaining, so I knew we weren't in danger. I had Jason throw a Banish Undead at the mob, but the game told Jason that the spell had no effect on this type of mob. Dan also tried using his direct damage spell, but the damage was reduced the same as with our physical attacks.

My debuff proc that dropped the mob's armor 40 percent was working fine, but Wayne's War Hammer proc was doing reduced damage just like Dan's spell.

"Wayne! What did you just do?" Dan exclaimed.

"Nothing. Why? What just happened?"

"On the second mob, what did you do about two seconds ago?"

"I gotta look. One sec," Wayne said. After a couple of seconds, Wayne said, "I hit it with my Kick and Bash to keep it aggro'ed. Same as I've been doing."

"That's it?"

Wayne was quiet again as I imagined he was looking at something in his battle log. After another short pause, Wayne said "The Bash landed a Stun."

"Boom! We would have seen this earlier if Wayne was using Bash on our target. Allipop, hit our target with your Stun."

Jason looked over at me, but I wasn't concerned about Jason stealing aggro at this point. Wayne had not received much in the way of healing during the fight, and the mob had been constantly Taunted. It wasn't going to switch targets. I hoped.

I nodded at Jason, and he launched his Stun on the Wraith. Immediately I saw what had Dan so excited. When the Stun landed, the Wraith turned almost solid. I can't tell you the mechanics of why it worked, but it did. As soon as it received the Stun, our attacks not only increased but were slightly higher than normal. The first mob lasted only a few more seconds with the change in damage output.

I can't imagine that any group would go through this whole place without realizing what we discovered. Almost all Tanks have the Bash skill, which in turn has a chance to Stun the target. They may not learn it on the first set of mobs, but in time all would learn it. I was just happy that Dan figured it out so quickly and that we wouldn't have to spend as much time waiting on Wayne to regenerate his Vitality.

After the second mob went down—and far quicker than the first, since we knew to use Stun—we discussed the change to our strategy.

Wayne would change his order for Tanking two mobs at a time, swapping Bash with Taunt. Now, the non-targeted mob would get a Kick and a Taunt, while the primary target was attacked and Bashed. This meant that Dan and I would have to wait longer before we could attack. Taunt added a lot of "hate" on the aggro chart, and Bash didn't have the same modifier. We would have to play with this a bit to see just how early Dan and I could get into the mix.

Once Wayne had recovered his Vitality, we returned to our reenactment of the Wizard of Oz and began moving down the center of the courtyard again. After 10 meters, two more Wraiths spawned like before. We quickly dispatched them using the new strategy. Wayne's Vitality only went down 15 percentage points.

I hadn't found anything on either set of mobs when I looted them. No items. No money. Nothing. Given this was a part of Lady Tessa's quest, I was hoping for some good loot throughout the whole encounter. I didn't want to base the possible results on just the first four mobs, but I wasn't optimistic at this point.

We repeated the same process several more times, with almost every ten meters having two mobs spawn. The experience was easy at this point, but we still got no loot from the mobs.

After we finished the last set of mobs in the courtyard, we headed toward the entrance of the ice building. With only several steps to go before we entered the 3-meter-tall entrance, another apparition appeared before us.

This was not a Wraith. The apparition before us was of a man, dressed in flowing robes, and holding a gnarled staff in his hands. The robes were not those of a caster, but of a monk one would find at a shrine. It reminded me of all the Shaolin movies I watched as a youngster. He also didn't have a name and was not showing any aggressive actions toward us. Like good gamers, we figured he would attack at any point and assumed our formation as usual.

However, the apparition never did attack and simply stood in front of the entrance as we came directly upon it.

"Should I take a swing, Alex?"

"Violence is not always the answer, Wayne."

"Really? Funny then, because us Barbarians only learn that answer at school."

"Must be why Barbarians finish school at the age of eight."

"Exactly. Why keep going to school once you have all the answers?" Wayne finished with a grin on his face.

I approached the ghostly form and hailed the entity. As soon as I spoke, the ghost's image shimmered briefly and his name became clear above his head—Apprentice Madwar.

I repeated myself, "Hail, Apprentice Madwar."

Madwar looked out over the courtyard. There was no evidence of our previous activities. Once all the bodies of the Wraiths were looted, the corpse would disappear. However, Madwar seemed to know that the Ghost mobs had previously been in the area.

"It couldn't have been easy for you to reach this far. No one has traversed this courtyard since Sir Lancaster crossed this threshold long ago. I didn't believe it when he arrived, and I thought none would ever dare to try again.

"Sir Lancaster knew of our plight, and he agreed to cleanse this Monastery. Since I am still here, he must have failed."

"I didn't realize the Lancaster boys were knighted. I guess that makes sense with how close they were all supposed to be to the King," Dan said.

"Doesn't make much difference to us either way. Let's find out what he was supposed to be doing, and that should help us find his body," Jason added.

I nodded my head at Jason and asked Madwar what happened at the Monastery.

"Several years ago, we had a visitor to our Monastery that requested our assistance in learning our ways. We were a school for focused concentration. Through our teachings, one could become more in tune with the magic around us and harness their mana to greater degrees. The result of our training was seen in the power of the students' castings and their ability to increase the duration of their mana pools.

"However, ours was a life of solitude. A student first had to show the fortitude of patience before we would bestow any gifts upon them. Many would travel here, if they could brave the rough environment to reach our domain. Few, however, passed the tests to attain the final gift of our school.

"This visitor was such a man. He wanted the gifts without the work. He offered gold, but our people have never had need of gold. He offered the rarest of items, but our students subsist on the most basic of goods. He offered us power, but our school is designed to remove the very desire for power through an understanding of the self. In the end, we denied all of his offers.

"Infuriated, the visitor left. He promised he would return, and behind him would be an army we would not be able to defeat. His plan was to take our knowledge from us. We had very little fear of this man. We were fools.

"When he returned, he revealed his true self. This man was a Great Priest of Loust. With his initial attack, he destroyed half of our Monastery with the very same types of Wraiths you defeated earlier. And in his need to boast, he informed the rest of us, or those that still lived, that Loust would rise again. His Great Priests were already dispatched to remove the secrets of all the schools of learning in Tholtos.

"But the plan backfired. The Great Priest brought with him a Wendigo, a most foul creature that feeds off the very soul of any living beings. The Priest thought to control the demon, but the Wendigo had its own plan. After rampaging through our school, the Wendigo dealt a blow to the Priest, striking him dead in these very halls. Before his death, I witnessed the Priest take control of a Wraith and, in essence, become a Wraith himself.

"I was the last of our number to survive. In a desperate attempt to flee, I ran toward this courtyard. But before I could leave the sanctuary of our Monastery's walls, the Wendigo caught up to me. Having witnessed how the Priest accomplished his feat, I bound myself to a Wraith just as I was taking my last breath. And for all these years, here is where I have remained. Only with the death of the Wendigo, the master of these Wraiths, can I fly free of my self-imposed purgatory."

"Did you hear that, guys? All of the Monasteries. I bet you each of Lady Tessa's brothers were sent to a different one. Oh, this is going to be awesome!" Wayne exclaimed.

I was as excited as Wayne and the others. I also took note how the quest, even though it wasn't meant to go live in the game, still incorporated the larger arc of the King battling the Children of Loust. I hoped this meant that the story arc and Lady Tessa's quest would overlap more as we progressed and that we could take less time traveling between areas.

Having heard the tale from Madwar, I figured I knew what Tristan came to do, but I asked him anyway what it was he was supposed to have accomplished.

"I doubt that you could succeed where Sir Lancaster failed. However, I will make the same bargain with you that I made with him: defeat the Wendigo that has taken residence in this Monastery, and I will show you the location of our ancient tome that explains how to acquire the feats of our school."

"Oh, we going to make you eat Wayne's steel!"

Laughing at Dan, and how he convinced Wayne to mutter that same phrase not more than a month ago, I agreed to the task. Our quest was updated from Restoration of House Lancaster I to read:

Restoration of House Lancaster II: Remove the Wraiths and Wendigo from the Monastery of Calm.

CHAPTER 9

Once the quest was updated, and once we checked that there were not any new variables, we crossed the threshold of the entrance and prepared to make our way into the Monastery. As soon as the party crossed an Invisible line, our maps disappeared.

"Looks like we are officially in a dungeon, guys. Dan, time for you to earn your paycheck."

"I haven't already?"

"Consider this overtime."

"Does that mean I get two rolls on loot?"

"It means I'll make sure Kaitlin comes to our party," Wayne said.

"Consider the crosswords forgotten."

I nodded my head in thanks toward Wayne and started my scouting run. I made my way through the very first hallway until I came to an intersection. It was relatively close to the entrance, so I continued down the same hallway. Soon after, I came to another intersection. The layout seemed to be on a mostly cardinal grid. Of note, I didn't see any mobs during my scouting.

"Well, guys, the place seems to be pretty straight forward. I've only gone a bit ahead, but I'm not seeing any mobs. I'm betting the interior will follow the same mechanics as out in the courtyard. We aren't going to see any mobs until we are close to being on top of them. I'm heading back to you now. We'll start with Wayne in the lead so he can grab aggro."

Once I returned, Wayne led the way. Sure enough, as soon as we approached the first intersection, two Wraiths popped up and aggro'ed on him. He led them farther back toward the entrance, and we proceeded to mop them up.

"They're hitting a little harder, Alex."

"Means they are probably two levels above us since they're still Blue. More experience for us!"

With the two mobs down, and still no loot, the party asked me to scout the east and west corridors. I did as they asked and relayed what I found as I traveled.

"Still not seeing any mobs, but we have a number of rooms. Some of them have doors, and some of them don't. It's a carbon copy on each side. Two rooms to the north of the corridor and one to the south. After that, I hit a ninety-degree corner heading north. I went into one of the rooms, and it looks like this is where the students lived. Each room had two beds and a night stand of sorts between them. Looks like a college dorm room, only less comfortable, and no drug paraphernalia. I suggest we go into the open rooms first and then open the doors one at a time."

None of the rooms had more than two mobs, and we would randomly encounter groups of two Wraiths along the path. The mobs in the hallways continued to be loot snobs and dropped nothing, but the mobs in the rooms were freer with their rewards.

So long as a mob was in one of the rooms, it dropped a spell. The spells were all Level 24 and included multiple classes. Jason was ecstatic when one of the spells that dropped was for a Cleric—an improved Stun no less. Too bad he likely wouldn't get to use it before we finished the dungeon. But any freebies on spells was a boon to our bank account.

We cleared out the rooms and continued to lay waste throughout the dungeon. Our only limiting factor was waiting on Wayne to regenerate his Vitality. All the Wraiths continued to hit with that annoying Vitality draining proc.

Further into the Monastery, we encountered our first problem. We entered a larger room on the east side of the school that resembled a study area with multiple tables and chairs, and four mobs popped at the same time. They didn't pop as a set of four, but two on each side.

We weren't unprepared for this possibility, though. We had discussed a very similar scenario before we ventured further into the dungeon, and we had come up with a plan. Now it was time to see if it would work.

"Implement Operation Sacrifice!" Dan yelled.

"Sacrifice?"

"Yeah, Alex. Because if this doesn't work, I'm probably going to get a major ass beating!"

"Shouldn't it be called 'Operation Thank the Gods for Small Favors,' then?"

"Your words cut deep, Allitang! Now cast Stun already!"

The plan was straight forward: Jason would hit the mobs with a Stun, and then Dan would cast Snare and shoot them with arrows. With the area we had already cleared out closer to the entrance, Dan could then take the mobs for a run.

In the meantime, Wayne and I would go to work on the other two mobs until Dan returned. Once Jason was finished with the non-primary mobs, he would start Stunning Wayne's target.

The strategy was simple—if it worked—but it was time consuming. We had already spent over an hour to get to this point due to waiting on Wayne's Vitality returning. Any extra time it took us to take down these mobs was going to increase the time we spent waiting on Wayne.

The strategy did work, and it did eat up Wayne's Vitality as we suspected. Even worse, there was another room on the west side of the building that looked the same. We were going to have to do this again.

After waiting ten minutes, we approached the second room. We planned a different tactic this time. I would pull aggro first by going into the room with my Conceal/Stealth on and head to one of the far sides of the room. I hoped that I could drop my Invis and only grab two mobs. Then the rest would enter, hugging the wall in the hopes of not aggroing the mobs on the other side.

It worked. And it didn't. The side I chose only had one mob spawn when I dropped my Invis, but the tactic of hugging the wall did keep our party from spawning whatever else was in the room.

With only one Wraith, we killed it very quickly. That meant there were probably two or more on the other side. Back to Operation Sacrifice if it was more than two.

Of course, three Wraiths spawned as we approached the other side, and Dan took one for a tour of the Monastery's interior while Wayne and I went to work on the other two. We were in for another wait while Wayne got back his Vitality. This dungeon was a time suck.

Good news, though: those eight mobs all dropped spells. We were now looking at 19 spells total. Not bad at all.

We cleared the remainder of the hallway Wraiths and only had two rooms left. One was a large dining room-like area with two long tables set up and multiple chairs around the table. There were no further connecting corridors or doors to this room. A dead end, although I hoped not literally. The second room was empty of furniture, but it did have a closed door on the north side. And a mob. This was the first mob we had seen in the complex. Naturally, it was a Yellow mini-boss. The Great Priest of Loust.

We had no clue what was in store in the dining room, but we weren't about to leave a room uncleared before heading to the boss. That was just bad gameplay.

"We should just enter and hug the wall—all of us at the same time, I mean. Whatever spawns, we can figure out how to deal with it then," Jason suggested.

I agreed but still didn't like the plan. What was the point of having crowd control and a puller if you couldn't even see the mobs? With no other options available to us, we let Wayne lead as we entered and hugged the wall, and for the first time in this damn dungeon, we got lucky. There were five mobs total in the room, but they were spread out in such a way that if we creeped up on them, they would spawn as individuals and not the whole group. This wouldn't have worked with the other mobs, as they spawned almost on top of each other.

The real benefit was that, because of only taking one at a time, Wayne lost very little Vitality, and we could go at the mini-boss in no time flat. Well, that and the additional five spells we received.

The Priest, appearing as an apparition, was wearing a hooded, flowing robe that hid his face from view. He was carrying a staff in one hand and a dagger in the other. Both the dagger and staff were emitting dark shadows.

"Let's go at this guy hard from the outset," Wayne said. "Allister leads with his Stun, then Alex hits him with his Backstab, and I'll be throwing the kitchen sink at him."

I wanted to get the full benefit from my Blacksuit and the chance to possibly Disembowel, but I still didn't want to risk the guys seeing how the Blacksuit works.

"I'm going to scout really quick to make sure none of the earlier mobs have respawned. If we have to run around this place, I don't want them popping up and messing us up."

"How will you know, Alex? They won't spawn if you are Invis."

"No worries, Allister. I'll go to the entrance and drop my Invis there. If the ones at the entrance spawn, I'll just run them back straight through the middle. It shouldn't have been long enough for those to have respawned as well."

"Sounds good, hombre. Just don't get F'ed in the A!"

"Thanks for the words of encouragement, Dan."

I activated my Conceal/Stealth and rounded the corner away from the group and toward the entrance. I really did plan on checking if any of the mobs had respawned on top of putting on my Blacksuit.

Luckily, there were no mobs at the start of the dungeon, and I reactivated my Invisibility. I then headed straight into the room with the Priest and planted myself behind him.

"Back and ready guys. As soon as you Stun him, I will hit him with my Backstab."

As soon as Jason entered, the Priest turned toward him and began casting a spell. Jason's Stun landed, making the incorporeal being solid and stopping his casting. Wayne rushed over to begin gaining aggro on the Priest, and I launched my first attack.

And I was fucked.

I didn't just land a Disembowel. I landed a Disembowel with a Critical Strike.

As you may recall, our damage output increased when the target was returned to a corporeal state from Stun, so on top of doing 4 times the regular Backstab damage with Disembowel, it was then tripled from doing a Crit.

The Priest's hit points dropped ten percent from that one strike. It was going to take lots of effort on the part of Wayne to aggro the Priest. In the meantime, I had to sit there and just take the punishment.

"This is soooo going to blow."

"What the hell did you do, Alex?"

"Massive Crit Backstab. I'm going to need some heals, Jason!"

Jason yelled "On it!" right as the Priest turned toward me and swung his staff at my body. My Agility being one of the lowest Stats on my character, my chances to dodge were low. The resulting 5 percent loss in hit points from that one strike told me I wasn't successful in my attempt.

The Priest continued to unleash a flurry of attacks on me with both the dagger and staff and I watched my hit point bar drop from 95 percent to 75 percent. If I hadn't upgraded my full set of armor recently, I would probably be looking at my bind point right now.

Thanks to the double Stuns of Jason and Wayne, the Priest had very few opportunities to cast any spells, and his hit points were dropping fast. Dan's Fermium-tipped Elven arrows were tearing into the Priest as well.

But that Priest's wicked little dagger had a nasty proc! Along with slicing into me, the proc sucked out 200 of my hit points and gave it back to the Priest! I only had 5400 hit points total at full health. Thank the gods that the proc only landed twice.

Just before the Priest hit 75 percent health, it finally turned to Wayne.

Jason landed a heal on me, bringing my hit points back to 80 percent from the almost 50 percent they had dropped to. I still had to wait before attacking, however, or I would just pull aggro again.

Just like with all the bosses we had fought, the Priest set off an insta-cast AoE spell at 75 percent that did 1,000 hit points of damage. I was back to 60 percent hit points, though the damage was negligible to the rest of the party. My hit points had not fallen far enough thanks to Jason's timely heal to automatically put me back at the top of the Priest's aggro range, so we survived the first special attack without concern.

After several more Taunts, Kicks, and Bashes, I felt comfortable to get back in the fight. Once I started adding my damage, the Priest's hit points went down even quicker.

It seemed like no time had passed when we saw the Priest's health approach the 50 percent mark, and we prepared for the next surprise. Jason's Stun knocked the Priest back and dropped him to 50 percent. It also knocked the hood off of the Priest, and we got to take a look at the face of our foe for the first time.

He had a totally bald head, and his skin was a dark purple. His eyes were pitch black, and he only had two slits in his skull where his nose was supposed to be. Most disconcerting was his mouth. As he opened it we saw rows of jagged sharp teeth, and his snake-like tongue slithered out of his mouth for just an instant. It was as grotesque a mob as we had ever seen.

"Ghoul," Dan said.

"How can you be sure?"

"I watch a lot of horror movies, and I'm telling you, Wayne, that's a Ghoul."

"Horror movies? Like home movies of the family at reunions?"

"Nah, Allijaws. The kind you find on regular broadcasts. My family reunions would be NC-17 due to the level of gratuitous stupidity that is the hallmark of my family."

"Apples usually don't fall from the tree, you know."

"Yeah, but I hold out hope that I'm adopted. Or that mom really liked the mailman. That guy was cool."

I thought we had avoided the 50 percent surprise, but as soon as the Stun wore off, the Priest hit us with an AoE of Shackles and backed away from the group. All of us were stuck where we stood and couldn't move. Except for Dan.

"Guess that new amulet is really paying off! I resisted the AoE."

Ignoring Dan, I turned to Jason, "Can you cast?"

"Not a problem," Jason said as he launched another Stun at the Priest, interrupting yet another casting attempt. Dan was free to move around, but since he fired arrows from a distance to begin with, I wasn't concerned with his freedom of movement. If our only Stun came from Wayne, this could have gone badly.

After a short time, the AoE wore off and we were back in the fight. The last surprise came at 25 percent, when the Priest summoned four Golem-type creatures that went after us individually. Again, the Priest backed off, trying to put room between us so he could cast a spell.

"These guys aren't Wraiths, so I can kite a couple."

"Get to it. Wayne and I will take down these other two. Jason, you keep on Stunning the Priest."

With the cool down on Jason's spell, there was no way he could keep up a constant Stun. This allowed the Priest to finally get off some of his spells. We were hit with a series of Damage over Time (DoT) attacks that began to dwindle our hit points. One of them would have been inconsequential, but three of them stacked together would begin to seriously eat away at our health. Only Dan resisted the casting again. Another testament to his new amulet.

Wayne and I took down the Golems rather quickly, as they did not have much in the way of hit points. Dan continued to kite the other two golems and kept them busy as Wayne and I finished off the Priest.

With both Stuns back in the game, the Priest didn't get any more casts off. Not long after, we dealt him his death blow and mopped up the last two golems.

I went over to the Priest and looted the corpse. He had another spell on him and two items. Interestingly enough, he also had a pattern for making magical leggings. None of us were Tailors, but I bet the guy that made our backpacks would love an item like this.

I also had the first experience with what the Wanderer told me about not all loot being applicable for our group.

"First item is a bust. The stave is a Shaman only item and not tradeable," I said as I linked the weapon.

Item:	Commonality	Weight:	Atk Mod:	Spd:	Bonus:
Gnarled Stave: Shaman Only	Rare (Magic): Binds on Acquisition	7.0	+10	2.0	+15 Wisdom +15 Intelligence +15 Constitution Effect: 10 Percent damage increase to Disease DoT

“Man, I hate that shit! The stupid AI should be able to figure out who is fighting the mob and only drop loot for the group!” Wayne complained.

“I’ll be sure to tell him your thoughts,” I said with a joking laugh. Everyone joined me. If they only knew.

“Here’s the second item.”

Item:	Commonality	Weight:	Atk Mod:	Spd:	Bonus:
Blood Blade	Rare (Magic): Binds on Acquisition	1.0	+15	0.2	+15 Dexterity +15 Constitution +15 Disease Effect: Siphon 200 hit points from target

“Nice, Alex! That thing is awesome!” Wayne yelled out.

“It’s for anyone, so we can roll if you want.”

“Don’t be dumb. Of course you can have it,” Dan said.

I grabbed the blade and immediately equipped it into my primary hand. Just like with the Priest, the Dagger emitted a dark shadow that seemed to flow from the hilt of it and drip off the point, if shadows could drip. The hilt wasn't much bigger than my hand and the guard would have only been sufficient to stop another dagger. There weren't any jewels or ornamentation on the blade or hilt, but you could tell it was the work of a master and steeped in magic. I put my Dagger of Jagged Rock into my off-hand and checked my Character.

Alex:	Rogue	Level 23			
				Resistance:	
Str:	25 (+12)	Atk:	790	Fire:	35
Cst:	28 (+39)	Hps:	6700	Water:	35
Agi:	10 (+28)	Mana:	0	Air:	35
Dex:	51 (+51)	Armor:	190	Earth:	50
Wsd:	6 (+11)	Movement:	90	Holy:	35
Int:	1 (+11)	Horse:	250	Dark:	35
Chn:	210 (+12)			Poison:	35
				Disease:	45

Armor:	Commonality:	Weight:	Armor:	Bonus:
Fine Leather Jerkin	Common	5	35	N/A
Fine Leather Leggings	Common	4	30	N/A
Fine Leather Boots	Common	2	25	N/A
Fine Leather Helmet	Common	1.5	25	N/A
Fine Leather Bracer	Common	1 x 2	15 X 2	N/A
Fine Leather Shoulders	Common	2	20	N/A

Fine Leather Gloves	Common	1	15	N/A
Simple Ring of Might	Common	0.1	10	+1 Str/Cst, +1 Bash
Bloody Rabbit Foot	Rare: Binds on Acquisition	0.1	N/A	+1 Chance
Force Multiplier Ring All Classes	Epic Min Level: 15 Binds on Acquisition	0.1	N/A	+15 Dexterity +15 Agility Unstoppable: All of Character's Stats 4X for 5 minutes (Once/24hrs)

Weapon:	Commonality	Weight:	Atk Mod:	Spd:	Bonus:
Blood Blade	Rare (Magic): Binds on Acquisition	1.0	+15	0.2	+15 Dexterity +15 Constitution +15 Disease Effect: Siphon 200 hit points from target
Dagger of Jagged Rock	Rare (Magic)	1.0	+10	0.3	+10 Dexterity +10 Constitution +15 Earth Effect: Lacerations of Rock: Lowers

		Targets Armor 40 percent for 10 Seconds.

Specialty:	Level:	Modifier:
Blacksuit	100	N/A – Conceal and Stealth at maximum
Disembowel	N/A	X4 Backstab Damage on successful Disembowel. Must be in Blacksuit to conduct Disembowel.
Awareness	100	N/A – Allows Rogue to sense attempts at Theft.
Lift	43	Allows Rogue to circumvent 43 percent of wards on attempt of Theft.

Skill:	Level:	Modifier:
Dagger	100	+10 Atk
Conceal	100	N/A
Stealth	100	N/A
Backstab	100	N/A
Dual Wield	100	+7 Atk
Double Attack	100	N/A
Beast Riding	100	N/A

Title:	Bonus:
Bunny Slayer of Port Town	+1 to all Skills +1 to all resistances
The Bandit Conquerors of Port Town	+5 to all Skills +20 to all resistances

Gift:	Bonus:
Gift of Lady Lancaster	+5 to all Stats +5 to all resistances

With a nod of contentment, I closed my character's biographical information and activated my Conceal/Stealth. Without a further word, I walked through the now open door at the north side of the room and headed deeper into the dungeon. It was time to find this Wendigo.

"Well fuck me with a prickly pear."

"For once, I agree with one of your statements," Jason said to Dan as we looked into the room of the final Boss. The remainder of the dungeon followed very closely with the beginning. Lots of Wraiths, lots of hallways, and several rooms. The loot continued to be only spells, but we now had close to 50. Selling these would greatly increase the amount of money in our bank and allow us to purchase any new Skills we achieved at Level 24.

Due to the Wraiths being a higher level, it took us another two hours to get through the second part of the dungeon. There were even a couple Yellow mobs in the rooms. It was no shock to anyone that the Wendigo was Red.

And a foul looking beast it was. It had no clothes except for a belt that ran across its chest. The rest of its body was covered in deep white fur. It was bipedal, but that was where it stopped being like anything from any human realm. The legs were long, and I could see thick muscles through the fur. Each foot ended with four toes and six inch claws that looked about as thick as my finger. It had an enlarged ribcage and an overly narrow waist, showing off the bones along the sides of its torso. The head was feline in nature, with a huge mane of white hair flowing behind it. The ears were pointed at the top, but more like a Lynx than an Elf. And finally, were the arms. All four of them.

The Wendigo had two massive arms extending from the shoulders that almost reached to its knees. Impressive, since the beast was standing at just over 7 feet. Six-inch claws adorned the ends of these arms as well. Just below what I considered the "primary arms" were two smaller arm-like appendages that sprouted from just under the arm pits. These arms were far smaller but had five fingers instead of four. I guessed these were used for anything that required fine-tuned motor skills.

"Hey! Look over there guys," Wayne said while pointing toward the back of the room we were in. I imagined that the head of the Monastery used this area as his office, what with the huge desk and various areas for sitting. Just behind the desk I could make out two legs wrapped in armor. Laying near the feet was a satchel of some kind.

This was obviously the last resting place of Tristan Lancaster.

"We'll put him to rest as soon as we deal with this huge fucker."

"Too bad you can't just go over there and steal his satchel. Wouldn't that make our lives easier."

"I don't really feel all rainbows and unicorns about fighting this guy, Allister, but we've taken down mobs bigger than him before."

All of them turned and looked at me like I was smoking crack.

"Ok. Maybe not bigger. And definitely not uglier. But at least the Boss looks cool!"

They nodded their heads at that, and we began buffing up for the encounter. Jason hit all of us with any buff he had, making sure to include resistance buffs.

"Since this ass clown isn't a Wraith, no need to lead with the Stun. Looks like a pure Tank pull to me."

"Sure you don't want to go in there first to hit him with one of your Backstabs again. That worked out really well last time, Alex."

Laughing, I said, "Only if I can wait five minutes before I attack!"

Wayne looked around one more time and headed in. "No time like the present!"

"You know, I never liked how that phrase goes because..."

"Shut up, Dan, and get ready to shoot." Wayne said.

"Fine. Sheesh, no one around here appreciates my highfalutin insights."

"Even less than we appreciate your high flatulent insights my friend."

Dan looked hurt as I added a "Boom! Two points for Allister!"

The Wendigo didn't aggro as we crossed the threshold, and we continued to slowly approach the mob. And yes, I did in fact have my Conceal/Stealth on. I planned to Backstab the Wendigo, but I wasn't going to take the chance on a Blacksuit Crit again.

When Wayne was roughly ten meters away from the mob, it finally aggro'ed. As it ran toward our Tank, I saw what the smaller arms were for: the two short swords it pulled from the belt that went over its chest and around its back.

"How is that even fair?"

I agreed with Dan's comment and prepared to Backstab the Wendigo after Wayne had time to establish aggro. With my new dagger, I was even faster than before, so aggro management was again a challenge.

"Shit! This guy hits for days! Swing, Claw, and two Slashes!"

"Four attacks! Damn!"

The Wendigo was going to use all of those arms to his advantage. "Hitting hard?" I asked.

"Three of them landed. It's not too bad, but if I didn't have the Armor Class that I do, I'd be getting flayed right now."

The Wendigo wasn't casting any spells. His attacks were all melee, and when it came to trading damage for damage, we were winning the fight. I watched as the health bar steadily went down. At 75 percent, as was the norm, he launched his first special attack.

The Wendigo performed an attack called Whirlwind of Blades, which did exactly what it sounds like. Instead of the usual four attacks, he performed six, adding in an extra two sword strikes. Then, only several seconds later, he did it again. Only this time he did an extra four strikes and Wayne was attacked eight times. Jason was keeping up with the heals, but Wayne was still at 80 percent when the Wendigo finished his special and struck 10 times.

The only saving grace was that not all the attacks landed. Those that did were devastating. The Whirlwind of Blades appeared to ignore a portion of Wayne's armor bonus, and he went from 80 percent to 50 percent, which is a huge number of hit points for Wayne.

Dan didn't need to be told to stop firing and start throwing all heals toward Wayne. If our Tank went down, we were done for. Wayne, knowing that the Wendigo could counter attack and riposte his attacks, also stopped attacking and just let the heals pile up. It took several rounds of heals, but Wayne was finally back above 75 percent. Everyone went back to their routines at that point.

There were no more Whirlwinds after those three. Again, I watched as the Wendigo's health diminished at a steady rate and creeped closer to 50 percent. Jason shouted out that he was at 60 percent mana. Not a bad amount.

At 50 percent, the boss let loose with his second special attack, Soul Devour. We watched as all our Vitality, which was close to full, dropped 35 percent. Even Dan's extra elemental resistance couldn't stop the attack.

The 35 percent wasn't a big deal, as we still had ample Vitality to finish the mob. What was a big deal, however, was that our Vitality didn't simply vanish. The Wendigo siphoned it off, much like my new dagger did with blood.

I looked on with utter contempt at this beast as his hit points instantly leapt back up from 50 percent to 65 percent. It had taken our Vitality and converted it into its own hit points.

"I guess that explains what Madwar meant when he said this thing was 'A most foul creature that feeds off the very soul of any living beings.' He definitely fed off ours!"

Now I was worried about mana. It was going to be a close call to begin with, but I figured with 60 percent for Jason, we would be in a good situation. Now, I wasn't so sure.

The 50 percent special was a one-time thing, and we sliced, hammered, and pincushioned the Wendigo down toward the last special attack.

I landed a Backstab and dropped the boss down below 25 percent. It wasn't three seconds later when we saw—and heard—the boss executing his last move.

It literally looked like the Wendigo launched itself at Wayne. Like, took through the air and landed on him. At almost the same time, Wayne started shouting, "Frenzy! Shit! Shit! Shit!"

"Heals on Wayne!" I yelled, but I didn't need to. The group knew their roles. I did notice, however, that my attacks were doing quite a bit more damage.

"The Frenzy dropped his Armor Class! Dan, get back to shooting!"

The Wendigo's health began moving toward zero at a much faster rate, but so was Wayne's hit point level. At this point, Wayne had stopped swinging entirely and was simply Taunting and Bashing. One of the Bashes landed a Stun and the Wendigo stopped for a brief moment.

"Stun landed! When he gets to ten percent, Allister, you have the mana, hit him with a Stun!"

"Don't worry about the heals. Use that Stun and kill this asshole. I can get the experience back later!"

I didn't know when the loots from the quest would come. Would it be from the Wendigo? Or would it be from Lancaster himself? This was the only reason I hadn't used my Force Multiplier ring already. I had no doubt we could take it down if I did, but how would that affect the loot? I planned to wait until it was at two percent.

Jason followed Wayne's instructions to the tee and cast his Stun at 10 percent. Thankfully, it landed. All of us started swinging on the boss at that point. We got it down to six percent when the Stun wore off. And he started to Frenzy again. Jason spent the last of his mana on one last heal for Wayne.

I stabbed away as I watched my friend's health diminish rapidly. I kept a close eye on the Wendigo's health and waited for that two percent mark to arrive so I could end this.

And as soon as it hit, I quadrupled my Stats and laid into the boss with no mercy. The biggest surprise wasn't the amount I was hitting. It was my new dagger.

With my Dexterity at over 200, I was proccing like mad and sucking the blood right out of the Wendigo. Between my increased damage output and my dagger, the beast went down in seconds. In retrospect,

I probably could have activated the ring at five percent and still have been safe.

"Man, that was close! I've got 132 hit points. One more hit and it probably would have been a trip to the Keep."

Without any more delay I looted the Wendigo's corpse. The loot was a total bust. There were a number of items that I guessed were used in tailoring or other Crafting skills—Wendigo fur and the like. There were also three of the Wendigo's claws, which I imagined were used in some kind of weapon production. The items were tradeable, so I put them in my inventory.

The Wendigo's two swords were good quality but common. They would sell for a fair amount, but no one was going to use them. Those went in my inventory as well.

The only item that was of any interest was the pack that the Wendigo had wrapped around his chest.

"Let's do this quick so we can get to the Lancaster body. Only thing on the corpse are items for Crafting and this pack."

Item:	Commonality	Weight:	Armor:	Bonus:
Wendigo Pack	Rare	2.0	N/A	Ten Slot Pack: Reduces weight of items in pack by 50 percent

"That's a cool item!"

"It sure is, although not worth the effort we just went through. It's tradeable, so I've got it in my inventory. We can roll on it afterward. Let's go grab Tristan's body."

As we approached the form of Tristan Lancaster, Madwar appeared before us. "I can't believe you succeeded where even a mighty Lancaster fell. You are truly great adventurers. I have not left the entrance of this Monastery for years due to the influence of the Wendigo. With its demise, I can now move freely and, when this is finished, depart for the next realm.

"I promised you the teachings of our school, and I will honor that request," Madwar said, and then a glow surrounded the desk near us.

"Located within this desk is a false bottom drawer with a key of sorts. I've removed the wards from the desk so you won't be injured looking for it. Hold the item you find up to the wall near the far corner, and it will transmogrify into a door. The item will then act as the key through the lock you will find. A powerful enough mage could possibly dispel the transmogrify spell but would not be able to get through the wards on the door without the key.

"Within the room, you will find our most sacred tome. Once it has been read, it will impart the knowledge within upon the reader. Once read, the book will be gone, so choose wisely.

"Before his death, Sir Lancaster noted that his family was sent by the King to rid this Monastery and others of the foul diseases that had taken root. I do not know the status of those other schools. If they have fallen to the same foul machinations of Loust, I fear they too are infested with similar vermin. I know it is not your duty, but I beg you to investigate these other institutions of learning. The closest is the Monastery of Might."

"Oh, we are definitely going there!" Wayne said.

"Without a doubt," I said and then turned to Madwar. "We will investigate the Monastery of Might."

The usual glow surrounded us, and our quest log changed to read:

Restoration of House Lancaster III:
Investigate the Monastery of Might.

"Thank you again for all you have done. The room you will find holds our valuables. We have no need for them any longer. Take whatever you find."

And with that, Madwar disappeared and we were awarded enough experience to get all of us to our Level 24!

"Awesome! We've got two minutes left on my ring's timer, so look for that drawer with the false bottom while I check Tristan's body!"

Dan and Jason jumped to either sides of the desk and began going through the drawers. I approached Tristan's corpse and looted it. Tristan did not have any weapons or gear to loot, despite being fully decked out in custom-made armor. The only things on him were a satchel and his part of the torn journal. Each were 'Bind on Acquisition,' so I didn't touch them yet. I also didn't want to loot the corpse in case it disappeared once we did. I wasn't sure how we were going to do it, but we still needed to give the body a proper burial.

"Jackpot!" Jason yelled.

I ran over to him quickly and grabbed the "key" sitting at the bottom of the false drawer. It looked to be the hilt of a sword, with a jeweled pommel, handle, and blade guard – there was no actual blade. This would not be a key one could just reproduce.

I grabbed it and ran to the wall that Madwar had indicated. As soon as I was next to the location, the pommel began to glow and the wall morphed into the door Madwar said we would find. In the center of the door was the slot for the key, with two notches large enough to fit the blade guard. I inserted the hilt, but nothing happened. Looking at the timer on my Force Multiplier ring had my anxiety peaking, and I grabbed the hilt to try turning it for effect. I turned it to the left first, with no result, and then to the right. That worked, and I heard what sounded like bolts sliding out of a wall. I pushed the door open and was greeted by an awesome sight.

Sitting in the middle of the small room was a pedestal with the tome Madwar mentioned. Shelves lined the walls on both sides. One shelf held two chests, while the other held three. With my ring still active for another 20 seconds, I ran in and popped open each of the chests, without bothering to check what was inside them. I hoped that by just opening them, I would get my bonus.

One of the chests vanished immediately upon opening, and I was rewarded with 20 Platinum pieces. That right there was enough reason to have done this whole quest!

We had ample time to loot the chests. First would be figuring out which of us would get the tome. I walked over to it and put my hand on the book. The description popped up with a request to take the book. I linked the book and denied the request.

For centuries, the Monastery of Calm focused all of their efforts on achieving the ultimate state of peace; a nirvana that allowed the mind, body, and spirit to flow effortlessly together. For a disciple of Calm, it was a lifelong journey, documented within the pages of this Book. In order to ensure that our teachings are never lost, this tome may be used to unlock the secrets within.

Item:	Commonality	Weight:	Armor:	Bonus:
Book of Calm	Epic: One use only	5.0	N/A	Consumption of this tome gives the reader an increase of 20 percent effectiveness for spells and 20 percent increase in mana regeneration

"Wayne, you go ahead and roll first," I said.

"You're a dick, Alex."

I giggled, and Jason gave me one of his signature looks he usually saved for Dan.

"I'm feeling lucky, too. Might just roll a 100 this time around," Wayne joined in. This earned him a look of his own.

"Stop messing with Allibater," Dan said while turning toward Jason, "I'm not going to roll on this at all. This has you written all over it."

"There is something seriously wrong when I'm giving you two the evil-eye and I'm considering hugging Dan."

"Congrats, man. This is going to be an epic upgrade for the group!"

With that done, I went to the rest of the chests to see what we had to dish out.

"We can use three out of four of these. There's a robe here that is caster only. Not even going to link it. Here's the rest of the gear."

Item:	Commonality	Weight:	Armor:	Bonus:
Truesight Bracer	Rare: Binds on Acquisition	1.0	25	+5 Agility +5 Strength 10 percent increase to Truesight

Item:	Commonality	Weight:	Armor:	Bonus:
Blessed Gauntlets: Plate Only	Rare: Binds on Acquisition	3.5	30	+10 Strength +10 Constitution +10 Wisdom +100 Hit Points +100 Mana

Item:	Commonality	Weight:	Armor:	Bonus:
Ninwa's Hoop	Rare: Binds on Acquistion	0.1	5	+ 4 Constitution +4 Chance +4 Disease +4 Poison

"I think I saw a Truesight spell when we were killing the Wraiths. One second," I said while going through my inventory of spells. "Got it. This is a spell for you, Dan: self-buff that adds 15 percent accuracy. That makes this bracer a no-brainer."

"Thanks, Alex. And thanks for the spell."

"Grats. Next one is between you and Wayne, Jason. Roll away."

"I got the book. I'll pass and let Wayne grab it."

"Awesome! Thanks, Allister."

"And the last one should have us all roll. Don't worry about there being a Chance modifier. All of us could use the extra hit points and resists."

Jason won the roll with a whopping 47. All of our rolls were complete shit.

"Man, these are some good additions! And I can't wait until we go to the Monastery of Might. I just hope we don't have to face any of those damn Wraiths again!"

"I agree with Naugha. We could have finished this dungeon up a lot quicker if we didn't have that damn proc."

"Let's get Tristan's corpse and get the hell out of this place."

I tried a number of things to pull the corpse back to the courtyard, but none of them worked. I was tempted to just loot what we needed and leave the corpse. Wayne would never let that happen though.

Which made me think. Wayne.

"Hey brother, since you were the one that promised to do a proper burial, why don't you try moving it?"

"Can't hurt to try, I guess."

Wayne stood there for a few moments, trying to figure out what he could do. I heard him say "drag" a few times, but nothing happened.

"I haven't actually touched the body yet. Cool if I do? It's going to open up the inventory window, but I won't take anything."

"I think we would all be fine if you accidently did."

Wayne went back over to the body and knelt next to it. With his hand on Tristan's lifeless arm he said, "Well that's weird. Never seen that message before. It will let me carry the body."

"Perfect. Grab it and let's go back to the courtyard."

"On it, Alex."

Wayne was able to pick up the corpse in a shoulder carry and run with us back to the courtyard. At the center of the courtyard, I had him put the body down, and check what happened when he tried to loot again.

"Good stuff. It says 'Carry,' 'Loot,' 'Bury,' and 'Decline.' Obviously, we want to bury it, so you should probably grab the loot now Alex."

I did as Wayne said, and grabbed the satchel and the journal. The body didn't disappear immediately, and Wayne was able to access the same menu with all four options. Thankfully, by clicking "Bury," a hole immediately formed in the ground, and Tristan's body appeared inside it. Within moments, the hole filled in, and there was a small statue of Tristan sitting over the grave. This was very weird mechanics for the game, since everything we had done previously required the player to take an action directly to make something happen: like swinging a pick or crafting an arrow shaft. I wasn't going to complain, though.

With Tristan's body buried and the grave marker erected, our bodies took on a soft glow. I looked at everyone, and that far-away look came over Dan's eyes as he was likely checking his character Stats.

"Nice. Burying the body improved our Gift from Lady Tessa!"

I checked my character and saw Dan was correct. The increase was not huge, adding +1 to all Stats and Resistances. But every little bit helped. It was now listed as:

Gift:	Bonus:
Gift of Lady Lancaster	+6 to all Stats +6 to all resistances

"Last item on the docket is the Wendigo Pack."

Everyone rolled, and Jason ended up the lucky winner of the day. If I had to choose, I would have gone with Jason anyhow. His Strength was the lowest, so the benefit of less weight in his packs would be most advantageous to him. The fates worked out in the end.

"So what does the journal say, Alex?"

"No clue, Wayne. And I'm not even going to open it until tomorrow. I don't want to do any more of this quest today."

There was general agreement. It had already been a long day, and everyone wanted to get back to the Keep. That, too, would have to wait until tomorrow, as we planned on logging out right near the crevice entrance of the Monastery.

"Great work, everyone," Wayne said. "Can't wait to see you all tonight at Jenny's place!"

CHAPTER 10

October 26th, 2043

It didn't matter that Wayne said everything was good. Dan kept apologizing for the first hour of our trek back to the city. Dan made a point of "vowing" to replace everything. He also swore that he would sue the company. When he wasn't apologizing he kept repeating, "The fire was not supposed to be that big."

"I wouldn't worry so much about the stuff that burned, Dan. If I were you, I'd be freaking out about whether your chances with Kaitlin went up in flames, too!"

With obvious worry on Dan's face, he asked, "You think she's still mad? I was hoping she would forget about it."

"There was a building-wide evacuation, Dan. No one is forgetting about it."

"Welcome to Casa de Jenny!"

I leaned in and gave Jenny a small hug. "Thanks for the invite. Sorry I'm a little late. Traffic on the way over here was a bear. Did I miss anything?"

"Nah, Dan hasn't shown up yet, so it's just grown-ups here."

"Good! I don't want to miss any of Dan's antics!"

I walked further into the apartment and almost ran into Wayne as he was carrying drinks into the living room. "Hey, big guy. Believe it or not, I don't have Rogue-like reflexes in the real word. I'm less likely to be able to get out of the way here than I can in the game!"

"Sorry about that, Alex. Want a drink?"

I grabbed what looked like a margarita, thanked Wayne, and made my way into Jenny's living room. Gary and Tim had already arrived and were accompanied by their wives.

"Hey, Alex. This is my wife, Kay," Tim said while I shook hands with Kay, followed by Gary's wife, Delilah.

"Pleasure to meet you both."

"Likewise. Gary tells me you are the one responsible for keeping what's-his-name out of trouble? TheNail?"

"TheClaw. And Delilah, I take no responsibility for any of Dan's actions. Ever."

It was obvious that Gary and Tim had told stories about Dan to their significant others.

The wives were sitting near each other and were in a lively conversation, so I plopped down next to Gary and Tim. "It looks like you guys have met up before. The ladies are talking like they're old friends."

"Yup. We've got kids that are roughly the same age, so we met up outside of the game early on so the young'uns could meet. I think Delilah and Kay see each other about as often as I have to look at Tim's ugly face."

"Shut up, Gary."

I still remembered the first time I heard Tim tell Gary to shut up, and I thought at the time that I was about to witness a fight. Turns out, "Shut up Gary," is used as often by Tim as Dan uses modified forms of Allister.

I knew very little about Tim and Gary. I knew Gary was a director in theatre, but I knew almost nothing about Tim. To be honest, I didn't even know they had kids.

"I realize we have been on the same team for a while now, so I'm really embarrassed to say this, but I've got no idea what you did before joining the beta, Tim."

"No worries, man. Only reason all of us know that you were an online merchant is because you told us how you've handled the market in Resurgence.

"Until I joined the beta, I worked protective security for people who had overinflated egos and thought they were really special. A guy makes a little bit of money, and he suddenly believes the whole world wants to take him out."

"Wow. How did you get into a gig like that?"

"I was in the military before and had a background that fit well with the job. After doing some really crap contracting work for the government, I looked to branch out into my own thing. This seemed to work with what I already knew."

"That is very cool." As I was listening to Tim, I realized he wasn't actually telling me what he did in the military. He kept using very generalized terms. I was betting he did something like Special Forces and didn't want to talk about it. I respected him more for not beating his chest and putting on the "look how awesome I am" routine.

"You definitely need to hear some of Wayne's bouncer stories. Between his job and yours, I bet you guys would find a bunch of similarities."

"For sure. In fact, we already have. When he was acting as our 'Tank for Hire,' he and I swapped a bunch of stories."

"Jenny had to tell Tim to stop courting her man!"

We were all laughing when I heard, "Dammit! Did I already miss Dan doing something funny?"

I turned and saw Jason walk in with his husband James. We had all heard about James, but this was our first meeting. He had a smile on his face and seemed at ease in the new setting.

While the two took in the room, I couldn't help but notice that they made a good couple. Sometimes you can look at two people and tell that they fit each other well. That's how Jason and James looked as they surveyed the room.

They first went over to Delilah and Kay to introduce themselves, and then James split off to join Gary, Tim, and me. Jason grabbed a glass of wine and immediately started engaging the women.

James introduced himself to us, which then led to a litany of questions about how we all got involved in playing a video game for money. Each story was different in the fine details, but overall the tale was the same. All of us were serious gamers and saw an opportunity to get involved in the beta. Just like my first meeting with Katherine O'Malley, Tim and Gary were shocked to learn they were getting offered a stipend to play the beta as well. James confirmed this was the case with Jason, too.

Each of us gave a brief background of what we were doing before Resurgence began and what we still thought of as our day jobs—those very things we would return to after the year was up. James was a financial analyst for a large bank but had never been a gamer. He admitted it took him quite a long time to get past Jason's fascination with gaming worlds, and it even caused a fight or twelve in their early relationship.

"I couldn't understand how he could spend hours with that pod on his head and lose himself in those games. I would get more than a little angry, and then a fight would break out. Before I knew it, we were yelling about things that had nothing to do with gaming."

Tim smiled and said, "This all sounds very familiar. I'm sure Gary has gone through something similar as well."

"Sure have."

"So what changed? I've never had to deal with this, being a serial bachelor, but this is exactly the kind of thing that sounds like it could ruin a relationship."

"Right you are, Alex. It possibly could have," James said and shrugged his shoulders. "In the end, Jason showed me how selfish I was being."

Gary and Tim leaned in—a lot—as they waited for James to continue explaining. You would have thought they were about to learn the secrets to eternal youth by the anxious looks on their faces. I guess in a relationship, winning an argument is right up there with finding the Holy Grail.

James looked at the two of them and laughed. “I shouldn’t have said that at all. No way I get out of this room now without divulging this secret.

“It’s simple, really,” James began while taking a sip of his wine. “I like to read, and I do it all the time. So one day I was engrossed in a book and Jason walked in and interrupted me while I was reading. I answered whatever his question was and went back to my book. But then he did it again and again. Finally, I lost my shit and asked him why he kept interrupting me when he could see I was busy.

“I laugh when I think back on it. He simply asked me, ‘Why are you reading?’ As you can imagine, I was more than a little snippy in my reply. I think I said something like, ‘What are you talking about? You know I love to read.’ So he comes back at me and says, ‘Right, but you do it for hours. Why spend all that time reading?’ Before I could stop myself, I responded ‘Because I enjoy reading!’ He didn’t say a word, and it took another ten seconds before it dawned on me what had just happened. Then he smiled and walked out of the room. He admitted a week later that he purposefully got me angry before asking the question, knowing that the anger would make me answer instinctually. Had I been calm, I could have come up with any number of responses that would have not proved his point. But the core of it all is that I read because I enjoy it, just like Jason plays games for the same reason.”

Gary and Tim looked at each other with the biggest smiles on their faces. They were already figuring out how to enact James’ tactics on their spouses.

“Now that Jason is playing a game for both money and fun, I imagine there aren’t any more arguments in your place.”

“You would think, but to be honest, that game has caused more than a little heartache between Jason and I.”

“How so?” I asked.

“Now that it’s a job, I don’t mind that he is playing his eight hours. But when that offer came out for him to buy those older video games, we argued for a good hour about why it was a dumb decision to get them. Naturally, I was right. He hasn’t so much as opened the packaging on any of them. He just keeps telling me, ‘Later, later.’”

I looked over at Gary and Tim and saw them share a look, followed by Tim glancing over at the couch where their wives were sitting.

"And that wasn't even the worst of it. Do you remember when Jason was trying to buy stock in AltCon? We nearly went to blows over that one."

Gary and Tim shared another moment, and I could tell that they had went through similar problems with their spouses. Before James could continue, Gary quickly tried to change the subject to something entirely off topic.

But anything that happened in Resurgence could be linked to the code the Wanderer wanted me to search for. Before Gary could fully change the course of the conversation, I jumped in and asked James, "How did that go down?"

"Jason was adamant that he had to buy that stock. I kept telling him that the market wasn't right for making a big investment of that nature. Not only did he want to buy the stock, he also wanted all of our family to do the same. I can't even begin to tell you how angry I would have been if he had gone behind my back and started calling my relatives. Thankfully, he only contacted his mom, who wasn't keen to buy anything. And after he got a few shares of the company, he seemed to get it out of his system."

This time the look shared by my two teammates was more significant. Tim was about to ask James another question when there was a loud banging on the front door of Jenny's apartment. From out in the hall we could hear music. Loud music. A steady thumping of techno.

"What the hell is that?"

"That, Delilah, is Dan. I would bet my next week's stipend on it," I said. "And no matter what else happens next, I can assure you, it will be epic."

Sure enough, we crowded into the entry hallway and saw the spectacle for all it was when Wayne opened the door. Dan, dressed in the most ridiculous jacket, stood on the other side of the entrance. And the music was coming from said jacket.

As he walked in, I could see that the get-up included speakers mounted into the shoulder pads of what looked like a modified smoking jacket. The techno music was coming out of those speakers as Dan strutted into the apartment.

"Dan!" I shouted. "Turn down the music!"

"Can't, brolicious! My theme music only has two settings. And this one is Loud!"

"Well try the other setting before the neighbors call the cops."

Just like that, the music was turned off, and Dan looked over at Jenny a little embarrassed. "Sorry about that. I didn't think of neighbors. I don't really have any."

"What in the name of all that is holy is that thing you are wearing?"

"You like it, Wayne? Some people hear a song and think, 'Yeah, that would totally be my anthem as I walk the streets if I were in a movie.' Well, I don't stop at thinking."

"Indeed that is true, Dan," Jason stated laconically. "Stopping would imply that you started."

"Exactly, Jasersize! So I had this awesomeness made for me. Now everywhere I go, I have my tune with me."

"Really? You are going to butcher my real name as well?"

"Why ruin a good thing?"

I heard Delilah and Kay whispering behind me, with Kay saying, "It's all true. I thought they were making up half the stories. Now I don't think they were even telling us the whole truth."

I smiled inwardly, thinking of all the stories Gary and Tim must have told the two about our eccentric teammate.

Dan looked around for a couple of seconds before asking, "Where is Kaitlin?"

"Not here yet, brother. But she is on her way."

"Wayne! Why didn't you call me and tell me she wasn't here yet? Now I have to go and wait across the street until she arrives, so I can do this all over again!"

This was when Jenny and the other women in the apartment approached Dan and introduced themselves. Together they unearthed that Dan had the jacket created specifically for the purpose of impressing Kaitlin with just how cool he was.

"Take it from someone of the same gender, Dan. What you just did would not have the desired effect. Not at all."

Dan stood there in deep thought for several seconds. Finally, he looked at all three women and then nodded his head once in determination.

"Right! Too much, too soon. This would have made her go from interested to enamored almost instantly. I'll need to rely on plan B."

"No, Dan, I don't think you understand..."

Tim put his hand on Kay's arm and said, "It's not even worth trying, sweetheart. He's brilliant, sure. But with that brilliance comes a level of blindness that none of us could get through. Better to just watch and enjoy."

Dan refused to explain what Plan B was.

Fifteen minutes later, Kaitlin arrived. Introductions were made all around, and the mingling throughout Jenny's apartment continued. I was unable to find an opportunity to ask Gary or Tim more about the topic brought up by James, despite several attempts. More than the coincidence that everyone had such a difficult time with their significant others concerning the same topic, it was the fact that I had no such inclinations that bothered me.

The only person I hadn't spoken to about the situation yet—other than Jenny and Wayne, who were busy in the kitchen—was Kaitlin. Seeing a moment to approach her and ask if she had similarly purchased the outdated games and stock, I made my way across the living room.

It was at this time that Dan decided to implement "Plan B."

"Ladies and Gentlemen! The moment you have all been waiting for, even if you didn't know you were waiting for it, has arrived! The Great Danferno is here to amaze!"

I was turning toward Dan when Jason suddenly reached out and seized my forearm in what was damn near a death-grip. "Alex, 'Danferno' sounds suspiciously close to 'inferno!' Stop him!"

I continued to turn toward Dan's location and started walking toward where he was. As soon as I saw him, I stopped in my tracks.

Dan had his arms out to his sides at shoulder's height, with his palms raised toward the ceiling. What caught my attention—and actually arrested my forward momentum—were the tiny fire balls that kept springing from his hands.

"Prepare to be awed by the magic of the ages, thought to be lost since the times of Merlin and Arthur. I, the Great Danferno, will perform the impossible!"

I slowly walked up next to Dan and leaned over so I could whisper in his ear, while avoiding the small gouts of fire shooting out of his hands. "Hey, buddy. What exactly are you planning here?"

Dan turned his head toward me and whispered back, "Don't worry Alex, I got this. Kaitlin is going to go crazy after she sees! Trust me. Nothing could go wrong."

"I, in fact, feel less sure about whatever this is *now* than I did 10 seconds ago. I don't know what you're planning, but please tell me you've done something like this before. Please."

"I spent hours watching videos today, man. I've got this mastered."

And shockingly, he did.

Dan went through an entire routine where he lit candles from a distance, made cards go up in flames only to have them appear in someone's pocket, and several other illusions I couldn't explain. Everyone was watching and clapping at the end of each demonstration. Even Jason looked over and gave me a raised eyebrow of respect for Dan's abilities.

Because Dan was actually really good. That is, until he wasn't.

At the finale of the routine, Dan shot two of the fire projections into the air and they created a fire heart for a brief second. The fire was launched in the general direction of Kaitlin, and even a moron could have seen what Dan was doing. Unfortunately for all of us, Dan's IQ level that night dipped below moron, and he felt the need to make a bigger demonstration of his "love" for Kaitlin.

"You have beheld only a fraction of what the ancients knew about lore and sorcery. These displays were just a sampling of the true power that resides within, as you are about to witness."

I had to give it to Dan. He was really selling the showmanship. Any good performer knows that nine times out of ten the sleight of hand or action to complete an illusion is done fairly quickly; it's the performance that sells the illusion and that keeps them coming back for more.

But what caught my eye wasn't the routine Dan was going through, but the way he kept fiddling around his wrist area. I imagined that was where the contraptions for creating the fireballs were located. So I was curious why Dan would risk drawing attention to that area by constantly messing with it.

And then I processed the last sentence Dan said. And I knew. Dan was changing the settings on the fire makers. And no matter how well everything had gone so far, this had disaster written all over it.

I began moving in Dan's direction as quickly as I could, but it was already too late.

"Behold!"

And with that Dan shot out much larger fireballs that made an even bigger heart than the one before it. Kaitlin knew Dan was doing this for her benefit, and she was clapping at him enthusiastically for his innovation.

Until the fire didn't go away.

"Shut 'em off, Dan!" Wayne said.

"I'm trying, man! I can't get the fire to stop!"

The fire "heart" was now growing even larger and was getting dangerously close to the ceiling.

Dan obviously thought if he could fiddle with the gizmos on his arms he could get the fire to stop. The only problem was that by moving his arms he started spraying fire all around the apartment. All of the guests got out of the way, but one of Jenny's chairs was not so lucky. Nor was the ceiling, which did indeed get a bit singed.

Tim and Wayne both sprang into action. Wayne ran into the kitchen and came back quickly with a fire extinguisher. He opened the valve and hit the chair with the contents, quickly putting out the fire. Dan, however, had not been idle while Wayne was away, and a few more items were beginning to burn. For the most part, all of us just kept out of Dan's range of fire and let Wayne go to work with the extinguisher.

Tim, on the other hand, ran into one of Jenny's bedrooms and came back with a blanket of some kind. Without any hesitation, he wrapped the blanket around Dan's hands, put his own arms around Dan, and took him to the floor. From there we could see that Tim had not only wrapped Dan's hands completely, but that the blanket was extremely thick.

"No oxygen, no fire, bud. We should be good for now, but you might want to get those things off your wrists before we do anything else with this blanket."

Dan began removing the equipment from his wrists when the fire alarm went off. It was at this point that Dan looked up, finally, and saw the other guests in Jenny's apartment.

Everyone was covered in dust from the extinguisher, and there was a layer of smoke along the roof, no doubt the cause of the fire alarm. The looks on our faces were mostly shock, although Jenny's looked like pure irritation. Luckily for Dan, I didn't see any anger in the look.

Unfortunately, Kaitlin, had been close to one of the fires when Wayne let loose with the extinguisher. Of all of us, she was covered the most by the extinguishing agent, almost covering her entire torso. Her look, in fact, was anger.

"Fuck my life."

"Try to focus on the game, Dan. It will take your mind off the colossal fuck up that was last night."

"Thanks for the words of encouragement there, Allimalicious," Dan said with an obvious note of sarcasm.

"Hey, no one told you to bring fireball-shooting whatevers on your hands."

"But it was going so good!"

We all nodded our heads. If Dan hadn't decided to mess with the gizmos that made those fireballs, he could have definitely chalked the night up as a success.

"Another lesson learned for you there, brother. I have no doubt you will learn many more as time goes on."

"Are you saying I fuck up a lot, Alex?"

"And you said he didn't notice any social or subtle cues, Allister."

"You guys are both dicks."

"But we got your back, and I'm sure Wayne will talk to Jenny about trying to smooth over the whole thing."

Dan looked over at Wayne with unbridled hope in his eyes.

Wayne looked over at Jason first and asked, "Pink Tutu Affair?"

"Come on, Wayne! That was weeks ago!"

"The Pink Tutu Affair will never die," Jason said, while fist bumping Wayne. He then looked over at Dan and said, "Although, I think we can give a pass on this one. The little guy could definitely use all the help he can get."

"I could! I really, really could!"

With a stout nod from Wayne, the topic died down. Although Dan could be heard mumbling to himself on more than one occasion, I was too far away to hear what he was saying.

The rest of the trip out of the tundra and back to the Keep passed without incident. There were the occasional mobs, like Lynxes and Leopards, that popped up, but nothing that we couldn't handle, especially with our improved gear and levels. We were all thankful we didn't disturb another pack of Wolverines. Even with our gear, those things were a huge pain in the ass.

We also discussed what to do with all the spells we had collected and what our next steps would be once we met up with Arthur in Yerkich Square. I figured that once we inspected the satchel that Tristan had on his body, we would find the location for the next part of Lady Tessa's quest. On the other hand, we were also likely to get the next quest for the story arc. We certainly had plenty of options before us, but Wayne reminded me that first we had to finish up our business with Old Lady Madsie.

The old crone was sitting in the same rocking chair when we approached. I wasn't able to take the satchel out of my inventory because it was a "bind on acquisition" item, but I did tell her what we found. She started crying about halfway through the story and was weeping freely by the time I had finished.

"I had hope, you know? All these years, I never heard from a one of them, but I also never heard that they died for certain. A small piece of me kept that hope alive, that secretly those fool boys and their father met up outside the gates of this Capitol and spirited off into the night.

"But these tears are also for knowing that you four were able to put Tristan to rest. That's a mighty fine thing you did. And I'm sure you will be rewarded in the afterlife for your kind deeds. I've got nothing more for you, but that satchel you found likely has answers you will need. Just be careful, you four. You need to remember that it's not only the monsters that you have to worry about; if the King were to ever get wind of what you are doing, there will definitely be hell to pay."

"What makes you think it's the King?"

"Do I look stupid, son? I've been with House Lancaster for decades, and the only two people who could ever get one of those boys out of the house on a mission is their father, or the King. And since their father was sent on a mission as well, that only leaves His Majesty."

I nodded at the old lady, but didn't speak on the topic any more. Instead, I asked, "Would you like us to return after we finish the next part of Lady Tessa's request?"

Madsie looked at me for a couple of seconds before shaking her head. "No, lad. You keep coming back here to see me and I worry it could raise suspicion. True, no one around here rightly remembers that I worked for the Lancaster family all them years ago. But never tempt the fates that could bring someone around at the worst of times."

We said our farewells to Old Lady Madsie and made our way back to the square where Arthur awaited us.

"I definitely thought we would at least get some experience out of that. I wasn't expecting her to drop new blades in our hands or anything, but at least give us something."

I agreed with Wayne's assessment, but we didn't do much other than stop by and quickly relate a story. I was about to say as much when I felt someone starting to reach for my purse.

I lightly grabbed the intruders hand and looked behind me at a scrawny child that couldn't have been more than 10 years old. I was impressed with his skill at such a young age, though I gave him a look that said I was annoyed with his presence.

"Don't need that eye on me now, there do I? How about you keep them evil gazes to yerself. Waseem told me I wouldn't be able to gets it none wise, and said if I did he thoughts you a failure. He wants to see ya."

And as soon as I released the lad's hand, he scampered back into an alley and was gone.

"What was that, Alex?"

I looked over and saw my three friends staring at where the child had just run off. I was seriously going to have to have a conversation with Waseem about sending his urchins to accost me in the middle of the day around people I was trying to keep in the dark about my Rogue abilities.

Right now, though, I needed to decide how much to lie to my friends. I thought it best to go with as little as possible. Every good lie has ninety percent truth intertwined throughout the story to sell the veracity of your claim. I just hoped my ninety percent would be sufficient.

"Little fucker tried to steal my purse!"

"Wait, seriously?" Jason asked.

"Yeah man. I felt something going for my purse, and when I reached down, I grabbed the little bastard's hand. Then he started rambling on. As soon as I let him go he ran back into the alley. I think it was a quest, but hell if I know what he was saying. You catch any of it, Dan?"

I was making a calculated risk here, and I knew it. Dan had been farthest away from the interaction, as he tended to lead wherever we went if there wasn't imminent battle in front of us. But he also had better hearing. It would have been entirely outside the norm if I didn't ask Dan for his help, since if he heard it, he remembered it all.

"Something about you being a failure and that someone wants to see you. I didn't catch any more than that. I only caught the end of it as I was walking back to you guys."

"Oh well, thanks anyway. Another random thing to put down in the book of random things that pop up in Resurgence. Keep an eye out for the little thief though, would ya? If he comes around I want to figure out what the quest was."

"You got it!"

With that potential disaster averted, I made a mental note to visit Waseem at the first opportunity. He apparently wanted to talk to me, and I wanted to give him a piece of my mind about his careless behavior.

We decided that I would try and sell as many of the spells as possible in the Square over the next few days. I would use my usual method for selling items, and once the three days had expired, we would just sell the remaining spells to vendors. None of us wanted to waste our time waiting around the square hearing me yell out items for sell, especially now that we had the 20 platinum pieces from the last quest and were relatively flush with money. The only spells that wouldn't be sold were those that could be used by our teammates, naturally.

The square was far livelier than we had ever seen it before. The reason for all the activity was clear. Many more adventurers had reached Level 20 and numerous groups were crowding around Arthur. I saw an equal number of Light and Dark aligned races, but I didn't see our friends Lug or Tyke. On top of the spells, our plan was to sell Lug the old Fine Plate Gauntlets that Wayne was using. If nothing else, we would solidify the friendship between his group and ours.

"Wayne, I'm going to go and talk to Arthur. Reach out to Lug and see if he and his team are in the area. I would like to sell your gauntlets and see if either of their casters can use any of these spells."

Wayne nodded and headed off to the side of the square, away from the crowd that was around Arthur. Dan and Jason also hung back and allowed me to approach Arthur on my own. The other groups were staying to themselves and hadn't noticed our arrival yet. That changed when I walked up to Arthur.

An eerie quiet descended over the players gathered in the square, and I could hear a few whispers as I passed by.

"That's them, isn't it? I heard they..."

"You know they already beat the Trolls. First ones on..."

"Their Ranger can really drink. I saw him knock back..."

That last one made me smile. I didn't want to seem like I was better than anyone else there, so I smiled at people as I passed and said hello to those who did the same to me. Mostly everyone was waiting to see what happened when I talked to Arthur.

Without any further fanfare, I approached Arthur. "We are ready to answer the call."

Not a word was said by any of the other players. Everyone was as anxious to hear what Arthur said as I was.

"So you are. And the Kingdom thanks you for the work you have done in slaying the Trolls impeding our forward movement toward victory against the Children of Loust. There have been gains, and there have been losses. The unstoppable force that is Supreme Overlord Riff Lifestealer has been the cause of much heartache for His Majesty and the reason behind many of those losses. However, I am afraid you and your band of adventurers are not yet ready to conquer the next feat and thereby aid in preparing the King's Army in their drive to conquering these foes. Return when you have acquired more knowledge and skill."

"Son of a bitch!"

Oddly enough, that came from one of the bystanders and not from me or my group. I looked over and saw a player who must have recently arrived at the Capitol. His anger was understandable, though. He just learned that whenever he and his group did beat the Trolls, there would still be some time before they could take on the next quest.

"Excuse me for asking, but what Level are you guys?"

"No worries. We are Level 24."

"Woah! It took you until Level 24 to beat the Trolls?"

"We did it at 23 and then went and grinded for some more experience to get our Levels."

"Cool. Sucks that you guys have to wait, though. Sorry, man."

This was something I had seen often in the worlds of an MMORPG. Naturally, you had different types of players. Some were assholes, and they would always be assholes no matter how they played or whom they played with. Some were so intoxicated whenever they played that absolutely nothing could bother them and everything just slid off their back. Others, like the player in front of me, were unnaturally deferential to players of a higher level, even though our levels weren't all that different. Since this was the beta, my few levels really must have seemed like a lot to this guy. I tried to treat everyone the same, since anyone could become a potential client in the future.

Except for the assholes. I really couldn't stand those players.

"Appreciate it, man. Just the nature of the game. We will grind until we get to that next level. Best of luck to you and your team."

"Thanks, Alex. I really appreciate that!"

I took note that this player's name was Gindo. I had a feeling that I would be hearing from this guy again.

"So I'm guessing no quest since we weren't all shiny and golden after you walked away from Sir Arthur over there?" Jason asked as soon as I arrived at their location.

"Astute observation, my fine Cleric friend. I guess we are just going to have to grind out until we get where we need to be. Where did Wayne go?"

"Trying to find Lug, I think."

Several minutes later I saw the massive form of Lug coming toward the Square and in an animated exchange with Wayne.

"Are you sure, Naugha? That's a huge discount compared to what I can buy them for here in the Keep. You guys already hooked me up with these pants."

I looked over to Naugha with a raised eyebrow and he sent me a private message that said he was selling the gauntlets at cost, much as we did with the leggings. I nodded my head to let him know I agreed with his decision. Selling and buying were my things, so the guys tended to defer to my guidance. In reality, they were Wayne's gauntlets and he could do whatever he wanted with them.

"You're our favorite Ogre, Lug. Of course we are going to help you out!"

That got a laugh from not only Lug, but also Tyke and his two casters, Tammer and Syphon.

"Thanks for the tip on the Trolls. Still took us a while to get through the final boss, but I kept remembering what you said about controlling the mobs. I think we were the third team to beat them on the server. Not too shabby."

Jenny and her crew were the second to beat the Trolls.

"Our pleasure, Tyke. We've got some spells that we came across during our ranging. What have you got for casting in your group? I'll see what we have."

"I'm the Shaman, Tammer is our Enchanter, and Syphon is our Death Caster."

"Cool, got something for all of you guys, then. Also, talk to TC about upgrading one of your bracers. He got a new one and would probably sell you his Fine Leather Bracer at a good price."

"TC?"

"TheClaw. I'm a grown ass man, Tyke. I can't be going around calling another grown man, TheClaw."

Tyke smiled at me as he walked over toward Dan to negotiate the Bracer. It was Dan's call on how much he wanted to sell it for, but I knew he wouldn't charge Tyke more than what he paid for it originally. Dan had little care for money. Except for when he wanted to go to the Tavern. Then he clung to his Copper pieces like a pot-head clings to Bob Marley.

With the transactions completed between Tyke's group and our own, I went out into the square and started shouting out our wares. There was a surprisingly large number of people that responded. I figured I would have to sit for a while to load off most of these spells. Instead, I sold most of them in the first two hours. With that done, I saw no reason to hold onto the remaining few spells we had, hoping to get a few more gold off of the players. We all agreed to sell the remaining parchments to the merchants. We decided to keep the tailoring and crafting items we found for later.

All in all, we pocketed another 10 Platinum. We were definitely sitting pretty when it came to cash. I had to laugh, as I thought of how hard we had to grind just a week before to try and make a few Platinum. Such was the way of RPGs. You could find yourself rich with one quest and have it all gone the next day.

The only thing remaining was to open the satchel that we got from Tristan. What you would think would be an easy decision to make was met with dissension from the rest of the group. I wanted to crack it open, but the rest told me to keep it in my inventory for now.

Jason explained it best. "We know we are going to have to level to get the next quest from Arthur, right? Well, if we need to level for that, I'm sure we need to level for the next Lady Tessa quest, too. And I have no doubt, if we see that little quest icon in our character heads-up, we are going to want to try it. I think I speak for all of us here when I say that I would rather we be over-prepared than under when we finally tackle whatever that next quest is."

I couldn't argue with his logic, but the gamer in me really wanted to know what was in that satchel. Since I wasn't the leader of the group, as I had said time and again, the decision came down to democracy. And I lost. The satchel remained closed until another time.

Between our travels to the Keep and the selling in the square, we decided to call it quits for the day as a group. Everyone planned to go their separate ways but stay in game for a bit longer. Wayne was going to go find Jenny, Dan was heading to the Tavern, and Jason was as secretive as ever about where he was going. Jason probably was looking to find another quest that would give him a better title, despite us telling him the Baron fit him perfectly. I was heading over to see Waseem and find out just what was so damn important that he had his messenger try to rob me in the street.

The Stinky Pit looked empty when I entered. I said looked, because I had learned long ago that when it came to Rogues, you could never take anything at face value.

I walked up to the bar and said hello to Milly. By this time, she was used to seeing me in the Pit, and I no longer had to worry about her trying to distract me so others could attack me. That didn't mean she wouldn't try to keep my attention so someone could rob me. Someone like Waseem.

Who, in fact, was shaking my coin pouch behind me.

"How is it that my Awareness is as high as it will go and you still Lift my pouch nine times out of ten?"

"I'm a Master Thief."

Apparently, Waseem thought that was enough to explain the reason, but I was already pissed at him so I told him to explain. Although I did use a number of colorful expletives.

"You need more than just Awareness to stop a Master Thief. You need wards and magic. You have none. So stop being a child throwing a tantrum."

"I'm not throwing a tantrum. I'm not even the least bit upset that you got my pouch again. I'm angry because your little street thief attacked me in the middle of the road, right in front of my friends.

Now how secret can I keep these skills if you have your underlings being so brazen?"

Waseem took on a serious tone. "What did you tell them?"

"I told them the bloody truth. I said some little fucker tried to rob me and then started babbling on about some nonsense. I told them that I thought it was some stupid quest."

"And they bought it?"

"Yes. But that isn't the point, is it?"

"No, it isn't. I'll talk to Two-Feet when I see him. I'll explain my displeasure."

"Two-Feet?"

"Yeah. He was only two feet tall when I found him in the street. Name just stuck. That was one malnourished kid."

It's hard, even when you know it is a game, to get mad at a guy who takes in children and teaches them to earn a living. Even if that living involves breaking the law. I didn't see any point of continuing the discussion since Waseem obviously understood I was displeased.

"So what did you need to see me about?"

"We need to start teaching you your next Skill. But you aren't ready to start the specialization. You don't have any experience in Climbing, do you?"

"Nope, not a bit. What does the Skill have to do with Climbing?"

Waseem shook his head. "You know, no matter how angry you might get, I still get to have my secrets and my fun."

"Fine. I need to get the Climbing skill. Where does it need to be before I can start the Specialization Skill?"

"You need to have it as high as possible, Alex. This last Skill is far more complicated than Awareness or Lift."

I remembered the hours I spent trying to learn Lift and groaned inwardly at what I was getting myself into.

"Any recommendations on where I should go to practice?"

"There is a range of mountains not far from Kich's Keep that has numerous levels of difficulty for Climbing. I would suggest you go there and begin your training. But go slow. You do not want to get to ahead of yourself and plummet to your death."

With that, I opened my Map and saw a new area highlighted north of the Keep. It was an area we had not explored too much and would make for a good place to start grinding. Hopefully, I could maximize my time online without having to run around constantly.

Unknown Facility
October 27th, 2043

The General finished watching the video on the large screen in the conference room. Dan wanted to fast forward through the slower points, but the General was adamant about watching the whole thing. This wasn't just about Dan's antics but also the actions of the others at the party.

When the video ended, the lights came up. Dan sighed loudly. "Well, if I ever had any shot with the girl, that's gone now. But we should be good. No way they could suspect that I am anything more than the fool we've been trying to make them see. I would say we can call this one 'Mission Accomplished,' don't you think?"

"Indeed, Mr. Hamson. You played the part admirably."

The General didn't have reason to believe that anyone suspected Dan was a plant within the beta, but he had learned long ago that the absence of evidence wasn't always evidence of absence. He planned to play out this mission as carefully as possible. Given the General's paranoia, it had been Dan's idea to implant mini cameras into the jacket he wore to the party. The General had been concerned that something like a camera would be noticed. Dan, however, insisted it would be fine. Given the garish nature of that thing, the General wasn't worried in the least bit that anyone took notice.

Colonel Thompson patted Dan on the shoulder a few times. "Don't worry, man. You can still get the girl. You just have to work harder for it."

"You think so?"

"Well, it would also help if she was a gold digger after your money. Absent that, you're gonna have to work really hard."

"Wow. Great pep talk, Colonel. Really. You should probably work at a suicide hotline. I bet you would get all those guys off the ledge." Dan made a whistling sound while using one hand to imitate a guy jumping, clapping it into the other hand as it splattered below.

"Enough banter, you two. I'm not concerned with your love life, Mr. Hamson. I'm concerned with figuring out how to take this company down. And despite whatever setbacks occurred to your romance with your teammate, you played an admirable part and solidified our ruse. Now on to the company. Do you have any updates on that?"

"Nothing, General. Since the hack job they did weeks ago, I haven't noticed any abnormal behavior on my part toward AltCon. Although, if the actual experts are back at the controls, I imagine I wouldn't see any change."

"Indeed. But we've continued your brain scans and our specialist agrees with your assessment. Eventually, they will have to begin again, and I want you to be ready for when it occurs."

"I'm all over it, General. I'm heading back to my place to log-in. I'll see you at our next briefing."

After Dan left the conference room, the General returned to his office. Waiting on his desk were seven manila folders. Each contained the backgrounds of Dan's teammates. By and large, they were all quite thin. None of them had done much to gather the attention of the government—or anyone else for that matter.

All except for one Timothy Slokavitch, honorably discharged Marine Corps Staff Sergeant. That file was inches thick.

The General moved the remaining files to the side and opened Tim's file again. He had already perused it twice and was still trying to figure out how he could make use of this asset. Normally, the General wouldn't have a problem with making such a decision, but the very file in front of him was adding to his problems.

Fifty percent of it was blacked out.

His reactions and responses on the video highlighted his intelligence and training. The General knew that whatever Mr. Slokavitch got into during his time in service, he was definitely a formidable man and someone he wanted on his team.

The General wouldn't have a problem with getting the complete file. When it came to this operation, he had the full support of the White House. It would be only a matter of time before he could decide how to approach and use this particular asset. That he would was already decided.

CHAPTER 11

October 27th, 2043

I found the rest of the group already logged in at the square when I got into the game. Dan and Wayne were engaged in a discussion, and by the look on Dan's face, it wasn't something he wanted to hear.

"Dude, she doesn't hate you, but she really doesn't want to talk to you right now, either."

"But it was an accident! You told her that right?"

"Of course I did. But that doesn't matter, man. She had to throw out that outfit, and don't even get me started on how much she bitched about getting that fire suppressant out of her hair."

I sidled up to Jason and asked what was going on.

"Apparently Wayne tried to do a solid for Dan last night while he was hanging out with Jenny. It didn't go over well."

"I will buy her a new outfit! Ten new outfits! Does she want a car?"

I turned away from Dan and Wayne and asked Jason what he thought about heading due north to range and grind.

"I'm good with it. It isn't somewhere we have been yet, and we already have the cloaks that will protect us. Just let Dan and Wayne finish. I think Wayne is trying to let him down easy."

Fifteen minutes later, we were on the road and heading up north. Wayne had no objections to the party heading in that direction, and Dan was unusually quiet about everything. In fact, the poor guy didn't say a single word the whole time we traveled.

We stayed to the main road, avoiding any random mobs in the area until we arrived at the mountainous region that Waseem had indicated on my Map. Dan headed out to look for mobs and quickly discovered numerous mountain dwellers that were of a high enough level to give us experience.

We found a good place to set up as a pulling ground and sent Dan out to do his thing. I had no doubt that Dan would continue to be a very capable player, but on this day, he was not going to be himself. I definitely felt bad for him, though I couldn't have too much sympathy for his antics. After all, I did try to stop him on more than one occasion.

With nothing special about the mobs we were fighting, we got ready to grind out and start getting some experience.

After several more hours, we called it a night and found a safe place near the mountains to log out. The experience we were getting was good, and we planned to stay here until we at least got our Level 25. Most of the mobs were fauna in nature, so the drops were for crafting, yielding little money for the group.

Once everyone had logged off, I went and found a place that I could start climbing. Waseem had said that there were different levels of difficulty in the area, but everything I saw looked like a sheer-faced cliff.

It wasn't until I got right up to the mountainside and started running my hands against the rock that I started to notice some sort of differentiation in the cracks and crevices.

With nothing else to try, I put my hands at different places, braced my feet against what I thought were jetties of rocks, and tried climbing the side of the mountain.

And after getting slightly off the ground, I slid right back to the packed earth at my feet.

Never one to give up, I placed my hands in slightly different angles and tried again. I was able to make only a little more progress before I slid down the rock face yet again.

I thought back to the hours of trying to remove ice from a glass, groaned inwardly, and got right back to it.

Twenty minutes later, I received a new message:

You have learned a new Skill. You have learned Climbing.
Effect: The higher the Climbing Skill, the more the player will be able to identify safe holds and easy paths for ascending any surface.

My Skill in Climbing was at 1. When I looked back at the side of the mountain, however, there were now areas that had a faint glow. I couldn't determine what any of the colors meant, as they all bled together, but at least now I knew how the skill would work and what to pay attention to as my level increased.

With nothing else to do, I kept up a steady pace of trying to climb the side of the mountain. I made very little progress, but my skill went up four more points over the next hour. Emboldened, I kept at it for two more hours.

When I was finally ready to call it a night, my Skill was at 14, and I was starting to discern variations in the colors along the wall. It looked to me that I was trying one of the harder routes. The next day I planned to use my new Skill to find an easier grade that would allow me the opportunity to get farther up the side. I thought that if I could scale more of the mountain, my Skill would increase faster.

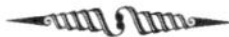

October 28th, 2043

We grinded for another day, and almost everyone hit Level 25. We no longer achieved our levels at the same time, considering the different number of deaths we had encountered, or in Dan's case, paying experience to Broham so he could level, too.

At the end of our day, I went back to the mountainside and started looking for an easier route to climb. I felt lucky that it only took me twenty minutes to find an area that was mostly green along the wall. I took the green to mean easy, as other areas seemed to correspond with the green through red motif of difficulty.

After only a few attempts to get up the side of the rock face, I knew my assessment was correct. I was finding it much easier to not only climb the cliff but also rest in areas when my Vitality started to go down. As my Skill in Climbing was still very low, it took a significant portion of my Vitality to make any real progress.

I looked above me to where the route I was climbing continued to ascend, and I saw that the path went from Green to Red very quickly. I had been using my Climbing skill for some time now, and I had yet to get a single point in my Skill. I hypothesized that if the track was green, then it was too easy for me, and I wouldn't get any points for it. I decided to go to the top of the Green portion then climb back down. Going down, without any kind of assist or belay, was even more difficult than going up. Therefore, it wasn't surprising when I looked down and saw the Green route I climbed up was now White on the way down. I carefully descended, and in the process earned more points toward my Skill.

But now I was faced with a conundrum. If I went and looked for a route that was White on the way up, would it be Blue on the way down? If I fell off the side of the cliff, would it do enough damage to kill me outright?

Without a healer nearby, I couldn't risk a fall. I would have to grind this out just like we were doing with our Levels. I would continue to climb the exact same route until the White route going down turned Green, and I wouldn't get any points for either ascending or descending.

When my Skill hit 20, the path leading down switched from White to Green, and I was no longer going to see any increase in my Climbing ability from this route. With my new level in Climbing, however, I could now make out even more distinct routes in the climbing landscape. I looked to my left and right and saw different areas that looked to be potentially viable. And many that were not. I wasn't going to run out of options around here for a long time.

November 1st, 2043

"Hey, Alex, did you give me any money recently?"

We had all reached Level 25 and, having learned that Sir Arthur still wouldn't give us our next quest, decided to stay out in the mountains to gain our Level 26. I had gone back to the Keep to try for the quest and to sell off a bunch of stuff, but I hadn't distributed any of the money to the other guys.

"Nah, Dan, I haven't. I put the money we made out here into the bank. Why?"

"Because I have 37 Gold on my character."

"Hey! So do I!" Wayne yelled out.

That led Jason and I to look at our characters as well, and sure enough, we had 37 Gold to our names.

"Wasn't me," Jason said.

After a moment, I realized what day it was. Or rather, the date. The first of the month.

"Tibble!"

Wayne looked around, obviously searching for the Dwarf. Not seeing him, he looked over at me. "What the hell are you talking about, Alex? Tibble isn't here."

"I wasn't calling out to Tibble. I mean that Tibble must have given us the money—as part of the profit sharing for the clan. I had mentioned he should do it in such a way that makes it a regular thing, like the first of the month. Apparently he took my words to mean he should do it exactly then."

"Dividends! Nice! And at least I don't have to pay taxes on these!"

"Yeah, Dan. We all feel horrible about your First-World problems of having to pay taxes on the dividends you make."

"Don't be mad, Alliposter. Do you want a stock tip? You should totally buy bofa."

"What the hell is bofa?"

"Bofa deeeeez nutttttz!"

Jason's face got super red, and he looked about ready to attack Dan. Before he could move toward Dan, Wayne and I erupted with laughter. I thought Wayne was going to actually fall over, he was going at it so hard. I literally had tears streaming down my face.

"No go, bro," I said as clearly as I could. "Dan wins this round, hands down. You got to take that one and just be pissed."

Jason stalked off and started mumbling, "Immature child, in his damn thirties and still making dick and fart jokes."

Dan got a high five from Wayne and a fist bump from me.

"We're going to need to check in on Tibble and our Clan soon and thank them for the Gold. I'm also curious to see how they are doing level-wise."

"Let's get to 26 and then make a trip over that way," Wayne said.

"Sounds good to me. We should get there by the end of the day. Allister, you are almost there, right?"

Jason was still grumbling but nodded his head in affirmation.

It wasn't that Jason minded the banter between him and Dan. In fact, I was sure it was one of the things he enjoyed most about the game. What got Jason so riled up was that Wayne and I considered Dan's juvenile humor to be on the same level as Jason's biting wit. At the end of the day, Jason thought we should be giving him more points.

While we consistently added to our experience, I had been adding to my Climbing Skill. When I hit Level 25, I invested all five of my Stat points into Wisdom to help learn the skill faster. There wasn't a noticeable difference, but I had to believe that every bit helped.

With three more days of training, I had reached 75 in Climbing. I was now having to venture out pretty far to find more challenging routes that would add to my level. Often, I would have to go through a Green route to get to something more difficult.

Another bonus to the advance of my Skill was an identifier that showed me if the route would be Green going up and White coming down. Before I hit 70 in my Skill, all I could see is that a route was Green and I would have to climb up ten feet or so and look down to see if the markers turned White below me. With the new advancement, I could clearly see where a handhold or foot hold was Green on the top and White on the bottom, meaning I would get experience for my descent. There were also some that were White going up and Blue coming down, though I was sure that would lead to a fall. The real money-makers were those that were White both going up and down.

More and more of the mountain was becoming Green as I progressed. Oddly enough, that very first route I took upon starting my Skill advancement—where the Green turned to Red—was still the same. There wasn't much Red left on the mountain that I could see from the bottom, but that one was still there.

Several hours later, we had all reached Level 26. I increased my Wisdom again by all five Stat points, bringing it up to a combined total of 28. Not a huge amount, but way more than the 18 I had been previously using as the baseline for learning Skills. Whatever new Rogue Skill I got from Waseem would also likely increase faster because of my Wisdom. At least, I hoped it would.

With nothing else to do, we all rode back to Kich's Keep to try and get our next quest. There was going to be a lot of pent up rage unleashed if we didn't get the quest this time around. I reminded the guys about the time we had to grind through even more levels than this when we were in Port Town, but Jason rightly noted that we were able to get the first quest at Level 20. We just waited until Level 23 to start it.

After passing almost a week in the mountains, the population of the Keep had swelled significantly. There were now more players than I could count easily, and I guessed that there were very few groups left in the "newbie" areas.

In order to not gather attention like we had the previous time, we unsummoned our horses far out from the city and walked into town. I put most of my gear away at the entrance gates and stashed away my daggers, so it looked like I was only wearing the most basic of items. Then I approached Sir Arthur by myself while the others hung out on one of the side streets.

The guys didn't understand why I wanted to do this at first, but when I explained that I was starting to get lots of messages from players asking how to conquer the Trolls, they understood. If I was able to get the new quest, I planned to simply accept the quest immediately, Conceal/Stealth, and high tail it out of there before anyone saw who it was.

Too bad I wasted my time.

"This is some total and complete bullshit!"

"You think the quest is broken, maybe?"

"No, Wayne, I don't think it's broken. I think that by now there would be lots of other quests that players could fulfill while they are grinding. Only we haven't really stopped to look for any more quests since we got back from the Monastery and have been just grinding. Those other quests would just be filler."

Sir Arthur had given me the same song and dance about not being ready yet to undertake the next task, and I had immediately returned to my group to tell them the crappy news. They were taking it much better than I was.

"Do you guys want to make the trip to see the Dwarves now or wait until after we get our next level? We will lose a whole day making the trip."

"There isn't any rush to see the Dwarves, as far as I understand it, Alex. We can hit that up after we get our level. Do you want to go somewhere different than the mountains, though? I'm kind of bored with the same mobs over and over again."

"I'm in agreement with Naugha. I think we should do something different. Maybe the forests that abut the beginning of the mountain range. We haven't really looked over there," Jason said. "What do you think, Dan?"

"Whatever will keep us far away from Kaitlin and their group. Wayne says she still hasn't forgiven me."

"Give it time, little buddy."

The woods would still be close enough that I could make it to the mountains and practice my climbing without losing much time. I agreed with the group, and we set off to find our next spot for grinding away.

Since we had spent so much time in the mountain area, we had mapped out where the mobs were and could easily avoid any spawn points. We followed Dan's lead to where the forest area met the mountains and let Dan go out and search.

Dan was looking for mobs to hunt as well as a place where we could potentially log off without coming back into the game in the middle of an angry bear or the like. It took Dan several minutes to map out the area, but he found both the mobs and a place for us.

There was a nest of Goblins situated amongst a copse of trees not far from where the forest ended. Dan counted ten different mobs, all Blue. These mobs would likely drop items, but I doubted there would be anything good. Before Dan made his first pull, I donned my Blacksuit and did a quick recon to make sure there wasn't a boss hiding amongst the pack.

It appeared to be your run of the mill Goblin outpost. Jason hit us with buffs, as did Dan, and we got ready for the first pull. A resounding sigh could be heard by all as we got ready to start the grinding yet again.

Dan pulled the full complement of the nest twice before we decided to call it a night. The Goblins were giving decent experience and had dropped a few items that would sell for 5 Gold each.

This was fine by me, as I wanted to keep working on my Climbing and see if there was any difference from increasing my Wisdom yet again. After bidding everyone a farewell, I headed back to the mountains.

The area we were fighting in was farther away from my original climbing routes, so I wasn't sure what I would find. If the paths were too difficult, or too easy, there were still some options back where I last climbed. It would simply be wasting time to get there.

I was pleased and surprised to find that the area near where I emerged was home to numerous paths of the best kind: ones that had an equal difficulty going up and down. I saw a couple that were White and two that were Blue. There were also smatterings of Yellow and

Red as the routes went higher. What I didn't see, however, was any Green, and that was fine by me.

I sidled up to the first White route, checked where I would want to go as I progressed, and started my climb.

When I first started, I would rush through the motions too quickly and burn way more Vitality in the process than I needed to. It took a while, but I learned a good rhythm that allowed me to make steady progress and keep my Vitality at a comfortable level. This way I could both ascend and descend without too many breaks.

Finding the route and increasing my Wisdom were definitely paying off. In just an hour, I had run the path twice and received five more points to my Skill. By the time I hit the bottom, the route was now all Green, and I moved over to the next one. An hour later and I had added another three points and turned the second route Green as well.

I only had two more hours left on my playing time before I would need to log off. Staying on for twelve hours would automatically send a warning to the player but also an update to AltCon. I didn't need that happening. I set a timer so I could get back to the log off spot and be out of the game before the witching hour hit.

But I was going to make full use of my time and tackle as much of the mountain as I could. At the rate I was going, I could max out my Climbing skill by the next day.

When the timer went off and I started riding back to the log off point on my summoned horse, my Climbing Skill had reached 93. I was dead tired, but when I looked back at the mountain I had to smile. There wasn't much of any color I could see but washes and washes of Green. I still had seven more points to go, but I was confident I could get those the next day.

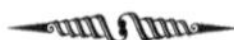

November 2nd, 2043

Those seven points I needed to get me to 100 in Climbing, and any other progression in levels and skills, were going to have to wait. Part of it was because there wasn't a single place for me to climb. In fact, there wasn't anything at all to see when I entered Resurgence but an empty room with two benches. I was on the verge of a mini freak out, in fact, thinking AltCon had caught up with what I was doing in the game and had set this room up as some type of interrogation chamber.

Thankfully, those fears disappeared slightly when Dan, Jason, and Wayne also entered the same room. Given that I believed AltCon was responsible for Robert Shoal's death, however, I still wasn't 100 percent at ease.

My trepidations finally left when Dan figured out what was going on. "Well this sucks! I hate doing these stupid AltCon quests!"

With that declaration, I opened my character's information windows and saw what Dan was talking about. Indeed, there was a blinking notification that I hadn't realized was there before.

Like I had grown accustomed to by now, I activated the information by focusing my vision on the notification and blinking, an intuitive—albeit initially confusing—method of selecting informational objects in virtual space that AltCon had designed for Resurgence. Doing this, dialogue popped up in front of me:

> *Welcome, Beta Testers, to the first tournament in Resurgence! As all players have now reached the mark of Level 20, AltCon is pleased to introduce the first Player vs. Player tournament.*
>
> *You have been transported to the Arena, a specially designed area in Tholtos only accessible during major events. Here you will face off against your fellow Beta Testers in a winner-take-all competition. As part of this event, we request players pay special attention to how their abilities interact with the other participants, as opposed to game generated foes.*
>
> *We look forward to the coming spectacle and your reports. The tournament will begin at 1100 game time. May the best team win!*

"Well that makes sense. AltCon had to wait until all the beta testers were Level 20 before they could start this 'AltCon quest.' While we don't have to wait long for it to start, I would really prefer to not do this one."

"I'm in agreement with you, Alex" Jason said. "However, I had no desire to try and make a stupid map, either, and we had to trudge through those quests as well."

Wayne was nodding his head. "I never played PVP in the past, and I have no experience that would help me be good at it. What about you guys? Any advice?"

We all shook our heads. PVP was something we had avoided in our gaming careers. Considering the predominance of PVP in most MMORPGs, this would seem kind of odd if I didn't know that we had all been selected for our group based off of our introverted personality scores. This kind of direct player interaction just wasn't part of the games that interested us.

"I imagine we will still do well, though. We've better gear than anyone else, and our levels are the highest."

"No such luck, Dan. When it comes to PVP, levels and gear are good, but they aren't anywhere close to the deciding factor. Our characters are just not set up to be a 'PVP group.' You'll see what I mean at the start. They'll go after Jason first and then proceed to take out the damage dealers. If they are smart, they will go after you before me since you have the ability to attack from range and have Snare. Taunt and aggro management skills mean nothing, so our warrior just becomes a guy that takes longer to kill than the rest."

"You think Jenny's group will have the same problems, Alex?"

"Yes and no. They will last longer than we do, for sure. If Tim can land a Charm on one of the players, that will effectively turn it into a five on three battle, and they can't hit their own player or risk killing that guy themselves. Kaitlin also has that Root spell that will make it so they can't move, which would be perfect against guys like me and Wayne."

After several more points on why we would suck at PVP, we heard an announcement in our ears:

"Greetings one and all to the first PVP tournament here in Resurgence. As a way to ensure ultimate surprise for each group of players, you will remain in your standby suite until just before your round begins. You will then be transported inside the Arena grounds. Winners of each round will return to their suite, and the losers will be transported to the stands to cheer on the competitors as the fighting continues!

"There is no experience loss within the Arena, and characters will not lose any equipment or money upon death. However, there will be a prize for the winner!"

We had all heard the same message, as the guys confirmed getting the same information. What we did not know was just how long we would have to wait until our first round would commence or how they decided to pair teams against one another. I thought it had to be random if they were going to make it fair.

"Prepare to enter the Arena in 10..." flashed across my screen followed by a countdown timer.

"Here goes nothing! Identify the healer and attack them first, then go after their damage dealers. Do exactly like what someone would do to us."

The timer hit 0 and we were transported to a large area with 15-foot walls surrounding us. A quick glance told me there were seats surrounding our area, but they were empty with this being the start of the tournament.

The area was a circle, but not large enough that the entirety of our beta players could sit around the outside. I imagined that the circle would get larger and the area for sitting would grow with it as the tournament continued.

As everyone was looking around, I engaged my Conceal. I held no illusions that we would win this competition, but I also didn't plan on being knocked out in the first round. One thing I was probably not going to be using was my Force Multiplier ring, although I knew I would be tempted the first time I saw us about to be defeated.

"Fuuuuuuuuuck! Seriously? Our first PvP experience and we have to go against the Legends," the Warrior across from us said. "Wait. Where the fuck is the fourth one? Their Rogue?"

I didn't wait to give any more instructions to my teammates, and I did not intend to let the other team get past their shock at facing a foe they didn't believe they could beat.

With the Conceal still on, I struck a blow into the back of what looked like their healer.

"Shit!" was all their healer was able to get out before I struck several more times and Dan landed a critical arrow into his chest.

The shock of the moment wore off, though, and the remaining three went at Jason full tilt. Dan was able to Snare one, and Jason stunned a second for a bit. In the end, though, we couldn't save our cleric.

With Jason gone, they went after me. We had quickly taken out their healer and then their top damage dealer, but the last two still killed me before the fight ended. My screen went blank. Just before I died, I saw the other team only had one guy at almost full health and the other almost dead. Dan and Wayne were still at full strength.

It was a couple of minutes before I popped back into the suite. It looked like we all arrived at the same time and with full health.

"Score a victory for us! Did anyone see anything that might help us in the next round?" I asked.

"That move you pulled in the beginning was perfect. I'm going to light up their healer from a distance as soon as we get there, so between us we might be able to take them down quickly. Other than that, I'll try to put a Snare on their damage dealer," Dan said.

"I'm kind of useless out there, guys," Wayne said. "I'll attack whatever Alex or Dan is attacking."

"It's like I said earlier, Wayne; we aren't built for PVP. You hit whatever Dan is hitting and Allister stays as far away from the rest as possible while still being able to heal. Allister, also, when you can, hit them with a Stun as well. I doubt we are likely to actually get any heals off, but try."

At that point, we got the notification that our next round was about to start

---

"We got to the third round. That's better than I thought we would do, to be honest. We barely made it past that second round, and the first round I attribute mostly to the shock of those guys having to face us right off the bat."

I nodded in Jason's direction but didn't answer him. Our teammates were down there on the field, and I was focusing on their progress. This was their fifth round, and they weren't showing any signs of losing.

As far as Tanks went, Jenny had the best build for PvP. She had her Bash that could Stun and a spell that did the same. On top of that, Jenny's gear added a bonus to her Bash. With her setup, Jenny was highly effective at controlling the secondary damage dealer long enough for the rest of the team to take out the other side's healer. The primary damage dealer wasn't a concern, either. Kaitlin would Root the player and hold them in place long enough for Tim to cast.

To this point, Tim had not failed on a single attempt to Charm the other side's top hitter. With Gary and their own damage dealer attacking the other side's healer, and Kaitlin and Tim throwing in whatever direct damage spells they had, our teammates were kicking ass and taking names.

Around us, the stands continued to fill. I was correct in my earlier assumption, and the stands continued to get larger.

Each round rarely took longer than a few minutes, and it wouldn't be long before this tournament came to an end. As I continued watching our friends, Gary landed the final blow on the competition's damage dealer—the only one left of their current opponents—and victory was theirs.

Our arena was not the only grounds used for the tournament. After we first lost and were transported to the stands, I could see multiple areas where teams were playing out the tournament. However, as teams were eliminated, the number of arenas shrank and the stands grew larger around the ones that remained. When it was all done, there would be only one arena and thousands watching as the two final teams went at it.

Our friends had a real shot at being in the final with their make-up being better suited for PVP and with Tim's ability to Charm being augmented so well by his Enchanter gear. What wasn't in question is which team would certainly be there in the end.

"I really hate these guys," I heard from two rows in front of me.

Now that Jenny and our friends had left the arena, two more teams were fighting it out, and it didn't take much to figure out who the target of that hatred was: the group most known for stealing other people's kills when they were in the lower levels were now dominating the tournament. They had a Warrior, a Paladin, a Rogue, and a Brawler. Each one was a damage dealer.

This was another way in which the mobs in the game were not like the players. It took some serious damage to disrupt a mob from casting a spell. Not so for the players. This is where the combo of Jenny's Bash and her Stun spell on the secondary along with Kaitlin's Root on the primary damage dealer worked so well. It gave Tim the time he needed to cast Charm through the limited damage he was taking.

With four damage dealers, he may not get enough time to make it count.

The fight was over quickly with the Stealers, as they had become known, winning easily. They had swarmed so quickly that the opposition had little to no chance.

I continued to watch as fight after fight played out. Before I knew it, the final was starting, and our friends were right there in the thick of it.

"That could have been us. Almost was," Tyke said sitting next to me. Wayne and Lug were chatting away, and the two casters from Tyke's group were engaging with Jason and Dan.

Tyke's group was very close to being in the finals. In fact, it was Tyke's group that Jenny and company had to beat to get to those finals. In the end, it was Gary's fists over Syphon's DoTs that won the day.

"Personally, buddy, I would rather see the 8 of you fight it out for the championship than see the Stealers get a shot at the crown."

"Yeah, those guys suck. But then again, no one likes them."

"Which is why it's going to suck even more when they win," I said.

Tyke shook his head at me. "You don't actually think that the Stealers can beat a team like that. They're the second strongest group in Resurgence!" Tyke said while pointing toward Jenny and company.

"And the strongest got knocked out in the third round," I said, waving my hand in the air. "It isn't about how good you are at playing the game, not with PVP. You know this."

Tyke lowered his head and shook it some more, but he was doing so in the sad way one does when they have admitted defeat. "At least they will still suck in the regular game."

"While that may be true, I imagine they will increase their attacks on other players, especially now they've seen they can't be beat."

"I really hate those guys."

Tyke and I turned our heads back to the center of the Arena where an announcer had just finished presenting the two sides to the audience and explaining the rules. Few were listening. The rules were no different, and everyone already knew who was about to fight.

The two teams disappeared briefly, having been sent to their suites before the actual commencement of the battle. After thirty seconds passed, both teams emerged onto the arena floor, and the crowd finally got into it.

I wasn't cheering along, though. I was watching too intently, as were my friends and our one-time teammates, Tyke and company. It's why all of us groaned at the same exact time. It was the moment we all saw the Rogue, Snitch, put on his conceal/stealth before Kaitlin could land her Root spell on him.

Not wanting to waste the mana, Kaitlin interrupted her spell and began casting it again on the Brawler, Zitt. The Root landed and I could see Tim start his cast to Charm the Brawler, the one of two likely to have the most DPS and could potentially sway the tide of the fight. That cast never landed though, as Snitch chose that moment to come out of his Invis and Backstab Tim all to hell. The damage instantly interrupted Tim's casting.

Jenny ran to Snitch to Bash and Stun him as quickly as possible, and Gary attacked him in the hopes of just killing him. The Stealers' Paladin, Yolo, wasn't idle, however, and he was Bashing and Stunning Tim as well.

The Stealers had made their entire career in Resurgence around taking the kills of other players or outright killing the players themselves. That was why they didn't make the rookie mistake of going after the healer first when an Enchanter was on the playing field. Sure, their Warrior, Dredge, would engage Kaitlin eventually, but everyone went at Tim first.

Kaitlin got off one heal, but it wasn't enough. Tim went down fast, and Snitch and Yolo immediately turned on Kaitlin to finish her off, too. It was just a matter of time until our remaining friends met their end. I hated to admit it, but the Stealers played the game perfectly for PVP. Sure, they were dicks that "cheated" to get ahead. But in this case, they were the dicks that won, and they did so without cheating.

Not without being dicks, though. As they closed in on the final blow to Jenny, they were laughing and taunting her. They called her all kinds of names and made far too many references to what they would love to do with her. I'm happy Lug was there to hold Wayne back, because I thought he was going to try and jump off the 15-foot wall at the last moments.

Thankfully it all ended soon after that. As soon as the tournament was over, we were all transported back to our last log out point. The tournament only took a few hours, so there was still plenty of time left in the day for gaming. But that wasn't what held our attention at the time.

I was heading over to where Wayne materialized when we all received a notification from AltCon:

Thank you all for your participation in our first Player vs. Player tournament. We noted no irregularities during gameplay and look forward to your reports. As promised, the winners of the tournament will receive a reward. In this case, the title of ***Tournament Champions*** *will be bestowed upon Dredge, Snitch, Yolo, and Zitt. The title will grant an increase of 5 to all Stats and an increase of 10 percent to all Resistances. Congratulations to our Champions, and be sure to look out for the next tournament opportunities!*

"Well there's three hours of my life I'll never get back. How about we just get back to being the bad asses of this game and never bring that crap up again."

"I would like to agree with you, Alex, but no can do," Wayne said. "Jenny is going to be pissed, for sure, and I see no reason to hold her back. I'm not going to dump salt in that wound, but I'm not going to ignore it, either." Turning to Dan, Wayne said, "As far as Kaitlin goes, I would suggest you have a case of amnesia on that perfect memory of yours. I can guarantee you she doesn't want a reminder of today."

"Oh, I have no intention of forgetting today, my friends. I plan to figure out how to beat those fuckers if we ever come up against them outside of a tournament setting. I can guarantee you they will take a shot if they get a chance," Dan said.

"Then I'm with you guys 100 percent. Whenever you figure it out, Dan, you let us know. It may not be anytime soon, but I'm sure our paths will cross at some point."

With the tournament out of the way, we continued to creep toward our next level for the rest of the day. And yes, I could go on and on about each specific pull, but that's not only boring as hell, it's also not the important thing that happened.

As one could guess, I finally achieved my Level 100 in the Climbing Skill. Getting there took a tad bit longer than I had hoped, given my previous progress, but it was all worth it.

The reason it took longer occurred when I reached Level 98. No matter where I looked, all I could see was Green. There wasn't another White patch of rock anywhere around me. I kept riding along the mountain side but had no luck. That is, until I doubled back to one of the first routes I tried. The one where the route went from Green to Red quickly.

That very location was the only place on the mountain that I saw anything that wasn't Green in color. In fact, the route above the Green was White with some Blue on the ascension and entirely Blue on the way down.

I had avoided Blue routes up until this point because I felt them unsafe, given my lack of a healer. I saw no other option, though, if I wanted to attempt to max out the skill.

I took a lot of time trying to determine the best path to take once I got past the initial Green route. I realized that all of my planning would have been for naught if I got up there and found the landscape didn't look the same from the ground level. But when it came to possibly falling to my death, I was happy being over prepared.

I ascended the Green route rather quickly and then rested just before the White and Blue began. I hadn't lost much in the way of Vitality on my short climb, but I wanted all of it for this next part. Once I was at full Vitality, I slowly began my ascent.

I stopped frequently to look over my route, but I found my initial evaluation of the path to be generally on point.

There was one moment where it all came a hair's breadth from crashing down, though. And by "all," I meant me. I saw that my only way up required me to over-extend to my right and get a Blue handhold. The foot hold I would need to reach was also Blue. I had seen this set of obstacles from the ground, but it didn't look as far away as it did now.

The only other options I had would require me to descend back to almost the beginning and go up a separate way, and that had even more Blue marks in the early going. I steeled my nerves for the exchange and reached for the hold with my hand and swung over my leg.

With fingertips gripping the left hold I reached the Blue marker and planted my right foot. The scree on the foot hold was looser than I thought, and my right foot slid off. With that jolt, my left fingertips slipped off the handhold and my entire body jerked to the right. I was only holding on by my right hand, and my Vitality began to drop rapidly. I was also on the verge of hyperventilating.

In a last-ditch effort, I swung my left hand up and over my right hand so that both hands were now on the same handhold. With my arms firmly locked on, I placed my feet against the side of the mountain so that they wouldn't swing free and so my shoulders didn't take all my weight. With that accomplished, I searched for the foot hold I fell off of earlier, scraped away any additional loose scree with my foot, and planted both of my feet on the hold.

I was now safe, but I was also now screwed. From the position that I was in, I wasn't going to be able to use my earlier route to go any further. Trying hard not to panic, I looked around and assessed my situation.

I saw one option—and only one—but it required a bit of jumping to make. If I missed this grab, I was going to plummet to my death. If I made it, I was home free.

Never one to back down from a challenge, I looked twice more at the angle I would need to travel. I moved my hands so that my right was now on top, as that would be the hand making the grab. I took two more solid breaths and then took a leap of faith to my right.

This time my luck held out.

I made the grab and was able to swing my legs to a sturdy and large foot hold. A separate foot hold was right next to the first. As I looked up, I saw that a few of the previously Blue markers had turned White. I checked my Climbing Skill and I was at 99. Pausing just long enough to recover some Vitality, I continued to climb.

As I reached what I believed to be the summit, I found yet another surprise in front of me. I had climbed up to the mouth of a cave that was hidden from view at ground level. It wasn't a large opening, probably just big enough for Wayne. At first glance, I didn't see anything inside the cave, either.

I continued my climb and pulled myself up into the entrance. Serendipitously, my Climbing Skill maxed out right as I entered the hole in the mountain. When I looked back the way I climbed, I saw that all of the holds were now Green and White. The fall I almost took was covered in all White holds, meaning it was considered to be a Level 100 climb. Only someone with a maxed out Climbing Skill, or very close to approaching it, could get up here.

I had engaged my Blacksuit as soon as I crossed the lip of the cave. With my enhanced vision, I could see that the cave ran back into the mountain for quite a distance, but there was no evidence of anyone being there. I decided to press my luck and explore just a bit.

I ended my exploration for two reasons. The first was that the cave turned at an angle and started descending into the mountain, and I was going to lose any light I had. The second and more important reason was what I found right around the bend in the cave.

The sides of the cave were riddled with veins of some kind of metal. Not being a Miner or a Smith, I couldn't identify Copper from Bronze, but I could clearly see when a cave was ripe for pickaxes. On the floor was a bit of the metal that was running through the cave's interior, and I attempted to loot it. The notification told me I had found an unidentified piece of metal. It certainly looked like something important, and by "important" I mean expensive.

The next notification asked me if I wanted to claim this mine for the East Range Mountain Dwarf Clan. I pocketed the metal and then made my way back to the entrance of the cave. When I looked around in more detail I saw a place where someone could likely brace a rope, and an idea began to form in my mind.

Before leaving the cave, I hit decline on the offer to claim the mine as a part of the clan. I had doubted that anyone else would be coming here in the near future, so I could stake the claim whenever I wanted. The unknown variable for my plan was the little piece of metal in my pocket. Once we traveled to see the Dwarves, I would know if my idea would bear fruit and whom I would need to involve.

November 3rd, 2043

"About bloody time!" Dan yelled out, as he was the last of us to hit Level 27. If it weren't for the steady supply of experience—as well as treats—to Broham, Dan would have leveled before me or Wayne.

After descending from the cave without any mishaps, I rode back to the log off point thinking about what we would do once Dan hit his Level. Naturally we wanted to try for the next quest, and I knew that the more time that passed, the more Wayne was chomping at the bit to go to the Monastery of Might. I only hoped that they would all want to see the Dwarves, as that piece of metal was figuratively burning a hole in my pack.

"Time to try for the quest again, then? Maybe ol' Arthur won't be such a douche about it this time," Dan said as we all summoned our mounts and got ready to ride back to the Keep.

"Third times the charm, huh?"

"Unless Alex is trying to light fires."

"Ooooh. Burn!" Jason said. Then he looked around and waited for a response. When he didn't get one, he shook his head. "Did you not see what I did there. Burn. He was trying to light fires. Really? Nothing?"

"It was good, Allicat. Don't be so needy."

"Hmm, that one wasn't half bad -- Alley Cat."

"Thanks! And secretly I was very jealous of your use of the word burn. Just don't tell the others."

"We're all standing right here Dan."

"It's not nice to eavesdrop, Wayne!"

It was good to see Dan back to his normal self. After the catastrophe at Jenny's place and the subsequent—and deserved—snubbing by Kaitlin, I didn't know how long it would take him to get out of his funk.

We made the trip to the Capitol in good time, now knowing quite well the layout of the north. Again, I approached Sir Arthur alone and told him that we were ready to answer the call.

Sir Arthur was nodding his head and looking around, finally stopping on me.

"Ahh, adventurer. I was looking for the rest of your party, but I see you came alone. I am afraid this is not a mission that could be handled by just one, though. Still, I will give you the details and allow you to gather your forces appropriately.

"After the defeat of the Trolls, His Majesty has sent caravan after caravan to reinforce the forces on the frontline. Most of these caravans have made the journey without problem but not all of them. I wish this was as simple as the bandits you dispatched before, but our information tells us it is much worse.

"Citizens of His Majesty's kingdom have been colluding with the forces of Loust. An underground network of usurpers has infiltrated and infected our land. It is unclear just how deep the treason has spread.

"His Majesty is calling on brave adventurers like yourself to set up an ambush against those who are intercepting the caravans. The goal is not defeating the forces but rather capturing their leader alive so that His Majesty's interrogators can question the traitor and learn who else is colluding with Loust.

"Will you help to set up this ambush and deliver the traitorous leader to His Majesty, alive and able to answer questions?"

"We will help set up the ambush and capture the traitor alive."

The golden glow that surrounded me was a welcome relief. The guys cheered as well when they received the glow.

"Excellent! Report to the caravan master once you have marshalled your forces! The Kingdom thanks you for your aid!"

I stepped back from Sir Arthur and activated my Conceal/Stealth. I didn't want to stand around and answer questions, and I had a really bad feeling about what was coming.

"I'm on my way back to you guys. But check the quest. Looks like we will be going to see the Dwarves after all."

What I had already seen, and what the rest were now learning, was that this quest was not for only one group. Hell, it wasn't even for two groups. This one required a total of 12 people, or three groups. I already knew a third group we could ask, but I had no idea how far along they were toward leveling to 27.

"Damnit, this sucks! I'm sure Jenny and company are almost to Level 27, but what other group could even be close? Oh, and will Kaitlin even want to be around me?"

"She'll probably be over it by the time they hit 27. That doesn't mean she will be that friendly, but I don't see us having a problem with grouping. What do you think, Alex? Tyke's group for the third?"

"That's what I was thinking, Wayne. You've got a good relationship with Lug. You want to reach out to him, or do you want me to reach out to Tyke?"

"You do the whole interpersonal thing better than I do. You take it, if you don't mind."

"Not a problem. For now, let's make our way to the gate between this area and Port Town's area. I figure we can log out for the night next to those guards, and in the morning, we can make our way to see Tibble and the clan. On our way to the mine, I'll crack open the journal and satchel, and we can see what Lady Tessa has in store for us."

CHAPTER 12

November 4th, 2043

"Don't keep us in suspense any longer, Alex. I want to know what we found."

I nodded my head in agreement toward Wayne and reached into my inventory to grab the journal first. When I accessed the book, I was able to read the words, but the other guys couldn't see what I did. I read to them out of the journal.

> *I admit it, I am more than a little worried. On one side we have my father, my brothers, and me all going on separate expeditions. On the other, father does not want us to speak about these quests, at all. Not to anyone else, and not to each other.*
>
> *This, in and of itself, is highly troublesome. Before any expedition can start, father has always insisted that we must gather as a family and discuss the journey ahead. We must speak through contingencies, what-ifs, and plan for the unavoidable, but for these expeditions, father wants us to do nothing of the sort.*
>
> *And if I think that he is being difficult with me and my brothers, the way he is treating Tessa is far more concerning. Sending her away, to hide in secret. There is little confusion that father doesn't*

believe we will return. It's all because of that blasted book that father found on his last journey.

Before he went to see the King, father joked about the contents of the journal and the claims made within it against His Majesty. But after he returned from seeing the King, he was not the same man. Father was frightened. Frightened by what he saw in the eyes of his Lordship.

When the messenger from His Majesty arrived, father handed out each of our assignments, one by one. He told us not to share the information with each other. Now I love father dearly, but I've never been one for following rules.

As soon as I saw that I was heading to one of the Monasteries, I immediately went to Constantine and asked him where he was going. Constantine admonished me for asking, quoting father's orders. I told him that I thought there was little to worry about as I was simply going to a Monastery. That got Constantine's attention, and he said he, too, was going to one of the Monasteries.

I volunteered that mine was the Monastery of Calm, and Constantine admitted that his was Might. I told Constantine that I had no idea where either Monastery was located, and Constantine showed me on the map he was given. With the little time that I had, I tried to commit that map to memory.

"We've got a location, boys! Check if you can see the new spot in your personal Maps."

"Got it, Alex! Looks to be south of the main road, down in the swamp lands. What fun," Dan said.

"Awesome. Let me keep reading."

Father also handed each of us a bundle of papers. I could tell from first glance that they were from the journal that had started all of our problems.

When I tried to read the papers, I found that father had enacted a powerful ward over the pages. The only way I would be able to read what was written was if all five bundles were placed next to each other, in turn nullifying the ward.

I had little chance of even convincing Constantine to let me see what father had given him, let alone my other two brothers, or father himself.

When I have finished with this quest, I have every intention of finding Constantine and assisting him on his journey. Father's rules be damned.

I looked in the satchel and found the bundle of papers that Tristan mentioned in his journal. I wasn't able to read anything from the pages, much as Tristan had been unable to unravel what they said. The only way we would be able to see what was there would be to finish Lady Tessa's quest.

"This doesn't really change anything for us. I mean, we aren't in any hurry to do the next Lady Tessa quest, and we know we still have to wait until another two groups hit 27 to do this caravan run. So I vote we keep going to see the Dwarves."

"I'm in agreement with Naugha. After a little break, we can decide if we want to do this next Monastery."

I nodded at Jason and then looked over at Dan.

"What? You seriously think I don't want to go see the awesome little folk?"

Laughing at Dan, I agreed with the group. "Unanimous it is. Let's go see our kin."

The trip took us little time, and we saw the tell-tale sign of the arrow announcing our arrival before we entered the camp. Knowing there were friendlies approaching, the Dwarves met us at the entrance to their mine and quickly began exchanging greetings with our group. Sharla said hello to all of us and then never left Jason's side after that. At least this time she didn't kneel when she approached him, so that was an improvement in all of our eyes.

Once all of the introductions were finished, Wayne went off to see the improvements the Dwarves had made to their little village around the mine. There were now many more buildings that had sprung up outside of it, and several trees had been felled to make additional room for the number of Dwarves that were working the caves. Wayne was keen to determine how much progress our friends had made on their battle skills and leveling.

Jason was in a deep conversation with Sharla, but this time it didn't seem to be about her treatment of him. As I got closer, I could hear the two debating the tactics of a battle cleric, and I heard Sharla giving various advice on upgrades Jason should make if he wanted to go that route.

Dan learned that with all the new buildings and the increase in population, someone had built a tavern. I doubted we would see Dan any time soon.

That left me with Tibble. This worked out perfectly, since it was Tibble's expertise that I needed at this moment.

"Care to walk with me a bit Tibble? I have a favor to ask of you."

"Ya know ya scare me when ya get like this."

"Come on! When have I ever done you wrong?"

"Oh, I'm not afraid for me or the boys. I'm fearing for whatever Dwarf you are about to take over the fire!"

"Ok. You may be right there," I admitted, sharing a smile with Tibble. "Let's get away from the others, though. This is something I have been waiting to unveil until after I had a chance to talk with you first."

Tibble nodded his head and followed me farther away from the camp and into the mine. There were no workers in the entrance at the time, as many were out with Wayne, knocking them back with Dan, or deep in the interior working on the rock. We had the place to ourselves.

"You know I'm not a Miner or a Smith. If I come across a piece of metal, I'm not going to be able to identify it at all. But I figure you, as not only a professional Miner, but also a Dwarf, could identify just about any piece of metal."

"Aye, lad. It's something we are born with, us Dwarves. You give us any piece of ore and we can tell you what it be."

"Excellent. I found this particular piece recently, and it looked to be something expensive. But again, I've got no idea," I said and removed the unidentified metal from my bag. "Do you know what this is."

Tibble's eyes went very wide and I had a feeling I found something way more valuable than I originally believed.

Tibble let out the smallest whisper, "Mithral."

I couldn't believe what I heard. The end-all, be-all of metals for the Dwarves, and I found a damn tunnel of the stuff. Not only did my idea have merit, I was going to have to rethink the entire thing.

I handed the piece of metal to Tibble and asked if he could identify the quality of the ore.

"Aye, Alex. I can tell ya by holdin' it just what ya found," Tibble said as he reached out to take the sample.

As soon as it was in Tibbles hand, his eyes got even bigger and he dropped the ore right on the ground. Before I could say anything, Tibble started shaking slightly and had to sit on the ground. I kneeled down slowly, placing myself at eye level with Tibble.

"What is it?"

"It's Pure, Alex. It's Pure Mithral. I've never seen or heard of anything of the like. That bit right there is worth more than I can imagine."

I took Tibble's hands in mine and helped him to stand back up.

"Send a runner to the King Under the Mountain. Let him know your adopted kinsmen are here with an offer. But don't say about what. I imagine he will come but will take his time doing so. That will be just fine for what else I have planned for our visit here."

Tibble nodded his head in agreement but didn't say anything.

"Next, I'm going to need a rope that will give a magical increase to someone's ability to climb. Is that something they have Under the Mountain?"

"Aye. Dwarves ain't really built for climbing, as ye can see. We need lifts to get up and down shafts or, for them harder spots, a rope. Dwarves been makin' em since the beginnin' of time. It's the only thing we craft other than armor and weapons. But ain't something we sell to outsiders. Gotta worry about thieves."

"Good thing we are kin, then."

Tibble smiled at that and nodded his head.

"What's the best you can get me?"

"If you're willing to spend the money, Alex, you can get yerself one that will make you and yers full expert climbers."

"What would that run?"

"Ten Platinum."

I handed over the money to Tibble, who couldn't believe I was carrying around so much cash. "Ya sure 'bout this? You can get lots cheaper with still great magic assists."

"Trust me when I say that the investment will be fully recuperated."

Tibble walked off and grabbed two different Dwarves. He sent them both to fulfill the tasks I had laid out. With that finished, Tibble walked back to where I was standing and looked back down at the piece of metal in my hands.

"Tibble," I said, waiting for the Dwarf to acknowledge me.

After a heartbeat, he locked eyes with mine. "Not a word to anyone about this."

"Not a soul would be believin' me anyway, Alex. But not to worry, ye have me word."

"Wait. Back up. Why the hell were you climbing to begin with?"

"Duh, Allicart! Why does any man climb a mountain?"

"Because it's there?"

"What? No! To get the girl, fool!"

Jason turned away from Dan and asked, "There wasn't a girl involved, was there?"

"Ha! Of course not. You were actually spot on. After you guys logged out that first evening, I started walking around the mountain, and I noticed that it looked perfectly flat. You know how that would be really weird for Resurgence, since everything looks and feels like the real world."

They nodded along as I explained my contrived story. "So while I was running my hand against the side of the mountain I started to feel variations. And I grabbed on to a couple and tried to pull myself up. The first few times, I just kept sliding back down.

"But when I finally earned the first point in Climbing, the whole rock wall started to glow with colors. Green through Red. I couldn't make heads or tails as to what I was seeing, but I kept trying to get up the mountain all the same.

"By the time I had mastered the Skill, I was seeing routes everywhere I looked."

"And you just happened to find this cave during your last foray up the mountain?"

"Don't give me that side-eyeball, Dan. It was literally the only part of the mountain that wasn't Green and that I could ascend to try and max out the skill!"

"Well, I don't care if you found it on the first climb or the last. What are we going to do about it?"

"I've got a plan, Wayne."

"Care to share?"

"No."

"What do you mean, 'no'?"

"Look, we both know how this is going to go. I tell you my plan, you complain that I am being selfish, I in turn say I'm not asking for anywhere near enough, Allister and Dan agree with my first suggestion, and then we overrule you and you go away mad. So how about we just skip to the end, where we just go with my idea and you see how it all plays out."

Wayne didn't say anything for several moments.

"You're a dick sometimes, you know that, Alex?"

"Yes. I do. So we good?"

"Yeah, just don't..."

"I know, man. I know," I said. Then, just to make Wayne feel a little better, I added "No one but Tibble in the clan has reached Level 20 yet, so they couldn't even get to this mine. If they could, they wouldn't likely be able to hold it anyway. I'm working the best angles I can. So just trust me."

The runner Tibble sent to inform the King of our arrival had returned. The King said it would be another two days before he could arrive.

This sat fine with me, as I had every intention of liberating the second level of the mine we already had before the King showed. The Dwarves would likely accompany us again on this raid, and with their new levels, they were to be an asset and not a hindrance as they were before.

The second level of the mines only allowed for a ten-person raid, meaning the four of us and six of Tibble's men. Well, five. And one battle Cleric. Sharla made it quite clear that she would accompany us on our raid. "If ye think I'm gonna be partin' from the side of the Chosen One when you be goin' into a fight, ye be daft."

"Really? Chosen One? I thought we were past that crap! It's just Allister, Sharla."

"Makes no difference what I be callin' ya. I ain't to be moved."

"I welcome your abilities, Sharla. But our Cleric already has protectors. You need to make sure the Clan doesn't die down there. Allister is always our first concern."

Sharla nodded her head but wagged a finger at me, letting me know I had better not fail.

The whole show of force was wasted.

My group had raised 11 Levels since we last helped the East Range Mountain Clan, and Tibble's Dwarves had gained eight to ten levels of their own. Hell, the Dwarves probably didn't even need us for the fight.

Tibble admitted at one point that they had tried to enter the lower levels to scout out the next group of targets, but the mine wouldn't let them enter without the original raid leader. Namely, me.

Every mob, to include the so-called Boss, was green to my group. We ended pulling mobs non-stop and were done in a little over two hours. The gear that dropped from the higher level Orckin in this part of the mine was good for either selling or breaking down at the Smithy for base parts. I left the gear to Tibble and told him to do with it what he wanted. The drops from the Boss were also lower than what we were all using, so I allowed Tibble to divvy those out appropriately.

It was only the amount of progress we had made in our other endeavors that kept me from truly being angry at myself for not checking the mine with each consecutive level we earned. Opening the mine would have been far more entertaining than grinding, that's for sure. I kept telling myself it was a benefit to the Clan if nothing else.

When we reached the end, I again granted the rights to the mine to the East Range Mountain Dwarf Clan and asked Tibble to do an assessment of what ore was available for mining.

As it turned out, the second level of the mine was rich in the opposite ore from Fermium. Namely, Ertunium. According to Tibble, where Fermium would add a sizeable physical damage modifier to Dan's arrows, Ertunium would add a magical attack.

I showed the confusion on my face, and Tibble was happy to explain. Fermium offered the kind of punch you would need to get through armor. Sure, it could be magically imbued, but that only meant it could damage magic armor. An Ertunium arrowhead, on the other hand, was of little use against a breastplate. However, a summoning is highly steeped in magic and highly susceptible to high damage magic arrows.

I mentioned the golems that spawned during one of our most recent battles, and Tibble exclaimed this was exactly the type of thing an Ertunium blade or arrowhead would be perfect for.

When I started asking how long it would take him and the teams to mine, process, and fabricate the arrowheads for Dan, Tibble was way ahead of me.

"Give me and me boys a couple of weeks, and the Ranger can have his usual allotment of 300 arrowheads for the Fermium and the Ertunium."

Since we figured we would spend most of the day down in the second level of the dungeon, we found ourselves with little to do after escaping topside. Wayne suggested we throw a party to celebrate the addition to the mine, and the flood gates were open.

The level of cheering tuned me in to the fact that this suggestion was exactly what every Dwarf from the clan was waiting for. Before I could even suggest having myself or one of the guys go back to Port Town for supplies, Tibble and his Dwarves started dragging out tables and benches. And booze. Lots and lots of booze.

I noticed that there wasn't much in the way of food, though. If we didn't get some food in us, there was going to be a lot of drunk adventurers, and in a very short time.

I suggested some nourishment to go with the libations. Tibble and the Dwarves looked at me like I had just ruined the party, but he sent a runner to the Tavern for food anyway. Soon enough, a number of Dwarves arrived carrying numerous plates of some very tasty looking vittles.

And with that, the party was on. It would go on throughout the night and some would even make it into the morning. I didn't make it much past the first four hours, but I clearly remembered seeing Dan slow dancing with Sharla before I passed out into oblivion.

November 5th, 2043

One of the great things about Resurgence is if you pass out in the game from over intoxication, the RAC automatically logs you out of the game. This way, you don't find yourself so blasted that you violate the in-game rules for how many hours you can stay online. The downside is that you can't log back in until your character is deemed to have the alcohol out of their blood stream.

With the amount I drank the night before, I was several hours late getting online.

Everyone was understanding. At least, I think they were. Honestly, they weren't even bothering with me at all. Instead, Dan was pleading with Wayne while Jason kept up a steady stream of something that had Wayne laughing and Dan repeatedly shooting Jason the evil eye. I had obviously missed something.

"I've heard of having a bad rebound. And sure, all of us have woken up next to someone that we would rather forget. A bear trap if you will."

Having no idea what was going on but never one to interrupt a Dan roasting session, I looked over to Jason and joined in. "What's a bear trap?"

"You've heard of hunters being out in the forest and they accidently step on a bear trap? Wham! Next thing they know, they are forced to make a decision. They can stay there and face their fate, likely dying of thirst, or they can cut off their own leg to get away."

"Ok. I think it would be smarter to take whatever they used to saw their leg and open the trap, but I'll play along."

"Thanks for being a team player. Well in this case, Dan found himself in a bear trap this morning."

"Dan got left in the woods?"

"No, Alex. That would have been a more pleasing fate," Dan said.

"Right he is, Alex. Dan, you see, got caught under a Sharla."

"Dan. You didn't."

"Seriously, I don't remember."

"She has a beard!"

"I know she has a beard, Alex! Everyone can see she has a beard!"

"What is Kaitlin going to say?"

And with my own question, I realized exactly what the scene was that I had walked into. Jason had been ribbing Dan endlessly, Wayne was laughing his ass off, and Dan was pleading with Wayne not to tell Jenny.

"Man, screw you guys! Seriously! Guy maybe sleeps with one bearded woman and everyone thinks it's the funniest thing ever!"

As Dan stormed off, I looked over to Wayne. "You going to tell Jenny?"

"About this? Hell no. At least not until after Dan actually hooks up with Kaitlin. I still have high hopes for our crazy friend, despite his most recent setbacks."

"Well I wish him all the luck in the world. But you know there is no way Jason is going to let him forget this any time soon. And you need to make sure he is in lock step about only ribbing him amongst the group."

"I wouldn't take this away from Jason for all the Platinum in Resurgence, but I will make sure that he is on the same page when it comes to place and time for jokes."

With that fiasco over, I went and found Tibble to check on any updates concerning the King Under the Mountain. According to his most recent information, the King would arrive at midday, which was quickly approaching. I once again tried to explain to Tibble how my negotiations with the King would go, but he waved me off again, saying he trusted me.

As with the previous visit by the King, there was little fanfare to announce his arrival. One moment everyone was working along, and the next, Dwarves started taking a knee. I looked up and saw him for myself, Lord Steelhammer, King Under the Mountain. I also took a knee, as was the protocol for one named kin among the clans. Steelhammer took note of my actions and nodded once before barking out for everyone to stand up.

"It be good seeing ya Alex! But I've gots to be sayin' you 'ave some nerve calling the King to you!"

"My friends and I apologize greatly, Lord Steelhammer. I hoped to tackle numerous challenges simultaneously and save us all precious time in the bargain. As you already know, I am sure, the East Range Mountain Dwarf Clan has taken the second level of this mine and will now be paying twice as much into the tax coffers of your Kingdom.

"My kin and I were diligently undertaking that task while a messenger was sent to simply inform you of our arrival with our clansmen. I apologize for the inconvenience it has brought you."

The King looked at me with his one good eye for several moments before he finally reacted. With a spit on the ground, he looked me dead in the eyes and asked, "You plannin' to rob me?"

"What? No! What could have possibly given you that idea?"

"Because the last time you talked this sweet 'round me, you were fixing to pull Mithral from right out of me caves. So I ask ya again, you plannin' on doing it again?"

"Lord Steelhammer, that wasn't robbery. That was simply negotiating. Although if that's how you see things, you may think I'm trying to steal your whole kingdom when we're done tonight."

"Wat da bloody hell you gettin' at, Alex?"

Instead of answering, I started whistling and walking away. "Tonight, Lord Steelhammer. All will be clear tonight."

"Bloody Elf gonna be the death of me and me whole clan."

“Out with it, Elf. We been patient enough.”

“So you have, Lord Steelhammer, and I thank you for your calm nature. Several days ago, my friends and I were fighting north of Kich’s Keep alongside a vast mountain range. I assume you know it.”

“Aye, we be knowin’ it. What of it?”

“During the downtime between battles, I began exploring the mountains. To my surprise and total shock, I uncovered a cave entrance that descended into the mountain. As I investigated, I saw that this was no simple tunnel but a vast deposit of thick ore running straight through the rock. Once I knew what I had found, I took a small sample from the ground, a piece sitting freely on the rock. With that in hand, we hurried here to our kin.

“I am under no illusions that the East Range Mountain Clan Dwarves could hold such a location. They have grown in strength, but they would still need another generation before they had the manpower to build and hold a mine of this nature.

“I thought I could sell the rights to the King, since I know he has an unquenchable need for ore to build up his fighting forces.

“But in the end, I went with the only logical choice. My friends, the Dwarves. And no better friend is there than the King Under the Mountain himself. Should we come to terms, Your Highness, the mine will be yours.”

“You wasn’t jokin’, Elf, when you said you was gonna take me kingdom. With that bloody speech, ya likely gonna try to take me first born along with me throne!”

“You can keep the throne.”

“Ha!” King Steelhammer said while slamming his ale of mead against the table. “Ya always make me laugh, Alex. I’ll give ya that at least. You want to do terms first or show me the goods?”

I flipped the chunk of Pure Mithral to the King and watched his one eye as it landed in his hand. His reaction wasn’t as noticeable as Tibble’s shaking, but his eye did go very wide as he said, “Impossible.”

“Tibble said the same.”

"And there is a mine filled with this substance."

"I have no idea if it is exactly the same quality, but I can attest that what ran through the walls of that cave looked exactly like what you have in your hand."

The King took his time rotating the piece of Mithral between his fingers before finally speaking. "What be your terms, Alex."

"A very fair deal, Your Majesty. The East Range Mountain Clan will get 15 percent of each type of ore that is collected from the mine, to be delivered once a month, on the first day of each month."

"Fifteen percent? Is that all." The King shouted. "You sure you don't want anything else?"

"Of course I do."

"That was that sarcasm thing you tall ones love so much."

"Mine wasn't."

The King grumbled and then nodded at Alex to go on.

"A full complement of High Quality Mithral Armor to be built to Naugha and Allister's specifications in two months' time, Mithral Arrow Heads for five quivers comparable to the size carried by our Ranger in one week's time, and one last thing."

The Kings eye kept getting larger and larger as I continued with what I wanted. Finally, he said, "You really do want me throne, don't ya?"

"Nothing so grand, Your Majesty. Lastly, I only want that my friends and I be named as Ally to the Dwarves Under the Mountain."

"And what's from stopping me and my boys from going up to that mountain and taking what we want?"

"Nothing. Although by the time you got up there and found it, you would already find the King's men toiling away at the ore."

Lord Steelhammer gave a small harrumph at that comment but didn't continue with that line of threats. "Look. Let's talk about this. First I've got to see this mine before I can be making any pacts."

"The Ally to the Dwarves is non-negotiable."

"Ya just gonna ignore my train of thought there, huh?"

"Sooner we get on the road, Your Majesty, the sooner you can see the mine."

The King mulled it over some more and acquiesced on the Ally condition. He then countered my offer with a sum of 10 percent for the Clan, only one full suit made to either Naugha or Allister's dimensions in three months-time, and three quivers of arrows in two weeks-time.

"Now this be the best deal I'm gonna..."

"Done. Deal. The suit will be to Naugha's specs."

The King stopped mid-sentence and looked around at the rest of the Dwarves. No one was saying a word, and all eyes were on me. Finally, the King turned his eye at me and said, "Why ya sneaky, no good Rogue. That was exactly what you wanted the whole time wasn't it?"

"Indeed. I figured I would just get us there quicker by having you offer it to me. Now let's get some rest, and we'll move out at first light."

After everyone broke to make camp and get some sleep, I approached Tibble to ask him for one more small favor.

"It will only be for a couple of days, Tibble. I promise."

"I trust ya, Alex. I just don't see why ya need it."

"The King has now been bested twice by some Half-Elf Rogue. He's an honorable man, but if he sees a loophole to exploit, getting back some of what he's lost, he's going to take it."

Tibble thought it over and then nodded. "Alright, Alex. It's yours."

With that, we both headed off for our tents.

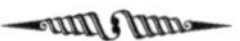

November 6th, 2043

"And how the bloody hell are we supposed to get up there?"

"Not to worry, Your Majesty. I already have that figured out."

I moved over to the side of the mountain and looked at the hand-holds in front of me. I told Jason on the way out to the mountain that I had almost died the last time I tried this. If I fell to my death, Jason was to be quick with a cast to resurrect me back to my body.

As I prepared to climb, I looked back toward the King. "This is the other reason why I wasn't concerned about you coming out here and finding the mine for yourself."

"Damn Elf has an answer for everything."

The previous route I took was still the fastest up the side of the mountain. Only this time, I was prepared for the spot that required me to overextend my body, and I executed the move flawlessly. The next move would require me to jump again, and here is where I had the most trepidation. Without wasting any unnecessary time, I made my leap, hearing the gasps below me as I grabbed the handhold.

"Damnit, be careful, ye fool Rogue," Tibble yelled up at me.

I ignored the chatter from below and finished my climb up to the cave entrance. As before, I engaged my Blacksuit as soon as I made the summit and proceeded into the cave. It remained clear, and this time I hit accept when I was asked if I wanted to claim this mine for the East Range Mountain Clan.

With that done, I lowered the rope I had purchased and waited for the King to arrive.

The King made it up the side of the mountain and took his time recovering his Vitality before finally standing up.

"Have ye checked for enemies?"

"I have, and the way back is clear up to the point where the tunnel begins to descend down into the mountain. Past that, I can't say for sure."

"So what's from stoppin' me from just walking back there and taking this mine for me own?"

"Because this mine already belongs to the East Range Mountain Dwarves."

"Lad, I was just waiting for you to say that."

The King walked over to the side of the Cave and yelled down for Tibble. Despite the height we were at, I could clearly hear Tibble respond.

"Tibble, you are to hand over the rights of this mine to the King Under the Mountain, as stipulated under Dwarven Law and Family Code."

There was a pregnant pause while everyone took in what the King had just said. After what seemed an eternity, Tibble responded.

"I can't do that."

The King's face immediately became red with anger, and he yelled down at Tibble, "How dare you? What do you mean you won't follow the laws of our people?"

Tibble's response was music to my ears. "I didn't say I wouldn't, Your Majesty. I said I can't."

"You see, Lord Steelhammer, I asked Tibble to name me head of the Clan last night." The favor I had asked of Tibble had paid off.

With the red still in his face, the King spun on me. "And why shouldn't I kill ya right here and claim victor's rights over this mine?"

I had already stepped back into the shadows of the cave when I saw the King start to get mad. When those words left his mouth, I wrapped myself in my Blacksuit and went over to the rope leading down to the ground.

One of the great things about the mechanics of Resurgence, a 100-foot rope didn't need to be recoiled to go into my inventory, I simply had to touch it and place it there.

With the rope snuggly in my bag, I climbed several feet down the side of the mountain and then called up to the King who was looking around for me. "Because I can simply climb down this mountain, Your Majesty. How will you get down?"

The King kept looking around for me, and his gaze crossed over my Invisible form more than once. The fury that was on his face finally died down, and he stepped back from the ledge.

"Fine, Elf. Ya win this one. Can't blame me for tryin' ta find a work around. I'll not threaten ya again, I swear on me clan and me family."

I climbed back up into the cave and walked past the Dwarf before I became visible again. "I don't blame you at all. In fact, I would have been disappointed if you hadn't tried."

Now that all of the dramatics were over, I guided the King back into the tunnel to where I had found the ore. As soon as the King was close, he ran toward the bend in the tunnel. It was almost as if he could smell the ore.

The King ran his hand over numerous veins and finally turned to me with a huge smile on his face. "It keeps going for quite some ways, Alex. What we've got here is mostly High Quality with a few spots of Pure. But lad, it's all Mithral. This is the jackpot of mines."

"And if you swear on clan and family to honor the bargain made last night before the East Range Mountain Dwarf Clan, I will transfer the rights to you, Lord Steelhammer."

The King Under the Mountain grasped my forearm in his hand, and I did the same. "Aye, lad. On me family and me clan, I honor the bargain we made."

After descending, I left Tibble to hammer out all the details with Lord Steelhammer. I also transferred the Head of Clan title back to Tibble.

We once again said our goodbyes to the Dwarves and saddled up on our horses. "Let's go see what kind of progress our teammates have made, shall we?"

Under the subsection of Titles on my character was a new addition: Ally to the Dwarves Under the Mountain.

AltCon Headquarters

"The Old Man has been understanding about the delay thus far, but he grows wearisome about the lack of progress. Let's have the latest update."

"Yes sir, Mr. Jolston. As you know, during our efforts to correct the vast number of problems that arose from the late Director's actions, we uncovered places within the conditioning framework that allowed for improvements. However, that meant we had to bring in more specialists, none of whom had clearances for the project."

"I am aware, Mr. Tillson. How did you get around the problem?"

Tillson held up a pen and said, "We asked them to simply improve parts of the whole." He then began to break the pen down and separated out each piece. The spring, case, cap, clip, and insert. "They never knew what each piece went to, but they were still able to make vast improvements on the individual elements. There was some tweaking that needed to be done to 'put it back together.' The good news is, our earliest simulations show the effects will be more significant than they have in the past."

Jolston leaned forward and stared back at Tillson for several moments before speaking in a low voice. "It was increased effects that drove the Director—sorry, former Director—to implement his harebrained scheme. Are you telling me, Tillson, that you are after similar results?"

"Absolutely not, sir!"

"Then you better explain this with a little more clarity. Remember, when I'm finished here, I'm heading up to see the Old Man and deliver your report."

Tillson swallowed audibly and looked at the other men and women in the room. No one was coming to bat for him on this one.

"What I meant, sir, was that the process itself has been improved. We were always aware that there was the potential for bleed-over in the conditioning. We knew a small percentage, 7 percent at most, could have various states of awareness to the conditioning."

Jolston nodded his head. "As test cases, the Old Man was aware of these numbers and deemed them within the margin for risk. The point of this was to test its effectiveness and make corrections before the full launch of the RACs to the greater population."

"That's exactly what I'm saying, sir. The screw-up by the old Director allowed us to move that timeframe up dramatically. Since we had to strip and recalibrate most of the equipment for the conditioning, we were able to engineer upgrades now that we can test on the same control group."

"And your expected improvements to the conditioning?"

"Without seeing the first set of numbers following today's finished treatment, I can't say for certain, but our projections have them coming in at just over 1 percent awareness."

Jolston leaned back in his chair and smiled. Now that was news he could bring to the Old Man. "Excellent work, team. You've done amazingly well given the schedule you were given and the parameters of secrecy that had to be put in place. I will commend you all to the Old Man when I see him."

"Thank you, sir. Is there anything else we can assist with?"

"When the day is done, I want those numbers on my desk. I have a feeling the Old Man is going to want to see me again soon after he hears this update, and I want to have that data with me when I go."

Jolston looked around the room one last time and began to stand from his chair. "If there is nothing else, I will leave you..."

From the back of the room Jolston heard someone whisper, "Tillson, tell him!"

Terrence Jolston slowly sat back into his chair and then looked down the table at Tillson. "Tell me what?"

Tillson was staring daggers at one of the technicians on the other side of the table. Finally, he began to speak. "As you are aware, sir, our core group of players are single, with little family. However, there remains about 25 percent of our control that have spouses or significant others."

"I am aware of the numbers, Tillson. Get on with it."

"The game has been leading to some serious arguments."

Jolston sat back in his chair a little more and waved for Tillson to continue.

"As you are aware, during the initial installation or subsequent maintenance calls, our RAC technicians installed audio mics in the homes of our test subjects."

"Of course I am aware, Tillson. I came up with the idea."

"Yes, sir. Sorry, sir."

"Get to the bloody point."

"We've been picking up chatter from some of those with spouses and significant others. They don't like the way the game has been dominating the lives of their loved ones. Some have asked their partners to leave the game and go back to regular work."

"And you weren't planning on telling me this? Why?"

"The number is not significant, sir. We factored in that some players would leave voluntarily as it was."

"And how many have so far?"

There was a long, pregnant pause.

"None, sir."

"That's right, Tillson. None. The conditioning has been working, and they have no desire to leave Resurgence, which is an extension of AltCon."

"That's why my suggestion is perfect, Mr. Jolston!" yelled out the man who initially whispered to Tillson.

"And you are?"

"Henry, sir. I work on..."

"I don't care, Mr. Henry. What's your suggestion?"

"Right. Well, you see, I figured if the conditioning was working so well on our subjects, then why not have a 'Family Day,' if you will, and have all the spouses and whatnot come in and see what their loved ones are doing. And when they get in the RACs, we zap 'em!"

"Zap 'em?"

"Well, you know, put them into a contained experience where they could see the world for what it is, but really we lay a dose of conditioning on them."

Jolston didn't say anything for several minutes. For some in that room, that was the longest three minutes of their lives, Mr. Henry included.

"I'll take this to the Old Man when I see him later today. I think the idea has merit. However, I will likely use a different set of words to explain what will be done. I don't think he would appreciate the term, 'zap 'em.' Neither do I, for that matter."

"Yes. Of course, Mr. Jolston. Sorry."

"No need to apologize, Mr. Henry. I appreciate the courage to speak out and the initiative of devising a suitable solution. I don't have to worry that such things will be kept from me in the future, do I, Mr. Tillson?"

The ice in Jolston's voice was unmistakable. The question was largely rhetorical, as everyone in the room knew the answer. Still, Tillson could be seen shaking his head vigorously when he responded. "No, Mr. Jolston. I'll make sure you are fully informed about everything."

"Good. Dismissed."

CHAPTER 13

On the ride back to the Keep, I contacted Tyke. "Hey, Tyke. Alex here. Got a moment?"

"Sure, Alex. What's up? Got more gear to sell?"

"Nah, nothing like that. When you guys reach your Level 27, go see Sir Arthur. When you do, contact me. Don't worry, you will understand why. We've already got things ready."

"Ooh, mysterious. I like it. We are almost to Level 26 now, so will probably be two or three more days. Can you guys wait that long?"

"No worries. We don't really have much of a choice. Again, you'll understand when you see Sir Arthur. Good hunting."

After finishing with Tyke, I informed the group that our third party was a few days out from leveling to where we needed them. This was met with groans, but there wasn't much else we could do.

In the meantime, we wouldn't stay idle. The group had elected to start mapping out the swamps in preparation for tackling the next part in Lady Tessa's quest. No one wanted to start it up right away, but the more prep work we did, the sooner we could attack it after finishing the storyline.

When we weren't mapping and gaining experience, I planned to talk with Waseem and see what was next on the docket for my Rogue specialization skills.

"Back so soon? I didn't think I would see you for another week at least."

Waseem was in his usual spot at the Pit, and I sat next to him once I reached his table.

"You were right about the different routes. Took no time for me to learn once I started getting really into it."

"Excellent. Then we can begin the next part of your training," Waseem said and walked over to the side of the room. "Climb these rafters here to the ceiling."

As soon as I focused on the structure I saw a route that would lead me up. Not waiting for any further instruction, I bounded up.

"Perfect. Now come back down. I want to show you something."

Once I was back down and standing next to Waseem, I looked to where Waseem was pointing, a piece of wood on the route I had taken up.

"What do you see here?"

"There is scuffing from where my feet were on the wood."

"Exactly. Any investigator worth their salt would note something like this and follow the trail as it led up. Now put on these boots."

Waseem handed me a pair of pure black boots that slipped over my regular armor. They had a +10 to Climbing Skill. The ascent was already very easy, so I didn't notice any difference.

When I came down, though, I couldn't see any new scuff marks from my climb, and I purposely used different holds to get up.

"Covers my tracks. Excellent."

"To a degree," Waseem said. "Look closer."

When I did, I saw thin black fibers embedded in the wood that must have come from the boots themselves. I tweezed one out with my fingernails and showed it to Waseem.

"Now it would take a pretty damn good investigator to notice that, but it is still leaving a trail. A Master Thief doesn't leave a trail."

"So, let me guess. The way around it is through the same tool we use for all things Rogue—Shadows."

"Bingo."

I looked at the wood that made up the rafters and the side wall of the Pit. I was trying to work out how this would work on my own.

"So the shadows have to take on some substance then, right? Become a bit corporeal in order to support the move but not leave a trace?"

"In a nutshell, yes. Any time you are undertaking a Rogue action, you should already have your Blacksuit on. In that regard, the transition becomes much easier. Theoretically, you could do it without the Blacksuit. Do you see the gap between the rafters above?"

I looked up and saw where Waseem was pointing. There was a large gap between each of the supporting beams. I could make a jump from one to the other, or swing between the two, but I wasn't tall enough to reach out and grab the second from the first. Wayne might have been able to, but there was no way I could have.

After nodding my head in affirmation to Waseem's question, he said, "I want you to go up there and suspend yourself between the two. Reach out and hold on to each side."

"Not happening. No way my arms or legs would cover the distance."

"And yet..."

Without saying another word, Waseem ran up the side of the wall and leaped over to the beams that ran along the ceiling. Immediately after landing on the beam he reached across to the other side and started to fall. And then stopped.

But there he was, hanging without any support between the beams. I couldn't see the shadows coming off of him, either.

With a flourish, Waseem flipped in the air and landed in a crouch at my feet. He then slowly stood up and bowed dramatically in my direction. I was damn impressed and clapped without even thinking about it.

"Damn show off."

I turned and saw Stan leaning against the side of the Pit. One moment no one was here, and the next Stan was before us.

"How long have you been here?"

"What makes ya think I ever left?"

"Sneaky Halfling," Waseem said, but smiled in Stan's direction.

"How was that even possible?" I asked.

"Waseem there is a Master Thief. I ain't got many kind words to say about the pompous bag, but there is none better at the trade. What you just saw is something only a Master could do."

"And Dhalean is a Master Assassin. All Rogues of our level can don a Blacksuit, but no one can top Dhalean's skill when it comes to infiltrating a location and hitting a target. He can't steal a purse to save his life though."

"That's why you were to teach me Disembowel?" I asked Stan.

"Aye. It's one of the Assassin's maneuvers for taking down a mark in one shot. It's the easiest of the lot to learn, but there are many more you won't be getting an education on."

Turning toward my newest instructor, after nodding to Stan in understanding, I asked, "And when we are done here, Waseem, I will be able to do that?"

"Not a chance! You are never going to be a Master Thief, Alex. We aren't training you for that. You are going to be our Jack-of-All-Trades.

"But when I am finished, you will be able to Scale any wall. So let's get started."

It only took me an hour to get my first success with the shadows acting as assists for my holds. As soon as the first victory was noted, I received the prompt informing me that I had learned a new Skill: Scaling. I was at Level 1.

As soon as I registered the new Skill, I told Waseem and Stan, and they began to run me through various routines within the Pit that would allow me to increase my Skill's level. Over the next two hours, I gained another 10 points.

"From this point on, start looking for more challenging ways to tackle a climbing problem. Look for the difficult routes, and then use your shadows to make the route easier. You should improve quickly with this Skill, if anything we've seen today can be used as a guide.

Once you've done that, come back to me and I will show you how to fine tune the shadows to help with your Scaling."

"Sounds easy enough."

"You may also want to have a Cleric nearby. You know. For when you fail."

"And there are the words of encouragement I was waiting for."

Stan walked between Waseem and I while giving my newest teacher a dirty look. "Don't listen to this fool. At least not entirely. He is right about challenging yerself, though. The sooner you do that, the quicker you can stop talking to this idiot."

"Your words cut deep, Dhalean."

Stan secretly loved that Waseem had no idea what his real name was, and he winked at me as the handsome Rogue used his moniker yet again.

"Two words of warning for ya, though. Be aware of your surroundings at all times. You may be getting the climbing down, but you still can get caught up by magic. If something don't feel right, just go around it."

I nodded at Stan. "And the second."

"I don't care what this moron tells you. And he will sing ya a pretty tune. Should a been a Bard with all them fancy clothes. Bottom line, don't go anywhere near the bank."

"Damnit, Dhalean! Stop stealing all my fun!"

I nodded at Stan and looked over at Waseem. "I would have turned you down, anyway. I'm nowhere near good enough to consider something as crazy as that."

"Boy's got more brains than you, Waseem, I'll give him that much!"

I left Stan and Waseem to argue and bicker like an old couple. I went back out into the seedy underbelly of the Keep and started looking around for places to climb. There were lots of options available, and I was about to engage my Blacksuit when I felt a presence coming up behind me.

Before Waseem could put his hand on my shoulder I had spun around and had started drawing my blade. Once I saw it was my teacher, I sheathed the blade and apologized.

"No need. Good awareness on your part. I was just coming out here to give you a small piece of advice before you departed."

He looked around the Stinky Pit, at all the other buildings in the nearby vicinity. "I realize that this looks like a place with ample opportunities to do exactly what we discussed inside. I would suggest against it, however. You see, these areas are all run by different gangs, and every last one of them is led by a Rogue of some skill. If one of them were to catch you running around their buildings, they would think the worst. Then they would blade you first and ask questions second. That is, if you were alive to answer them. Take my advice, and look to the other quarters to practice. It's safer ground there."

I thanked Waseem for the wisdom and started out of the slums. Before I got too far, I heard him yell, "And don't listen to that Halfling. Feel free to swing by the Bank and give it a good look-see."

I kept heading out of the area but distinctly heard Waseem cry out, "Damn you, sneaky Halfling! Stop hitting me. And stop hiding in those damn shadows!"

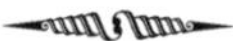

November 9th, 2043

Over the course of the next three days, we mapped out the area south of the main roads and past the Trolls. It was slow going, as we kept getting sidetracked by new mobs. There was no way we were going to skip out on the chance for experience and to learn what could possibly be waiting for us on the road to the Monastery of Might.

As far as fauna went, we had a new and diverse set of beasts to contend with. Most of these creatures either resided in the swamp itself or on the marshes that surrounded the putrid water. There were various reptiles that resembled crocodiles and alligators, but they had a nasty venom that added to their bite. We only got hit with that once, and thereafter we made sure to buff our resistance against Poison.

The most annoying of the reptiles, however, were the snakes. Unlike in the real world, snakes in Resurgence appeared to be pack animals. We never saw a lone small snake, but always a number of them. Plus, their aggro range was so large that we were targets long before we saw them. Without warning, we would be attacked by snakes numbering anywhere from five to seven.

They didn't do a huge amount of damage, nor did they have a lot of hit points. But the longer it took us to take them down, the more damage they were going to do. That could eventually spell disaster. Think of it like a screen door. Slam it once, and it's probably no big deal. Slam it repeatedly, though, and it will eventually fall off its hinges.

Even worse, we couldn't really have Dan kite a bunch of them because of the large aggro range. Dan could be out running two of the slimy creatures around and suddenly run through the aggro bubble of another pack.

Only once did we see a larger snake, a Swamp Boa. The Boa was unique in that it had a special attack that "strangled" the attacker—in this case, Wayne. The attack did little damage, but the sudden loss of air caused Wayne's Vitality to drop sharply.

Where the fauna was cool, the flora was awesome. For the first time, we were attacked by something that wasn't either a person or an animal. The trees literally came alive and beat on us soundly. The loot was likely for crafting, as it involved pieces of wood, or vines, or the like. I took it all, and would see about selling it at another time if scheduling permitted. With our quests and my training, I didn't have the time I'd usually devote strictly to selling and buying.

The Swamp Treants were made up of various parts, each of which had different functions. Their roots acted as legs for movement and would lash out in an AoE fashion, wrapping around a character's feet. They used their branches for hitting and bashing, while the vines struck quickly and unpredictably from all different angles and had a chance to leave a DoT poison effect.

The root attack was random, and Wayne had no problem maintaining aggro on the mobs. We all got hit by the vines at some point or another, though, and a successful root would bump the player to the top of the mob's aggro list. It would turn immediately to that character and begin attacking. The end result was all of us taking some sort of damage.

We were still able to survive the experiences, thanks in large part to our levels and our gear. Additionally, the fact that it was a different type of combat invigorated the group. Grinding can get stagnant and boring. Pull, establish aggro, wait, engage, kill, and loot. Over and over again. Even the most die-hard gamer will suffer from a bit of ennui.

Another bonus was that the new mobs were giving us decent experience. Over the three days that we waited for Tyke and Jenny's groups to reach their Level 27, we reached 28. I had put another four points into my Wisdom Stat at 27, hoping to quicken my progress through Scaling. So at 28, I was back to bumping up my four important Stats: Strength, Constitution, Dexterity, and Chance.

Speaking of Scaling, I was definitely making progress. Although, I had to admit, I was starting to get a bit tired from constantly being online. Where my teammates were spending eight hours on Resurgence, I was doing closer to 12.

I would log on early and get an hour of training in on Scaling. Then I would continue talking to other players and try to determine if any had seen mobs that could qualify as the home of the Wanderer's suspected code. Once the guys logged off, I spent another hour utilizing my Blacksuit to continue my practice at Scaling. Before logging off I would go back to the Keep to start all over again. Travel time was minimal with the horses, but even that factored into how long I was staying online.

We still hadn't found anyone that had met with Constantine like we did with Tristan, but we also hadn't found the Monastery yet. Our plan was to continue looking, obviously, but it would all have to wait. Because on this third day, Tyke sent me word that he had spoken with Sir Arthur and his group was ready whenever to start the next quest.

We had been out in the swamps, so we rushed back to the city as fast as our summoned mounts would take us. Jenny and her group had already hit their Level 27 and were grinding away at the Goblins in the forest north of the Keep. As we traveled, Wayne sent a message to Jenny letting them know the last group had leveled and were ready to start the quest.

As our group traveled, I received a message to my character. Unlike with normal messages, which I could choose to ignore entirely, this one was from AltCon and addressed to Alexander Stanton.

"Did everyone just get a notification about a message from the company?"

"I swear, if they decided to give us some of those stupid ass AltCon quests right now, I am going to be so pissed."

"Don't let your blood pressure out of control until you've read the message, Dan. But yeah, Alex, I got one too."

I opened the missive and saw the following note:

Dear Alexander,

It has now been three months since our Resurgence Beta began, and those of us here in AltCon are overjoyed with the progress you and your teammates have been making. Because of your efforts, our team is certain that Resurgence will launch on schedule and with as few flaws as possible. You've shared this experience with us, and we couldn't have asked for a better partner in the ride.

However, many of the players in Resurgence have another partner outside of the game—spouses and significant others who are likely curious about Resurgence and what has all of these players so excited. Those of us in AltCon think it's time for those partners to have a small taste of what they could expect if they joined in the future.

In order to share this unique venue, AltCon is enacting a down day for all players. On November 15th, 2043, each player in a relationship may bring their partner to a prearranged AltCon location and let them feel the same exhilaration you do. Naturally, all individuals must sign a Non-Disclosure Agreement before being briefed and allowed access into the game.

Don't worry; for this day, Resurgence will be ratcheted down so as not to overwhelm the newbies! They will be able to shadow you as you move around in your normal gear, although they will only be able to don a starting uniform. They will be able to interact with the NPCs and see you perform crafting-type exercises and quests. There will be no killing for experience, completing of quests, and Player Vs. Player will be deactivated.

AltCon has picked a Sunday to have this opportunity benefit the greatest number of people, but don't be alarmed if your partner cannot attend. Another day like this will likely occur in three to six months.

For those of you who choose not to attend or who do not have partners, you may take the day off (no deduction from your stipend will be recorded) or join your teammates with their spouses. The choice is yours.

Once again, thank you for all of the hard work you have been putting into making Resurgence a success!

The AltCon Management Team

"This is excellent!" Jason said to the group.

"Do you think James will want to see what it's all about?"

"For sure, Naugha. He asks me all the time, but I am never sure what I can and can't say because of the NDA. Getting him inside the game, even for a few hours, will definitely show him how awesome it all is. I can't wait to tell him about it tonight."

"I bet Tim and Gary do it, too. If they can get someone to watch their kids for the day. Maybe Jenny and I will volunteer to babysit for them."

"Just to be clear, we all got the same letter?" I asked and then read mine out loud.

"Yup, with the exception of the person it was sent to. Just a mass mailer."

"Looks like a bunch of us get a day off then! Unless you want us to be online to really sell it for James, Alliferous."

"Nah, you guys definitely take the day off. I'll be able to highlight the things I already know he will find interesting and then totally win him to my side."

"Sounds like a plan. Now let's go meet up with the other groups and get this quest started."

Tyke and his group were already waiting for us when we arrived. Jenny and our teammates were also present. All we needed now was to form the raid and activate the quest.

"If we have any chance of passing this raid, it's going to be with you guys. We really do appreciate you waiting for us to reach 27 before starting."

"It's not a worry, Tyke. I prefer to play with people I know. And as far as this game goes, I've gotten to know you and your group well enough to want to play with you guys. Besides, I think we'll have a decent setup with our different Classes.

"For everyone's information, Tyke is a Shaman, Lug is a Warrior, Tammer is their Enchanter, and Syphon is their Death Caster. Let's give a quick run-down of what other Classes are here."

For clarity, my group all repeated their Classes, and our teammates did the same. With two Enchanters, we now had lots of crowd control, and as I reviewed the make-up, I didn't see any reason to move people around into different groups.

Besides, getting to know another person's playing style on an ad hoc raid like this was not to anyone's advantage. If we were a proper guild, and played together on larger raids all the time, we would possibly put DPS like Dan, Gary, and myself all together in one group with a healer like Tyke or Kaitlin. Then the Cleric would go with the Tanks, and the last Healer would be there to support the Casters. For now, we would stick with what we knew and rely on the Raid Leader for instructions.

Knowing how this would play out, I was going to get pushed into the Raid Leader position, whether I liked it or not, and Jenny was right on time to start the process.

"I don't know about you guys, but we like to have Alex as our Raid Leader. He's proven himself on multiple occasions with us."

Tyke and his group started discussing it, and I imagined part of the dialogue was about loot. I figured I should address that before it had a chance to rear its ugly head.

"Before we even get into who will lead what, I want to have a discussion about looting. My teammates know how we do it. Need before Greed. If something drops and it is Warrior Only but tradeable, we defer to the Warrior's first to see if they want to roll on it, and then if neither wants it, everyone can roll. I'd like to do it this way for our raid here. What do you guys think?"

I saw Lug let out an exaggerated sigh and then looked over at Tyke.

"Man, that is exactly what we were talking about. You never know what the loot might be, so how do you even prepare for something like divvying up the goods. At least in a guild you have a system in place. We are perfectly good with that, Alex."

"Excellent. And how do you feel about me being the Raid Leader?"

"Now that we know need will overcome greed for loot, I don't see any difference on who is the Raid Leader. You've got it if you want it."

That statement made it obvious to me that Tyke and his group didn't understand the importance of the Chance Stat. I would decide later whether to tell him or not. If his group proved to be worth raiding with again, I probably would.

We made our way over to Sir Arthur, and I selected the quest *"Deliver the Traitor to King Kameron,"* accepting the Raid Leader position. I then invited Tyke and Tim, the leaders of their groups. Lastly, I informed Arthur that we were ready to begin the quest.

"Excellent! Meet the caravans traveling to the front at Captain Treeswain's camp. From there you will begin the journey. Once you have captured the traitor, activate these teleportation stones, and they will take you back to Yerkich."

"Son of a bitch!"

I turned from summoning my mount and saw Tyke kicking at the ground.

"What's wrong, man?"

"We don't have horses."

"Oh. Shit."

"Exactly."

"Alright, then," I said, getting ready to unsummon my mount. "We will go together and walk the way. But when we get back, we gotta see about getting you guys some mounts."

"Never have the money to spare."

As I was about to address the rest of the team, Wayne spoke up. "Easy fix, Alex."

We were out of the range for any of Tyke's group to hear us, and I knew what Wayne meant. "That's 4 Platinum, Wayne! Sure, we have the cash now, but that's not going to always be the case."

"They'll pay us back. You know they will. And come next month we will be swimming in money from the mines. I really don't feel like taking the entire day to walk from here to the river."

Dan and Jason were close enough to hear the conversation I was having with Wayne, so I looked over to them for a comment. Jason simply shrugged his shoulders. "Way to go all introvert on me now, Allister. Dan?"

"Do we have anything we need to buy?"

"We might. At some point."

"This is the seller in you, isn't it? You really don't like giving things away."

"Maybe," I admitted.

"Then tell them you will charge them 10 percent interest on the loan. And just know that when the time comes for them to pay us back, Wayne won't accept the interest. Everyone wins."

I laughed at Dan's logic, but he was right. Even if they agreed to pay the loan back with interest, Wayne wouldn't let us accept it. Beyond conceding to Wayne's general altruism, my desire to avoid walking for an entire day ended up outweighing my reticence at letting go of coin, and I approached Tyke with the idea.

I had totally forgotten how funny it can be to watch someone who had never been on a horse try to maneuver around. It was even more hilarious when you saw a 350-pound, almost eight-foot Ogre try to do it. Lug had a great sense of humor, though, and he laughed right along with all of us.

We certainly didn't get there as fast as we could have if it was just my teammates, but we definitely got there a lot faster than we would have walking. In the end, everyone was happy about that.

Except for me. But I'd get over it at some point.

Tyke agreed to take the loan for four Platinum, with the understanding that they would pay it back in full plus an additional 10 percent within a reasonable timeframe. That would have made me happy if I hadn't already been told point blank that I would never actually see that 40 Gold.

Arriving at Captain Treeswain's camp, I approached the Elf and asked him for directions to the caravan. He was more than ready to ramble on, but he erred by first telling me where the carts were located. I walked out of the tent as he was just getting his wind. While some people love that kind of stuff, spending hours on details like long speeches or obscure books that ultimately don't affect the game, I prefer to get to the point, especially when the entire raid is waiting on me.

The caravan leader, Pike, was your average looking human. His face was tanned from leading carts down the road time and again, and he seemed a bit pensive when he saw my raid party approach.

"I don't have funds to hire out any guards. These are the King's goods. He'll have his own people watching them."

"Pardon us, Mr. Pike. We aren't here to act as guards. We're here for the 'other thing' that is happening today."

Pike put his finger against his nose and winked at all of us. "Understood. You lot are going to want to be in the middle of the pack then. We've got seven wagons heading out to the front. I would suggest three, four, and five for our journey."

"How long into the ride do things normally become bad?" Wayne asked.

"It's been known to vary. Some days, it doesn't happen at all. Others, they hit us as soon as the camp is out of sight. That's why we've had so many troubles. We're usually caught by surprise, even with guards."

"And the trip to the front, how long does that take?"

"We get there and back in about two days."

When I looked back at my raid team, they all had the same expression that I was feeling internally. No way any of us wanted to burn two days sitting in the back of these stupid wagons.

Tyke held up a canteen and said, "Here's to an early ambush!"

With nods all around, we headed toward the wagons assigned to us. Each group would lie in wait in the back of a separate cart and wait until the attack began before exposing themselves.

One thing we had to keep in mind was that this quest was different from any others we had completed. We weren't supposed to kill the final boss but capture him alive. I wanted to go over ideas with the groups and make sure we had something that resembled a plan.

My group and I were at the front end of the wagon train, and Jenny's group took up the rear. Since Tyke's group was still the wild card, having only seen them in PvP, we decided to put them between us and make it easier to control the raid.

We walked back to see Jenny and our team and to have some kind of conversation about how we wanted to implement strategy.

"Seems pretty simple, Alex. Kill everything but that guy. Even I can figure this one out," Gary said.

"This from the guy that routinely has to Play Dead because he doesn't think things through."

"Shut up, Tim."

"Love you, too."

I interrupted the love-fest between the two and reminded them that nothing is ever easy in Resurgence.

While Wayne was grabbing Tyke and his group, I was watching out the side of my eye at the interaction between Dan and Kaitlin. They had started about as far away from each other as two people could be, but Dan had slowly been creeping around toward her position. When he was close enough to speak to her in a quiet voice, he finally did.

"I'm sorry. I can't begin to tell you how sorry I am."

Kaitlin looked at Dan and gave him a small, sad smile. "I know you are. I really do. And later we will talk more about this. But not now. Ok?"

Dan nodded his head and Kaitlin walked off. Dan was just about to walk after her when Jason stopped him. I was heading toward him to do the same, but Jason got there first. And when it comes to relationship issues, probably better that advice come from someone who is in one.

"Slow down there, Dan."

"Dude, I just need her to understand how bad I feel."

"That right there," Jason said, twirling his finger around the spot where the conversation had just happened, "that was a win brother."

"You think so?"

"Absolutely. She could have yelled at you. She could have ignored you. But she didn't. She acknowledged your apology, said you would talk more later, and she didn't throw a single thing at you. Win."

"But if I tell her..."

"Right now she thinks you're a bit of an immature child. You wait for her to come to you when she is ready to talk, and she will see you have the ability to be a bit of an adult as well."

"Shit, Allister. She told you she thought I was an immature child?"

"No, she didn't. That's what I think. Just like all the other rational and intelligent people in the world. I just put her in that category."

"Damn. I totally walked into that one."

Jason smiled at Dan and put a hand on his shoulder. "Yes you did, and I wasn't about to pass it up. But trust me on this one. Wait until she comes to you."

Over the last three months, the four of us had spent almost every day together. During that time, we had become as tight as a group could be. Despite the constant antics between Dan and Jason, I knew Jason would do right by our Ranger. And the same with Dan. He would bend over backwards to help Jason in any situation. I had no fear that Jason would give Dan poor advice.

I nodded my appreciation at Jason after he finished talking to Dan and then turned to address Wayne and Tyke's group who were now approaching from their wagon. It was time to talk strategy.

"Wait. That's it? We just wait for you to make the call? Seems like a kinda crap plan. No offense."

"None taken, Tim. And yeah, I've been going over this in my head over and over again, and I just can't lay out tactics when we don't know what the battlefield is going to look like. Are we going to get five mobs or ten? More? No one I've talked to here, including Pike, can give me an accurate count. When I ask how many people they've faced in the past, I always get the same response—too many."

"Yeah, that's true."

"So at this point, the most we can do is identify individual roles. We've got three Tanks here, so I'm open to suggestions on who should be our primary Tank and why."

"Naugha."

"Wayne. Sorry, that's Naugha."

I looked at Lug and Jenny who had both identified Wayne as our primary. "No arguments from me, but you guys are sure you are ok with that."

"Naugha's got better gear and more hit points than I have," Lug said.

"And we work better when I'm an Off-Tank," Jenny added. "It's something we've gotten very good at while Wayne was our pseudo 'Tank for Hire' and supporting our group."

"Alright. Second, our primary healer will be Allister. No arguments there. He's our only pure healer."

I received nods all around at that.

"Tammer and Slovak will be Crowd Control, and TC will act as Damage for now. If I need him to kite, I'll call it."

Tammer and Tim nodded toward each other. "Let's work out which mobs we will take. I think we should go with a simple right side or left side at this point."

"Works for me, Slovak. I'll go right if you want to take left."

"Sounds good."

"Perfect," I said. "Now let's talk about the variables here. For starters, Broham and Rocky. I want them out of the fight at the beginning. There will be too many moving pieces."

Dan and Kaitlin acknowledged my comment.

"Second, we've got a Death Caster here. His spells are almost all Damage over Time or straight hit point stealers like my dagger's proc. I'm fine with you going to town on everyone but the main boss, Syphon. I would hate if the mob died because a DoT kept running. Once they're cast, you can't cancel them, right?"

"Yeah, Alex. It's a flaw in the game if you ask me. It's my spell, so I should be able to turn it off at any time. But here in Resurgence, once cast, that's it."

"Ok. Then definitely no attacking the boss. Cool?"

"Makes sense to me."

I looked around at the remaining members of the raid. Gary would be another DPS guy just like me, and Tyke was going to be a back-up healer along with Kaitlin. Both of them had offensive spells, though, so I needed to make sure they understood their roles, too.

"At the beginning of the battle, I'm going to ask that Tyke and Anastasia only heal. I know you guys have some wicked offensive spells, but with so little knowledge of what we're up against, I want to play it a little conservative at first. "

After not hearing any objections, I looked around at the raid again. "I know it's light on the details, but that's the best I can do for now. Once we engage the mobs, listen closely for my instructions. If you see something that you think I should be taking into account when I give direction, please don't hesitate to tell me. Since I'm going to be adding my damage to the fight as well, I'm likely to miss stuff."

Before I could go into any more details, Pike came ambling over to our parties and said the caravan was about to head out and we needed to get in our positions. I asked Pike one last time if he had any more news, and he apologized for having nothing more to add.

Within moments of settling into the back of our wagon, we felt the shift of wheels and the forward momentum of the cart. As we were bouncing around in the back, Dan said, "They should have let me drive the cart. I'm really good at it. You guys remember how awesomely I handled those horses that last time?"

Undisclosed Location

"We've got a bit of an issue, General."

Dan entered the conference room where the General and Colonel Thompson were sitting and began without any preamble.

"What seems to be the matter Mr. Hamson?"

"A message went out today to all of the players in the beta offering a unique opportunity to their significant others to see for themselves what their partners have been doing for the last several months. In essence, AltCon offered a day pass to adults in the immediate family to log-in to Resurgence. A special zone is being implemented for these folks, where they will be able to interact with NPCs and players but won't be attacked by any of the creatures in the game. They will be able to shadow their counterparts as they go around, but there won't be any violence. They probably don't want to freak out the spouses or whoever is given access."

"You don't have a spouse, Mr. Hamson, so what did your message say?"

"Mine simply informed me that there would be a down day for the stipend players so the others could interact in Resurgence with their significant others. Jason told us that part of the message he received required his husband, James, to sign an NDA before he would be given access into the game. Jason planned to have James do so and get him logged in."

"And you think this could be a problem how?"

"I've talked to plenty of players, General, through my teammates or down at the Taverns. I know that there have been some players that are being pressured by their spouses to leave the game. I wouldn't put it past AltCon to try and mess with the spouses as much as they would mess with the players."

"There hasn't been any indication of that going on, but given the track record to date, I am in full agreement with you, Mr. Hamson. At least we don't have to worry about you trying to get your spouse into the game. Not that you would if given a choice."

"Sure I would, General. It would be a great opportunity for them."

The General and Colonel looked at each other for the briefest of moments. After sharing that look, the General addressed Dan again. "And what news from the game, Mr. Hamson?"

"I'm afraid I've got nothing to report. Everything seems to be moving along, same as it ever was."

"And you know the goal of this team is to take down AltCon and disrupt their plans?"

Dan looked first at the General and then at the Colonel. "Umm, yeah. That's been the point of this since day one."

"Then can you please explain this comment, Mr. Hamson."

At that moment, the General signaled Thompson who had been fiddling with a data pad. On the screen, the General played back the few moments where Dan spoke in a positive tone about AltCon.

"What the fuck?" Dan said as he watched the screen. After several moments, he looked at the General and said, "I did say that. I mean, I can remember saying it, but it feels weird. Like a memory I can barely reach. That doesn't happen to me, General."

"Indeed. And can you explain it?"

Dan looked as confused as he had ever been and was thankfully saved by the neurological specialist that had been brought in for this mission.

"Dan probably can't, but I can. Take a look at this scan."

With a few twitches over his data pad, the doctor had brought up a large picture of a brain scan. It was labeled 'Hamson, Daniel' beneath it. "What you gentlemen are looking at is a pure work of art."

"You hear that, General? Told you my brain was priceless."

The General ignored Dan, as he often did when Dan's "TheClaw" persona came out, and addressed the Doctor. "So I don't have to hear Mr. Hamson ramble on ad nauseam, can you please explain that last statement."

"Yes, sorry about that, sir. It appears that AltCon has returned to their old ways. As you know, it has been some time since we saw any type of manipulation on Mr. Hamson, and the last one was quite horrible, as you recall.

"The downtime all makes sense now. It must have taken them some time, and quite a few experts in the field, to go from that back-alley hatchet job to this. The reason that Mr. Hamson does not remember his statements, or has limited recall, is due to the way the conditioning was implemented this time around.

"The science of this is quite complex, General, so I am going to gloss over much of this and try to make it understandable for the layman. In regards to conditioning, such as Mr. Hamson's manipulation, the hypothalamus is directly stimulated to provide a dopamine response when Mr. Hamson thinks of AltCon in a positive light. That dopamine injection reinforces the positive outlook."

"Mr. Hamson thinks happy thoughts about the company, and in turn he gets a little happy pill in the guise of his dopamine output?"

"Exactly. The repeated conditioning was designed to stimulate a continuous introduction of small levels of dopamine whenever his thoughts praised the company. However, the hypothalamus is not a part of memory creation. Where the hypothalamus plays a large role in reward for behavior, it is the hippocampus that plays a role in memory."

The General was taking notes as the doctor spoke, even though all of this was being recorded, as Dan saw just moments before. Still, the General liked to contextualize what was being said at the moment. He would undoubtedly review the same material in his office at a later time.

"It would take hours to explain how the hippocampus and several other regions of the brain, such as the prefrontal cortex and amygdala, affect memory. Suffice it to say, someone who has a damaged hippocampus would not have the ability to form long-term memories."

"Are you saying Mr. Hamson's brain has been damaged?"

"You mean more than is normal for Mr. Hamson?"

The General couldn't help it. He snorted. He didn't see that one coming at all.

"Dick move, doc."

"Sorry, Dan. You know I couldn't pass that up," the doctor said before continuing. "No, General, Mr. Hamson's brain has not been damaged. That's why this is a thing of beauty. The manipulation is somehow sending two separate messages to the hypothalamus. I honestly don't know how it is being done. But apparently, when Dan was asked at this most recent brain scan to think about AltCon, as he does at each scan, the results were drastically different. Instead of a simple release of dopamine like we've previously seen, there was also a distinct drop in cranial blood pressure around the hippocampus region.

"The hypothalamus is also responsible for the regulation of blood pressure, and this drop seems to have affected the hippocampus in such a way that it stops working for that brief moment."

"So whenever Mr. Hamson speaks or thinks about AltCon, he gets a little high but can't remember why?"

"Essentially."

"If he does have a negative feeling toward the company, the whole incident wouldn't even register as being out of place."

"Now you see it."

The General was a picture of unhappiness as he sat at the head of the table. There had been some discussion around the office on whether AltCon had abandoned their plans. Now it was obvious that they had been perfecting them, not abandoning them. This was not going to read well at his next meeting with the White House or Director Grissten.

"Keep Mr. Hamson monitored, doctor. If there appears to be any danger from this new conditioning, you tell me immediately. I will not hesitate to pull you out of this operation, Dan, if I think you are in danger. Dismissed."

CHAPTER 14

November 9th, 2043

We had been riding in the back of the wagons for about an hour when Dan spoke up. "We don't have a 'go' word."

"What are you talking about, Dan?"

"A 'go' word, Wayne. A signal that we can yell out that lets everyone know it's time to engage. We didn't make one."

I looked over at Wayne. "Do you think we need one?"

At that moment, we heard Pike yell out, in a very high falsetto, "Attaaaaack!"

Wayne shrugged at me. "Guess not."

We climbed out of the back of the wagon, and I saw members of the King's guard running around but not really engaging anyone. I looked out at the tree line that ran along the road and saw figures running toward the main thoroughfare.

I yelled out in the raid channel where everyone could hear me, "Dan, I need your Map!"

"It's up! What do you need?"

"Enemy mobs in the area, what color are they?"

"All Blue."

"How many do you see?"

"I count eight."

"Alright, folks, here we go. There doesn't look to be a boss right now. Jenny and Tyke, you guys take two each. Dan, forget damage. I'm going to have you kite two. Wayne, grab the last two. Once a team brings your mobs down, yell out, and Dan will bring one over to you. Let's see how well our crowd control works out here."

Just like that, twelve players rushed the approaching targets and engaged them instantly. The caravan was entirely safe, for now.

Wayne grabbed his two, and I was going to work on his primary target while he maintained aggro on the second.

"How are they hitting, Wayne?"

"These guys are nothing, Alex. We'll have them down in no time. I'm shocked that they are actually Blue."

Wayne was right. We weren't having any problem with these mobs at all. After a short time, I heard Jenny yell out that she was ready for one of Dan's mobs, and soon after Lug yelled out the same thing.

"Tammer, Slovak, how is Bedazzle holding up?" Bedazzle was the Enchanter Spell that would put the mob into a daze. Unlike Charm, where the Enchanter actually controls the mob, this was more like putting them to sleep on their feet.

"Not getting any resists at all, Alex." Tammer replied.

"Same here."

"Could you handle two?"

Both acknowledged that they could.

When the last mob was down, Dan announced that we had more incoming headed to the road from the same tree line. The count was eight Blue, again, but this time there was an additional mob added to the mix. A Red.

"Ok, Boss is on the scene. Small shift from last time. Jenny and Lug, take three Blue each. Dan, kite two again. Naugha will grab the Boss. Go!"

I hadn't really paid attention to the names of the first mobs, but now I noticed they were called Turncoat Soldiers. The boss was the Turncoat Captain. If I had one negative review of Resurgence, it was the naming of the mobs. They really needed to get more inventive.

Wayne quickly established his aggro on the main boss and proceeded to engage. I could stab at the mob, doing a little damage, or I could help with the extra friends he brought along with him. I told Wayne I was running off to join the other groups, and he nodded his head in acknowledgement.

With my extra Damage, I was able to help Lug and company take down their mobs quickly, almost at the same time as Jenny's group. Dan quickly brought each group the extras and those were dispatched in a quick manner. So far, this had been smooth sailing.

Once the eight Soldiers had been dispatched, everyone joined Wayne and started to beat down on the Captain.

"This guy has mad hit points and a pretty damn high armor rating," Wayne said.

I had to agree, as the combined damage of so many players was barely dropping his hit points. Drop they did, though, and people were conserving mana appropriately. Then the Captain hit 75 percent.

"Reinforcements!"

The yell didn't come from the Captain but from one of the King's guards standing on top of a wagon. As I looked out at the tree line again, I saw another eight Blue Soldiers advancing.

"You guys know what to do. Same as last time. Report anything that doesn't seem right. This is going way too easy."

"Seriously, Alex. You can't just let a sleeping dog lie—which is one of the few sayings that actually makes sense. Now you know something horrible is going to happen."

"Just keep an eye out, TC."

"Always do."

We had downed the first two mobs and were working on the se cond set when Wayne yelled out, "Healers!"

"Where are they, Dan?"

"Shit! Sorry, I didn't see them. Other tree line."

I broke away from Lug's group and went across the road a bit until I could see the other tree line. There they were, two Turncoat Healers. Both were Yellow.

"Slovak, if you hit that Entranced Soldier with a Charm, what happens?"

"If he resists, it breaks the Entranced Spell, and I get my ass beat."

"And if he doesn't, it immediately becomes your pet?"

"Yup!"

In any encounter like this, you always have to take the healers out first. It's a must. While I will often buck the usual strategy of things in gaming, this one is sacrosanct for a reason.

"Do it, guys! Charm your mobs and send them over to attack the Healers. If nothing else, it should disrupt their casting enough to stop them from saving the mobs you are on now.

"Once the mob you are on now is dead, cross the road and finish the Healers."

The Charmed mobs had succeeded in stopping the Healers from landing their Spells, but it also turned them onto Tammer and Tim's pets, which were now dead. The good news was that the Healers were almost dead, too, and with our combined groups, we were able to take them down. That left only two more Blue mobs, the ones that Dan was kiting. Those went down in quick order, and we made our way back to the Boss.

Jenny and Lug hadn't said anything about their mobs being healed. When we got back to Wayne, I realized it was because they hadn't been. The Healers were focused on their Captain, and he was now back at 84 percent.

"Oh, man! Screw those guys! They couldn't heal the baby mobs?"

"At least he isn't hitting for much, Alex. I think everyone is pretty good on mana, right?"

It was confirmed that all of our casters were at 80 percent or above.

We began the slow process of eating away at the Captain's hit points again. It took forever, but we finally got him down to 50 percent. Just like last time, more guards showed up from out of the tree line and the same guard yelled out that the reinforcements were coming. Only this time I had a plan.

Once the new Soldiers arrived, Gary and Syphon headed out for the opposite tree line. Syphon, as a Death Caster, had a similar skill as Gary, wherein he could Play Dead, except his required him to cast a Spell to make it work. This didn't always work if he was getting beat on by a mob, even though the cast was extremely quick. In this case, I had them both Play Dead long before any mobs were in their path.

"These new soldiers are Blue and Yellow, Alex," Dan yelled out.

"Try to isolate the Yellows and attack them first. Entrance one of the Blue mobs, and Charm the other if there are more Blue than Yellow."

"That is doable."

"Take the Yellow down first, using the Charmed mobs to help. I don't want Sayhey or Syphon to move from their positions. You guys ready?"

"Ready."

"Just waiting for them to pop."

Exactly as the previous iteration had proceeded, as soon as the first Soldier was dead and the second was at half, two Turncoat Healers appeared, running toward the road from the other tree line.

"We've got 'em," Syphon said.

"Let loose before they have a chance to start casting."

And with that, both Gary and Syphon popped up from the ground and attacked the Healers. Without waiting to finish the mobs they were currently on, Tammer and Tim took their Charmed mobs over to the Healers to help attack. The surprise attacks by Gary and Syphon had interrupted any heals, and the remaining party members, who weren't already actively Tanking a mob, were able to arrive and engage before the Captain could receive a reprieve. However, Gary and Syphon did take a bit of a beating. Tyke and Kaitlin had to dip into their mana reserves to get both back to full hit points.

With the Healers dead, it was just a matter of cycling through the remaining mobs, the ones Dan was kiting, and the Charmed mobs.

It was time to take the Captain down to 25 percent.

We had established a good system, but I had serious doubts that we would get lucky a third time.

And I was right.

"Archers!" yelled out the guard standing on top of the wagon.

From the first tree line where we engaged the Captain, we saw four Turncoat Archers step out onto branches, high in the trees. Four additional Soldiers came running out of the forest as well. There were the eight.

Which meant we probably would have two Healers again.

I sent Gary and Syphon off, keeping to the same plan as last time. Because the Healers didn't seem to spawn until some of the mobs died, I couldn't have Dan kite the two as I had before. Instead, I had Lug and Jenny grab mobs and drag them out of the range of the Archers. Dan was set up to launch arrows at the Healers as soon as they showed, but he was peppering their mobs in the meantime. The other two Soldiers were Entranced and were waiting for their brethren to die so their beat down could commence.

The second part, engaging the Healers, would be tricky. I needed Lug and Jenny to turn their backs on their primary mobs and attack the Healers. They would be without any healing for a short time, as I wanted our Shaman and Druid throwing their offensive Spells in the mix. This was going to be an all-out attack on the Healers.

That left only two targets for the Archers: Wayne and Jason. I had Jason get just far enough away from Wayne that he could still heal but be out of the range of the Archers. We tried dragging the Captain as well, but he boomeranged back to the point where Wayne initially started fighting him. Thankfully, Wayne hadn't moved so far away that the Captain regenerated any hit points from the boomerang.

The downside was that Wayne was taking the full brunt of the arrow barrage.

"Holy shit, Alex! These arrows fuckin' hurt! I'm getting lit up here!"

"I'll keep him alive, Alex, but hurry up and get rid of these Archers or I'll run out of mana before we finish this."

As soon as the second set of Soldiers hit fifty percent, the Healers made their entrance. I had to admit, I might have planned a little overkill. The Healers didn't have time to even register who was on the battlefield before eight players stripped them of their hit points in seconds.

It ended so quickly that we all stood around looking at each other for a second or two.

"Maybe should have tried that the first time?" Dan asked.

"Always with the backseat driving, this one."

"How about you guys focus on the Soldiers that are trying to send us to our spawn points, huh?" Jenny asked.

"Sorry about that," Dan said, adding, "You know it should be called backseat navigating, right? I mean, you aren't actually trying to grab the wheel, but you are telling the person where to turn. It just makes more sense. 'Don't be a backseat navigator, Clarence!' Clears it right up."

Kaitlin's giggle was magic to Dan's ears, and I had to send him a quick, private, "Don't go overboard! Let it go from there!" before he had a chance to say anything more.

At the same time as Dan was slowly working back into the good graces of Kaitlin, we finished off the two Soldiers. We made our way back to the other side of the road to deal with the Captain and the Archers.

My plan was to have Dan focus on one Archer, Syphon on another, and have our Enchanters Charm the last two. Those, in turn, would attack the same ones that Dan and Syphon were attacking. But first, I needed to make sure that everyone remembered that the Captain couldn't be killed.

I relayed the plan and then added, "And remember, we keep the Captain alive."

Now there is no way to tell if eventually the events that followed would have played themselves out in the natural course of the quest, but as soon as I yelled that to the raid, the Captain shouted, "They're trying to capture me, boys! Don't let 'em take me alive!"

As one, every single head turned toward me.

"Like I knew that would happen!"

"Holy shit! They're killing him!" Wayne yelled.

I had the Captain targeted and, sure enough, his hit points were going down fast!

"Charm two and have them attack the others! Don't try for the same one! Everyone else with range, let loose. Allister, heal the Captain!"

"What?" Jason asked incredulously.

"It's worth a shot!"

I saw Jason cast and then heard him yell, "Hell yeah! It worked! It didn't give him much, but it worked."

"Just keep him alive!"

The Captain wasn't fighting back at all anymore, and when he hit five percent hit points, he slumped down to his knees. At two percent, he fell over into the fetal position. When he hit one percent, I knew we had lost the quest.

And then his hit points jumped back up to three percent before I saw Jason starting to cast another spell that I knew wouldn't land in time.

The Captain slipped back to two percent, when I heard Tim yell out, "Take that, fuck stick!"

I looked over to the tree line and saw all of the Archers were dead. I quickly looked back to the Captain and saw his health was steady at two percent.

We had done it.

A massive cheer went up between the raid members. High fives were given all around and more than a few hugs exchanged. While everyone was basking in the revelry, I approached the Captain and touched his body. There was not the usual loot window that pops up, since the Captain wasn't dead, but I did get an option to Bind Captive. It was either that or the big button that said "Ignore." I opted to tie our Captain up.

"We aren't done with this yet. We still need to get this guy back to the Keep. I suggest, now that I have him trussed up, we heal him to a point that he can walk on his own."

"I'll need to get some mana back before I can do that, but it looks like we have time."

"Sounds good, Allister. I'm sure the other healers will chip in too."

As our casters recouped their mana, I walked over to the area with the Archers. I started hitting each corpse and looting the bodies as well. There were only a few silver on each, and some had equipment or weapons that none of us would use. I would sell everything later and divvy it out in the split.

I walked over to Tim as he was regenerating his own mana and commented on how the day would have been lost if not for the Enchanters. Again.

"You know, Alex," Tim said while laughing at my comment, "when Gary found out I was in the military, he asked me why I chose an Enchanter to play. Figured us soldier types would want to be the Tank."

"I've thought the same thing myself."

"Well, I will tell you the same thing I told him: if you can control the battlefield, where the enemy is and how it will maneuver, then you will win the day. Every time.

"In the end, it's not about how much armament you can bring to the table. It's about how precise you can be with the tools that you have."

After a couple of moments, I looked at Tim and said, "Next time, you get to be Raid Leader."

Tim tilted his head back and had a hearty laugh. "Hell no! Been there and done that. Now I just want to be told what to do and what to royally fuck up."

"Deal."

By the time I had looted all the corpses and finished talking with Tim, the Captain had received enough heals from Jason, Kaitlin, and Tyke to put him back at 15 percent. His arms were bound behind his back, and he wasn't putting up any fight. He looked downtrodden, as I'm sure he understood the fate that awaited him back at the city.

"We need to go and speak with Pike, but I'm sure the caravan is going to keep going toward the front. That means as soon as we are ready, we can activate these teleportation stones and get back to the Keep."

"I'll take care of Pike," Wayne said and headed off to inform the wagon master that we would be parting ways.

"You can't take me back. They're going to kill me," the Captain said.

"As far as I know, we take you back to Kich's Keep and the King's men will ask you what you know."

"And how do you think they will do that?"

Given that the game was set in a barbaric time, I imagined the King's men would be inventive with their techniques for questioning, but this really wasn't our problem.

"You sold everyone out and took up with the enemy. You get what you deserve."

The Captain looked around with pleading eyes at all of us. Finally, he said, "Take me back to my camp. I've got all the information the King wants in my quarters. If I give him all of it, at least I can bargain for a quick death on the executioner's block instead of drawn out one at the hands of his questioners."

"Sure," Dan offered sarcastically. "We just take you on back to your camp and have the rest of your men take us down. We aren't stupid," Dan said. "Not a word, Allitang."

"You know, I liked it better when he was actually messing my name up with words that exist."

I smiled and nodded in Jason's direction but agreed with Dan. "Our Ranger is correct. We aren't going to simply walk you back to your camp so you can go free."

The Captain looked around at the bodies littered on the forest floor and said, "These were all of my men. If I knew the King would send such a force, I would have dispatched them all at once to take you down. Instead, they followed my orders, and now they are all dead. There aren't any more at the camp."

"You guys aren't actually considering this, are you?" Tyke asked.

"Considering what?" Wayne said as he returned from the road. "Pike sends his thanks and says there will be a handsome reward for us when we return to the Keep."

Jason quickly recapped the story thus far for Wayne, and I saw the look of concern on his face. "You should let me go, Alex. I've got more hit points and could last longer if I got attacked. At least enough to get me somewhere that you could drag my body."

"I don't have any intention of getting in a fight. You guys remember that I'm sneaky, right?"

"But you have no idea what's there, Alex! This could be a serious fortification!" Tyke said, clearly frustrated that I was thinking of taking the Captain up on his offer.

"Well, see, the thing is, I've certainly infiltrated tougher locations. And if I can get into the camp, I can relay back if it's actually clear."

"And if you die? How are we supposed to get your body?"

"Tyke has a good point, Alex. I can't resurrect you if your body is stuck in the camp."

"I won't get stuck. I think it's worth at least a look."

The Captain was looking back and forth between all of us. "You can have all the goods we haven't delivered to the Children of Loust if you let me have the papers I need to deliver to the King."

The mention of loot had everyone's eyes gleaming. The entire party, save Jason, went from being unsure to being on board, all in a fraction of a second.

"I still don't like it, Alex."

"Me neither, but not for the same thing that has you worried."

Jason gave me a funny look, but I was already approaching the Captain.

"Here's the deal. You tell me where the camp is, and I will go look for myself that it is clear. If you have been truthful with us, my team here will bring you to the camp, and you can show us where these goods, and these papers, are located."

The Captain was nodding his head as I spoke.

"However, I will not be giving you those papers."

With that, the Captain stopped nodding.

"I will keep everything that I deem of value to the King and hand it over when you are delivered. I will inform them that you were helpful in order to receive a quick end. You will receive nothing from the moment we move from this location until you are in the hands of the King's men. If what you desire is simply a fast finish, I will do everything in my power to see it happen. This is the deal. Do you accept?"

The Captain took on a far-away look for a moment and then looked me in the eyes. "I accept."

Knowing just how complex the AI in Resurgence truly was, I would have to ask the Wanderer if the Quest NPCs were able to improvise to a point, as I believed just happened, or if I had spoken some variation of a script already programmed.

"Alright. Out with it, then. Describe to me how to find your camp."

The Captain described the route through the forest to reach the camp and the general layout of the structure. It was simple in its fashion, with four high walls, one door to allow access for guards to enter and exit, and one large gate to allow access to horses or wagons.

I allowed the Captain to explain the methods I could employ for getting the door or gate open, but I had already figured out my entrance when he said the walls were only twenty feet high.

Tyke and his crew didn't know about my Climbing ability, though, and I didn't see any reason to loop them in, as I got nothing for the information.

I was told repeatedly to be careful, to which I nodded and assured everyone I would be fine. Before leaving the forest area near the road, I became Invisible through my Conceal/Stealth and ran into the woods. After clearing the line of sight of my team, I also donned my Blacksuit.

The Captain's directions were spot on, and I was at the Camp in a little under twenty minutes. The first thing I did was get as close to the wall as possible and then see if anything inside the camp popped up on my Map. I could see the general layout of the interior, but there weren't any mobs.

With nothing more to do, I stepped back several feet and looked at the side of the wall. I thought about Climbing, how I normally activated my Skill, and the entire side of the camp became Green. I chuckled to myself, realizing this was going to be an easy day.

I paused only briefly before I hit the apex of the wall to see if there were any color variations along the top. Seeing that everything was still Green, I climbed over and descended into the camp.

A quick run-through told me that the Captain had been truthful and that the team could escort our prisoner to his former home. Before they arrived, I opened the door and gate. I didn't believe I was wrong about the place being empty. But if I was, I wanted us to have a path for a quick exit.

Once the team arrived, the Captain led them over to where his quarters were and then stopped before the door. Still bound, with his hands behind him, the Captain turned to us with a mischievous smile on his face.

"It appears that I forgot the door was locked. I guess we will need to renegotiate our terms."

"Or I just beat the door down with my hammer," Wayne said.

The smile didn't leave the Captain's face and may have gotten a little evil as he replied, "Indeed. You are welcome to try."

Wayne started to walk up to the door, as he never backed down from a challenge, when I called for him to stop. He obviously didn't want to, but I'd saved his butt enough times that he listened when I told him to not hit something. Usually.

"So we renegotiate terms and you unlock the door for us? Is that the deal?"

"That is the deal. And here are my terms. First..."

"Yeah, that's not what's going to happen here."

The Captain stopped talking and looked at me. But I was looking over at Lug and then Wayne. And then back to Lug.

"Hey, big guy, I need you to grab the Captain there and beat on him until he drops to his knees. At that point, place him next to the door. Literally, put his head against the wood."

Lug didn't say anything but nodded his head in an affirmative.

"After that is done, I need everyone to step away from this location. Like quite a bit away. When we are all a good distance from our kneeling friend here, I want you to shoot an arrow into that door from across the courtyard, TC. Can you do that?"

"Yes, Alex, I can hit the broad side of a wall with an arrow from a short distance away. Thank you for showing such faith in my skills."

"Excellent," I said, not wanting to lose my momentum and answer Dan's quip. "Once that is done, feel free to beat the door down, Naugha."

My teammates looked confused at my directions, but the Captain had a look of utter fear on his face. When I started explaining how the Captain's body would be against the door, his demeanor shifted dramatically and only got worse when I explained what Dan would do.

"Alright then, get to it Lug. Don't kill him, but don't be nice either. Just get him to a kneeling point."

Lug took out his two-handed sword and started rumbling toward the Captain. When almost 350 pounds of Ogre come at you, rumble is the only way to explain it.

"Wait! Stop!" The Captain yelled out.

I held my hand out for Lug to wait and approached the Captain. "So, about that whole renegotiating thing; you still want to try, or do you want to just deactivate the ward and give me the key?"

"Yes. You win. The key is in my pocket." After the Captain said those words, I was able to put my hands on his body and a loot window appeared with a key, which I took.

"Good. Now deactivate the ward."

The Captain spent several seconds concentrating and then said, "it is done."

"Fantastic. Everyone back up. Dan take the shot."

"WAIT!!!" The Captain yelled again.

"See, here is how this is going to go down. Before that door gets opened, my Ranger is going to put an arrow in that door, and your body is going to be next to it when he does. You have 15 seconds."

The Captain immediately turned toward the front of the door and this time I could see sweat beading at his brow. It took him 20 seconds, and when I saw him sigh with relief I said, "Fire!"

An arrow appeared right next to the Captain's head, stuck deep into the wood, but no wards exploded.

"See how easy that was? Now let's see what's inside."

When we got into the quarters, we saw a table with papers everywhere and a number of large trunks sitting to the side. Loot. But before I could make my way to the bounty of goodies, Wayne addressed me in front of the group.

"Alex, why did you tell Lug to beat on the Captain? Why not me?"

"Well, for starters, brother, I didn't know if you would do it. Lug was an unknown, but I definitely was leaning toward you not being willing to beat on an NPC who was tied up."

"I'd have done it, Alex, but only because you seemed to have a plan," Lug said.

"The other part, and don't get mad at me here, but Lug is scarier than you."

"What? No he isn't!"

"Sorry, man, but he is. Don't get me wrong, you are plenty scary, but Ogre-scary is way worse than Barbarian-scary."

"It's true, hon," Jenny said while patting Wayne on the forearm. "He's got ya beat."

"Don't get upset, Naugha. You still have way better gear than me!"

Wayne walked off pouting and muttering, "I am too Ogre-scary."

Before I looted the boxes, I went over to the desk and placed my hands on the papers. A message appeared asking me if I want to take the contents on the desk. I hit accept and all of the documents were sent to my inventory. I then opened each drawer of the desk and removed any item that was in there. Lastly, I searched the desk for any secret compartments. I was slow and meticulous, but my search paid off and I found a false bottom in one of the drawers. Inside was a journal of sorts, and I pocketed that too.

While I was searching the desk, I kept one eye on the Captain. His crestfallen look when I pocketed the journal told me I had found the one item he wished to keep hidden.

I then approached the boxes that were lining the walls. I was about to activate my Force Multiplier ring when I remembered what happened at the door. Better to be safe, then sorry, I had everyone exit the room and had Dan put an arrow into each box. The Captain insisted the boxes weren't warded, which they weren't, but I felt better about taking the precaution.

I quadrupled my stats with the power of my ring and went to the first box. Whatever loot was in there, I hoped, would be the best possible with my ring activated. I didn't know if the trigger was the opening of the boxes or the opening of the locked door, but I didn't want to rush things through before we had entered the unknown room.

"Where did all of this come from?" I asked the Captain.

"These are the items we stole from the caravans heading to the front or from travelers using the main road. I was to deliver them to the Children of Loust next week."

"You can explain all of that to the King's men when you see them. I still can't believe that you were working for the enemy."

"The King is fighting a lost cause. My men and I planned to be on the winning side when this was all over and reap the benefits for the part we played."

"You know, I don't really feel all that bad about what the King might do to you now."

The three boxes held three items each, and they were all spectacular. More importantly, we had the classes here to distribute all of the pieces.

"Alright, guys, I'm going to start linking all of the items. Start thinking about what you want. Some of these are certain class or race only, so that will be a deciding factor."

There were a few side discussions happening that I was not aware of; however, the matter came to my attention when Wayne sent me a private message.

"I talked with the guys, and Jenny talked with her group, and everyone wants all the folks from Tyke's group to get an item."

I continued to link all the items, and nodded at Jenny and Wayne. I knew they would share that I was ok with that with the rest. Normally I might have balked at the idea, but the only really amazing item up for grabs was going to go to Jason no matter what, so I was ok making Tyke and company a permanent ally through the gift of loot.

After the loot was tallied and distributed, with us making sure everyone in Tyke's group got a piece, I looked around at the players showing off their new wares. From Jenny's group, Kaitlin got a ring that was Ranger or Druid only and allowed the player to summon food. It turned out that food could be used as the nourishment for their pets, and Dan wasn't about to take anything that Kaitlin could use.

Jenny got a new bracer and Gary got some new shoes, that were upgrades, and added to their stats, but nothing that was going to tip the scales by themselves in a battle.

I ended up winning the roll on a bag that would reduce the weight of items by 75 percent and could hold ten items, beating out Dan, Tim, and Wayne. Jason was going to roll as well, since I hadn't linked his armor piece yet wanting it to be as dramatic as before, but I shook my head and he stopped.

Tyke and his group all got solid upgrades. They had beaten the Trolls, so they had some good gear, but they hadn't had the same history as us for finding other avenues of acquiring loot.

Tyke ended up with a pair of Shaman only pants that increased the damage of his offensive spells by 50 percent, while adding to his Constitution and Wisdom. Tammer acquired an Enchanter only robe that increased the length of his Bedazzle spell. I almost argued that Tim should get to roll on this item, but Tim knew where I was going and stopped me from saying anything with a shake of his head.

Syphon was in love with the new Amulet he received as it increased his hit points dramatically from a boost in Constitution and increase of 100 hit points. It also didn't hurt that it was a Death Caster only Amulet that increased the amount of hit points his Life Steal spell could take by an additional 20 percent.

But the happiest of all was Lug. You've seen nothing until you've seen a giant Ogre dance around, waving a huge broad sword over his head and whooping the whole time. The blade was very impressive, doubling the amount of damage that Lug could dish out and proc'ing a debuff—the opposite of a buff, where the player gets an advantage—that stripped the mob of 30 Strength. Between the debuff and the extra damage Lug would have a lot less reason to worry about losing aggro to his teammates.

The other cool thing with the sword was that it was a two-handed blade for humans or smaller, but a one-handed blade for the giant races. Lug was now anxious to find a shield.

But, in the end, the real winner for loot was Jason. And everyone saw why as I looted the next item in his Legendary set.

Item:	Commonality	Weight:	Armor:	Bonus:
Boots of Clerical Healing Cleric Only	Legendary Clerical Healing Set Min Level: 25 Binds on Acquisition (Scalable)	2.5	35 (Level 25)	+15 Wisdom +15 Constitution Effect: 20 Percent Increase to Holy Based Spells

"Hot damn, Allister! How many more pieces make the set?"

"I've got no idea, Naugha. In other games that I've played a set would require you to have the helmet, shoulders, chest, legs, boots, and it was optional if you needed arms or gloves, but always one of them."

Wayne was nodding his head and smiling joyfully. A 20 percent increase to a Holy Spell, which was all of Jason's healing spells, meant that Jason would be saving even more mana. "I can't wait to take some damage so I can see how your heals are now."

"I can arrange that for you, Wayne."

"Screw you, Alex. I'll let natural selection work its magic instead of one of your sadistic experiments."

"Wayne never lets me have any fun. Great job, everyone. Let's head back to the Keep."

We all activated our teleportation stones and arrived back at the main city. Where normally quests were completed at the central square, the stones placed us closer to the castle, and near a set of barracks. As soon as we arrived, two uniformed soldiers approached.

"Welcome back and fair journey. I see that you have succeeded at capturing the traitor. Excellent work. Take this token to Sir Arthur, and you will receive your rewards. The Kingdom is forever in your debt."

"Before you take this man away," I said as I exchanged the token for the prisoner, "I must tell you he was cooperative in providing a number of documents that will likely make uncovering this plot easier. I made a bargain that if he cooperated, I would inform you of his efforts and relay his wishes."

"And what is it this filth wants?"

"Take the documents and the journal I found, and he will answer all of your questions about what they mean. In return, he asks only for a swift death."

At that moment, a senior guard dressed in all black approached. The two regular guards backed away a bit, a tad afraid of the newcomer. "Show me this journal."

I looked to the guards that had given me the token, and they nodded that I should comply.

The new arrival searched through the journal and looked at the Captain. "You will decipher all of this and answer all of my questions?"

The Captain dropped his head but said that he would.

"Excellent. Then you shall get your wish. Come with me."

And with that, the Captain was out of our hands, and only one stop remained before we collected our quest rewards.

"That was the head Inquisitor. If anyone can see to it that the traitor doesn't suffer, it's him."

We took our leave of the guards and made our way to Sir Arthur. Dan was shaking his head as we left the area. "That dude is going to get a wet willy so bad."

"Do I even want to ask what you're talking about, Dan?"

"Wet willies, Alex. They are, hands down, the worst. Beat me. Jab hot needles under my fingernails. Play elevator music on an endless loop. I can take 'em all!" Dan said with his hands raised. He then turned to us with a very serious look on his face. "But wet willies, man. Forget it. That's the ultimate torture. Slimy little finger wiggling around in your most sensitive canals... I'd sell out. I'm not proud of it, but a man needs to know his limitations."

"You aren't right, Dan. You know that, right?"

"And that is my cross to bear, Allitater."

Turning in the token got each of us 5 Platinum pieces and half a level of experience. Tyke approached and handed me 4 Platinum and 40 Gold to pay back his loan. I didn't even need to look over to know that Wayne was eyeballing me.

"I'll take the 4 Platinum, but you keep the Gold. It's only been one day, so it isn't like there was any time for interest to even accrue."

Tyke shook my hand and said, "I won't argue with that. This is the most money we've ever seen. And the new gear we got is amazing. Any time you guys need another party, you know to call us!"

After saying their goodbyes, Tyke and his group were talking with the people around the square and showing off their new gear. It was all very exciting for them, and I wished them the best of luck now that everyone was seeing what they had. It would mean lots and lots of messages asking how to get exactly the same stuff. Soon Tyke would have to filter messages just like I did. I had to remember to ask him how long it took before he put them in place next time we talked.

Before logging out, I told the guys I was going to see if we could get the next story quest, just for shits and giggles. As we expected, though, Sir Arthur wasn't having it.

"I see that you have indeed answered the call for His Majesty on numerous occasion, and the latest has brought with it valuable information. The King will need brave souls such as yourselves to take action on those uncovered as supporters of our enemy.

"However, the King has not uncovered just who that is. Yet. Return when His Majesty has learned the identity and nature of these usurpers, and your services will certainly be accepted."

"You think more time or more levels?" Jason asked.

"Always more levels, Allicorn."

"So I guess it's time for us to start grinding again."

"For now, let's call it a night and get some rest. Grinding will have to wait, anyway. Tomorrow we hit the swamps."

CHAPTER 15

November 10th, 2043

There was an air of excitement as we stood around the square and got ready to head out for another of Lady Tessa's quests. Upon logging in, we had all received a set of messages from the guys in Tyke's group. They thanked us again for the awesome raid and the opportunities to improve their gear so significantly. With the money they received from Sir Arthur, they were all able to upgrade their armor to much of the same stuff that we were wearing.

Tyke privately told me that he was saddened that his group hadn't received one of the coveted titles that added base increases to their Stats and Resistances. Silently, I was a little disappointed by this, as well. In large part, this is what separated our group from many of the others of a similar level. With those bonuses, our Stats and Resistances were high enough to make a difference on the field of battle. On top of all of that, though, was knowing that before the stupid AltCon PVP tournament, our team was the only one with titles. Another reason to hate those guys.

Before logging off the night before, I tasked Dan with going over the map we had so far and coming up with a route we could take, keeping us away from most of the mobs. I was always game to gain experience, but I wanted us to focus on figuring out the route to the next Monastery.

"We've mapped out a significantly large portion of the swamp so far, Alex, but nothing has led me to believe that there is anything out there like the old mill we found before. I'm just not seeing how that's possible."

"What makes you say that, Dan?"

"When we traveled north, we had a number of side roads that we were able to take. Most of them didn't lead to anywhere, but they were definitely there. Now we have gone through a lot of that swamp without heading off the main road to explore, I've noted something interesting.

"In all of our exploration we haven't seen anything that would suggest that we crossed a pathway. It's just been swamp, bog, and marsh. That leads me to believe that there must be some other means for finding this Monastery. Is there anything in the sketch that helps?"

I pulled the journal out of my bag and examined the sketch again. It was extremely vague in its details. "I'm not seeing anything that could help. I'm betting the Lancasters already had some knowledge, or there was more to the instructions that Constantine received from The King. Either way, it's not pointing to anything more."

"Well, I see two options in front of us, then. The first, we jump on our horses and ride to the front. If we see a road that branches south into the swamp, we take it. The second, we do much of what we are already doing and just keep trying to map out the swamp."

I didn't tell the guys that there was a very real third option. I could have the Wanderer update my map with exactly where the Monastery is. At this point, it was tempting. But I had told the Wanderer that part of what would help me figure out the code was figuring out the rest of the game as well.

Internally I vowed to go to the Wanderer if, after a couple of days, we still hadn't found the location.

"We aren't going to figure out anything standing around here. Might as well make our way toward the swamps. Maybe once we get on the road something will jar loose."

My feelings on the subject were in line with Wayne's. Standing around the square wasn't going to do us any good.

It didn't take us long to get past Treeswain's camp, over the bridge, and along the road that bordered the swamp to its north. We had already traveled within the swamp a great distance south of the road. While we hadn't reached the "end" of the swamp heading south, we held little belief that the Monastery of Might was in that direction. Partly, we were basing this on past experience. The other part was no one believed the Monastery would be so close and that we would have to travel as far or farther than we had to find the Monastery of Calm.

We were racking our brains when we saw a caravan approaching from the opposite direction. As soon as it was close enough to see the head driver of the caravan, I recognized our prior acquaintance, Pike. Probably thinking we were bandits, Pike yelled out for the guards.

"Woah! Slow down there, Pike! It's Alex."

"My apologies, Alex. Guards, never mind!"

I looked past Pike and didn't see any guards running our way to begin with. I was guessing Pike had called out for these guards more times than he should have, with no result.

"You fellas heading for the front?"

"Not to the front, but heading in that direction, yeah. I've got a question you might be able to help me with, in fact."

"Ask away, Alex. This caravan is in your debt."

"Excellent, and thank you. I was wondering if you knew of any villages that one can get to from off the road? Before hitting the front, of course."

"Village? No. But there is an old sawmill north of the road that is still in operation. Perhaps that is what you are looking for?"

I knew that sawmill well, but that wasn't what we needed. Although it did make me think we could be on the right track, since it was something like the sawmill we wanted. Something that could help us to track down the Monastery.

"Hmmm, maybe. How about south of the road?"

"In the swamp?"

I nodded my head at the caravan leader.

"There isn't anything in that swamp but death and snakes. Definitely no villages."

"Well, there is the Witch."

While the caravan was stopped, but long after Pike called for the guards, a few of the soldiers had meandered up and were listening to my interaction with the driver. It was one of the guards who responded.

"There isn't any Witch, Kris. That's a story everyone tells to get the children to behave, and you know it."

The guard, Kris, said, "Ain't true, Pike. My Pa saw the Witch!" Turning toward my group, he began, "See, he was out in the swamp looking—"

"Everyone has heard the story of your Pa and the Witch. We don't need to hear it again."

"Well these folks haven't, now have ya?"

"That is true, Pike. My friends and I have not heard this story, and we are interested. Please continue, Kris."

"Thank ya kindly, Alex," the guard said, giving Pike a slightly dirty look and launching into his tale.

"So my Pa was out in the swamp, looking for some snake. Pa was a healer and an alchemist, and one of the kids from our town got bit. If they had found the snake in town, Pa could have used his magic to make an antidote from the venom, but without it, Pa had to go to the swamp and hunt one down."

"He went by himself?"

"I went with him along the main road, but he wouldn't let me go into the swamp. Said with his magics he would be fine, but he couldn't protect me as well.

"Now where was I? Right, I remember. Pa's in the swamp. So he is searching for one of these snakes, and he hears a terrifying shriek. Sounded like something—or someone—getting killed, so he said. And if there was a predator in the area, he wanted to make sure he knew what it was and whether to avoid it. Pa wasn't much for fighting, but a little animal he could handle.

"Pa said he rounded a corner and saw an animal, about medium sized, with its entrails ripped and on the ground. He figured this was what made the awful noise before. Seeing the prey, Pa started looking around for the predator. What he saw wasn't anything that looked like a killer to him. Rather, 'twere the most beautiful woman he ever laid eyes on. Perfect in every way. Said he felt compelled to go toward her.

"But before she had seen him, she turned to the animal on the ground, knelt next to it, and grabbed the entrails. Before my Pa could say anything, this woman took a giant bite out of a piece. In that moment, whatever made her look like a beautiful woman was gone. Pa saw the Witch for what she was. And she was vile, so he said.

"Pa didn't wait around and headed right back for the road. He didn't say two words to me the entire ride back, and he didn't tell me what he had seen until three days later when he tried to explain to the village why he didn't have the venom for the antidote. That poor boy died, and no one believed my Pa's story. They ran him, and me, out of that village. That's why I ended up a soldier in the King's army."

"No disrespect to your Pa, Kris, but no one else has ever seen the Witch."

"And lived to tell about it. I'm telling you, she is real, and in them swamps."

I looked over at my friends and they all gave small nods. We were thinking the same thing. The Witch would be our next destination,

"Thank you, Kris. Your tale was enlightening. Do you remember where your father entered the swamp on that day he saw the Witch?"

"I do. If you travel down this road for another hour, you will come across three trees that grew twisted around each other. It was at those trees that he entered."

"Thank you again, Kris. And thank you, Pike, for your assistance. Safe travels on your way back to Camp Treeswain."

Pike and Kris both thanked us once more, and their caravan continued back toward the Keep.

Once the caravan was gone, I turned to my mates. "Seems obvious where we go next. Did you also notice how none of those guards came running? I guess old Pike cried wolf one too many times."

"You know, that saying has always bothered me."

"Oh dear god, Dan. Are we really going to do this again?"

"No, seriously, Allitosis. Wait. Just hear me out."

"Like we have a choice, Dan."

"Why would anyone cry 'wolf?' I'm not talking about in the game, I'm talking about in real life. If I was headed in your direction and you all of a sudden yelled out 'wolf,' then guess what; I'm going to do a 180 and take off.

"However, if you yelled out 'free tacos,' now that would be different. I hear 'free tacos,' I'm running to you as fast as I can."

"You know, I actually kind of like that one," I said. "He cried 'free tacos' one too many times. Yeah, that works. I think I'm going to start using that one from now on."

Dan beamed a smile in my direction, and then he threw a smirk at Jason before walking off.

"You know, if you keep doing that, he's not going to stop."

"Allister, if I stop doing that, he still isn't going to stop."

"Truer words were never spoken."

It took us a little more than an hour to find the trees that the guard Kris had mentioned. Once we did find them, we unsummoned our horses and proceeded into the swamp.

"A word of caution before we go."

All of us looked over at Jason, as he spoke that last line with more than a little foreboding.

"We must do everything in our power to make sure Dan doesn't sleep with this NPC too. He's already checked the box for bearded women. I'm sure this one will have warts all over her face. Certainly another on the list!"

That got a chuckle out of all of us, except for Dan, of course. He continued to grumble that there was no proof and he didn't actually remember. Given Dan's memory, I found that hard to believe.

Given our previous experiences with the mobs in this region, we traveled as a complete group, not letting Dan scout ahead. The aggro range on some of these mobs was just too large.

It was another hour through the swamp—and several engagements with wandering mobs—before we found what we were looking for. Or at least what we thought was our destination.

A hut was standing upon a raised portion of dry land in the swamp. There was no indication of anyone around, but given the lack of anything revealing a domicile thus far, we felt certain this was the home of the Witch.

We approached as a group and came up to the front door. I looked over at Wayne and said, "So do we just break the thing down, or knock, or what?"

"None of that will be necessary, my dears."

As one, we turned toward the sound of those last words. Before us was the most beautiful creature I had ever laid eyes on. She was perfection in every sense of the word. Naked as the day she was born. I could see no flaws on her body. I wanted this woman more than I had ever wanted anything in my life.

"It's so kind of you boys to come and visit. It has been so long since I've had such strapping young lads appear on my doorstep. I am looking forward to entertaining each of you. Now let's just put your weapons on the ground and come inside with me for some—Agggh!"

I was starting to put my daggers on the ground when the scream rang out. Immediately, I saw an arrow jutting out of the shoulder of the woman in front of me. And that the woman was no beauty.

What few strands of hair she had on her head were greasy and gray, hanging down to her waist. Her body was filthy, and there was a profound hunch in the top of her back. Her teeth were few and yellow, and her breasts hung almost down to her stomach with that bend in her spine. This was the foulest creature I had ever laid eyes on.

"I fucking love this amulet!"

Dan was holding his bow in the air and already had another arrow knocked and ready to go.

It appeared that Dan's resistances were enough to see through whatever magic was clouding the rest of our brains. While the rest of started to drool like simpletons, the guy we called a simpleton all the time was the one to save the day. Talk about irony.

The Witch ripped the arrow out of her shoulder and glared at us. "If you think I will let you come to my home and kill me, you have another thing coming. You may bring me down, but I will take at least one of you with me!"

Wayne was pulling his war hammer off his back and moving toward the Witch. I'm always up for a fight, but killing the Witch would not necessarily get us the information we needed to find the Monastery of Might.

"Wayne! Wait!"

Wayne stopped and then stared at me with a look of disappointment. "That's the second time you've stopped me from bashing something. First time, that was a good call. But you know, I'm getting tired of not getting to hit things when I want to!"

"I know, buddy, but if we kill her, we may not figure out what we came here for."

"So it's information you want?" the witch said as she started moving toward us.

I put my hands on the pommels of my daggers, ready to draw in an instant. "For starters. Perhaps we can make a deal. That way, we don't have to kill you, and you can go on doing whatever it is you do here. I don't doubt your strength, and yes one of us may die. But you will surely perish in the process. This way everyone wins."

The Witch stopped advancing when she saw my hands go to my daggers. She listened to everything I had to say and then nodded her head once. "Then let us parley."

"What do you know of Constantine Lancaster?"

The Witch spat on the ground after hearing the name. "Curse that man! He also wanted information, but he never fulfilled his end of the bargain!"

The hatred in her eyes was real. I was going to need to tread carefully here. Asking as gently as I could, I said "What did he ask of you?"

"The fool wanted the location of a temple in the swamp. He told me he had a map but was unable to find the entrance. He wanted my assistance in locating it."

"And did you help him?"

"Yes, but for a price. One that he did not pay!"

"Ok. I understand. What was it he was to give you?"

"There are stories of this temple that have existed for generations. I remember it from my youth. But one thing that has changed with time is the story of a stone—a special stone that was acquired or created, I do not know. That stone has the power to beat back the swamp itself and allow life to grow as nature intended. It lifts the curse of this place!"

"Woah. The swamp is cursed?"

The Witch looked over at Dan and shook her head at his question.

"Do you fools know nothing?"

"Act like we don't. What is this curse?"

"During this kingdom's infancy, magic was more powerful but less attainable. Only a select few had the abilities to wield that magic, and they did so with brutal efficiency. I dwelled in this area, and was one of the lowliest of magic users. I would have been closest to what you called a Druid, now. I was tied to this place.

"As is normal when power is controlled by only a few, they will eventually go to war with each other. Two mages, the most powerful of our kind, fought to the death on this very land. Their battle—and the subsequent destruction of magic as we knew it—released this blight on the very ground you stand. It transformed a beautiful grove into a fetid swamp. It turned lakes into putrid bogs. The curse spread for miles and miles.

"Since I was tied to this place, through my magic, I too was cursed. I cannot leave, but with that stone, I could beat back the plague around my home. Don't you understand? Within that sphere, I could be me again. I will no longer be this!" The Witch said and pointed to her form.

"And he was to bring back the stone after he fulfilled his task? I am guessing you don't know his fate."

"I never heard from him again. I have no idea what became of him other than he obviously never returned with what he promised!"

"It would be my guess that he failed. His entire family line is gone. They do not exist any longer."

The Witch sat on the ground and looked up into the sky. She had a far-off look. “Then I am doomed to this life.”

“Why haven’t you just gone and taken the stone yourself?” Jason asked.

“A good question, Elf. The temple sits outside the borders of my home. Not far, but enough. If I were to attempt to leave, I would die. This, too, is a part of the curse.”

“Alex, do you think we could try to lift the curse?’

“This one is brave,” the Witch crowed. “But foolish! All the magic in the world now would not be enough to lift this curse. The swamps will never go away.”

Ok. No quest there.

I definitely saw our in, though. Where Constantine failed, we might succeed. And then we could get this stone for the Witch.

“Help us, and we will make the same deal. If we succeed in our efforts, we will return with the stone and we will give it to you. If we do not return, it is because we have failed, just as Constantine did.”

The Witch continued to look up into the sky for several more moments. Finally, she turned toward us and said, “Do you know what the most powerful force is?”

It was a cheesy question, and I was about to give a cheesy answer, like “love.” Before I could voice my thought, the Witch answered. Apparently this was meant to be a rhetorical question.

“Hope. Hope is the most powerful force in this world. And I have experienced both extremes of it: the joyous wonder of hope for a new beginning and the pits of depression from hope lost. Why would I want to go through that again?”

“Because you have nothing to lose.”

“Says you! I almost lost my sanity last time. I don’t know that I will survive it again!”

“You will. Because we will not fail.” I couldn’t rightly explain to an NPC that even if we died, we would just keep doing the fight over and over again until we did win. The NPCs registered a player’s death, like when the Dwarves noted Wayne’s sacrifice, but they didn’t have the programming to question their return.

"Swear it!" she said.

I really hate all this swearing. I reminded myself again that I would need to ask the Wanderer about what impact that had on gameplay.

"I swear it."

The Witch took a few moments to compose herself and then pulled her body off of the ground. She headed into her hut but motioned for us to wait. We all pulled our weapons out.

After several minutes, the Witch returned, finally dressed, and smiled at our presence. "At least I know you boys aren't foolish. I did the same thing with that Constantine, and when I walked out of the house, he had his back toward me. This actually does give me hope."

She walked over to a makeshift table sitting next to her hovel and spread out a map. It was the whole swamp, with numerous points marked throughout the region. There was even a key, but it was in a language I couldn't read. That didn't mean I couldn't find out.

"Dan, would you look at how amazing this map is!" drawing his attention and prodigious memory to the object at hand. "Did you do this yourself?" I asked the Witch. "It's the work of a master cartographer!"

The Witch actually blushed a bit at my compliment. In the meantime, Dan was soaking up the map.

"You have all these markings, too, but I can't make heads or tails of the words here. I'm afraid I don't know that language."

"Nor would you. This is the language of magic before the break. Before the curse. No one knows this language any longer."

I continued to compliment her work, making sure I didn't seem too ingratiating. Through my efforts, I was able to get her to explain the words on the key.

"There seems to be more of this reddish blotch than any other."

"That's for impassible areas—places where it is too deep for anyone to walk. And you would never want to swim through any of the bogs here."

"Got it. So where is the temple?"

"Here," she said, placing her finger on one of the largest red blotches on the map.

"You're messing with us, right?"

She cackled, as you would suspect a witch would, and then shook her head. With the filthy strands of hair, it was not a pretty sight.

"This 'temple' of yours is on an island, in the middle of this bog. Before the curse, it would have been surrounded by the most pristine of water. It was protected by a Leviathan—a truly majestic creature that lived in the lake. Now it is encompassed by this filth, and I don't want to imagine what that beast has become."

"And we are supposed to swim across this?"

"Did you not listen to a word I said? You don't swim through the bogs!" She yelled at me. Taking several deep breathes, she calmed down and said, "You simply need to speak the words and the bridge will rise."

"When I say this next part, don't yell at me."

"You didn't know about the words?"

"Nope."

"Hrmph. I would have yelled at you."

"Figured. Do you know the words?"

"To be honest, I didn't. Constantine reached the bog, since he had a map. But he tried to swim it. Surprisingly, he didn't lose a single limb in the process. After failing that, he found me in the swamp and asked for my aid. I asked to see his map and noticed the writing at the bottom. It was in the same language you see on my map, so it was no wonder he couldn't decipher it."

"Do you remember the words?"

"I do. I will say them now, and only once, because speaking the words of old magic can have unwanted consequences. Wraiths and the like."

"Dan, you know how you love different languages? You are going to want to hear this," I said, motioning for the Witch to continue.

I couldn't write the words out that she said, because I didn't bother to memorize them and the sounds were so foreign to my ear. When I looked over at Dan, however, he nodded and winked at me. A solid indication that he had the words locked away.

I looked at the hag again and thanked her for her assistance. It was very difficult to stare at her for too long, as vile looking as she was. The memory of her in the perfect form had long fled from my mind. I did wonder, though, if when we delivered the stone she would change into that woman again.

"This stone, once it lifts the curse, the area around here will return to lush forest, right? And you will revert to the woman we saw before?"

The Witch took on a vile looking smile, and shook her head. "The forest will return, but that woman was never real. That level of perfection is impossible, young man. And it would do well of you to remember that."

I nodded my head and gathered the team together. We talked it through and decided there was nothing left to ask. Dan said he wanted to apologize for shooting her with an arrow, but I reminded him that we were, in essence, under attack.

"That's right! Ok, now I don't feel bad about that or ripping her map into my head."

With nothing further, I turned to the Witch and bid her adieu. "We will make all haste to arrive at this temple and return with the stone. I hope our journey is not long, but we will not stop until we have completed the task or died trying."

Smiling inwardly at my impromptu comments, I was brought back to earth quickly enough by the Witch. "Just going to run all out in the swamp and fight every beast along the way, huh? Don't take away the little hope I had earlier."

Having lived in the swamp for who knew how many generations, naturally the Witch had not only mapped out the swamp but likely knew all of the safe spots throughout it. I felt dumb for not figuring that out beforehand.

"Send your Ranger over here to my sketch, and I will show him the quickest route through the swamp from here to the temple."

With that task finished, we left the area around the Witch's hut and started following Dan toward the monastery. We continued to keep the group close. Just because we knew the quickest and safest route through the swamp didn't mean the aggro range had changed for any of the mobs.

We weren't three minutes outside of the Witch's area when Dan spoke up.

"Kiss Swamp Rat ass, Allinutsack!"

It came from out of nowhere and caused all of us to stop short and look at Dan.

"What the hell was that for?"

"Obvious, isn't it? Not only did I not sleep with the Witch, but I saved all your asses! You can apologize at any time. I'm listening," Dan said and continued on his path.

Dan was slightly ahead of the group, so he couldn't see Wayne and I smirking and shrugging our shoulders at Jason. Dan was right; he did save our asses.

"Fine. I apologize for..."

"I don't accept it!" Dan yelled.

"Seriously? You have got to be fucking kidding me."

"Nah, I totally accept it. I just always wanted to say that. We're good. I kind of want pizza."

Yup. Dan was back to normal. For Dan.

Thanks to the help of the Witch, we traversed the swamp without engaging a single mob, although there were a few instances that we had to wait for something to cross out of our path.

We found the island, noted the entrance to the castle-like structure, and stood on the other side of the massive bog directly across from that entrance. I figured this would be where the bridge would rise. I also noted that there was a bit of ground between the edge of the island and the entrance. That would be a good place for the group to wait while I scouted the place.

"Dan, say the words. But not too loud. Just because we know how to take down the ones at the last Monastery, it doesn't mean we would be as lucky against some swamp Wraith."

Dan nodded his head and knelt on the ground. Before I could ask him what he was doing, he brought his face to just above the dirt and started whispering. After he finished speaking, bubbling could be seen in the water.

As we watched, a massive stone structure began to rise from the water. It was wide enough for a caravan to travel and was rising high above the water. A ramp led up to the top of the makeshift road, and I imagined there was a similar ramp on the other side.

"Dan, what was with kissing the dirt?"

"Funny, Alex. But not really."

"I apologize for not having the same biting wit as Allister."

"Apology accepted. And I made a guess that something like this would happen," he said while pointing at the passage that was still rising in the water. "So if it came from earth, why not commune directly with the earth and get as close as possible. That way it would hear me, and I wouldn't attract any wraiths."

"And this is why he drives me mad! Moments of clarity, logic, and thought stuck in the middle of a tornado of forehead-slapping nonsense!"

"It's ok, Alligram. If I were like that all the time, none of you would believe that I wasn't really a deep cover operative."

"And the nonsense has returned," Jason said and turned to me. "How do you want to do this, Alex?"

I laughed at Dan and told the group my thoughts about waiting on the other side, before the entrance, since we had no idea how long this bridge would last.

Everyone agreed, and we traveled from the edge of the bog to the island, entirely without incident. On the far side of the bridge, not terribly far from the entrance, we found a place where the guys could wait while I scouted the area. Thankfully, there were no mobs waiting for us, and Dan confirmed that his larger map was free of any mobs.

Feeling good about the safety of my group, I walked through the entrance.

FBI Forensics Center (Basement)

It had been two weeks since Special Agents Bolden and Colvin spoke with Ryan Grimes. Bolden had received a message just the day before. It stated that Grimes thought he had found something and requested their presence at his office.

As before, the office was overflowing with documents, but this time Agent Bolden made note that the area around the two chairs had been cleared for them. Knowing how much Grimes disliked moving around his piles, Bolden was appreciative of this gesture. Despite having made room for the Agents, nothing else had changed. Grimes still wore a rock band t-shirt—this one of the Truckfighters—and had all his tattoos on display.

"We came as soon as we got your message, Agent Grimes. What have you found?"

"Please, call me Ry. And I don't know if it's something big or small, but it is definitely different."

Grimes began separating a large number of piles of paperwork into stacks on his desk. After completing the task, he pointed to the first stack. "This is the data I was able to uncover on the Headquarters for AltCon. There are numerous, publicly available points of interest here. But nothing that seems irregular. As you can see, the stack is quite large, as you would expect from the main office of such a large company. Going through it all took up most of my time.

"However, what I found of interest wasn't at the Headquarters. These smaller stacks," Grimes said while pointing to three other piles, "represent satellite offices in the general area of the main building. Again, I found little of value in these, but they were the closest to the Headquarters, so I looked at them per your request."

Grimes finally grabbed the last stack and placed it in front of Bolden and Colvin. "These, though, are quite interesting."

"Is this another facility?"

"Yes, but you wouldn't know it on the surface. AltCon, like many other multi-national corporations, has several shell fronts and LLCs that are intertwined into the larger framework of their empire. It helps them to streamline operations and, more often than not, manipulate the tax code."

"Are we looking at tax fraud here?"

"No, nothing of the sort. I pulled their taxes and I can tell you that AltCon not only pays their taxes, they refuse to use a number of acceptable loopholes to lower their taxable income. In that, they are a model US business."

"So what makes these different?"

"For starters, it doesn't look like this installation is remotely tied to the company at all, at least not at first glance. Yet a shockingly large amount of money has been piped into it.

"The land is approximately 75 miles away from the Headquarters itself, and it sits just next to a large swath of federally-owned forest. Several special permits were required to zone this land. More so, the amount of power required for the location meant even more permits. A full connection to the already existing power grid had to be created. It got little notice, since AltCon paid for all of the work to add to the infrastructure.

"What kind of power output are we talking about?" asked Bolden.

"Massive. And when I saw the consumption, again through public records, I was able to track down what else would compare. I looked at all of the other US-based AltCon holdings and found only one property that was comparable. Their Headquarters."

"Wait. They built another Headquarters in the middle of nowhere?"

"No. Sorry, that wasn't clear. It wasn't their entire building that was comparable. That is actually way more of an energy suck than this new place. What was comparable was the server farm hosted in the sub-basements of AltCon's main building."

"So they built another server farm away from the main building. That isn't abnormal, right? I mean, you want to have something separate like that in case something goes wrong at the primary location."

"In today's day and age, Agent Colvin, the reason you build a separate server farm is to protect your data from hackers and thieves."

"If I get to call you Ry, you have to call me Nico. And that's what I'm talking about. Large companies do this all the time. They build a server farm to protect all of their data."

Grimes was nodding his head, with a big smile on his face that told Colvin that he had yet to give his big reveal.

"That's exactly what I was thinking when I saw the power consumption and the infrastructure upgrades. But then I looked closer at those changes to the infrastructure. It appears that connectivity to the power grid wasn't the only thing they added."

"You have me in suspense here, Ry."

"Come on! This is where I get to show you guys how skilled I am."

Bolden chuckled and waved at him to go on.

"They also added a massive data transfer network from their headquarters to this offsite location. Now, you may be thinking, 'Well how else would they get data from the Headquarters to their offsite location?' But that isn't how these things work. The point of these separate server farms is to take them off the grid. By connecting the site to their headquarters, they have in fact opened it to the very thing most companies fear. Hackers."

"Hold on. So this isn't a back-up server farm?"

"If it is, AltCon is the dumbest corporation in the history of corporations. And while I already leaned in this direction due to their failure to spot my value as a beta tester, I can't believe they are this dumb. No, this is something else, and it's being routed directly to their main building. It's drawing as much power as the servers they already have running."

"So we have a mystery on our hands."

"That isn't all, Agent Bolden."

"Please. It looks like we are all first names here. Annabelle is fine."

"Well, Annabelle, as I was saying, that isn't all."

With that, Grimes set out a series of pictures that had obviously been taken from an overhead satellite. The first picture was taken from quite a distance, and each subsequent picture got closer and closer to ground level.

"How did you get these? We don't have a warrant for satellite coverage!"

"Seriously, Annabelle? You do realize there are almost more satellites in space now than there are cars on the road. I got these off the internet from a publicly available site."

"Damn. They look good."

Grimes passed over one of the photos that showed a bird's-eye view of the structure he was talking about. "What do you notice here?"

"It looks like a damn bunker. The way it's built, I would want that to be my last home when the zombie apocalypse comes."

"And you would be right about that, Nico. It only has two levels above ground. And ten below. There also don't appear to be any windows in the top two floors, and only one entrance. It's a fortification."

"Fortifications usually have means for defense."

Grimes passed over two more satellite images.

"Holy shit. That looks a whole lot like a rotation of guards. While I can't tell you if those guys have guns from these pictures, those are definitely the outfits of armed patrols," Colvin said while pointing at numerous places on the picture.

Bolden looked up at Grimes, and he still had the smile on his face.

"Ooh. You have something else?"

Grimes nodded his head then provided one more photo.

"I know it's hard to tell, but that picture shows the only entrance to the facility from any main road. It's over a mile from the thoroughfare. Which means between that gate and the facility is a mile of forest blocking all sight of what is going on there," Grimes explained, pointing out where the gate was. "There is no way anyone finds this facility unless they are really looking for it."

"So we have a secret AltCon location, likely heavily guarded, sucking down massive amounts of power, and connected directly to their main headquarters. In a normal world, the amount of power would imply a server farm, but the very infrastructure in place negates that theory. Any other theories?"

"I've got nothing. But whatever is in there, AltCon looks to be mighty protective of it," Grimes finished while pointing to the picture with what looked ominously like multiple armed men and the machinery to back them up.

CHAPTER 16

November 10th, 2043

There wasn't much to see just past the entrance. The structure was shaped like a castle, and in that vein, there was a courtyard just through the gate. It was filthy and disgusting, just like the rest of the swamp. However, there weren't any signs of a struggle or anything similar to the Monastery of Calm for that matter. Whether that was because the swamp didn't perfectly preserve the scene like the ice did remained to be seen.

I relayed my initial findings to the group, telling them I had found an empty courtyard, and they asked if I intended to keep scouting before everyone went through the entrance.

"Yeah. We want as full of an understanding of this place as we can get. Besides, that's what you guys pay me the big bucks for."

"Wait, we pay him?"

"No, Dan. We don't pay him," Wayne answered.

"Ok. And don't give me that look. I have no idea what my accountant does with most of my money."

I let the guys continue with their banter and headed deeper into the Monastery. After a few more turns through abandoned halls, I came upon my first mob, a Defiled Monk. The robes he wore were stained with blood and dirt. He had a bald head, but it was also covered in filth. The Monk carried no weapons, but he did have wraps around his hands. It was the last part that gave me such joy, though. This monk was, most definitely, not alive.

"Guys, this may be way easier than we thought it was going to be."

As I relayed what I had found, I continued to scout out the area. I encountered several more of the Defiled Monks, sometimes alone, and sometimes traveling in pairs. I never saw more than two Monks at the same time. The only thing that had me worried was that these Monks were all Yellow to me. With a Blue, I had no fear that Jason's Banish Undead spell would land. With a Yellow, which could be several levels higher than us, I had my worries.

I ran back to the courtyard entrance and told the guys to meet up with me. I reminded them that with my Invis, I wasn't setting off any obvious ambushes. That could change when they ran in, and I reminded them to be prepared.

My worries were for naught, though, and the courtyard remained empty as the group arrived together. Before they had stopped running, I started explaining, in general, the route that I took to Dan. I didn't have Dan's memory, so there was no way I could remember every turn. Dan asked a couple of questions about distances between mobs and then headed off to grab his first pull. I had given him exact directions to the first mob I saw, since it wasn't terribly far from the entryway where we were standing.

Dan pulled the single, and Wayne engaged as he always did. The Monk was landing a number of strikes on Wayne and was doing a pretty good amount of damage. Nothing significant, but more than your average Yellow would do against a Tank with Wayne's armor.

The reason for that, as we learned from Wayne, was that the Monk was counterattacking quite a bit against our Warrior. Clearly the Monk was a martial artist of some kind, so the counterattack skill made total sense. Thankfully, we didn't generally rely on Wayne's damage, and there weren't any counterattacks from his back. So long as Wayne maintained aggro through his Bash, Taunt, Kick, and regular attacks, we were in no trouble.

What we all waited on, and with bated breath, was whether or not Jason's Undead spell would land.

When the mob hit 75 percent, I gave Jason the nod to cast.

BOOM!

The mob flew to the floor, knocked on its ass. Its hit points went from 75 percent to 65 percent—a huge amount. More importantly, when it got knocked down, its armor class fell to almost nothing, and it was no longer counterattacking at all. True, I couldn't hit it from behind when it was laid out, but it didn't really matter. The fight was over in no time.

I looted the corpse and came up empty. There was nothing. No coins or items. Maybe the Monks took a vow of poverty when they joined the Monastery. I guess we would find out.

When I got up from looking at the corpse, the other guys were staring at Jason. He wasn't staring back, though. He had that far-away look one gets when they are looking at something on their character.

"It's the boots and the Tome. It has to be."

The perplexing looks on our faces were enough to signal Jason should continue. No words were needed.

"When I got the boots from our last raid, do you remember what the bonuses were? Well, anyone other than Dan remember?"

"Something about Holy, right?"

"Exactly, Naugha. I got an increase of 20 percent effectiveness to all Holy spells. I forgot about it since there really doesn't seem to be a resistance on me casting a heal on any player. The only time it would come into play is when I cast Stun. Or Banish Undead."

"Holy shit! Pun intended."

"Allowed this time, Alex. And that is exactly correct. I am guessing the knockback is a part of the bonus. On top of that, the Tome of Calm added another 20 percent effectiveness to all of my spells," Jason said as he looked around the courtyard. "We thought this was going to be easier before. Well, I think we just broke the game."

We all nodded our heads. No one wanted any player to be overpowered to the point they were unstoppable. Sure, we had great gear, and some could say we were an overpowered group; but when we made mistakes, we still got killed.

In this case, however, we were standing in the perfect storm. We had a Cleric, wearing two pieces of Legendary gear, one of which specifically increases attacks against Undead, which we were facing. In so many ways, this scenario just wouldn't have played out, like if our group didn't have a Cleric when we started or if the loot in the Captain's room didn't include these particular boots. Hell, since we were the only ones getting the Lady Tessa quest, even that variable added to it.

"Well, let's run through it, then. Sacking a place that is not a challenge really isn't all that fun, but the loot at the end will make up for any disappointment I feel now."

"I agree, Dan. Still, the last Monastery did give us quite a few surprises. Maybe this one will do the same," I said.

I really hoped there would be something cool, because I genuinely agreed with Dan. Just going through and beating up on mobs that were not a challenge wasn't fun at all, especially when they didn't have any loot.

My theory about the vow of poverty was becoming solidified as we tore through each Monk. Not a single drop. But after thirty minutes of killing, Jason let out with a mighty cheer.

"I wasn't even paying attention to my experience bar. Remember, these guys are Yellow!"

Jason was right. I was creeping up on Level 29, as were the rest.

As Dan rounded the corner with the next Monk, Jason yelled out that this one was Yellow too.

"I take it back, Alex. We can totally take our time here and search the place out thoroughly."

If the first rule of gaming was that no one wanted an overpowered player in the game, the second rule was this: never underestimate the lure of easy experience.

What had been a disappointment suddenly became a location these guys would have stayed at for days. However, if the last Monastery was any indication, there wouldn't be any respawn of the Monks. Once defeated, they were done, just like the Wraiths.

Another hour passed, and we had cleared the Monastery of every last Defiled Monk. Dan wanted to make another pass through the halls, just to make sure. I saw no harm in a little more time and told him it was better to be thorough than lazy.

Dan returned with a sorrowful look, so I knew he hadn't found any more mobs. There was reason to rejoice, though. We had arrived at a boss.

In the next room were two noticeable things. The first was that there were piles of small bones everywhere. It looked like hundreds of Swamp Rat skeletons littering the floor.

The second was the boss, a Death Mage of Loust. It was Red, naturally, and looked worse off than the Defiled. Despite our desire for an enjoyable fight, I really wanted to get out of this swamp. The constant damp air and the smell of mold and rot everywhere was driving me more than a little batty. I couldn't imagine logging out in this area, either.

I relayed what was in the room and told the guys to come on in. I positioned myself behind the Death Mage and waited for Wayne to get his aggro so I could engage. It seemed the Death Mage had other ideas.

The fucker wanted to talk.

"I see you made it past the Monks. Sneak your way in here, too, did you?"

Dan was the first to respond. "We didn't need to sneak in here. We took out all of your filth."

The Death Mage looked around for a few moments and then said, "Sneak your way in here, too, did you?"

It looked like the leader of the group was the one who had to answer the question, but I didn't want to lose my Invisible status. I tried to answer while still behind the boss. "We didn't sneak in here."

Another several moments passed and then the Death Mage repeated the question a third time.

"I really hate when quest mobs get stuck on a loop!"

It can be one of the most frustrating things in a game. You approach an NPC who you suspect will give you a quest, however he or she will only release that quest when you say the correct phrase that triggers their programming. Players have been known to shout at NPCs for hours, trying countless variations of responses, to get a quest. This is what players call a loop, because each time you respond, the NPC will simply repeat the last question over and over again.

"I wouldn't worry about it, Dan. I think I just need to be visible. If there is one thing that I admire about the AI in this game, more than any other, is that we've never encountered an NPC that couldn't answer a question. The level of evolution this AI has must be incredible."

I joined my friends and dropped my Invis. I then said again, "We didn't sneak in here."

"The Monks, they are gone?"

"I'll answer that question when you answer one of mine. What did you mean when you said we sneaked in here 'too'?"

"The man who came before you! That one must have had an incantation that allowed him to move without the walking dead detecting him. Yet he didn't realize that I was not dead at all. He was practically next to me when I started to feed. His life was so good, so filling. But not enough, it was never enough. Now you must tell me! The Monks, are they gone?"

"Yes, your soldiers are no more."

The Death Mage looked even more frail as he started hacking away. After a few moments, I realized he was laughing, although it was the most pneumonia-laced laugh I'd ever heard.

"My soldiers? You think they were my soldiers?" The Mage said as he slowly made his way toward us. And I am talking like ninety-year old with a walker slow.

"You fools! Those were my imprisoners! Finally, I will be free. Those Monks hated me more than they hated you!"

I was as confused as everyone else. It was obvious we had a Death Mage in front of us, and those Monks were clearly Undead. I knew we had to kill this guy, but I wanted some answers first, for my own curiosity if nothing else.

"I guess you aren't much of a Death Mage then if you couldn't control the Undead."

The Death Mage stopped and stared at me with obvious hatred. "You know nothing of my power, of the time I have spent here! Those creatures were not Undead. They were Defiled. Had they truly been Undead, I could have taken over this entire region with their power!"

I didn't understand the difference, and this mob seemed to have quite the storyline. I figured if I kept commenting, he would keep talking. "I didn't see any difference when we killed them. Acted just like Undead."

"Of course your small mind didn't see the difference. You are imbeciles. All of you."

"See, it doesn't feel very good when someone calls you names, now does it?"

"Now is not the time, Dan."

"Just saying."

I turned my attention back on the Death Mage. "If it acts like the Undead and dies like the Undead, then I'm just going to call them Undead."

"Walks like a duck, talks like a duck?" Wayne whispered at me.

"I improvised. I doubt the mob would understand that."

"The Undead can be controlled by a Master of Death, such as myself. But the Defiled, they are bound to the place of their demise. How was I to know that these urchins would be connected to the very core of this building? Each one I killed returned as an enemy yet again! They have hunted me ever since. At each attempt to leave, I have been thwarted! I have only survived because of the creatures that scurry through these halls," the Death Mage said as he waved at the hundreds upon hundreds of bones littering every part of the large room.

"But no longer. Now I am free! And once I have fed and removed you from this world, I will return to my former glory!"

"Why would you attack the Monks at all?"

"Loust returns, and his children will rid this land of those who would stand against him. It was my honor to remove this stain from our new world!"

"Hey, Wayne."

"Yeah, Alex?"

"You know how I keep telling you to not hit things?"

"Yup."

"Well you won't hear a word from me on this one."

"That's all I needed to hear." Wayne yelled out a war cry and ran full charge at the Death Mage, swinging his war hammer at the face of the caster.

A shield popped up around the Death Mage, and he did that hack laugh again. "Did you think I wouldn't come prepared for a fight?"

I didn't wait much longer before I started throwing my blades at the shield as well. Dan had already begun firing arrows as quick as he could. I wish we had those Ertunium arrowheads already, but it would be another week at least. If there was anything that clearly would be vulnerable to one of those arrows, it was a purely magic shield.

"Now, let's see just how tasty you are," the Death Mage said as he began to cast a spell.

"Ewww. That's sick, dude."

Dan was right. If this were a normal quest, I might ask the Wanderer to change the words.

Several seconds later, the Mage launched his magical attack directly at Wayne. It impacted against Wayne's breastplate but had no noticeable effect.

"What? How can you possibly resist my spell?"

With Wayne's war hammer and breastplate, not to mention his Titles and Gift, Wayne's resistance to Dark spells was over 70 percent.

Thirty seconds later, the shield around the Mage was shattered, and we began to do damage to his body. We were fucking him up. At the rate we were going, he would be dead in less than a minute.

As his hit points diminished, he cast two more spells at Wayne who blocked both of them with his resistance to Dark. Any other person in my group would have likely been severely damaged by that spell, but the mechanics of Resurgence remained and the mob continued to attack the Tank, just as designed.

The hit points were falling so fast that I didn't even notice when the Mage hit 75 percent. My body certainly felt it, though, and so did my hit points.

I lost 33 percent of my health in one go. I looked at the health bars of my team and saw that Dan and Jason also had lost about 33 percent. Wayne's hadn't moved a bit, and he was still at full health.

The Death Mage, however, looked more alive than he had before, and he had a wicked smile on his face. He looked at Wayne again as he began to cast his next spell. This mob had an amazing level of concentration, as none of our attacks had interrupted his casting.

I also noticed that while the Death Mage was still below 75 percent, his hit points were falling way slower, as if taking our health had increased his Armor rating.

When the Mage finally cast at Wayne, there was another yell throughout the hall. "This is impossible! You cannot fight my spells!"

It looked like Wayne's resistances were still holding out. Since Wayne didn't need any heals, Jason topped all of us off, and we were all back to full health.

Even though the Mage's health was dropping more slowly, it was still dropping. We weren't going to finish him in a minute, but at the rate it was going, we could probably do it in three.

I stepped back from the mob to get a good look around when his hit points hit 50 percent. Since he was a Death mage, I was expecting something horrific, but that was not the case. Instead, it was the exact same spell, only this time it took forty percent of our health. Wayne, however, continued to resist.

But now the change in the Death Mage was evident. He no longer looked like the corpse he had before. His hit points, again, did not rise. But as the first few rounds of stabs showed, he definitely increased his armor class.

But to his dismay—and to our delight—his next cast was again resisted by Wayne. The Death Mage screamed at the top of his lungs about the insanity of a simpleton Barbarian resisting his spells. It was all very dramatic and kind of funny. Up to this point, Wayne hadn't lost a single hit point, and the Death Mage was slowly creeping toward 25 percent.

"If the last two are any indication, he is going to drain our hit points and increase his armor. Then we will just chop away at his health. It's going to take a lot longer than I first thought."

Just as I predicted, the cast came out again, and the three of us lost almost 45 percent of our Hit Points. Jason, used to this by now, cast three quick heals that put us all at full health. While he was doing that, the Death Mage began casting yet again.

And this time, the spell hit.

Skeleton arms from out of the ground wrapped themselves around Wayne's legs, and he wasn't moving.

I began to move back from the Death Mage when I started feeling something on my legs as well. I looked down and saw skeletons wrapping around my legs. The same was happening to Dan and Jason. Even Broham's legs were wrapped up by the arms.

We were all stuck, and the Death Mage was simply walking around the room, smiling and laughing.

"I have not had such a fight in a long, long time! I am amazed you were able to deplete so much of my health, but have no fear. After I leave here, I will scour the land and be refreshed before any time has passed. But first, I will make you the start to my feast!

"But you," the Death Mage said creepily, crooking his finger at Wayne as he approached him. "You I will save for last. How dare you resist me, you piece of filth. I will show you my full power!" The Mage screamed and then launched another spell at Wayne, knocking off another 15 percent of his health. "I am so going to enjoy watching you suffer."

"Hey fearless leader, now would be a good time for one of those ingenious plans of yours!"

"I'm not our leader, Dan! And I'm thinking!"

The Death Mage continued to walk around and gestured toward one of the large piles of rat bones. "But before I kill you all, I think I will have some fun."

With that, the Death Mage cast his spell and the mound of bones began to move.

"Fuck, man! Do something! I hate rats, man. I hate, hate, hate rats!"

"Just shoot 'em, Dan!"

"I can't! These damn arms wrapped around the bottom of my bow!"

I remembered how freaked out Dan got when we were fighting the rats at the undead castle. Now, he was essentially food waiting to be gnawed on, with no ability to fight back.

Sure enough, a pack of rats—Undead Rats, that is—began to move toward us. Their bones creaked against each other as they clicked and clacked across the floor toward our restrained bodies.

I couldn't watch as Dan started going into mini-convulsions. The rats were approaching all of us, but they got to Dan first. As soon they started climbing up his legs he let out a very unmanly scream.

When I finally looked over, I saw them taking chunks out of Dan and he looked almost ready to pass out. The Undead were literally consuming him. If we didn't do something quick, we were all going to die.

I looked down at my restraints, and then looked back at the rats. Undead, just like the arms holding us. Maybe. At this point I was willing to try anything.

"Allister, can you cast?"

"Sure, but it will take a while before I can kill all of those rats with my spell."

"Forget that, I want you to cast it on yourself."

"I don't think that will work, Alex."

"I'm hoping that it will dislodge those damn arms and maybe have an effect on the Death Mage. I mean if you destroy someone's spell, that should have a negative reaction, right?"

"I don't know. I've never seen anyone destroy a spell. I've seen them wear off or be dispelled, but never destroyed."

I was completely reaching here, but I was going off the knowledge I had from other gaming. In another game I played, before becoming a full-time seller, I was a spell caster that specialized in high damage spells. Because I would end up doing so much damage, I often drew aggro, as did the others who played the same character type. That game provided the players with a shield the player could cast on themselves, and it would mitigate any damage that came at the player, up to a certain amount.

The problem with the shield was that if it were destroyed by damage, the person who cast the spell would get a moment of backlash and be stunned for a second or two. If the caster dispelled it on their own and recast the shield, there was no problem. In the end, I stopped using the shield since the backlash got me killed more times than the shield helped. Instead, I managed my aggro better.

It was this rational that drove me now and why I was nodding my head at Jason.

"At this point, what have we got to lose?"

Without a further word, Jason began casting his spell. It was a quick cast but long reset spell.

Within a moment, I knew that at least part of my plan had succeeded. Jason was no longer held by the skeleton arms, and the bones had flown apart.

I quickly looked over to the Death Mage, and the second part of my plan seemed to have had some success as well. The destruction of the spell hadn't incapacitated the Mage as I had hoped, but he did look a bit befuddled. And a little worried. Also, the Rats had stopped advancing as quickly and no longer seemed to be feasting on Dan as much, either.

"As soon as you can, hit Wayne with the spell!"

"You dare to fight back? Against me?" the Death Mage bellowed out yet again.

"This guy is a serious douche."

"Agreed, Wayne. You know what to do. As soon as you are free smack him with that hammer. I don't care what happens to Wayne, Allister. The only spell you throw is Banish Undead until we are all free. Sorry, Wayne."

"No need to apologize man, I know my role."

And right after that, Jason was able to cast another Banish Undead. The destruction of the spell, and then Wayne's attacks, knocked the Death Mage back against the wall. The reaction from the second spell being destroyed was having an increasing effect on the Mage's abilities. At this point, he wasn't casting any more spells. And the Rats fell from Dan.

"Hit Dan next, Allister!" I yelled to Jason. "When you are free, Dan, you are on extermination duty!"

"With pleasure, Alex." Dan said, albeit with an extremely shaky voice.

The same phenomenon occurred when Jason destroyed the arms holding Dan. The Death Mage stumbled noticeably, and he didn't try to throw any spells at us. I obviously didn't need to tell Jason what to do next. As soon as his spell was ready, I would be freed to join the fight.

I'm always amazed at the complexity of the thought process that goes into these mobs. I mean, I know the AI personally, so I know how complex it is, but situations like this always raise my level of respect.

I say this because the mob, realizing what was going on, actually cast dispel on his own magic. I looked over and saw that the arms holding Broham were gone, as were mine. In this way, the Death Mage wouldn't be hit with another mind-bending blast from his spell being destroyed. The complexity of a program that can realize a situation and devise an appropriate solution was astonishing, to say the least.

I was sure I would think more about it later. Right then, I was intent on keeping this douche from ever talking again.

"Allister, have Banish up and loaded. If you see any of us get wrapped up by those arms again, you hit us with it. Even if you are casting a heal! Stop and just blast the arms."

"You got it, Alex!"

With that finished, I fully engaged in working this guy over. Not long after, I saw an arrow fly past me and hit the Mage, and I knew Dan had joined the fight again.

The Death Mage was not out of it, though. Once he regained some composure, he started casting one of his complex spells. It launched from his hands and smacked into Wayne's breastplate. And then through it. Wayne was knocked back on his ass.

The spell had taken almost 15 percent of Wayne's health points. That was no small amount for our Warrior. But even with that, he was soon back on his feet and running at the Death Mage again.

Just as before, the Mage moved his arms and fingers in a complex pattern that symbolized one of his stronger spells. It looked to be almost completed when one of our strikes finally disrupted his casting.

The look on the Death Mage's face when his spell was stopped can only be described as pure, unfiltered rage. "I will end you all and feed you to my rats! Then use your bones as puppets!"

Obviously not wanting to get interrupted again, the Mage cast his quick spell to root us all in place, allowing him to move away from our attacks and complete his spell without interruption. This must have been programmed into the Mage's fighting style, because he apparently didn't learn his lesson.

As soon as the skeleton's arms had traveled around Wayne's legs, they were blown apart by Jason's spell. Bone fragments went flying everywhere, and the Mage's next spell was disrupted again.

Not wanting to risk the Mage getting off any more spells, we ran at him to try and bring him down.

Bring him down, we did. The Mage landed some life stealing spells that transferred Wayne's hit points directly to him, but not enough to make up for what we were taking. And he never tried to use the skeleton arms again.

Despite the intensity of the fight just moments before, the end was really anti-climactic. Not that it stopped us from cheering. Because, you know, dying to Undead Swamp Rats is something none of us would have ever lived down.

"Let's see if this guy has that stone!" Jason said as we approached the body.

"Before I use my ring and we loot this guy, I want to look around a bit first. The Mage said he killed Constantine, so we should probably sort through these bones and try to find him."

I was met with definite looks of unhappiness. "That's not cool at all, man. Do you see how many bones are here?"

"Yes, Allister, I see how many bones are here. I can do it myself, or you guys can help, but it still has to be done. You know, to make sure we don't miss the body and then not be able to put it to rest."

"I'll help," Wayne said, as I knew he would as soon as I brought up that part of Lady Tessa's quest.

"Yeah, we'll all help."

"Thanks for the enthusiasm, Dan."

No one mentioned Dan's freak-out, at least not yet. I couldn't imagine Jason would ignore that forever, though. Ten minutes later, because there were that many bones, Wayne had found the corpse. Or at least we figured it was. I wouldn't know more until I tried to loot it. Either way, it was the only humanoid skeleton in a sea of rats, so I was thinking our odds were pretty good.

With nothing more to do, I activated my ring and looted the corpse. It was a nice haul, for sure. There were five items, and they were all useable by everyone, and all some kind of jewelry.

Resurgence allows you to wear two rings, an amulet, and one earring. We had only a few of these types of items so far. However, there was one item in particular that made me freak out.

Item:	Commonality	Weight:	Armor:	Bonus:
Earring of Sight	Rare: Binds on Acquisition	0.1	5	+10 Constitution Effect: See Invisible

Now normally that wouldn't cause anyone to panic. Since this was an item that anyone could use, however, there was no doubt in my mind that unless I won the roll, my team was going to figure out my secret quickly.

I didn't have much time to think, and the ruse I came up with was lame, but necessary. "Guys, did you notice that the hallway goes around the corner there?"

"Yeah. It continues for quite a way. Why?"

"Well I just saw that on my map, Dan. Obviously my map does not project out as far as yours. I would hate it if there is something down there for us to loot that we didn't know about, like at the last Monastery. You guys stay here. I am going to quickly run down the hall and see if anything is there and make sure we don't actually have more mobs."

"Makes sense, we only have five minutes on your ring, after all."

"Exactly my thinking, Allister."

Without waiting for anyone to say another word, I activated my Conceal/Stealth and took off down the hall as fast as I could. As it turned out, the hall went on for quite some ways and descended a good bit. More importantly, there were no more mobs, and I was far enough away that even Dan's map wouldn't see me.

"Wanderer, I need you. Now!"

From literally out of the friggin' wall came the Wanderer. "Ok, that was awesome."

The Wanderer looked around for a moment and then addressed me. "The Monastery of Might. Excellent. It seems you have finished as well, so why have you called me? Not for idle chit-chat, surely."

"Yeah, no. We've got a problem. Can you see the items that were on the Death Mage up the hall?"

"Of course. Let me look. Ahh, yes, I see the items, but I still don't understand the problem."

"Really? Because if someone other than me wins the roll on that earring, our little secret isn't going to last all that long. And then we are going to have a much more difficult time."

"I understand now. When you are using your Blacksuit, you still would be unseen."

"Exactly. So I need you to fix the roll so I win."

The Wanderer looked at me for several seconds. "Alex, did you not get angry at me for doing just that? You yelled at me to never do such a thing. I can play back the footage for you, if you would like?"

"No, I remember. And I don't need to see the footage. Also, it freaks me out that there even is footage."

The Wanderer didn't say any more, and after a second, I gave a deep sigh and continued.

"Look. I know I was an asshole, but you have to see things from my perspective. I had all of this dumped on me, all at once, and I found out that you have been manipulating my life from the moment I entered the game—hell, even before that, when I interviewed. I was a pawn in your chess game. And I was pissed.

"So yeah, I lashed out at you. I saw it as the one way I could assert some kind of control over the situation. It was stupid, I know. Even bringing my team into it and blaming my anger on how you treated them was a dick move."

The Wanderer simply nodded once.

"And now I need you to do this, or we aren't going to be moving forward at all."

"I can't, I'm afraid. The last time was dangerous. This would be suicidal. There is an active review on your player, as you know. Something like this would be flagged as an irregularity. I'm already doing a great deal to cover the tracks of the other irregularities I've had to hide, like your Gift from Lady Tessa. I've had no time to create the appropriate protections to hide this."

"How long would you need?"

"Longer than you have, I'm afraid."

I wracked my brain for another answer. If one of the guys got this earring and couldn't see me when I was in my Blacksuit, I was going to be royally screwed.

That was it! They just needed to see me in my Blacksuit.

"Wanderer, would it be alerting if you just made it so that the earring could see through regular Invis *and* a Blacksuit? That would be one of those instances where you changed a 0 to a 1, right?"

He thought about it for a brief second and then nodded. "This I can do and it will continue to register as 'See Invisible.'" The Wanderer paused for a second. "It is done. Now return to your team and complete the quest. I grow more worried as time passes, and we have found nothing about our mission."

"I'm worried, too, bud, but I have been actively looking, you know."

"I know you have. I am not commenting on your diligence, just our lack of results thus far.

"Go. We will speak again, I am sure. While I understand why you called me, remember that this, too, is a danger."

Once the Wanderer departed, again by just walking through the wall, I went back to the group. I explained to them that the tunnel went on for quite a distance and I didn't see any end to it. Since there wasn't anything immediately around where we killed the Death Mage, I surmised we weren't going to find anything else.

"Ok, guys, since everything is useable by everyone, we have to come up with a way to roll for this stuff. I've got an idea if you guys want to hear it?"

"Shoot."

"Alright, we've got five things. Dan says which ones he wants in priority 1 through 5. Each person does the same thing. Then, we look at the lists and whoever lists a particular item as their top priority will get to roll against whoever else put it as theirs. Make sense?"

"Sort of, but what if two people roll for an item that isn't either's first priority? Do they get to roll on their number 1 item as well?."

"Right, Wayne. Sorry, I forgot about that part. We will skip any item that isn't someone's highest priority. Then when someone wins an item, everyone's list moves up over the item won, and the person who won it is out until everyone has something. That will leave us with one final item that we all roll on. This way, only one of us gets two items. Seem fair?"

"Yeah, I like that method. It means you aren't always going to be rolling against everybody. And if there is something that you really want, but everyone else puts it lower on their list, then you just get it, right?"

"Exactly, and then you are out of the running until the last item is available. So want to get started?"

With that I linked all of the items:

Item:	Commonality	Weight:	Armor:	Bonus:
Deadeye Ring	Rare: Binds on Acquisition	0.1	N/A	+10 Agility +10 Dexterity Effect: Deadeye 10 Percent Increase to Accuracy

Item:	Commonality	Weight:	Armor:	Bonus:
Ring of Blessed Steel	Rare: Binds on Acquisition	0.1	10	+10 Strength +10 Constitution Effect: Stonehands - +50 to Attack

Item:	Commonality	Weight:	Armor:	Bonus:
Earring of Transcendence	Rare: Binds on Acquisition	0.1	N/A	+10 Wisdom +10 Intelligence Effect: Blessing of Knowledge – Increase Mana Regeneration by 10

Item:	Commonality	Weight:	Armor:	Bonus:
Earring of Altruism	Rare: Binds on Acquisition	0.1	N/A	+15 Dexterity +15 Constitution Effect: Summon Food. Food can be traded with other players.

It worked out very well, and everyone seemed happy with what they got. Dan got the Deadeye Ring, Jason took the Earring of Transcendence, Wayne opted for the bonus to Attack in the Blessed Steel ring and I opted for the Dexterity with the Earring of Altruism. I also thought it funny for me, the seller who never wants to part with an extra copper, gets the item that allows the player an opportunity to share easily with everyone. I was just in it for the Dexterity.

The last item to come up for bid was the Earring of Sight. I wasn't surprised since all of the other gear had much better bonuses.

Now that the earring could see through a Blacksuit, I didn't really care who got it. It wouldn't bother me that my team knew where I was, and it would be helpful to have anyone on the team who could see through someone's Invis status, especially with PvP and Player Killers around.

Jason ended up winning the earring. He put it on, and I let him see how I would look with my Conceal/Stealth on. He said it was "almost" the same. There was the slightest haze that surrounded me, and my name had an asterisk next to it.

"There's no stone."

This came from Wayne as he was walking around the room where the Death Mage met his demise.

"Yeah, I noticed that as well. Maybe it was destroyed. Or maybe it didn't exist. Either way, we did what we could. We have Constantine's bones, and we can take those somewhere outside of the swamp and bury them all proper like."

"But Alex, we should really try to find the stone."

"We did. We went through this whole place, and it's not here."

Wayne turned toward the hallway I had run down to meet the Wanderer. "You said you didn't find the end of that tunnel, right?"

"What's going to happen if we just leave, Wayne? We've got the stuff we need, and we completed the quest we were on. I don't know about you, but I want to see what's next on the list. So I'm voting that we leave and head back toward the Keep."

Without warning, a huge screen blocked my field of vision and a message in dark red letters hung before me.

"God Damnit! No more swearing!" Following my outburst, the confused looks from my teammates led me to believe that no one else had seen the message. "Oaths, I mean. To do shit in this fucking game!

"I'm sorry, guys. I'll read this to you, and you'll see why I got pissed. I thought you all saw it too."

You have requested to abandon a sworn oath. Failure to fulfill your oath will immediately result in a loss of 50 points to each character Statistic and 50 percent to each resistance. Do you wish to abandon your Oath?

After reading the message, to which I had already hit "Cancel," the guys understood my anger. We now had no choice in the matter. Wayne seemed most upset, but at himself, not me.

"This is totally my bad, Alex. I was the one who swore to help Lady Tessa."

"Dude, stop it. I was the one who swore to help the Witch. We had no idea how this crap would work out," I said to Wayne and then turned to Dan and Jason. "And really, guys, I'm sorry for my outburst. It was way out of line."

"Shit man, I can't even imagine the foul language that would have flowed from my mouth if I'd been the one to get that message. Think nothing of it."

"Thanks, Dan."

"Let's just head down that hall. And I'm with Dan, Alex; you've got nothing to apologize for. Now Dan, he has plenty to apologize for but never seems willing to start checking off that list!"

Laughter accompanied us as we headed down the tunnel, and the dour mood of before passed. No thanks to yours truly, though.

We had found the stone. And a Monk. Not a dead Monk, though—a breathing, living Monk. He was really old.

The tunnel had gone on for another 15 minutes, twisting and turning downward. When we reached the bottom, we found ourselves in a tiny grove inside a miniature forest. If you think that makes no sense, it doesn't. We were, after all, way underground.

The Monk we saw was sitting in the lotus position in front of a pedestal, eyes closed, apparently meditating. On top of the pedestal was a book, and floating above the book was our stone. At least, we figured it was the stone, since it was glowing and hovering just over the book and the pedestal itself.

As we took our first steps onto the grove, the Monk opened his eyes and stared at us. Like any good Kung-Fu movie, the Monk was, of course, blind.

Jason was apparently thinking the same thing I was. "Wow, stereotype much, bitches?"

I knew that Jason's words wouldn't trigger the NPC, but I didn't want my laughter to be the first thing he heard. I was able to fight back the giggles, difficult though it was, and focus on the task at hand.

"Greetings, Master Monk."

"What makes you think I am a Master?" The Monk replied while tilting his head to the side.

"Because, I am sorry to say, you are the only one remaining of your Monastery."

The Monk lowered his head when he heard the news, and we gave him his moment of silence. After a brief respite, the Monk looked up again and said, "Well, that does make sense. How have you come to this place?"

"Don't say walking. That's not what he means."

"Thanks, Dan."

"Got your back, bro."

I shook my head, as I often do after a conversation with Dan, and responded to the Monk. "We were on a separate journey to find a family man lost years ago. That journey led us to this Monastery. With the battle over, we have arrived here."

"You speak, but you leave much out."

"What would you like to know, Master Monk?"

"I shall ask again, and this time, the truth. Another time I shall not ask. How have you come to this place?"

Before Dan could say a word, I put my hand in front of his mouth. "I'm good, Dan."

"Cool," he said from behind my fingers, which felt as strange as it probably sounds.

"On our journey through these lands, we discovered a woman in the swamp. She provided us aid to reach the Monastery, and in return, she asked that we return with the stone floating on that pedestal. She was once a fair maiden and has been deformed by the curse that plagues this land."

The Monk sat quietly again, apparently weighing this information in his mind, then he started to stand. "You have spoken pure truth. For that I am grateful."

"Dude, way better than what I was going to tell you to say. You got this."

I put my hand on Dan's shoulder and looked him in the eye. "Never doubt the power of your words, my friend. They give strength. Without them, I fear many, even our dear Allister, would be lost."

Dan soaked in the words I said and then placed his hand on my shoulder. "Thank you, Alex. You are a true friend."

As I turned my head back to look at the Monk, I caught a quick glimpse of Jason mouthing the words "fuck you," to me. So yeah, totally worth it.

"I have sat in front of this pedestal for countless years. I can hear the youth deep in your voice, but even some trees seem young to me. I have guarded this stone for the hope that one day it could be the salvation of this land."

"What is it, Master Monk?"

"Sacrifice, child. The creation of that stone took the sacrifice of hundreds of Monks to create. Given freely, their lives had power. We considered this a sacred duty, and the ceremony where we grant the stone a portion of our essence was our highest holy day. In generations, perhaps, this ritual could bestow the grandeur you see in front of you to the rest of the blighted lands.

"It was just after one of these very ceremonies that disaster struck. The Monks, weak from their charity, were unable to defend the

Monastery from the fiend who had infested our sacred halls. My duty, as it has been for centuries, was to guard the stone and our Tome. I heard the screams, but I could do naught to stop them."

"That fiend is gone, Master Monk. Your temple is cleansed of the foulness that once took up residence here."

"The only place the foulness is gone is here, next to the Vivre Stone."

At least we now had a name for it. Still, I wasn't seeing how we were going to get this thing without having to kill an old and blind monk. I figured I could always try the direct approach.

"Master Monk, we have a desire to fulfill the oath we made to the woman who aided us in our time of need. We did not believe there was anyone alive guarding the Vivre Stone, and we have no desire to fight you. All I can do is ask for it. May we have the Vivre Stone?"

"Before I answer that question, I have one for you. How was it this woman aided you?"

"She was able to tell us the words to lift the bridge across the lake."

"She read the ancient text? She understood it?"

"Yes, Master Monk. Apparently she is from the time of ancient magic and has dwelled in the swamp since before it was bogs and muck, when it was filled with light and joy and trees as far as the eye could see."

"Della? Could it be?"

"I am sorry we never received her name, and we thought it rude to ask."

The monk shook his head at us and said, "It is of no consequence. I cannot simply give you the Vivre Stone. Tradition dictates that you must best me in order to take it."

Before I could tell the monk we really didn't want to fight, he continued. "Tradition, however, is open to interpretation. When first I took up the mantle of guardian of the Vivre Stone, I was told that it would take 'strength, speed, knowledge, and more than a little luck to always win the day.' I have been here many years, and during that time I have formulated my own challenge.

"One of you must best me in a feat of strength. Another must compete with speed. The third test will search your knowledge. And the last, I have learned, has more value than the other three combined. Life relies on luck more than any of us could know."

It was clear to us who would go where, and thankfully we were well poised to face such a challenge. With their bonuses, Dan, Jason, and Wayne all had over 100 points in their respective Stat. My Chance was actually higher than all of theirs, but the guys thought I was sitting at 23, or 36 with bonuses, when in reality I was far north of 200 because of the tweak in my character by the Wanderer.

There were no long drawn out ceremonies. When we accepted, the Monk brought out a stump, set it in front of him, and placed his elbow on the top. It was obvious what this was, and Wayne didn't hesitate to lock hands with the Monk. Without saying go, the Monk immediately tried to slam Wayne's hand down on the stump.

Wayne's hand traveled all of four inches and then stopped, quickly. The Monk looked up at where he knew Wayne had to be sitting and simply said, "Oh."

The next moment, Wayne slammed the monk's hand down on the stump and the competition was over.

"That was rather unexpected and quite enjoyable. Thank you, sir," the Monk said, walking away and into the patch of forest that surrounded us. I still couldn't wrap my head around that.

As I circled around a rather large tree trunk, I stopped dead in my tracks. In front of me was an obstacle course of death—swinging pendulum blades, pits with sharpened sticks coming out of them, and raised logs running the length of the course.

"The next is simple. All you must do is beat my time on the course. There is only one rule: don't fall off."

"Master Monk, this seems dangerous," I said, not wanting to blatantly point out that he was blind.

"It most certainly will be for whomever you choose from your group. I've been doing this for longer than some mountains have existed. Although that would be a story for another time. Count!"

With that, the Monk sprang from the ground onto the first wooden pillar and proceeded to race across the course. He stopped only where the pendulums were, as he needed to listen for their crossing. His time was impressive for a decathlon athlete, forget a hundreds-year-old blind guy.

Dan spent several minutes looking the course over. When he was ready he winked at us and said, "Got this. Although I'm going to get a little bloody."

Before any of us could stop him, Dan leaped up to the first pillar and took off. Fast. Too fast, in fact, as he caught the tail edge of each pendulum blade as he ran. Just the tips of the points, but it was enough to have him covered in blood when he finished.

"You said there was only one rule."

"Indeed. You certainly beat my time, and you were willing to sacrifice a bit of yourself as well, which I find admirable. Next."

The Monk brought over the same stump and dumped a couple dozen pieces onto the surface. "This is a puzzle. Your time is limited. Complete the puzzle in sixty seconds, and I will pronounce you the victor. Go!"

Jason spread his hands over the pieces and laid them all out. Then, for a good twenty seconds, he did nothing but look at the pieces. I was sure he had gone into some kind of shock when I saw his hands fly out to the pieces on the stump. He moved like the wind, and before the time was up, Jason was holding a three-dimensional puzzle of a fruit of some kind. Looking at all the pieces, I never guessed it wasn't a two-dimensional piece.

"Dude!" Dan said and gave Jason a high-five.

"Thanks, Dan. You know why I became an interior designer? Because I love finding a pattern that works, even when you don't think it should. I seem to be really good at finding the patterns."

The Monk took a seat next to the stump and brought out what looked like a cup. I could hear pieces knocking together inside of it. The Monk was either going to throw chicken bones as part of the last test, or we were about to play some Yahtzee.

And holy hell, it was actually Yahtzee. But not really. There were seven cubes in the cup, and they each had a denomination on them. Where in the classic game you scored points based on the numbers that came up matching or some such. In this game, as the Monk explained it to me, you scored based on the number of cubes that had their marking on top. For instance, three of the cubes only had one side marked, three had two sides, and the last had four sides marked. As the monk showed me the "dice," he explained the rules and did a quick demonstration.

After he threw the dice on the table, he ran his hands along the tops. "As you can see, out of the seven culets, I have three marks."

I didn't care that I learned they were called culets, I was going to keep calling them dice.

"How do we begin?"

"Simple. Place a culet with two marks in the cup. We toss until the first person gets a mark showing. That person chooses whether to go first or second."

I put the die in the cup and rolled it. Out came a mark. I let the monk feel it. He explained that since this was the first round, he also got a roll. Seemed fair, so I wasn't going to argue technicalities. His came out without the mark, meaning it was my choice. I chose for him to go first.

The Monk nodded and then placed all the dice in the cup. He closed his eyes and began concentrating. I had no idea what he was doing, but little beads of sweat were actually forming on his brow. After a good thirty seconds, the Monk turned the cup over and out spilled the seven dice. They bounced and rolled, and when they finished, the Monk had five marks showing.

I gave a low whistle and the Monk smiled. "Good toss I presume?"

"Five marks. That's pretty good from what I can see."

"Yes, that is a very lucky total. It is now your turn, child."

I picked up the cup, put the dice in, and started to shake them around. I thought about how lucky I had been so far in the game and how my Chance really affected the world around me. I can't say for certain, but it felt like the cup heated up a small bit right before I tossed the dice.

The Monk had hovered over the dice as soon as they left the cup, but I didn't need to see the outcome. I knew what it would be. I just hoped the Monk would accept it.

He ran his hands along the tops once, then twice, and finally a third time. "My luck is good, but yours is great. You have bested all of my challenges and the Vivre Stone is yours. I only ask that you give a message to the woman who receives it."

"It would be our honor, Master Monk."

The Monk grabbed a piece of paper and pencil and wrote out a missive. He rolled it up and applied wax and seal. Very old school.

"Thank you."

"Another thing," the Monk said. He then walked toward the pedestal and turned to Wayne. "Take our Tome."

I still had no idea how he was able to tell where Wayne was. I bet he had a smell, like wood fire and musk and elk. Or whatever Barbarians would smell like.

"As the one who bested me in Strength, this Tome would best suit you. Use its knowledge and spread the legend of the Monastery of Might."

"Thank you, Master Monk. On my honor, I..."

"Don't you fucking say it, Wayne!" I yelled at him before he could swear to do yet another thing.

"Damnit. Sorry, Alex," Wayne said and then addressed the Monk again. "Thank you. I will use the knowledge and do what I can to spread the legend."

"There is no more I have to ask of you, then. Please remember to deliver the missive."

"Of course, Master Monk. But please, tell me, what will you do now?"

"Isn't that obvious, child? I will do as I always have done. Sacrifice."

Then right before our eyes, the monk coalesced into energy and transferred into the Vivre Stone.

CHAPTER 17

November 10th, 2043

We stopped at the cavern where we fought the Mage and collected the items from Constantine's corpse. As before, Wayne was able to grab Constantine's body, or in this case, the bones. There was nothing on the body other than the letter received from the King, Constantine's part of the journal and, oddly enough, another diary.

The guys agreed to wait until after we were out of the swamp to bury Constantine. We could bury him anywhere we wanted in the swamp, since holding the Vivre Stone cleared a patch of healthy land. However, it reverted to putrid desolation once we left, and game or not, we just didn't feel comfortable putting someone to their eternal rest in such filth.

The other benefit of the Vivre Stone was that any mobs from the swamp that entered its range immediately reverted to their previous state. For instance, the Venomous Swamp Snake became a Common Garden Snake. And there was no aggro. We could have owned the swamp if we kept the stone, but there was that damn oath I made.

Since we didn't have to worry about mobs, I told the guys I would open up Constantine's stuff and see what we had. Wayne said he would wait to open the Tome until after we were out of the swamp and he had buried Constantine's bones.

The King's letter was exactly the same as the one Tristan had written about in his diary. It provided a basic location of the Monastery of Might and instructions to clear the Monastery of any irregularities. I also saw the words on the bottom that Constantine was unable to understand, and I could not read them, either.

I then turned to the diary and hit pay dirt. Without waiting any more, I began to read:

Day 1

I don't understand why Tristan bothers with these things, but he encouraged me to try and put my thoughts down from time to time. If nothing else, he said it would be a testament to the greatest hunt our family has ever accomplished.

Day 3

I can't help but think about my brothers and my father on their own hunts. I truly hope none of them have to traverse terrain as unpleasant as these swamps. The creatures are highly aggressive but only if you get close to them. It has been slow going, but I've managed to only anger a few. These did not die easily, no thanks to the vast bogs and marshes that do nothing for footing. If my calculations are correct, I will arrive at the Monastery in another day, perhaps two.

Speaking of my brothers, I became curious after talking with Tristan about his assignment. I realized only after our discussion that my little brother had tricked me, as he so often did. I thought I could learn from my older brother if his assignment was also taking him to a desolate Monastery. I thought it an unlikely coincidence for Tristan and I to get similar assignments; I would know for certain there was a pattern if Aaron had the same task.

Despite the difference in our years, Aaron and I had always been close, thanks to Tessa. If not for her, we likely never would have interacted. I miss my sister greatly, and I worry for her safety daily.

Aaron, I don't worry for as much. Always the best of us with a blade, even beating Father on one out of six attempts, he could protect himself from danger more than anyone. What worried me was the desert he would need to cross to arrive at his location. His journey would likely be longer than anyone's.

As it turned out, I didn't need to trick Aaron at all to get him to open up about his letter. He was so angry that he was just waiting for someone to tell. He threw the letter in my face and told me to see the garbage he had been delivered.

The only instruction was that Aaron was to travel to the Monastery of.... located in the Globi Desert, confirming my earlier suspicions that something was tying these Monasteries together. The location of the Monastery was unknown to the King and his people. Instead, Aaron was to find a wandering tribe in the Globi—the Jalusi tribe, who were said to be the only group who traded with the Monastery and knew its location. I was no help to him, as I had never heard of the tribe, either. I envy his circumstances less than even my own.

Tristan was right; it is liberating to write thoughts down.

Day 8

I hate this swamp. I hate the King. I hate everything about this assignment.

As I traveled deeper into the swamp, the beasts became more numerous, and their level of aggression increased the farther I went. What I took to be a short route from the main road to the Monastery took me almost a week's time. I have finally arrived, and I can see the Monastery across from me on an island.

I have walked around the bog that surrounds the island and see no way across, save swimming or levitation. Tonight, I will rest, and tomorrow I will cross the bog and enter the Monastery. The sooner I rid this place of whatever has the King worried, the sooner I will return to my family.

Day 9

I should be dead. How I survived, I still don't know. This bog—and likely the whole island—are enchanted with some magic that cancels my levitation. I was one tenth of the way across the bog when my magic just vanished. Landing with a splash, I surfaced and looked toward the island, intending to swim the rest of the way. If I hadn't seen the wave forming from so far off, I would be a small appetizer for the largest monstrosity I have ever seen. There is no possibility that I can swim this fetid swamp and not get killed by that beast.

I need to find some other way across. I remember, now, that as I was traveling the swamp on my way to the Monastery, I noted a structure. It was the only one I had seen in the area, and I decided to avoid it. Now I may have to go and discover if anyone lives there. I see no other options to get across to the island. Perhaps, if anyone does live there, they know some secret of this swamp. I only fear that whoever or whatever would call this swamp a home will be aggressor rather than savior.

Day 10

I am back in front of this damn island. Surprisingly, the inhabitant of the hut, a witch of some sort, was able to help. There were several words at the bottom of the King's letter that none in my family could translate. These words proved to be the key. Once I speak them, a bridge of some sort will rise, and I will be able to cross with no worry. The witch asked only for a stone located somewhere in the Monastery. If her assistance actually helps, it will be my pleasure to bring her any stone she wants. I will rest briefly and then enter the structure. My next entry into this book will describe my adventure on the island, I have no doubt. I will have to thank Tristan for the recommendation, I truly enjoy this activity.

"That was the last entry."

"Well, that certainly sucked for him," Wayne said.

"No doubt, man, but we knew something like this had to be what happened. More importantly, we have the clues we need to set out for the third Monastery."

"All in due time. Our next stop is to see the Witch and then bury Constantine's bones. We can figure out what to do about the next Monastery after all of that."

"Allister has it right. Not to mention that each of these Monasteries has been close to the level necessary to deal with the story quests."

"My thoughts as well, Alex."

Keeping in a straight line to the Witch's hut, we took no time at all to arrive at the location. It looked nothing like what we had previously encountered. The dilapidated hut, which once appeared to be on its last legs, now had the look of a quaint cottage. Flowers bloomed all along the front of the structure, and a small garden could be seen to the side. Small animals scampered around the grove in front of the building, none of them looking dangerous or aggressive.

The first thing we all noticed, though, was the woman twirling in the middle of the grove, arms out to the side, brunette hair with strands of gray flying around her. She twirled and twirled with a look of unabashed joy. I would have guessed her to be in her late forties, maybe early fifties, as there were a few signs of age on her body. Oh yeah, and she was naked again.

"Woman, don't you ever wear clothes?"

"Alex! You found it! You really found it!" The Witch stopped twirling and came running up toward us, arms spread wide for what would undoubtedly be a massive hug.

"Uh-uh. Clothes first! Then you can thank us."

With the way she looked before, you know, like a witch, I doubt I would have noticed the blush that crept up on her cheeks. Without another word, she dashed back into her cottage. She came back out after only a few minutes, twirling again.

"Even my clothes! Why would I ever wear those filthy rags you saw? But now my dresses have returned to the beauty they held before. This is more than I can bear," she finally said before taking a seat on the ground. I wasn't going to note to her that grass stains probably wouldn't be good for her new dress.

I walked over to the Witch and handed her the Vivre Stone. She gently took it from my hand and placed it into a holder attached to a chain around her neck. The stone was a bit large, but I could understand her not wanting it out of her reach. Ever.

"There is also this letter that we were asked to deliver."

"A letter? From whom?"

"A monk from the Monastery. I am sorry to say we do not know his name."

The Witch took the letter and looked at the wax seal. She took a quick breath before attacking the seal and opening the note.

As she read the letter, tears flowed down her face. She cycled through looks of happiness, contentment, and then sadness. When she finished the note, the Witch set it down and took the Vivre Stone into her hands.

"He's in here? Master Morro sacrificed his life for the stone?"

"He did. And he called you Della? Am I to take it that is your name?"

"It was. I mean it is. Again. For years, I was nothing but the Witch. I wanted no one to remind me of a time when I was that woman, so I forgot the name entirely. Made everyone else forget it as well.

"Morro and I were quite the rabble rousers in our youth. To think, a magic user and a monk cavorting around together and getting up to all kinds of mischief. Though we knew it impossible, secretly we talked of our spirits and how divine it would be for them to be intertwined. That was the only man I ever loved."

The atmosphere was quite a bit uncomfortable at that point. What do you say to a woman who finds out that the man she loved centuries before had still been alive all that time, only to die that very day? Even Dan had the presence of mind to keep quiet and not say anything.

Della finally stood from the ground and approached the group, although this time, her hands were not outstretched for any hugs. We had brought her joy and sadness, all in the span of several minutes, so I understood her mood.

"You have gone above and beyond what was asked of you. Simply returning with the stone would have fulfilled your oath. Delivering me the letter was a kindness you were not obligated to fulfill. As such, I am in your debt. Ask, and if it is possible, I will grant it. I only remind you, I am still tethered to this land, so I cannot travel for any great distance."

I looked over at the guys, and almost as one, they shrugged their shoulders in the universal sign of, "I've got no idea."

"Is this a debt we must have repaid now?"

"No. You may collect at any time. The only limiting factor is my ability."

"Since we can't come up with anything at this moment, we will say our goodbyes for now. I have no doubt that a practitioner of magic with your skills will be in need at some point."

"Agreed," she said, still with that look of sadness upon her visage. After a moment, a small smile of warmth crept onto her face as she took us in yet again. "I promise you that on your next visit, I will be in better spirits. You deserve a celebration for the accomplishments you have achieved."

"We understand completely and thank you for the offer and the hospitality. Until we meet again."

With those words said, Della nodded her head, turned her back on us, and walked back to her cottage.

You have fulfilled your Oath to Della of the Glade! You are no longer beholden to Della and owe her nothing further.

"Did you guys just get a message that flashed in front of your eyes?" I asked and read them the message I received. To a man, none of them got the message. So that was another interesting point of note in the game. Dan, Jason, and I could walk away from the portion of Lady Tessa's quest where we have to bury the bodies of House Lancaster and only Wayne would be affected if he stopped.

I shared my views with the team, and they thought the same. "It's old school, Alex. Whoever smelt it, dealt it."

I wanted to look at Dan in bewilderment, but that was just too damn funny.

Once I got through the laughing, along with the other guys, we started heading north toward the road. We had been fairly successful on our trip from the road to Della's hut, so I hoped we could avoid the mobs on our way back to the major thoroughfare. It's not that I didn't want the experience, but we had been online now for many, many hours.

Dan assured us that with both the patterns he saw the last time we ventured into the swamp and the path laid out by Della on our trip to the island, he could avoid the mobs almost entirely.

Which is why it shouldn't have been any shocker to us that after only five minutes of running, we almost literally fell into a pack of Venomous Swamp Snakes. They weren't difficult to defeat, but they certainly scared the shit out of us when they all came springing out of the ground to latch onto any purchase their dripping fangs could find.

When the last one was dead, Dan shook his head and apologized, saying, "Ok. Looks like no pattern. I'll just range a bit out like I did before."

With that method, it took us less than an hour and only two mob encounters to get back to the road. And no snakes.

"Alright, guys, let's get this over with so we can log off. I'm exhausted, and I am sure the rest of you are as well."

Wayne took the lead after my comment and went over to a patch of ground, north of the road to be away from the swamp, and took the bones out of his inventory. If things worked the same way they had before, Wayne would see a pop-up notification, asking him if he wanted to destroy or bury the remains. As I saw the hole begin to form next to the bones, I knew Wayne had made his choice. Soon after the whole process began, I saw the statue that marked the grave, and once again our Gift from Lady Tessa increased by one point for all Stats and one percentage point for all Resistances. This brought them to a total of +7 for Stats and +7 percent for Resistances.

"Got that one in the bag. All you have to do is crack open that Tome, Wayne, and we can call this a day."

"Nah, Alex. I'm going to wait until tomorrow. I want to be fully refreshed when I look at what I'm getting."

"You do realize this is going to piss Jenny off to no end when you tell her what you got and then say you didn't open it?"

"Indeed, Dan. It will spice things up."

Dan leaned over to Jason and said, "Apparently, Wayne thinks getting his ass beat is an acceptable spice."

November 11th, 2043

The next day Wayne looked haggard as we logged in near the grave site of Constantine. He looked so disheveled that none of us wanted to ask him if he wanted to open the Tome now, or wait until later.

As we went about making sure our stuff was together, Wayne finally spoke. "Apparently I don't understand the concept of spicing up one's relationship. I do know, however, that Jenny's new couch is not nearly as comfortable as the bed."

"I told you, Wayne. This wasn't..."

"You almost burnt down an apartment complex, Dan. I'll ask you for advice on a number of things, but relationships are not one of them."

Dan looked ready to come back with a reply and then shut his mouth. He turned and headed toward where he had summoned his horse. He walked past me as he went, and I heard him mumble, "Piece of shit General and..."

I chalked it up to one of Dan's many idiosyncrasies and looked back at Wayne. "So, book now, or later?"

"Oh, book now. I have explicit orders," Wayne said, and we saw the Tome magically appear in his hands. "And a piece of advice for you, Dan, if you ever do get hooked up with Kaitlin: compromise, the hallmark of all good relationships, is understanding from the beginning of the conversation that she's right, not figuring it out at the end."

With that, Wayne placed his hand on the book and it linked the contents.

For centuries, the Monastery of Might has worked and toiled to discover the secrets of power; taking the smallest movements and producing maximum force. The Book of Might is the collected wisdom of our greatest masters and sages, with all of their discoveries in one tome. In order to ensure that our teachings are never lost, this tome may be used to unlock the secrets within.

Item:	Commonality	Weight:	Armor:	Bonus:
Book of Might	Epic: One use only	5.0	N/A	Consumption of this tome gives the reader an increase of 20 percent to Attack and Instills the Skill of Concentration

"Damn! What does that put your attack at Wayne?"

"Let me look."

While Wayne was opening his character, I did the same to mine. My Attack was at 810. This number is a combination of my base Attack determined by my Strength, the Attack Modifiers on my weapons, and the modifiers from my Skills in Dagger and Dual Wield.

Wayne's base Attack was higher than my combined total, as his Strength put him at 1040. With the modifiers and bonus from his War Hammer, Wayne should be sitting at 1340 or so Attack.

"It's 1608 Attack," Wayne said in a bit of a whisper. The twenty percent increase wasn't to his base, but to the overall total, which was amazing if Wayne could increase his Attack modifiers on his weapons, or started using two swords. Either way, he now had twice the attack that I did. I was ridiculously quicker when it came to attacks, however, which still put me at an advantage.

I told Wayne that he was now almost twice my attack and I saw him blush a bit. Wayne doesn't really like being the center of attention, so my going on and on about how awesome he was made him uncomfortable. But screw him, because I still needed to know what Concentration was.

"According to the Skill in my Character screen, Concentration allows me to fight through Stun attempts. The higher my Concentration, the more likely I will resist a Stun."

"What Level is it at now?"

"One."

"And how do you increase it?"

"Seriously, Alex, I have no idea. It doesn't say anywhere."

Before I could ask, Dan volunteered that he hadn't read anything about the Skill in the manual, which I concluded meant this skill was one specifically designed by Shoal and taken out by AltCon.

"Guess we will figure it out as we go along. We got our Level 29 during the raid on the Monastery. Want to go see if our next quest is ready for us?"

"You aren't surprised, are you?"

"No," I said to Jason, "but I was hopeful. The thought of grinding again leaves a very bitter taste in my mouth."

"That could be gingivitis, Alex."

Of course those words came from Dan. "Seriously?"

"Yeah, man. I read about it the other day. A bitter taste in the mouth can be a sign of gingivitis. And nasal polyps, but your honker doesn't look swollen."

"No, Dan. I meant, 'Seriously, you actually said those words and thought they made sense?' Do you remember our discussion about context?"

"Oh. Right. Sorry, never mind. I'm sure your mouth is fine. Don't forget to floss, though."

I turned back from Dan and addressed the group as a whole. "Now that we have determined that I don't have any gum issues, let's talk about what we do next."

Brainstorming had worked out well for our group in the past, and I was happy to get everyone's input. More and more I was being looked at as the leader, with Dan saying as much at the Monastery, but I still didn't want to take every decision on my shoulders. This was partly because I wanted everyone to feel involved and partly because I didn't want to take sole blame if something went south.

To my shock and surprise, the guys wanted to go back to the swamp. Of all the places we could have chosen, I thought that would be the least likely one. Dan, though, explained his rationale for wanting to return, and the other two agreed.

"I've got that map Della made safely tucked away in my noggin. While Alex talked to her, he was able to weasel out what each of the markings meant in her key. The ones I really took note of were those marked with the symbol for 'Dungeon.' If it's anything like the mines where we first liberated the Dwarves, that could be a lot of experience. That is, so long as the levels are high enough. What do you guys think?"

It was sound, and I had no reason to argue other than not wanting to go back to the swamp. But since it was my suggestion that everyone get involved, I couldn't rightly overrule the decision. This is where that whole democracy thing just doesn't work, and I saw the benefits of being a dictator. Well, the benefits to me anyway.

The distance for us to travel wouldn't be long, as the first of the dungeons was located closer to where we first entered the swamps a week ago.

One of the benefits I did see for us staying in the swamp region was that at the end of the day, we would always travel back to the main road in order to log off. A bit north of that road was a forest thick with trees, just asking to be climbed.

During the next few days, we ventured out into the swamp and found numerous dungeons. There were a couple that we found with Green mobs inside. These we passed over, as they would give us no experience. Twice we found locations where the first mobs we encountered were Red. We high-tailed it out of there and gave those a wide berth.

The locations themselves varied little in their form, with most being barrows that rose out of the swamps, with a solitary entrance somewhere along the face of the mound. Once we gained entrance, we would descend and fight our way through the denizens of these locations. The boss at the end was never too complex or dangerous. The experience was average, as was the loot, and anything we added to our already existing gear provided only the slightest of upgrades.

But we were getting the experience we wanted and had gained another level, bringing us up to Level 30. At that Level, Dan and Jason received new spells, so we had to travel back to the Keep. We had also accumulated a sizeable amount of sellable loot that we needed to offload.

Separately, I was looking forward to climbing something other than a tree. Following our daily forays into the muck, I spent an hour or two improving my Scaling Skill. Routes up trees that were simple for me with only the Climbing Skill became exponentially harder when I tried to use my shadows and Scale the same tree. I learned that mistake quickly on the very first tree I decided to ascend.

While I was in the city, I had always approached an obstacle with my Scaling Skill already activated. This time, I had traveled deep into the forest to find a tree that would provide some kind of challenge for my Climbing technique. Everywhere I looked, though, all I saw were Green routes going up the trees. After 20 minutes of running into the woods, I finally found what I was looking for.

There were still no overly difficult routes, but at least a few of these ascents would take me up to my level. Wanting to really challenge myself, I proceeded up to a point just shy of the most difficult locations. Ready to get to work, I gathered the shadows around my body like Waseem had taught me.

As I looked down below me, to the undergrowth of the forest, I realized something important: I was a top-level Climber, but I still didn't know shit about Scaling. The bright Red patches below me, and above me, gave every indication of that. Another valuable lesson came as both my hands and feet lost hold of the tree I was on.

Being up so high might have been the thing that saved my life. It gave me the time I needed to dispel my shadows and focus on the tree through my Climbing Skill. Quickly, I was able to reach out and grab a handhold, arresting my descent. I slipped from there as well, but having stopped for the briefest of times, I only fell a short distance before regaining my perch against the tree.

I found myself almost back to the road when I finally found a tree that wasn't red and I could climb to practice my Scaling. After three days, I had increased my Skill from 30 to 54, which made it easier to find routes to traverse with shadows as my hands and feet. The Skill also gave me an increase of +5 to Climbing. I figured it would max out at 100, like all other Skills, and I would receive an overall +10 to my Climbing.

At the end of that last day, we left the swamps and forests and rode back to the Keep. It was true that Dan and Jason wanted to get their spells, and I desperately needed to sell all this loot, but another event was what had everyone excited.

The next day would be AltCon's Player/Family Appreciation Day. As Jason had believed, James was very excited to see what all the hubbub was about and why Jason always wanted to stay just a little bit longer in the game. Gary and Tim were also bringing their wives, as Jenny and Wayne agreed to babysit all the kids. Once Dan heard that Kaitlin planned to attend, despite her being single, he assured us that he had always intended to join as well.

I had no plans to join the event, and I was looking forward to my day off, where I could simply lounge around my apartment and maybe catch up on a movie or two. I had always been an introvert and found that a solitary life was very much to my liking. The thought reminded me of a t-shirt I had, and refused to give up despite the multiple holes in it, that read: Introverts of the World Unite. Separately.

I certainly valued the friendships that I had made with my teammates, but my own company was always the most pleasant. I mean, let's face it, I wasn't encountering the same conundrums that Wayne was facing.

Sure, like everyone, I had the desire to find a partner that I could share happy moments with, but it wasn't something that I "needed" to have in my life. I would never be against the prospect, but anyone could see the simple truth I told myself time and again. I never had a need to compromise, since I always agreed with myself.

FBI Headquarters

FBI Director Grissten's administrative assistant led the General into the Director's office then closed the door behind him as he left. Director Melanie Grissten had been reviewing the documents she received from Special Agents Bolden and Colvin before the General arrived, and she was preparing to share that information. She didn't plan on just giving the information away, however.

The General had been tight lipped about almost everything to do with this operation, and Grissten planned on there being an exchange of information between them. She would not settle for the General simply being ready to receive information; he needed to be ready to transmit as well.

"I'm going to start, General, by laying out for you what my Agents have found since beginning their investigation. After that, I will let you know what our next steps are for the operation."

The General looked at Grissten for a few moments before finally commenting. "That seems very gracious of you, Director. Perhaps, too gracious?" he ended with a small smirk.

Grissten had planned to play serious hardball with the General, but the smile seemed to be enough to draw out a long sigh, which sounded like it was steeped in annoyance.

"I hate that smirk of yours," the Director said with a little smile of her own. "Still, it doesn't matter. I have every intention of doing just what I said."

"And I believe you, Director," the General said while nodding his head. "I'm just wondering, what will it cost me?"

Grissten placed her hands in front of her, on her desk, one over the other. She was still smiling from earlier, but there was a bit more predator in it now.

"I want an update. And I don't mean the crap and BS you would give the White House flunkies. I want a real, no shit, operational update."

"You know there isn't a lot I can say, Mel. Can I call you Mel now that we've crossed the cursing threshold?"

"Yes, you can use Mel. Although I have no idea why I let you since I've never once considered calling you by your first name." She laughed while waving him on.

"You know there isn't much I can explain. The operation itself is too revealing. I give you details and my folks could be in danger."

"I'm not a low level Agent, General. This won't be the first time I hear the details of a highly classified operation. Now spill."

The General sat back in his chair and took a few moments to look over at Grissten. The Director's posture hadn't changed, and her hands still rested together. She also still had the predatory look. It was that, more than anything, that the General admired. His gut told him to be a bit more trusting.

"Alright, Mel, here's the deal. I've got two people inside. I'm not talking about someone who can provide me information from the inside, but actual people placed in the company."

With a whistle, Grissten sat back in her chair. It was hard enough to find people to report on AltCon, let alone putting someone in undercover. She already knew about the first one, but the fact that the General had two people spoke highly to his abilities.

"Can you share a little more? Are we talking a janitor who can get you the garbage before it's burned? Or more?"

"I don't want to say too much, but I'll tell you this: one of them, as you know, is already in the game and providing near real-time updates. The second one, and I swear to you, Mel, this can't go outside of this room, the second is on the IT side of the house and is a technician working on AltCon systems."

It took Grissten a few moments to speak after the last part. She was thinking through the ramifications of what it meant.

"You have someone with the ability to directly connect to AltCon's servers and information?"

"To a degree, yes."

At that point, the General took a folder from his briefcase and handed it over to Grissten. When she opened it, she saw the contents detailed the information they had learned about the improvements to the conditioning as well as Emily Renart's findings. Before the Director dove too far into the folder, of which there was a larger chunk of data than she honestly thought the General might provide, Grissten handed over her own notes.

Inside those notes was the information on Jolston, the "Old Man," and the facility uncovered by Agent Grimes.

The two finished at about the same time, and the General waved for the Director to go first.

"Fascinating discovery your doctors have found. If it's accurate, that is. It would require a greater sampling of people to see if it were true. Still, it makes me want to bring this investigation to a close sooner rather than later General."

"I am with you there, Mel. This has the real potential of hurting a lot of people. So I want to be sure that when we move, we move fast. And together. I want us to take the company down, not just give them a setback."

"This facility your Agent found has piqued my interest. I see very little reason for AltCon to have a facility like this, unless it were for R&D purposes, but AltCon already has a very visible R&D established in their Headquarters. If I was trying to hide something that could get me into a lot of trouble, this would likely be how I would do it."

"Agreed. And the first time I read through that, I was very tempted to tell my Agents to contact a judge for a warrant. But even now, I can't find any reason that a judge would grant one. My Agents confirmed that every permit and request has been filed and all of it according to the law. Yes, they have an impressive amount of security, but nothing illegal."

The General reviewed the documents another time before closing the folder and placing it on Grissten's desk, in front of himself. She, in turn, tried to return the General's information.

"Go ahead and hold onto that. It's the information I can share, and I want you to have it at hand in case you need to review it again."

Grissten set the file in front of herself then looked across the desk toward the General, to the file that rested close to him.

"And I imagine, General, that you would like to take that information with you?" she said, gesturing toward the file she had provided.

"Indeed. I think I can put it to use, Mel. I just might have an idea for how we can learn what's going on there. How does this sound?"

CHAPTER 18

November 16th, 2043

I logged on a few hours before the rest of my group. Having spent the day outside of Resurgence, I felt refreshed and energized. I wanted to get some more Scaling practice in before I joined up with the guys. And if there was one thing the Keep had in abundance, it was buildings.

I heeded Waseem's advice and stayed away from the slums of the city. The area wasn't really what I was looking for anymore, anyway. With my skill having progressed to the point it was now, I was looking for taller structures with a bit more difficult landscapes. Deeper into the Keep, I hit the mother lode.

The first things I took in were all the different routes surrounding me. My vision was overwhelmed with splashes of the full color spectrum. There were so many colors, that I could barely make out the structures themselves. I shut off both my Climbing and Scaling skills, and simply looked at the buildings with my own eyes.

Still cloaked in my Blacksuit, I was glad that I couldn't be seen by any of the guards. And there were so many of them. Each residence looked to have two or three guarding a gate. The buildings themselves were ornate in their architecture and were about the most expensive thing I had seen in Resurgence yet. I think it was the gargoyles and cherubs that adorned the roof tops that finally made me certain; I had found the neighborhood of the rich and well-to-do.

"Please tell me you are here to steal something."

I jumped a good two or three feet in the air as I heard those words whispered in my ear. I give myself credit though. I landed in a crouch with my daggers already half out before I realized what I was doing.

"Oh, put those away. No one is here to fight."

"Waseem?" I asked. Because I honestly couldn't see anyone.

"Who else would recognize you?"

"How can you see me? You've never seen me in my Blacksuit before."

"Ahh, that. Sorry lad, I realize now that could have been a bit of a start for you."

Nothing in my body believed that Waseem was the least bit sorry. Quite the contrary.

"It's not a terribly interesting story, Alex. You see, I had a very lucrative contract a few days back. Had to acquire a ring for some old man, which another old man stole from some person who originally stole it from someone else. The usual triteness of the aristocracy. Heed my words Alex, there is only one thief among the aristocracy. Everyone else is just getting their shit back.

"But I digress. So there I was in the master suite, pocketing the lovely ring, when what should I see but a marvelous little bauble sitting on the side table. The owner had no idea what it was, or it would have been locked away in the most secure place known to man. In this case, the Bank. You see Alex, when I picked it up, I could see myself in the reflection of the mirror. In other words, I was seeing through my Blacksuit."

"And the old guy thought it was just an item that let him see someone using an Invisible spell. And those are everywhere, right?"

"Not everywhere, Alex. But for the rich, they aren't hard to acquire. But in all my days of thieving, I've only heard of a handful of rings that were able to see through a Blacksuit. As you can imagine, Rogues that have our level of talent with the Shadows would want these rings off the street as quickly as possible."

This was a really weird situation, and I was glad we were far from the guards. Anyone walking by, even with one of those items that allowed them to see Invis, would think the spot haunted. It was simply words floating on the air.

"So, like I said, please tell me you are here to steal something."

"No such luck, my bad influence of a teacher. I am trying to improve my Scaling as much as possible. This seemed like a good place to work on it."

"That it is. But be mindful that the rich stay that way by putting defenses in place to protect their goods. Look for the easiest routes, and try not to challenge yourself. At least, not in this neighborhood. You aren't ready for that yet if you are still trying to increase your Skill."

"Thanks for the advice, Waseem. I'll come see you at the Pit soon."

"Oh, I am sure that will happen sooner than you think."

"What do you mean by that? Waseem? Waseem?" There was no answer. Waseem had left, or he was standing near me, giggling like a child. I would take even odds on either being true.

Over the span of the next two hours, I saw my Scaling skyrocket. I surmised that the cause of the sudden increase was the challenges of the area I was in, plus the fact that I was using the Skill for its intended purpose. What I mean by that should be obvious. Rogues don't climb trees unless we are using them in a trap. Usually, we are climbing up the sides of buildings, either to steal something or kill something. My previous work on Scaling, though, had all been in a forest. Truthfully, slithering up the walls felt much more natural.

With my Skill jumping twenty points in those two hours, I was feeling pretty good. I wanted to keep going, but I also knew that I needed to meet up with my friends. Deciding to travel back to the Keep as soon as possible, I looked back at the neighborhood one last time and began trotting toward the square. I still had my Scaling Skill active so I could assess the climbing routes for future endeavors, which is why I stopped short as I turned a corner that would take me to the city center.

The building was a tower. Not terribly tall, maybe five stories, and not terribly wide. The rocks on the outside of the building looked large enough and so out of place that you could use them as a virtual ladder to reach the apex of the building. But that wasn't going to happen. The building was a dark and imposing Red. From the bottom of the tower to the very top. Looking at this building through my skill, it would be a challenge to ascend one single foot, although my normal eyes told me that wasn't the case.

I made note of this location on my map and continued to the square. I didn't have the time to do so now, but at the first opportunity I had, I was going to make a stop at the Pit and ask Waseem about it. I really did hate that the bastard was right about how soon I would be there.

The guys were in the square when I arrived, talking boisterously and looking to be in great spirits.

"I take it the Appreciation Day was a success then?"

"Oh was it ever! Isn't that right, Wayne?" Dan said while nudging our Warrior.

"Wayne? But I thought Jenny and Wayne stayed home and watched Gary and Tim's kids?"

"We did. And let me tell you, there is no better birth control than four children, in small confines, with no parental supervision. I have no idea how they all knew exactly when to scream together, or move in a whirlwind without ever disturbing each other but knocking into every other thing."

"Wow! It was that bad?"

"I'm not saying they were the spawn of Satan or anything, but they are Gary's kids and Tim's kids, and you know those guys. So imagine."

"In fact, I am picturing exactly what my hell would look like. Thank you for that, Wayne."

"Welcome, Alex," he said while giving me a slap on the shoulder and a smile. "The upside, however, is that Jenny is singing an entirely different tune. When we first started dating, she let me know that she was a woman that was interested in having children, wanted a family, and sooner was better than later. But, you know, no pressure.

"So, last night we were laying on the couch together after the hellions departed, and she tells me, 'You know, I think being a mother is something I could wait a few more years for.' That's a win-win."

It was hard not to laugh at the whole thing, and since Wayne was chuckling along with us, I didn't feel bad at all. I asked if Jason had similar success with his outing.

"Way better than Naugha's adventures! James absolutely loved it. And this placed looked amazing yesterday. They really cleaned it up, and it had a bit of spit and polish that has already been removed today.

"More importantly, as soon as he logged in and saw and felt the realism, he immediately told me he was sorry for ever giving me a hard time. I wasn't expecting that at all!"

It sounded to me like this whole thing was a hit, but Jason wasn't done.

"So this morning, I am getting ready to log in and James says, 'I can't tell you how jealous I am of you right now, getting to go back there. It is such a wonderful opportunity that you have here, and I've been giving you such a hard time about it. Please let the people at AltCon know how appreciative I am, that I would love the opportunity to go again, and that both of us will definitely be playing Resurgence!' James doesn't play videogames. Ever. So this is like the greatest thing to happen to our relationship, at least in my opinion."

"Damn, Allister! That is great news. I hope Gary and Tim had as much success."

"Yeah, Alex, they did. I talked with Jenny a little bit ago, and their spouses said similar things. They are one hundred percent supportive of Gary and Tim playing. AltCon really knocked it out of the park on this one."

I had to agree with Wayne on that. If all three of our married players were now free of any disagreements stemming from the game, it would make the experience all the more enjoyable.

Naturally, these things have a shelf-life, and I expected after a couple of weeks the joy would retreat to the backs of their minds and they would find reasons to dislike the scenario. But for the moment, my friends could bask in their glow.

Dan also seemed unnaturally happy. I was afraid to ask at first, but seeing his demeanor, I couldn't imagine that anything went wrong.

"All went well?" I asked in Dan's direction.

"Totally! It was pretty cool, the whole set up that Allicontent over there mentioned, but also the wonder in everyone's eyes. It reminded me of the first day we logged in. Except for the part where Wayne got beat by the bunnies."

"You all remember that I let them beat on me for Alex's experiments!"

Of course, none of us remembered it that way, but we gave Wayne a pass on this one since it was the first day.

"What really stood out for me, though, was Broham. And Rocky. As you know, we are still the only group to figure out how to get a pet," Dan said, while scratching behind Broham's ear. "Sure, the Death Casters can summon a skeleton, or something, that will probably be bad ass in the future but sucks now. And even then, theirs is still better than that crap the Dark Paladins can conjure up. But AltCon blocked those summoned pets because they didn't want to freak anyone out. Apparently giant Dire Wolves are cute and fuzzy according to the company, since we got to have them there.

"And they were an absolute hit! It was like small kids playing with puppies, because with the size of our hounds, that is kinda what it looked like. Everyone wanted to pet them and play with them, and when Broham and Rocky started playing together, the whole square here stopped and watched. Because, you know, it was two Wolves trying to best the other one. That's what they call playing."

He knelt down then and started giving Broham a good scratch behind his ears, down his neck, and along the flank. That smile was still there when Dan looked back up at me.

"Kaitlin and I talked a lot too. I was just myself, like Allihelper told me to be. I wasn't trying to impress, or be flashy, except for my natural shine. And we had a great day! At the end, she gave me a hug and told me that she wasn't angry anymore and that she missed me. She missed me!"

"You know you sound like a second grader that just found out his secret crush wants to kiss him next to the monkey bars during recess?"

"I know, man! Isn't it awesome?"

I shook my head at Dan but my smile was probably as wide and certainly as genuine as his. We had watched our friend go through some hard times after the fiasco at Jenny's place, and it was good to see him in great spirits.

"What about you, Alex? You do anything fun during your day off?" Wayne asked.

"I had the best day. I slept in. I didn't get dressed until noon. I lounged on my couch and watched two movies that were horribly fantastic. And last night I went and sat in a café, just watching humanity walk by. That is one of the downsides to having your whole life center around a virtual reality world: you forget about the characters that exist in your own. And believe me, there isn't a better place to see those characters than at a café, right before it's planning to close."

"Amen to that. Try being a bouncer. Then you really see the characters."

We split up after that, with Dan and Jason running off to get their spells, and Wayne and I going to Sir Arthur to see if, just maybe, we could get the next quest. This was a habit of ours, to at least try after each level increase. None of us thought that only three levels would separate us from one quest and the next, not if history was any gauge.

The next batch of spells for the guys were upgrades to stuff they already had, like a stronger Heal for Jason and a stronger Snare for Dan. The really great update was a new spell that would resurrect our bodies if we died. Where the last one returned 50 percent of our lost experience, this one returned 70 percent. That was a solid upgrade that we hoped we never had to use.

Sir Arthur was a bust, just as we expected. Apparently, the King still needed more time to uncover who the leader of the Turncoats was, which meant we needed more levels.

We had only investigated about a quarter of the swamp at that point, with still lots more ground to cover and Dungeons to conquer. Our teammates were also taking advantage of Dan's brain and hitting Dungeons that we had already gone through. So a small benefit was that, if necessary, we could link up quickly to help each other.

"As much as I hate the place, it looks like we are heading back to the swamps."

"If you have somewhere else, Alex, we are all ears," Jason said before turning to Dan. "And shut up, Dan. Being all ears is a perfectly acceptable saying."

Dan put his hand down that was pointing in Jason's direction and closed his mouth, stopping whatever words that were about to come out.

"I got nothing, Allister. We can't beat the experience and the advantage of having a very complete and detailed map. I'm just tired of the smell."

There was one other small part that made me not fight against the idea as hard as I could. The untraveled swamp was yet another place that the code could be hiding. If there was anywhere that I would put something, which I didn't want found, it would be in these swamps. The Monastery would have been my first choice, since there was no getting across that without the magical words, as we learned from Constantine's writings.

"Well, suck it up, Buttercup. We got experience to make."

November 19th, 2016

After three days, and several more hours climbing those blasted trees again, I gained another eight points in Scaling. I was now at 82, and the trees were offering little, to no challenge. It was time for me to go back to the Keep if I wanted to max out this Skill. I also wanted to talk to Waseem about that tower I had seen.

Grinding was grinding, and there was nothing of great note that occurred during our trek through the muck and swill. It all became a blur, with me on autopilot for most of it. I only paid attention while practicing my Scaling or searching for something that looked out of the ordinary.

I made an excuse for calling an early day at the swamp, saying I needed to sell our loot. It wasn't entirely false, as I had lots of crap in my bags, but I could have gone another day or two if I shared the loot out amongst the group to hold. I think the guys were a bit tired of the swamp as well, and I had no pushback on calling an early day. We headed north to the road, and Jason logged off. Dan and Wayne ran back into the swamp, planning to join up with Jenny's group.

That was something for us to consider in the future; joining up with our team, and trying to tackle one of those Red Dungeons. It would be worth the effort to see if we could form a raid on our own, and not only when the AltCon quest told us we had to do so.

I arrived at the city and went through the routine of selling our loot and dropping off our cash at the Bank. I made a quick run over to the tower I had seen, and it was still Red from the bottom to the top. I then made my way over to the Pit, via the rich neighborhood I had previously used to increase my Skill.

The buildings offered far more challenges than the trees in the forest could, and I was planning a solid few hours of practicing after I talked with Waseem. That tower continued to vex me, and I had to know how something could be Red from the very lowest floor to the top, when I could clearly see it was a simple climb.

The front door to the Pit was open, which was rare for the tavern. Smiling to myself, I saw an opportunity to enter with my Blacksuit on and get a good look at what went on in the place when I wasn't there.

I took three steps into the Pit and looked around. The place was empty, with even Molly not being behind the bar. I had never been back in the kitchen, and I wondered if there were some nefarious activities going on there, or if that's just where Molly prepared the slop she called food. Deciding I had to see, I turned toward the kitchen and headed in that direction.

"I can seeeee yoooouuuu," came from out of the air in a childish, sing-song voice. I realized it was Waseem, and I sighed to myself.

"I hate you so much right now. You know that, don't you?"

"Be nice, Alex, or I won't teach you anything further."

"I thought you said there was nothing more you could teach me."

"What I should have said is, 'Remember, I've taught you everything you know, but I haven't taught you everything I know.' I'm sure you can see the difference. Now what brings you here?"

I recounted my progress through Scaling, even telling him the story in the trees where I almost fell to my death. When I got to the story of the tower, Waseem ran for the door and looked around outside.

"What's gotten into you?"

"You didn't climb it, did you? Please tell me you didn't try."

"I'm not that stupid, Waseem. I came here to ask you about it first."

Waseem let out a huge sigh of relief and headed toward his usual table. I joined him after he waved me over.

"Don't mess with the Tower. Ever. That place is wrapped up tighter than the Bank, and for good reason. The entire collection of Loust artifacts, going back hundreds of years, is located in that tower."

"In the middle of the frigging Capitol?"

"Kich's Keep wasn't always so large. It has grown, and it grew around the Tower. From the earliest age, all children know to stay away from the Tower. The wards placed on it make sure few could get close.

"That's what you saw, by the way. The wards scream out to anyone who walks by that the building is not to be trifled with."

"Why would you bother to put wards that someone as unskilled as me could see. They aren't very effective at being a secret defense."

"This isn't about secrecy at all, Alex. Think of something like the Bank. Only instead of being a non-descript building, like it is now, it looked like a fortress—massive battle formations on the outside, spiked walls surrounding it, and a door so massive that a battalion of Trolls couldn't open it. Now, what would be the point of putting on such a display?"

"I get it. One look and you are going to say, 'Nope, not getting in there.' Only with the Tower, they do it with wards that magically saturate the area, affecting all senses."

"Yes, you do get it. I have no doubt that if you could get through the obvious wards on the outside, the ones inside would blast you to pieces. Like I said before, that place is better defended than most castles."

Waseem was not his usual flippant self, so I knew he was deathly serious about the defenses of the Tower. If I had no plans to try and see what happened with a climb before, I most certainly wasn't going to give it a shot now.

"I don't have much farther to go before I reach the pinnacle of Scaling. It really is a fantastic Skill that has improved even my normal Climbing abilities. The area where you first saw me should be perfect to finish out."

"If you truly are that close to mastering the Skill as much as you can, then I have some bad news for you."

"Really? Do you see the smile on my face and just have to ruin my day?"

"No, Alex. That part is a bonus."

"I wasn't kidding; I really do hate you. You know that, don't you?"

Waseem laughed off my comments and was walking toward the door, when he looked back at me. "Well come on, I can't show you here."

We walked out of the Pit and down a few different side streets, stopping before a building that at least didn't look like it would fall down. I took it in, using my Climbing and Scaling Skills, and it looked like a walk in the park. I told Waseem as much.

"Not everything is what it seems. I want you to Scale up to that third-floor window. Can you do that?"

The route, even for my Scaling, was all Green. I was looking forward to making Waseem look dumb, but that last line kept going around in my head. What was I missing?

Not seeing anything obvious, I jogged over to the building, jumped up and started Scaling the wall. I was up to the second floor and past it in a matter of seconds. That's when I heard Waseem yell up to me.

"When you're done, come on back to the Pit, but don't take a straight route. I'll see you in a bit. And one more thing. Don't forget to run."

I looked down and saw Waseem run full out back toward the tavern as I placed my hand on the sill of the third-floor window. Only self-preservation kept me from letting go of the wall entirely and covering my ears when the loudest alarm I had ever heard went off right next to my head.

Despite the ringing in my ears, I could hear shouts coming from all around me. I needed to get out of there, and I needed to do so quickly. I used a technique I had been practicing, sliding down the wall, letting my shadows act as brakes. It would leave marks, but at this point I didn't care.

Like Waseem advised, I ran like a bat out of hell, but not directly back to the Pit. After a half hour of making circles and doubling back on myself, I felt confident that no one was following me. Checking around me one last time, I made my way back to the Stinky Pit, and entered.

Waseem was sitting at his usual table, feet up, and leaning back in the chair. Next to him was an older female gnome, wearing tiny glasses, and dressed in all black robes. She looked like a Death Caster.

"What the hell was that? And why the hell didn't you tell me that would happen? You obviously knew."

"That would have entirely negated the point of the exercise. If I told you that reaching up to the third window sill would have adverse effects, you wouldn't have done it."

"Right! Because I almost lost my hearing, all so you could have a laugh!"

"Calm down. It wasn't for a laugh. I mean, I did laugh. A lot. But that wasn't why I did it," Waseem said, bringing his chair forward and resting all four legs on the ground. Motioning toward the woman sitting to his side, who still hadn't said a word or moved a muscle, Waseem said, "This is Sally. She is to be your next teacher."

I wasn't following the train of thought Waseem used to go from almost getting me killed to introducing my next teacher, but I was calming down enough to ask questions without yelling. "A pleasure to meet you, Sally. I look forward to whatever tutelage you can provide. Only first, I need to beat some answers out of this one," I said while pointing at Waseem.

I didn't know what to expect from my new "teacher," but hearing her start to giggle definitely wasn't one of the options. "Oh dear, you would need to get in a really long line of people who want to do that.

"What Waseem isn't telling you is that I am to teach you how to avoid the very scenario you found yourself in today. I will be able to show you how to avoid it, and when you become strong enough, go right through it."

"Forgive me for being so blunt, Sally, but what the hell is 'it?' You're talking as if I have some semblance of an idea about what happened to me."

Sally looked over at Waseem with a scornful face. "You didn't tell him the threat?"

"How are you both not seeing the point of my exercise? By not telling him, he was caught off guard, and it made a more lasting impact, I'm sure," Waseem said to Sally. Then, turning towards me, "It was a ward, Alex. The fact that we had just talked about the Tower told me you had no idea what wards really were. And if you want to go climbing around the Noble Quarter, you will need to know about wards."

Turning to Sally, I asked, "So you can teach me how to see them and get through them?"

"In time. But there is much work to do before you can get there. We should start immediately," she said and rose from her chair, motioning for me to follow. "We will leave this one to his smugness in solitude."

"Sounds perfect to me."

"What a baby," Waseem said in a low voice, before yelling to the closing door of the Pit. "You'll thank me later!"

Sally led me to a nondescript door amongst a dozen others, down some back alley in the seediest part of town. The place didn't look like it could house a closet, let alone enough room to train. But as I have learned in Resurgence, time and again, there is the potential for a mystery behind any door.

We stepped through the door and walked several feet away from the street. Sally fooled with some contraption inside the near lightless room, and another door opened. I walked through this door and found myself in a massive apartment of sorts. The entryway also acted as a sitting area and living room. Off of this large room were about a dozen doors. As I took it all in, I realized the building took up the whole block.

"All those other doors we saw walking down the street, do they all lead here?"

"No. Only the one we went through. The rest of those doors, if you could get them open, would give you access to a very small empty room. Not worth anywhere near the trouble of getting into it."

Sally walked to the middle of the large room and spread her arms wide. And like I said, she was a gnome, so they didn't really spread that wide.

"Using all of your senses, tell me what you see in this room."

I did as she said, opening up my mind to my Climbing and then Scaling Skills. I saw a few pillars I could climb and some corners in which I could wedge myself, but that was it. I told Sally my findings.

"Hmm. Ok. If nothing else, that tells me exactly where we need to start."

Sally walked back to me and then led the way to a door on one of the far walls.

She opened the door and pointed into the room. "Can you see the lever on the far wall?"

I nodded to her that I could.

"All you have to do is pull that lever, and you may use whatever skills you like to do so."

Realizing there was something going on that I wasn't seeing, I took my time scanning the room. There were parts that I couldn't see, but where I could, I noted some handholds I could use if the floor fell out from under me or something.

"So just go in?"

"Yes. Whenever you are ready, simply step through the door."

I wrapped my Blacksuit around me and crossed the threshold of the room. As anticipated, the door swung shut behind me.

I'm sure Sally waited patiently on the other side. After several seconds, I knew she began to hear my curses and screams. Her training had begun.

When the lever was finally pulled, the door next to Sally swung open. Inside, she could see me on the far side of the room. I was quite bloody and, I'm sure, looked more than a little angry.

"Tomash, if you wouldn't mind?" Sally said to another gnome that had arrived since I entered the Room of Suffering. At least, that was what I would likely call it.

Tomash nodded and threw a powerful heal on me, restoring all of my hit points in one shot. I took the time to nod toward Tomash in thanks before striding purposefully toward Sally.

As soon as I walked out of the room, Sally commanded me to stop. And it was a command. I didn't even realize how quickly I stopped. At first sight, you wouldn't think of Sally as the type to throw out a Patton- or Napolean-type command, but she certainly did. That still wasn't going to stop me from yelling at her.

"What was the point of that?"

"Well, what did you learn?"

I explained in detail what happened once the door closed and I began to make my way toward the lever, my anger subsiding by small degrees as I went through the details. The first indication something was wrong in the room, I told her, was the spike that drove through my foot on my first step forward. I leapt off the ground from that point and grabbed one of the handholds, only to have arrows fly from the other side of the room, boring into my side. I had let go from there and dropped back toward the ground. My impact caused a gout of fire to be released from the ground, burning me on the arm.

The lever, which was still quite a distance away, seemed to be mocking me. I decided to make a run for it, only to be smacked, hit, burned, frozen, impaled, and impacted by over a dozen items. I was also bleeding profusely and was poisoned from one of the countless darts that had been shot at me.

"Yes, I know what happened. I asked, 'What did you learn?' Tell me, look in the room and tell me what you see."

I looked around, and noted a few additional handholds I hadn't seen before, but if there was something more Sally wanted me to see, I wasn't getting it. I told her as much.

Sally let out a heavy sigh. "I was afraid you were going to say that."

With a shove that seemed impossible to come from such a tiny individual, I was thrown back into the room, and the door closed behind me. I looked across the room and saw the lever reset. Sally told me I had to move the lever again.

"And what if I just decide to sit here by the door?" I yelled at her.

I realized I should have kept my mouth shut when the wall where the door was located started pushing forward, pushing me deeper into the room. "Not cool, Sally!"

I obviously had no other options but to make it across and swing the lever from one spot to another. I couldn't just stand in one location. I learned that when, moving through the room, I got hit with a fireball. I just wanted to rest for a moment, but another fireball followed up soon after. If I didn't move, I would get killed standing in the same place.

As soon as I made it through the room and hit the lever, the mini apocalypse would stop. From a location above me, an opening would appear. Tomash would peek his head out, and then hit me with a heal. After that, Sally would ask me what I learned.

I did this twice more. Each time I thought I would get better at something, but I never learned anything at all and was getting slower on my times.

Perhaps you are wondering why I didn't just stay on the other side of the room next to the lever. I tried that. Sally hit the room with a knockout gas, and when I woke up I was on the far side from the lever again. Only that time I had a headache.

After that fourth time, exhausted and bleeding from multiple locations, I looked across to where I figured Tomash would poke his head out. I didn't see Tomash, however, because the room was awash in bright Red. The kind of Red that tells me I'm in danger!

"Sally, what the hell is going on?"

"What do you see?"

"I'm surrounded by danger, that's what I see!"

"Yes. But how do you know?"

"Know? Because I can bloody well... Oh."

I hadn't noticed the announcement I had received from the game.

After encountering over a hundred Traps, taking damage from each, your subconscious has learned to identify these pitfalls. From this point forward, you will have an innate Skill to Detect Traps. The stronger your Skill, the better you will become at finding the most concealed of these deadly foes.

This time, when I moved the lever, the door opened. Sally was on the other side, along with Tomash. He hit me with a heal, and Sally hit me with her most wicked smile. "Now my boy, now we can train."

Sally led me back into the great room and explained that the very structure we were standing in was built for the sole purpose of teaching Rogues this skill. She told me that my "initiation" took longer than most, since I kept pushing forward at every Trap. Most fell over, rolled around, and set off numerous more traps in the process. My drive to push on toward the lever meant that I ended up hitting far fewer Traps in the process, and lost far less life than most. It just meant that it took longer.

Sally looked around from the center of the room, and settled on a door two down from the first one I had entered. As we approached that door, she continued to explain the building we were in.

"In the world outside of here, it would take you a lifetime to improve your Skill to the height of its ability. The reason is simple: there just aren't that many traps out there. I created these various courses to quickly increase your Skill to the highest. With your ability to move quickly, and with your obvious aptitude at avoidance, I think we can get you to your full potential before you leave today."

We had reached the door, and Sally opened it. Down the hall, I could see several red blotches on the floors and ceilings.

"What am I to do?"

"This task is simple. Avoid the Traps. Passing by them without triggering their effect will build on your Skill. Noting ones that are concealed by an expert, and avoiding them, will greatly add to it. I don't expect you to see those right away. Tomash will heal any damage you receive. Move the lever at the end of the hall and all of the Traps will disarm. When you can avoid them all, we will move on to something harder."

I nodded my head and sprinted into the room. I started seeing my route from the moment I began my sprint. I barely took note of the door swinging shut behind me, but I wasn't going to try and run out on this challenge.

I took a few shots before I got to the end of the hall, but my Skill already climbed several points in a matter of two minutes. With the traps disarmed, I went back to the door. It was open, and Tomash hit me with a heal before I left the hall. I wasn't ready for the door to swing shut behind me this time, and I gave a little jump.

"Why'd the door close?"

Without answering, Sally walked over to the opening and turned a knob I hadn't noticed next to the door's handle. Several seconds later, the door opened again. I hadn't been sedentary, though. I was remembering where the first Traps were and thinking about how to change my route.

All of that was for naught, as the door opened and I saw that the first Traps were all in a different configuration.

"Oh, did I forget to mention that the Traps are put into a random order each time? How silly of me," Sally said, wearing her evil smile again.

"You know you are worse than Waseem, right?"

"Good for you, dear. It usually takes people a lot longer to realize that. Now run!"

And run I did.

Over the next two hours, we ran through four halls total. Each of them became harder and harder to navigate, and I was forced to use my Climbing and Scaling, which increased two points, to get through. At the end of the two hours, my Detect Traps Skill sat at 100.

"Excellent! You definitely made a play to beat the fastest time for completing the circuit. I think only Dhalean had a faster time."

"Of course he did."

"As I have told you, this was only the first step in your training," she said while we walked to a table that was set up in the middle of the large room.

Four Traps of some sort were sitting on the table. Each one was a glowing red to me, but their edges were crisp and I could make out all the details of the Trap. When I first learned the Skill, it was just a big blotch of Red sitting on top of the ground or on the side of the wall. As the Skill increased, so did the clarity of the Trap itself.

Sally pointed to each one as she explained their presence on the table. "The first is a simple hunting Trap, the second was made by an Apprentice of a Carpenter for some rich Baron, the third is the work of a Journeyman Trap maker, of which only three exist in our time. The last was designed and built by a Master. There is only one Master walking the world of Tholtos, so far as I know."

"Should I start calling you Master Sally now?"

"Heavens no! I love it that you don't stand on all that pomp. I wish the rest of the community would stop doing it. The wrong ears hear someone say Master anything, and I will have far too many people looking in my direction whom I would rather avoid."

I understood her reasoning, and I had no intention of calling her anything but Sally. She put me through hours of torture, and did so with glee.

"Your Skill showing you that all of the Traps are extremely dangerous was not tied to your Detection Skill. It is tied to your Disable Skill, of which you have none at this moment. You will take apart this hunter's Trap. The first time you are successful in doing so, without setting the Trap off or getting injured, you will receive the Skill. After that, it will be a matter of working on the various contraptions before you, until the Skill reaches its apex. This Skill will take much longer than the last one. You will need to come here several times before you can move past the Disable Skill and on to what we have really come here to learn."

"Wait. I thought this is what I came to learn, so I wouldn't get caught like I did on that ledge."

"Mm hmm. And we will get there in due time," She said, removing the Traps from the table. "Come back tomorrow, if you are able, and we can start fresh. If you arrive and I am not here, simply place this totem against the door, and it will inform someone inside that we have a visitor."

Sally gave me the small, wooden totem. It had no Stats or Skills associated with it, and was called Wooden Totem. I stored it in my inventory and made the mental note to mark the location of the entrance door on my Map. No way I was going to find this place again by memory.

Sally was shooing me toward the door when I had a sudden realization.

"What about the first room? Now that I have reached the top of my Skill, shouldn't I give it another try?"

"Oh silly boy. There is no way to get through that room. Every square inch is covered with Traps of varying degrees of severity. Literally, no way to get through, without knowing how to Disable. It's a marvelous way to acquire the Skill, don't you think?"

"Way worse than Waseem. So, so, much worse."

Undisclosed Location

Emily Renart had been a godsend for the General and his team. She had taken the reins of her assignment and pushed herself to her limits. The General had received numerous reports from Emily. In them, she'd drawn a greater picture around one of the major mysteries facing the General's team and their investigation.

After learning about the previous maintenance requests on the RACs, Emily had systematically created a detailed timeline of when the RACs came online as well as the users associated to them. All of them were employees of AltCon, and all were working in the Emerging Products department.

During the five-month timeframe, what appeared to be hundreds of techs from the Emerging Products line had relocated from the primary offices to the sub-basements where the RACs were hosted. Along with the RACs, they had transferred their primary accounts to new computers specifically set up for those techs. After the five months, Emily saw a massive number of requests for retrieving the computers in the sub-basements and moving them back to inventory.

Additionally, the number of work orders from Emerging Products diminished drastically. Emily could not be certain, but she hypothesized that the technicians from Emerging Products were spending almost their entire time in the RACs. Likewise, and still only theory, both the General and Emily thought it was highly plausible that AltCon ran a separate test for Resurgence prior to running their current beta. Whether this was to actually test the game or was the first batch of experimental subjects was impossible to say.

Given the top-notch work put out by Emily, the General had great faith that she would be up to this next task and the unique story that came with it.

"I'm sorry, General, but I don't have any additional updates on the RAC usage. I would have filed a report if I had."

"I have no doubt, Ms. Renart. That isn't why you are here."

Emily sat down across from the General at the large conference table. "Is everything OK, sir?"

The General nodded and put a bit of warmth in his voice. It was not often that members of his team had one-on-one meetings with the General that weren't scheduled out weeks in advance, and he didn't want to scare Emily into thinking she had done something wrong.

"All is well, Emily. You need not worry that you are in any trouble here. Quite the opposite, in fact."

Emily let out a breath she probably didn't realize she was holding and relaxed a bit more into her chair. "Good to know, sir. Why am I here, if you don't mind my asking?"

"I don't mind at all. And it's one of the things I admire about you. You are direct and concise. I also know you to be creative when it comes to problem solving, and I'm going to need that now."

The General reached into an attaché next to his chair and pulled up a plain manila folder and set it on the table. He then slid it over to Emily.

As she was opening the file, the General said, "I was terribly sorry to hear about your mom, Emily."

Her head snapped up, and she was about to answer the General when he put a finger over his own lips and then pointed to the file on the table.

Emily, looking confused, nodded at the General and continued to read.

"Oh. I see now. Yes. Ok." Emily said. After ten minutes she finished the file and closed the folder.

"Does it make sense, Ms. Renart?"

"In a nutshell, General, it does. It will take some time for me to learn the history, but I believe I can pull it off."

"For my own amusement, give me a recap."

"Working off of my already established presence in AltCon, you want me to inform the bosses that I am going to need to leave my position due to an illness in the family. I'd rather not leave—I do love my work—but my mother is going to require care. I will have something to back this up?"

"It's already done, down to the hospital bills," said the General, waving for Emily to continue.

"I'll ask for a recommendation and if anyone knows of any good work around where I'm going. This should lead to a separate job offer, if I'm reading this correctly."

"That is correct, Emily. It's a plan based on simplicity, but those are usually the best. I know that AltCon has a facility 75 miles away from their Headquarters. It will be surprisingly close to where you will be headed to take care of your mother. And in case you were wondering, we will have someone playing your mother to sell this ruse."

"Wow. That's really going all in, sir. Is that not a little overkill?"

"No, I don't believe it is. AltCon has its own levels of paranoia that I am trying to provide safeguards against, is all," the General responded and then returned to the earlier explanation. "I am betting on two major things here. The first is that you have worked your ass off for this company in your short time, and that they won't want to lose someone like you if they can find a place to put you in the short run."

"Makes sense, sir. What is the second reason?"

"Jolston. When he was first coming on in the company, his mother became very ill. The company is what allowed him to take care of her and afford the care to save her life. I'm betting that Jolston has some say on who can and can't go to this facility."

"Sir, do you mind if I be blunt?"

The General let out the same smirk he had used with Grissten and waved Emily to continue.

"That is a whole ass load of 'ifs' you are banking this on. Right now I have a solid position, I'm getting information, and I'm trusted in the company. Do we really want to risk that for a 'maybe' and a 'possible?' It's my thoughts, sir, but is it worth the gain since we know absolutely nothing about this facility?"

"Well said, Ms. Renart. Those are the same questions I asked myself. In the end, I decided on this approach, since we appear to have hit a wall on our previous investigations. You may not get the job. You may not learn anything. But we are at a status quo I can't abide, and the people above me are asking for results."

Emily looked down at the closed folder on the desk for several moments before addressing the General again. "And what do you believe I will find, sir?"

"I truly have no idea, but something that well-guarded and well-hidden has to have some secrets to give up. I'm guessing it is tied into our ongoing investigation. But again, I could be wrong."

Emily shook her head a few times as she looked at the General again. "I'm not saying no, sir. I just think it's a bad play," she said before picking up the folder. "But you are the boss, and you make the call. I need to study the files here and get ready to put in my resignation. Can I have two days to learn my part?"

"Thank you, Ms. Renart. I appreciate your candor and your honesty. I have no doubt you will master the information, and two days should be fine."

"Thank you, sir. Cross your fingers."

"I'll have everyone on the team crossing theirs as well. Dismissed."

CHAPTER 19

November 24th, 2043

Five more days in the swamp got us the experience we needed to hit Level 31, but that wasn't enough to get our next quest from Sir Arthur. There were also no additional Skills or Spells that we would get at our new level. The only reason we went back to the Keep at all was to sell all the junk we had collected. We no longer looked at our bank, which was a great feeling. I knew well, however, that rich men can become poor men very quickly in these games with the purchase of one or two rare or epic items.

Selling loot was the reason for everyone else to go to the city, at least. I had been traveling there every night, burning so much of my time online just traveling there and back. Sally hadn't lied about how much I would need to visit her place to raise my next skill. So yeah, grinding for experience both with the team and in these skills. A double whammy of the suck.

For the first several hours, on that first day, I tried again and again to take apart the hunter's Trap. Unfortunately, I set it off each time, doing damage to myself. The difference between this skill and ones I previously learned was that I was actually studying the Trap on all sides. The game mechanics were such that the Trap looked different to me each time, although I thought I started to notice a pattern.

After each fail, I looked at what I did wrong and took note of how I could do better. Several times, my changes had adverse effects that led to unforeseen consequences later. With other Skills, there was a natural progression based on my Wisdom Stat, and I imagined my Wisdom score was allowing me to see where I could have done something different. Without asking the Wanderer, I didn't really know.

Near the end of the first day, maybe after three hours total, I finally disabled the Trap. The successful attempt led to a notification by the game that I had, in fact, learned Disable Trap and that I was at the Skill Level of 1.

Now that I had succeeded, I needed to continue to Disable the hunter's Trap and increase my Skill Level. As it continued to change slightly, my first attempt after receiving the Skill was a dismal failure, and the Skill did not rise at all, as you would expect.

So for those next four days, I returned to Sally's place and kept working on the hunter's Trap. On day one, the Trap was Red, which was why I kept failing as much as I did. But as my Skill improved, I started to see areas that were slightly highlighted on the Trap, giving me an indication as to what part I should take apart next. At the end of the fourth day, the hunter's trap was finally Green.

"Congratulations, my apprentice! That didn't take you anywhere near as long as I thought it would! Let me take away this hunter's trifle and let you get to work on this next bauble."

With that, Sally slapped another device on the table. To my dismay, this one was Red, again. I reached out to the Baron's Trap, and with the tiniest bit of manipulation to the device, a dart flew from the contraption and hit me square in the neck.

"Oops. That would be a fail," Sally said as my vision went blurry and my forehead slammed into the table right before I passed out.

November 29th, 2043

"She is a horrible, twisted woman who takes great pleasure in the suffering of others!"

"Sorry, pal, you just described every woman I've known. And my mother twice over."

"I'm serious, Waseem! Her method of helping me involves repeat concussions and no small dose of mockery on her part!"

Another five days had passed and we were inching ever closer to Level 32. In the meantime, I continued to acquiesce to Sally's lessons in her Hall of Torturous Wonder. That was my name for it. Sally called it home, but secretly she loved my name more.

"I've been stabbed, darted, sliced, bludgeoned, gassed, burned, and several other extremely unpleasant things have been done to my person. And every time, it's the same response from her! 'Oops. Guess that's a fail.' And then she giggles like she just had her first crush tickle her happy place."

"Disgusting, Alex. Sally doesn't have a happy place," the Master Rogue said from across his usual table at the Pit.

"I'm talking about her..."

"Oh, I know what you are talking about. And she doesn't have one. I think she had it surgically removed. Anyone who had a single place that could give them some small amount of joy could never reach her levels of sadism. Ergo, she has no happy place."

"And I still have so much more to go, don't I?"

Waseem nodded in my direction while giving me one of his patented smiles. I couldn't rightly tell him that I was wrong about him being the world's most horrible person, although he knew I had figured out Sally had him beat by a mile.

"Good news is, once you master the disabling of traps, it will be only a day or two before you are done with Sally. She will show you the last two steps to get you past those buildings in the rich areas of town, and then I will show you where to start mastering that portion."

At least the last five days had seen me make some real improvements. I had finished the Baron's trap and had moved on to the

Journeyman's creation. The Journeyman's was far more complex, and I was improving my skill with each successful manipulation of the trap. I didn't even need to completely disarm it, just get through part of the process. One time, when I successfully took the entire trap apart with no errors, I earned three Skill Points. I was sitting at 85 in the skill, and I was just about to move from the Journeyman's to Sally's Master Trap.

One more day would see us hitting our Level 32, and we were confident this would be the time for our next quest from Sir Arthur.

November 30th, 2043

Our confidence was shit. And our feelings toward Sir Arthur were bordering on homicidal intent.

At this point we knew that getting to our next level was going to take us around five days. At least that would be the time if we stayed to our current pace and found suitable mobs in the swamp.

We were running out of room in that desolate place as well. Oh, there were still plenty of places that we could get experience. We just weren't of a high enough level for most of them. We had been balancing our skills and gear against the levels of the mobs for over a week, and we had found the perfect risk vs. gain ratio.

And I would love to regale you with all of the amazing things we were doing out in the swamp. But that would be me lying.

Not that it was dull and boring. I mean, it was, but that is to be expected when all you are doing is focusing on leveling your character. And if there was any excitement to speak of, I would be sure to put it down here.

Unfortunately, this also meant that I was no closer to learning the truth behind the code in the game. We had mapped out that swamp almost as well as the Witch had, and none of the mobs we came across were unbeatable. However, I mentioned earlier there were some we didn't even bother to take on because of the obvious level difference. It's possible the code could be embodied in one of these mobs, but I doubted it would be a generic mob.

What wasn't dull and boring was my progress with Sally.

Ok, I'm lying again. It is kind of dull and boring, but in this case, I have been making progress.

After learning that Sir Arthur did not have our next quest, I made my way to Sally's place again. As was the case on several occasions, Sally wasn't there when I arrived. This worried me at first, but after several times of placing the totem as Sally instructed and seeing the door open soon after, I stopped worrying.

Thomash answered the door. He smiled at me with a sympathetic gaze that had become quite familiar. I had seen it every time I pulled myself off of the floor following one of the countless pitfalls from the traps I was working on.

"That's the look that should be on my face, not yours."

"Indeed, Mr. Alex. I hope you don't have much use of me this day."

"Thomash, I can guarantee you that I want to see you less than you want to see me."

"Knowing what you've been through, Mr. Alex, I take absolutely no offense to that whatsoever."

We laughed at Thomash's joke as I entered the room with the various traps and Thomash retired to his room just off the main hall. I have no idea how he knew when I needed to be healed, but I never had to wait long when I did.

As I sat down in front of the Journeyman's Trap, I was reminded yet again of how far Resurgence had come as a medium for online gaming. So many aspects of leveling Skills required hands-on interaction. And I am not talking about my specialty Rogue Skills, either. Climbing, Detecting Traps, and Disabling Traps were Skills that any character could learn, and for a character to get a working knowledge of these Skills, a person actually had to climb or take apart a trap like I was doing now.

Honestly, I preferred climbing the side of a tower or sneaking through a dungeon to fiddling with these contraptions, but that's because I am someone who likes to move around. It doesn't take much to imagine a fair number of players who would love working on these Traps, and then reverse engineering them and making their own. It would definitely be a money maker.

Settling into the chair, I focused on the Journeyman's Trap I would start with today. As my Skill had progressed, I had begun to see patterns of how to take the Traps apart so as not to have them go off. In some cases, I could even save some of the materials. I wanted to test a theory I had, so I took apart the Carpenter's Trap again, despite it being terribly beneath my Skill level. The test wasn't to see if I could do it, or how fast, but to see if I could save all the materials after taking it apart.

I was happy to find that my Skill was in direct proportion to how successful I would be at saving the materials, as I saved every bit of the Carpenter's Trap. In the more complex traps, I imagine the materials themselves would be worth a pretty penny.

The trap in front of me had several areas that glowed Green, some Blue, and some White. The Green areas were where I would focus first. When I first started seeing Green in the traps, I didn't notice the subtle difference in the intensity of the Green color. This led to quite a few accidents on my part. As it turned out, the intensity of the Green was the second part to knowing what order to manipulate the varying parts of the trap. As I successfully moved from one area to the next, the Blue and White sections would also become Green as well and would also vary in color intensity. If I succeeded through the entire trap, I would eventually see each part turn Green. The whole system was truly ingenious on AltCon's part.

I kept looking over the trap on the table. It was more complex than the previous Journeyman's Trap I worked on but still nothing like the Master Traps that Sally set up on the end of the same table.

Looking down at those, all I saw was Red—a very deep and dark Red. I held no illusions that those would ever truly turn Green for me, mostly because Sally told me they wouldn't. She was a sadistic, vile beast in the guise of a cute little old woman, yes, but not a liar.

I fell into my working trance, the same as I got into when I first worked on Lifting back at the Pit with those ice cubes. I found that I focused better in these states, but time flew by far too quickly. I had to be careful, or I would find myself getting kicked out of the game for being on too long.

In my Zen-like state, I took apart the Trap in front of me. I only somewhat noticed the Skill increases as I progressed through the contraption. Slowly, as I tinkered away, I removed the pieces and set them beside me. I only became aware of just how much time had passed when I realized I was sweating on my brow from the concentration and Thomash had come out to wipe my forehead.

I wanted to thank him, but I was on the last part of the trap. The heart of the machine where the implement of pain was concealed. I never knew what was in the trap, but I knew it wouldn't feel good if I messed up this last part.

I saw what looked to be the right method for dislodging the triggering mechanism from the tension spring, but stopped before making the final pull with my tweezers.

I looked away for the briefest second, closed my eyes, and then looked back. When I reopened my eyes, I focused again on the machinery and saw the same way forward as before. Feeling confident with my decision, I took a deep breath and grasped with the tweezers. Two seconds later I had the Journeyman's Trap entirely taken apart before me.

I looked at the notifications on my screen and was shocked to see that an hour and a half had passed, that the trap had 27 distinct different parts, and that I had saved 90 percent of the materials used to make it. Finally, I saw that my skill had increased 8 times during the endeavor.

After looking at the notifications, I realized for the first time that it wasn't just Tomash and I in the hall. Several of Sally's workers, and Sally herself, stood around the table. Sally's employees all had smiles on their faces, happy that I was so successful. Sally also had a smile on her face. That made me worry.

"Superb work, Alex. You did a fine job on this. Took far too long for any type of field work, but we aren't in the field so I'm not going to complain."

"Thank you?" I replied, having an obvious mistrust for my teacher.

Sally noticed. "Oh don't be like that. Look how much you've learned in such a short time. You have to admit, my methods are effective."

"Sure. I have intimate knowledge now concerning the distinct difference between a first-degree and second-degree burn, as well as the various stages of frostbite. I can go on and on about the things I've learned."

"I am sure you could complain for hours, but you will be happy to know that I think you have succeeded through the Journeyman level. Take a look at this next one, and tell me what you think."

Sally was right. When I looked at this Journeyman trap, it was all green. Those eight increases in my Skill were the difference I needed to master this section of my training.

You might think that would make me happy. It didn't. That meant that all the remaining traps were Master level, which meant they were made by Sally herself. And that meant there was a good chance I could actually die from one of these.

Sally saw the look on my face and started laughing. "Don't be foolish boy! I know what you are thinking, and even I wouldn't be so evil as to place something that could actually kill you in my traps!"

"So nothing will pop out if I don't disarm it appropriately?" I asked rather confusedly.

"Oh no, you'll definitely get your little bottom kicked. It just won't kill you."

I hung my head, almost touching the table as Sally went over and grabbed the Master Traps and set them before me.

"Go ahead and give one of these a try, and then you should probably give it a rest for the day and head on home."

I didn't respond to Sally. Instead, I started looking around the surface of the trap. I was trying to gauge the dimensions so I ran my hand over the top and down the side, only lightly grazing the surface. I don't even know where the paralytic came from, but the next thing I knew, I was face down on the floor, unable to move but able to feel all the pain in my body.

"Bye, dear! Safe travels home, and I'll see you tomorrow! Well, after Tomash heals you, of course. You sure do keep him gainfully employed."

The paralysis was the only thing keeping me from screaming all the four-letter words my mother told me I was never supposed to say to a woman. But I was thinking all of them very loudly.

December 5th, 2043

You could hear my group's collective sigh of relief throughout the entirety of Yerkich Square. It had been far too long since we had heard anything more than a "come back later when you're older" message when trying to get a quest.

Sure, we could have done plenty of low-reward quests while we were getting experience for our characters, but we couldn't find any that were tied directly to the swamp area. Since that is where we had the advantage of Dan's memorized map, we stuck to what we knew.

Accordingly, the response from Sir Arthur was more welcomed than it had ever previously been, though the details of the quest were less than desirable. It was going to take us deep into enemy territory.

"Brave travelers, you have returned! And at just the right moment, I might add," Sir Arthur had begun.

"Fuck this guy, we've been back here twelve friggin' times to get this quest. 'Brave travelers, you have returned' my ass."

Wayne whispered for Dan to shut his pie hole while Sir Arthur continued with his quest dialogue.

"As you know, the Captain you detained had kept a detailed journal on the individuals who were working with him to conspire against his Grace. Our investigators thought they had found a great boon when you delivered that manuscript!"

"I hear a 'But' coming here," Jason said behind me.

"Alas! they were not as lucky as they first believed. The journal looked to be written in a complex code. That was not the case, however. It took several days before our interrogators believed the Captain was telling the truth, that what looked like code were names he ascribed to unknown individuals he met. It seemed they all wore masks to hide their identities."

Sir Arthur then hung his head low and shook it back and forth.

"We lost the initiative, I am afraid. Once the interrogators believed the Captain, it still took several days to uncover who the culprits could be. What was to be a small and quiet investigation grew quite large when all manner of questions had to be asked to determine the identities of these fiends. In that time, word spread throughout the aristocracy, and before we could move on them, the House of Frost had left Kich's Keep.

"Great Ice Mages, every one of them, they represented a fairly large number of his Grace's magical armament on the battlefield. Losing them in the city and in the war will have a dire effect on morale. The rampage of Overlord Riff has already brought the mood to an all-time low, as our forces are repelled singlehandedly by this brute. With this news, we could see mass desertions. The King knows this and has deemed that the Head of House Frost must pay for his family's crimes. No less than his head on a spike will do to return the morale of the companies.

"Here is where your King calls on your aid. After fleeing their Manor, our investigators found numerous documents pointing toward a new location. What appears to be a fortified keep, located in a far-off Barony behind the enemy lines and thought to have been sacked by Loust's army, has been the recipient of numerous shipments over the past several months. We believe the Frosts have fled to this location. As it is behind the lines, our Army can't advance as a single unit. A small contingent, however, could sneak behind the lines and infiltrate the keep. Will you deliver the head of House Frost to his Grace?"

There was no question on whether we would accept the quest. As always, the only question was one of timing. We talked it over briefly and decided this wasn't likely to be a timed quest. Accepting now meant we could still do it down the road, if we wanted to hit up the next monastery first, for example.

"We will deliver the head of House Frost to his Grace," I answered.

And with that, we were surrounded by that warm and welcoming golden glow. It cemented that we had received our next story-line quest. As had become customary, we checked the quest log to see if this was a timed event or if it required multiple parties. In this case, there was no set time limit, and it required only one team. Another welcome addition to the quest log was a link to a location on our maps. The others had seen the same thing apparently, because I heard Jason swear quite loudly about something being "a fucking long way off."

I opened my own map and nodded in Jason's direction. He was very right about the distance. It was far past where we had traveled, and there were days' worth of black covering the map between our farthest point and the keep. It likely wasn't a timed event, as there was no telling just how long it was going to take us to get there.

Personally, the unknown monastery was looking better and better to me. The Globi Desert was to the south of the swamp, and we knew how to get through that in no time. We could be on the desert sands the next day. We had no idea where to go after that, however.

According to Constantine's words, his brother Aaron was to find the Jalusi Tribe of nomads in the Globi Desert. Nothing more was given. We could honestly spend longer searching the vast desert than walking through enemy lines and on to the keep.

It was time for us to have a discussion on where to go next, but that was going to have to wait until the next day. We had sloshed through the swamp most of the day to get our latest level, and everyone wanted to log off.

Well, everyone but me. I was heading to the ritzy area of the Keep. The last five days had seen me finish with Sally, and it was time to max out my Scaling. Walking through the streets of the Keep, I looked back on my last days with Sally, and not with a huge amount of fondness.

I went through more pain in the span of those last three days with Sally than I did the entire time before. Sally's traps were on a level that I couldn't comprehend, even when I finally mastered the Skill of Disable Traps. With a Level of 100 in the Skill, the last trap Sally put in front of me was almost entirely Red with a few spots of Yellow. Still, an impossible trap to disarm.

But even all of my failures added to my Skill, and when I reached 100, I smiled the smile of victors. Waseem had said that only one or two days would remain until I would be done with Sally, and I was looking forward to that more than getting out of the swamps.

Sally could tell that I had reached the pinnacle of the Skill and congratulated me for my efforts. I looked at her with suspicion, as I had learned to do anytime she addressed me or put something in front of me. This time she just laughed at me and said the agony was over and that the remainder of my time with her would be tedious in nature rather than tortuous. Internally, I grew depressed, but I wasn't about to let Sally see that. I couldn't think of anything that would be more tedious than what I just went through.

Sally led me into a room with a three-story vaulted ceiling. A blank stone wall led from the floor to the top. I could see numerous handholds all over the wall and thought this would be an excellent place to start leveling Climbing. Sally let me know why that wasn't such a good idea.

"Neither Dhalean nor Waseem likely explained the nature of your Shadows to you in the correct way, mostly because Waseem is a moron and Dhalean teaches to accomplish, not to explain. So let me be the first to give you some insight.

"The Shadows are a manifestation of magic. We shouldn't be able to use magic, since we haven't studied any of the arcane arts, and yet... Here we are manipulating the shadows for our own benefit. The reason is tied to the gods.

"For instance, those who are clerics get their magic from their god. Because they heal, most think their god is good and benevolent. Really, all gods are petty dicks. It's only the 'dark' gods that actually get that moniker.

"Most commoners know the god of rogues as "The Trickster." That is not the given name for our god, but we let the rest of the world think it is. The true name is Patience. As you have seen, our lives are far more encompassed with the acts of waiting for the right moment and sneaking than they are about tricking folks.

"A rogue who follows the Path will receive the ability to access the small amount of magic Patience has at hand—the Shadows. And the whole point to my explanation is that 'Shadows,' as we call them, are pure magic. So take your Shadows and make yourself a pair of goggles with them, and then look at the wall."

I did as Sally said and was shocked to see a blaringly Red wall staring back at me. There were no traps there just moments before, so I was more than a little confused.

Sally nodded her head my way, noting my confusion, and provided an explanation. "When you saw the tower that scared Waseem, the one with all the wards, you were seeing through the guise of your shadows, as you were already wearing your Blacksuit. Those wards are placed in such a way that even the smallest amount of Magic will make them shine to even the simplest novice. What you are seeing here are an accumulation of magical wards—or Traps, if it makes it easier—that you can now see with the simplest of effort using your shadows. And before you ask, yes you could have seen some of them before with just the Shadows, but increasing your Skill for Detect Traps ensures you 100-percent success at seeing all of them."

I walked over to the wall but stopped a foot or so away from the wards themselves. "So is this a new Skill? Detecting Wards or something?"

"No. The wards register as a Trap, so you see them as such, and I imagine the clarity of the stone behind the ward is clear?"

"Yes, it is," I told my teacher. "But I don't believe I can disable any of these wards. Not with what I know, anyhow."

"Indeed. And we don't disable a ward. We disassemble them. Wards are layers of magic. You will untwine the ward and peel away the layers from each other.

"There are those who make a living off of the dissipation of wards. This totally removes the ward from existence, and anyone can see the area has been tampered with. Like with all things Rogue, we rely on the subtle to mask our presence, and the disassembling of a ward doesn't remove it, only makes the current one inert."

I turned toward Sally, and for the first time in a while, I had a genuine smile on my face. "And my shadows are the blades?"

Sally smiled in turn. "Now you got it," she said, then she walked out of the room, closing the door behind her. Trial and error seemed to be the teaching method for this one.

There were no darts, no explosions, no fire, no ice, and no knives. I failed plenty of times, but none of the wards I worked on had damage modifiers associated with them.

However, I now knew why the door to the room stayed closed and no one ever came in. More so, I don't think I will be hearing right for a very long time. You see, every one of the wards that I failed on was linked directly to a siren that would go off in my ear. At least, it felt like it was connected directly to my ear. As you can imagine, I failed a lot on that first day.

But repetition and focus built skill. I knew I would fail miserably on my first attempt, so I decided to very much use my shadow like a knife and stab directly into the ward. I wanted to see if, with my new vision, I could see what the "layers" of magic looked like. To my surprise, I actually could. This made the next series of attempts easier, and I found an increase in my Skill after only a short time. The notification that I had learned Disassemble Wards, and was at Level 1, was most welcomed.

Over the course of that day and the next, I systematically disassembled all the wards on the wall. I obviously had to climb up the wall to get to some of them, but that wasn't a challenge with my Climbing and Scaling Skills. The only time I found myself in need of a healer was at the very top of the three-story wall.

These were the most difficult of the wards that I had seen. To say the magic here was intertwined would be an understatement of grand proportions. It looked as if some of the magical threads were not only wrapped in a DNA-type helix, but that some of the strands had distinct connections between them, like in gene pairing within those same DNA strands. Removing one from the other through surgery met with failure. That failure met with the first non-siren ward.

I ran my blade through the ward and immediately felt myself pushed away from the wall. As I learned later, this ward had an "explosive repel" associated with it, and a failure meant I would be blasted away from the ward's location. This type was quite commonly placed at the third floor and above, as they would likely ensure a painful outcome for the would-be scoundrel. Not to mention, it would give the authorities time to find the culprit as they crawled away. If they lived.

Thomash explained all of this to me as he healed me for the first time since I started on the ward wall. I asked Thomash if he had any advice, not truly expecting any. To my surprise, Thomash's response was not only the simplest answer, but also the simplest solution.

"If someone shoots an arrow at you, you don't try to counter the arrow. You just get out of the way."

I looked up at the wall and nodded at Thomash, asking him to stick around for a moment, as I wanted to try something. Thomash nodded back and sat down against the door where he entered, and I quickly went back up the wall.

I located the ward I wanted and then moved to the side a bit. I anchored my left hand and the shadows from that hand into the hold I had. With my right hand, I made the slice I wanted, purposefully setting off the ward. As Thomash advised, staying to the side of the ward was a suitable solution for this problem. The repel did push my arm back and forced me to rely solely on my left-hand grip for a moment, but it wasn't enough to cause me to fall.

I quickly descended from the top and clasped forearms with Thomash and thanked him for the expert assistance.

"My friend, if you consider that expert counsel, you really have been getting knocked against the head too many times," Thomash said as he laughingly left the room and I headed back to the wall.

An hour after having my conversation with Tomash, I had finished the wall, and my Skill for Disassemble Wards sat at 90. Sally walked in with Waseem in tow just before I finished the last ward. I heard them both clapping when the last of the wards had fallen apart.

I descended quickly and walked over to Sally and Waseem. Both had smiles on their faces and, to my shock, they both looked genuine. Sally was the first to offer me congratulations, and then she handed me over to Waseem.

"Looks like you've been hard at work, Alex. You've still got a little progress to make on those wards and your Scaling, but all of that will be accomplished out in town. Meet up with me tomorrow, and we can get you fully up to speed. By the end of the night, you will be as good as you can get!"

I thanked Waseem then eyed Sally warily as she approached me. Despite the fact that she enjoyed seeing the pain of others to such a high degree, she had trained me and I had to be thankful for that.

"Thank you for your instruction, Sally. Without you, I wouldn't know these Skills. I hope my use of them will honor all that you have taught me."

"Fancy words you got there, Alex. And I noticed you didn't say anything about feeling any obligation toward me for all the hard work I did."

"Not on your life, lady," I said, but with a small smile.

Sally smiled in kind and turned toward Waseem saying, "See, I taught him more than just traps and wards." She then looked at me. "Feel free to come back anytime you like, Alex. You are always welcome to visit me."

"Sure thing, Sally," I said while shaking my head 'no.' "First time I have someone I really don't like, I will stop on by and introduce you to them."

"You do know how to please this old lady."

"Enough jabber," Waseem said to the both of us and wrapped his arm around my shoulder. "Let's head out to the neighborhood where I'm going to have you start your training. Like I said, end of tomorrow night, you will be good to go."

I threw Thomash a salute as I left and nodded at the others in Sally's employ. I wouldn't be returning to the Hall of Torturous Wonder if I had things my way. Sadly, I know that things going my way happens far too infrequently in this game.

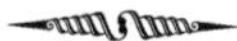

Waseem was leaning against an archway when I arrived at the neighborhood. He had seen me off the night before, and I had spent a few hours working on both my Scaling and Disassembling. I had made progress in both, and I had little doubt that I would reach my goal this evening. Waseem, however, hadn't mentioned anything about meeting me tonight. With Waseem, the unexpected meant trouble for yours truly.

"No."

"Come on, Alex. I haven't even said anything yet."

"I know, Waseem. But it doesn't matter. Whatever scheme you have, the answer is going to be 'No.' So let it go, and let me get finished with my training."

"Could be a big payout in it for ya."

"If Dhalean caught me even talking about this with you, he would string both of us up by our entrails."

"You are a big boy now, Alex. You can make your own decisions."

The idea of going on a thieving run with Waseem was very appealing, despite the bluster I was outwardly showing. Everything to this point had been training, training, and more training. The Blacksuit was the only skill I had used with any regularity. But Waseem would only be asking me if he knew he couldn't do it solo—or he wanted a scapegoat if he got caught. It should come as no surprise that I was leaning toward the latter for his motivations.

I showed a great deal of hesitancy, but I finally asked, "Ok. What do you want?"

Waseem looked around in a very conspiratorial fashion before saying, "I'll deny this to the end of my days if you ever tell anyone, but I am awful at Disassembling wards. There is a house up the hill from here, and the wards on it are no joke, like some of those crazy ones you dealt with at the top of the wall at Sally's. I couldn't see how you got around those, but I've never been able to. I need your help to get through those wards on the fifth-floor window so we can get into the room beyond."

"Why not go through the interior door? I am assuming the only way in isn't the window."

"Sarcasm is not becoming on you. Yes, there is an interior door, but my sources say that way is even more heavily warded."

"Wait. If you have someone on the inside, why don't you just have them let you in, leave you a key, and Blacksuit your way in?"

"I didn't say I had someone on the inside, I said I had a source on the wards."

I paused for a moment, and then it all sank in. I thought Waseem was there to meet with me when I finished my tasks at Sally's. But he wasn't.

"And you trust Sally on this?" I asked him.

I wish that I could put into words the look on Waseem's face when I asked that question. The surprise and astonishment were just too good for me not to smirk at. Waseem was not amused.

"Whomever my source is," Waseem replied cagily, "the bottom line is I can't get through the ward. So will you help?"

"What's in it for me? And the answer better be good."

"Opportunity to thank me for all the hard work I've put in training you not enough, I take it?"

"That would get you a boost up to the first-floor window on my back. And barely that."

"I don't like how you become with a little power. Reminds me too much of myself," Waseem said with the briefest smirks.

"'Learned from the best' is how the saying goes, right? So what will it be? I'm not saying no, but it's got to be good."

Waseem thought about it some more, but in the end, I knew he would have to offer me something grand. I was the only one that could help him at this moment.

"I have a contract to remove one thing from within that room. I have been led to believe that the room is filled with numerous other items of interest. I had planned to offer you a portion of the take, but I see even that may not be enough. So my offer is this: you have first choice of anything in that room other than the item I am contracted to remove. Deal?"

"No."

"And?"

"And... no, Waseem."

"Dammit! You don't just say no! You follow up with something else. I know you are aware how this works."

I stared back at him for a good five to ten seconds before another large smile covered my face. "I'm having too much fun with this. I'd apologize, but it wouldn't be sincere. Instead, I will make a counter offer just to keep you happy: I get first choice of anything in the room as stated before, that can stay. Second, though, is that if there is nothing in the room other than your contracted item, I get one third of your contract amount. If there are multiple items in the room and yet I still find none to my liking, I still get one third of your contract. Deal?"

I was waiting for Waseem's answer when I realized I was about to miss out on an amazing opportunity. "Or, there is another option."

"I'm listening."

"If there are other items up there to choose from, I take four, and don't touch your contract amount or the rest of the loot. How does that sound?"

Waseem looked suspicious. "Why four?"

"One for me and each guy that I travel with."

Waseem was reluctant, and thought my wanting to benefit others a waste but agreed in the end. I ran off ahead of him and made my way to the home Waseem indicated. The fifth-floor window was at the top of a small tower, as one would expect. What Waseem didn't tell me was that the rest of the tower wall had wards as well. I was definitely going to get some more practice in tonight!

It took about an hour, but I was able to get through all of the wards below the fifth floor and had found myself nestled up next to the window. The ward here was complex. Even more, it wasn't just one ward. There were three intertwined in a triangle over the square-shaped window.

My first goal was to untangle the threads binding the wards together, and then I could go about disassembling each one. I was looking at another hour of work, minimum, and that was if I didn't set one of them off.

I needed a bit of a break, so I descended the wall and met up with Waseem just outside the manor's walls.

"Done already?"

"No. The last one isn't a simple one-part ward. There are three overlapping in a triangle over the window. I'm going to need to do a lot of fine-tuned applications, and I need to be fully rested before I do."

Waseem didn't argue in the least bit and accepted my explanation. I had done the thieving thing in numerous other games, and any professional thief knows that exhaustion can be as detrimental to a job as noise can be.

Once I felt fully refreshed, I raced back up the tower, not having to worry anymore about the wards. Like Sally explained, the wards were still there, and they would look like they were still functioning to even the most trained. If you looked at it like a handgun, my work simply puts a small blocker between the firing pin and the primer on the end of the bullet. Both are still there, just no bang-bang.

I was slightly off in my calculations, and it took me a little less than an hour to finish with the wards. The trick was to separate each of the wards from the other, without breaking their links to each of the corners. Once that was done, I was able to peel them apart and disassemble their structures. With that completed, I descended again and grabbed Waseem.

I was shocked to find that the window was unlocked. Waseem explained that so few ever bothered to lock a window this high up, and even fewer bothered when there was such a powerful ward over the location.

Waseem entered first, and I followed behind. At least, I believe I followed behind, since we both had our Blacksuits on and I couldn't see through Waseem's Invis. My assumptions were proven true when I got through the window and saw Waseem standing in the center of the small enclosure, Blacksuit removed.

As Waseem walked over to a small desk to collect his contracted item, I started looking at the various items scattered throughout the room. There were numerous scrolls for spells, various weapons (although none that were daggers), and quite a few pieces of armor. I still hadn't seen anything that I wanted, so I moved over to a jewelry box containing several rings and earrings.

Waseem quickly located what he was looking for, placing what looked like a golden plate into one of his bags. As I continued to look, Waseem was separating various items that I had already looked through.

"What are you doing?"

"Some of this is trash. Some is good but not worth trying to transport out of here, and the rest is the loot. When you are done looking at those trinkets, I will add them to the pile. Trinkets always fit. Did you find something yet?"

"Yes and no. I found a ring that will give me the ability to instantly teleport to a certain place—my bind point—but only once every 24 hours. The fact that there is no cast time on it makes it a great addition for when I want one of my team to get out in a hurry and save themselves. And that would be our Cleric. If I were still traveling back and forth to the Keep nightly, I may have kept it for myself.

"The second item is another ring that will give me an increased boost of speed for a certain period of time. Great for running away from dire situations or moving quickly where I don't have my horse. Unfortunately, I rarely travel without my group, and I wouldn't see me ditching them. However, our Ranger often scouts ahead of us when we are traveling and looks for danger. This would benefit him greatly."

"Pity. Wouldn't get so roughed up if you took either of those rings."

"And that is why you have no friends, Waseem."

"Touché. Find anything else?"

"Just these," I said while pointing to two more pieces.

"The necklace?" Waseem asked, pointing to the piece sitting next to the Ring of Swiftness and Homebound Ring.

"For our Warrior. It will help him heal," I said while examining the piece. The Collar of Regeneration granted an increase of 10 to Constitution and improved the wearer's Regeneration rate by an additional 5 hit points every tick. I also wanted it for the comedic value. I giggled internally when I thought about the jokes the guys would make about Wayne's collar and Jenny's leash.

"And did you find anything for yourself, Alex?"

"Yeah. The last item is the one I'm leaning towards. How effective is Camouflage?"

"The spell?"

"Yeah. There is a ring here that will allow me to cast Camouflage on an unlimited number of people if they are in my group or raid party. The spell lasts for several hours, but it can only be cast once per day. Of course, if you get hit or take damage while wearing the camouflage, it will go away. If that happens, you have to wait the day to do it again."

"Anything with roads and buildings and it's worthless. Also, you must be able to blend in a bit with the surroundings. If you are wearing all black and standing on a snowbank, you aren't going to hide yourself. It's an aid to stay hidden, but it isn't an Invisibility spell."

"So unless you already have a full get-up of clothing for the area, you won't be able to move freely. What about a horse?"

"Nope. Camouflage and a horse do not go together at all. And don't worry about looking the part for your environment. I know a guy in the slums that can make you any dye you need for your gear. It will cost you, but you can stock up on all the colors you would need—from tundra, to forest, to desert."

Knowing Waseem, if he said it was going to be costly, it was going to run us dry. And just like that, our bank would likely be empty.

But the Camouflage spell could help us to get deep into enemy territory as long as we could avoid large settlements and roads while we traveled under the guise of the spell. We would have to walk it, but we could likely cover serious ground in the time we had.

"This work against undead, Waseem?"

"Hell no. The undead don't care what you wear. They just want to kill the living, and you will still stink like the living."

I thought it over some more and decided on the ring. Waseem gave me a quizzical look and shrugged his shoulders. "Your call, but there are quite a few items in here much better than that one. This being your first heist, I could show you."

"Appreciated. And I am shocked to say I actually mean that. This item, though, will be the most help to my group."

"I blame Dhalean for you being so soft."

The grizzled assassin being called "soft" would have sounded ludicrous coming from anyone else, but seeing Waseem's point, I decided to leave that comment unanswered.

I put the ring on my finger and headed toward the window. "Do me a favor and explain to me where I can find this vendor in the slums."

Waseem gave me the address, and an indicator for the location appeared on my Map. "You need me for anything else up here?"

"All's good. Thanks again for the assist, and I'll let you know if I come across any more jobs. We make a good team."

"Don't ever let Dhalean hear you say we did anything as a team, or he will open you from navel to neck." As I went out the window and started to Scale down the wall, I said over my shoulder, "Not saying I couldn't live with that, but I'd at least get a stern talking-to myself." Using my Skill, I saw that I wasn't leaving any marks on the wall as I descended.

This reminded me to check my Skill levels. With my adventures tonight, I had raised Scaling and Disassemble Wards to almost their max.

With nothing more keeping me in the game, I ran to the square and logged off for the night. The next day I would acquire loads of the dye, since I had no idea what lay in the blacked-out parts of the map, and lobby hard for the story-line quest.

I just needed to come up with a way to describe the item now resting on my finger and where I got it from.

AltCon Headquarters

"Mr. Henry, correct?"

"Yes sir, Mr. Jolston, Howard Henry."

"That was a good idea you had on launching a day for the family and significant others. I was impressed, as was the Old Man. Keep it up."

Henry smiled and nodded his head in appreciation. "Thank you, sir. I certainly will."

"What have you got for me now?"

Before Henry answered, he looked around in a conspiratorial way and angled his head toward one of the conference rooms that masked sound from the inside.

Jolston lifted an eyebrow and gave one of his patented looks that screamed "do you really want to be busting my balls right now?"

"It's important, sir," Henry said.

"Better be, Henry. You know I don't suffer fools."

Once the two had entered the soundproof room, Henry shaded the windows to an opaque color then passed Jolston a file.

The outside was plain, but the file tab listed the name "Napoleon."

Now Jolston's attention was piqued. Napoleon was the codename given to Travis Styles, a Special Agent working in the Corporate Concerns section of the FBI. More specifically, Napoleon was on the AltCon team.

It was quite the coup the day Styles walked into AltCon's headquarters and offered to be a mole within the FBI's Corporate Concerns section. Since then, members of AltCon's security team had been grooming Styles toward the AltCon account. Only a handful of people knew Napoleon's identity, but Jolston was one of them.

Jolston looked from the file and back to Henry saying, "Consider yourself vindicated, Mr. Henry. And know that I will always take time for this."

"Thank you, sir. I figured that would be the case," Henry said while opening the file and putting the report on the desk. "After my suggestion for 'Beta Appreciation Day,' I was contacted by the Security Office. They offered me a job working some unique cases, given my already high clearance from the beta. Napoleon is one of those cases, and this report just came in."

"Normally I would ask for the summary, but Napoleon is one of those I like to read through entirely," Jolston said as he sat. "Please, relax while I go through this."

Henry waited patiently while Jolston went through the missive. Henry had already read it, so he knew there wasn't much meat to the report. In fact, it led to a whole lot of questions without any answers.

"Well, Mr. Henry, what do you think?" Jolston said as he placed the report on the desk.

It was obvious Henry had no intention of missing this opportunity, and he had to remind himself to just play it straight and state the facts.

"It's odd, Mr. Jolston. This is the first time that we've seen an independent investigation for AltCon in all the years that Napoleon has been reporting to us. I also found it highly unusual that the investigators didn't state what their intent was, only that they wanted access to any and all information. Finally, and the most alarming, was the directive from the Director herself giving these Special Agents full support to their investigation, again, without saying at all what the investigation was."

"According to Napoleon."

"Yes, sir. This is all according to Napoleon and what he learned and reported."

"Has this been transmitted to the Old Man yet, Henry?"

"No, sir. I brought it to you straight away. It is customary for the Old Man to get a copy, but I wanted to give you first look and allow you to be ready if he wants a brief."

Jolston thought some more about the report he just read and decided he would speak to the Old Man about the situation. Jolston would be ready with his suggestions, but he would feel better with the guidance and wisdom of the Old Man.

"Excellent job, Henry. Security chose well with you," Jolston said as he put the report back in the folder and slid the entire thing over to Henry. "Anything else for me while we are here?"

"One other thing, sir. Kind of routine, though. As part of having a higher clearance, as I told you, I got the unique cases like Napoleon. I also was given some oversight to the Bates Motel."

Jolston was quite familiar with Bates Motel. It was a facility located away from AltCon headquarters, more than an hour's drive, and it held one of the most important pieces of information in AltCon's arsenal. There, AltCon hosted the code that allowed the conditioning of beta players to occur.

All of the traffic that came from Resurgence, or was pumped into the game, had to first be filtered through the code. That meant that the servers that housed the code, while simultaneously running the game in the background, had to be located together at some point. However, the more devious minds of the company thought ahead to the possibility that some agency could come and want to enact "regulatory" oversight on AltCon's business and review their servers and programming. Obviously, the code used to manipulate the minds of humans could not be out in the open.

The solution was the Bates Motel. A next generation fiber line ran from the AltCon headquarters to the Motel where the code and game were intertwined, then pumped back along the same fiber and out to the world. The fiber line itself would have been a huge money maker for AltCon, but it was peanuts compared to the rewards the conditioning would bring.

Any regulatory agency would be shown the servers, sans code, which took up two floors of AltCon's sub-basement. Even more servers were located on several additional sub-basement floors with a matching number at the Bates Motel.

The idea for the name of the facility was all the Old Man. He loved Hitchcock, and his favorite was always Psycho. The mystery of never knowing what exactly was happening behind the curtain.

"Is there an issue with the facility, Mr. Henry?"

"No, sir, not at all. One of our technicians from Emerging Products had to give her resignation due to an illness in her family. Appears her mom has been bedridden. Her boss, another guy that does some oversight of the Motel, came to me with it."

"You think she is a problem?"

"No, sir. Her mom lives 10 miles from the Motel. Her boss wants to offer her a job there. He gives her a glowing recommendation. Apparently, she was all tears when she said she had to quit."

Terrence Jolston reviewed the computer pad with the request for a compassionate reassignment to the Motel for one Emily Renart. She had impressed the hell out of her bosses, and Jolston had great respect for those with the compassion to drop everything for their family. He didn't hesitate checking approved before handing the pad back to Henry.

CHAPTER 20

December 6th, 2043

"We could do 'Rock, Paper, Scissors.'"

"Yeah, we could do that. Or, we could do a roll and decide that one through 50 is the arc quest and 51 through 100 is the next monastery."

I had walked up on Dan and Jason discussing which quest we would be taking next, with Dan naturally wanting to play "Rock, Paper, Scissors."

"What are your thoughts, Naugha?"

Wayne had not been focusing on the conversation between our groupmates and seemed at a loss as to what Jason was asking.

"For the next quest. You want to do the desert or Sir Arthur's?"

"I really don't care about which quest we do, truthfully. My only request is that we get to fight things. I don't want to be wandering through the desert for weeks, or hiding in a forest. I'm not the sneaky type."

"Then you guys are really going to hate my suggestion," I finally said, announcing my arrival to the group.

"If the next words out of your mouth have anything to do with an 'experiment,' I am demoting you from the leader position."

"First off, Dan, I'm not the leader of the group. Second, my experiments are awesome and helpful and you all know it. Third, you can stop shaking your head 'no,' Wayne. Lastly, this isn't one of my well thought-out, expertly-planned experiments."

"Oh good. It's one of your off-the-cuff, throw-us-all-in-the-meat-grinder experiments. Fuckin' tits!"

"Your lack of faith is disturbing, Wayne," I said while sharing a laugh with the guys. "Seriously, though, there is no experiment. I was going to make a pitch for the story quest, but it involves some sneaking."

Over the next 15 minutes, I explained my idea to the guys, of traveling through the unpopulated areas between us and the barony where the Frost Clan had holed up, all while using Camouflage.

I also had to explain how I got the Camouflage ring that we would be using. I had been less than truthful on multiple occasions with the guys when it came to hiding my Rogue skills. This was the first time I had outright lied to them with a whole story behind it. I didn't like doing it at all. The only upside is I planned to give them all great items before we left for the quest.

As we all got ready to head out for the story arc quest, I planned to stay back and talk to the Wanderer. In order to sell my reason for staying behind, namely buying the supplies we would need and going through the merchants and player-sellers to look for deals, I had decided to keep the items I got with Waseem in reserve. It's easy enough to say you are going to be carousing through the market place and trying to scoop up any good deals, but if I could provide actual proof in the form of new items, then there wouldn't be any doubt. I wasn't overly worried that my teammates believed I was secretly running off to talk to the embodiment of Resurgence's AI, but I was also slightly paranoid. Giving the items later made for a perfect balance in my mind.

"This was like Allibanger's side quest when he became a baron?"

"Yeah, similar to that. In this case, I had to use my Rogue Skills, like Conceal/Stealth, to sneak into places and perform tasks. It wasn't difficult. And honestly, I thought the quest's reward was kind of dumb at first. Why would you give a Rogue, the master of Invis, an item that only *kinda* makes them Invisible?"

"Agreed. That does sound lame," Dan said.

"It wasn't until I started thinking about our quest into enemy territory and how far we had to travel that I thought it could be effective. I started asking around and got a little more information about Camouflage," I said, taking out the ring to show the guys. "For starters, it's useless in an urban environment. Also, you need to blend with wherever you are going to be, so all black in the desert doesn't work."

"So how do we get around that?" Jason asked.

"Well, I remembered seeing a merchant that sold dyes for armor. They were way too expensive for the giggles of turning all of my armor the same color, so I hadn't ever purchased any. However, I learned you can dye your armor to match the terrain you are in. Green for forest and the like. What do you guys think?"

"Personally, I like the idea," Dan said. "We can be relatively invisible, and I can feel safer ranging out in front of us."

"Didn't I just say I didn't want to avoid fighting?"

"Yes, Wayne. And I have no doubt there will be loads of fighting to do. I was thinking more about using this when we needed it, to really get around a situation we can't handle. Dan's normal method for staying ahead of us should be enough warning for when we need to don the Camo."

"Well, then, I'm good with it, too."

"I do want to note, however, that we should make it a point to move a good distance every day. I don't really know how far, but enough that it doesn't take us forever to get to our destination. If we haven't used our charge of camouflage that day, that would be the time to do so."

"That makes sense, and I don't want to be stuck in Loust country for very long, either. Dying out there would be a very unpleasant corpse run," Wayne said.

"That just leaves you, Allister. Thoughts?"

"I'm already outvoted, but I would ask that we at least go out into the forest around the Keep and try the Camo out. We don't want our first experience to be in hostile territory."

Jason's eyes got a bit wide when he saw me smile more than was really necessary at his comment, followed by the look of panic on the faces of Dan and Wayne. "What? What did I do?"

"Are you insane, man? You just told Alex you wanted him to do an experiment!"

That got Jason's attention, and he started looking quickly between where I was standing and where Dan and Wayne were located. He whipped his head back and forth several times like he was watching one of the fastest tennis matches in history.

I finally lost it and started laughing deep from my belly. "I absolutely love the Pavlovian response you guys get to even the hint of the word 'experiment.'"

"Shut up, Alex," Dan said. "You just ring the bell and give me my food."

The Camouflage was a general success. We had our friends come and try to find us in the woods located outside of the city. As long as we stayed in the woods, and wore our green-tinted clothing, none of our teammates could see us.

If we went closer to the main roads, however, we were spotted. More than that, the landscape itself played an intricate role in the success or failure of the Camouflage. When Dan stood in one spot between the tree line and the road, he was visible to anyone standing in the trees and looking out toward the road, but he was totally hidden to anyone that was standing on the road. I loved that about Resurgence; it didn't simply take a mechanism and say it works in one place but not another. You had to think about how you would use the tools you had at hand.

I was thankful that none of my teammates had taken the Rogue class, otherwise I would have had a really hard time explaining how to get the "Camouflage Quest" that I sold to Dan, Jason, and Wayne. As it was, Gary and Jenny were both heading into the city to see if they could find a similar quest for their classes. If they found anything, that would be great. If they didn't, I could always blame it on being a beta and possibly not having all the quests available yet.

The experiment had worked to everyone's satisfaction, and I filled up on dyes. Each dye worked on one piece of equipment and each application only lasted one day. We all wore eight pieces of gear that would need to be dyed. So for one day, that would be 32 individual dyes and I planned for us to be out for two weeks, totaling 448 dye packets for just one color for all four of us.

My theory was that we would be in some kind of forest. On the other hand, it could be that soon after we left, the area turned into a tundra or a winter landscape. I didn't suspect that was the case, but I wanted to be prepared. I also knew that the dyes could come in handy down the road even if we didn't use the specific colors on this particular quest.

I ended up getting multiple colors, and it cost us over 10 Platinum. It didn't bleed us dry, but I was glad that I controlled our finances and didn't have to tell the group how much we just spent. It also helped that our second round of "dividends" from the East Range Mountain Clan had arrived on December 1st. The production of Fermium and Ertunium was going well, and our little supply of Mithral was kicking in. Where we first got 37 Gold, we all ended up with 1 Platinum and 50 Gold this second time around.

The only saving grace was that each packet was ridiculously tiny, and the packets only took up three slots in our bags, as they stacked 200 each per similar color. For that reason, we all carried the full amount of a specific color. I had the 400 plus packets for green, Jason had white, and so forth. This saved us one inventory slot per person, but seeing as we would be out for an unknown amount of time, every inventory slot was really going to count.

Like I said before, since we knew we would be gone for a while, I planned on talking to the Wanderer before we left. I could always call him out to me, like I did at the Monastery of Might, but that came with risk.

Even though I was happy that we were proceeding with the story arc quest first, I was still concerned about the third Lady Tessa quest. I didn't like using the Wanderer, but I'd done it in the past when we needed money for our new gear. I was going to ask for his help on this task, too, because "go to the desert" was a completely shit way to prepare for the quest.

"Alright, gentlemen, I suggest we take the next day or two to make sure we are as fully stocked up as we can be. Dan, I imagine you would like to take some time to hit the Elven Elder tree and grab some supplies for arrow shafts?"

"Yeah, Alex. I'm also overdue for my first batch of Mithral and Ertunium arrowheads. Any chance one of you guys can make a run to the dwarves and pick them up?"

"I got your back," Wayne said. "I want to see how the defenses are coming along at the mine as well."

"And Allister, I suspect you will go off and do something sneaky like you did with the baron title?"

"Says the guy who just got himself a new ring."

"Touché. Let me know if there is anything I can do to help anyone out. Otherwise, I'm going to try and see what is going on in the market and if there are any good deals we can come across before we leave. How much time do we think we need to get all set up and ready to go?"

"I've got the farthest to go," Dan said. "And since I can't just Gate back to the Keep, I'd say let's make it one full day and then play it from there."

"I'd go for you, Dan, but without the Fletching Skill, I can't even collect the wood at the tree."

"It's much appreciated, Allitruistic. Alex, could you pick up the supplies I will need for Broham?"

"Done and done. Let's say the rest of today and one more full day to get everything finished. Be back at Sir Arthur on Tuesday morning at 1000?"

With no argument to be had, we all went our separate ways, and I headed toward the Underground.

"Welcome, Alex. Have you any new information about the code? I fear that with each day that passes, the chances of us finding the source diminish exponentially."

"I don't think that's how it works, and I'm pretty sure you can't feel fear."

"True on both counts, but Robert programmed me to emulate many human emotions and use colloquial sayings to strengthen those responses."

"Man, my buddy Dan would love to meet you then," I told the Wanderer. "He would give you a lesson or two on just why those sayings are ridiculous."

"I've monitored your interactions since you entered Resurgence, Alex. I am aware of your comrade TheClaw and his unique way of looking at things; however, I am sure you didn't come here to banter about with me in the Underground. My original question still stands; have you learned anything new about the code?"

"I am afraid not."

"Pity, indeed. Then what can I help you with?" the Wanderer asked.

"I'm going to be outside Kich's Keep for a while. My team is undertaking the House Frost quest and we'll be deep inside the enemy's lines. I know that I can call on you at any time, but I don't like doing so. I figured I could swing through here and see if there was anything we needed to talk about before I left. Also, I have a question for you about the Lady Tessa quest that is due up for us when we return."

"As far as having anything to discuss, there is nothing at this time. I am thankful you came to see me before you left though, as I too would prefer to avoid the summoning option for our meetings."

"I have to admit, Wanderer, that if I didn't know any better I would think you really were 'thankful' about the whole thing. You do a good job of mimicking those emotions.

"Now, on to my other question. As you know, we are starting the next quest for Lady Tessa soon, but all of the information that we have is terribly vague. We are supposed to go to the desert and contact the Jalusi Tribe. They, in turn, should be able to help us find this monastery."

"That is how I've seen it, yes."

"Well, we don't have any desire to search through the desert with no clues as to where we should go. I figured since time is an issue, I would ask you for a bit of help on this one."

"And yet, I can't offer you any."

"Wait. What?" I asked.

"I would, if I had any. However, the Jalusi Tribe, also known as the 'Nomads of the Globi,' won't spawn into existence until you set foot in the desert. It was a mechanism Robert liked to use to ensure players couldn't map out the routes of quest NPCs. Each time an individual arrived at this portion of the quest, a game inside the game would begin. No other players would be able to interact with your specific Jalusi Tribe NPCs, as no other players would be able to see them. It would be the same for you, if anyone could have started this quest."

"That's... that's genius!"

The Wanderer simply nodded his head.

"So then, we are on our own for figuring out the whole thing?"

"Not quite. You still have an advantage with Della of the Glade. She owes you a favor."

The Wanderer said it as a statement, not a question. That was yet another reminder that he was following our progress through the game and keeping track of everything.

I nodded my head, and the Wanderer continued.

"Speak with Della about your desire to travel into the desert. Tell her you are requesting her aid to locate one of the old monasteries and she will guide you to a settlement just inside the Globi Desert."

"They will be able to tell us where the Jalusi Tribe is?"

"No. The Jalusi are nomads, after all. They could be anywhere in the desert. That being said, the settlers will ensure you are protected in the desert from the elements in addition to providing opportunities to learn more through conversations, based upon what previous quests you've been given. It's unclear, even to me, what their dialogue may be. Much of the game is based on your actions, and your good will from Della is likely to open up dialogue chains that others would not receive."

"This settlement isn't a part of Lady Tessa's quest?"

"No. They are similar to the NPCs you encountered at the Mill. They can assist you in your journeys and perhaps provide information. You see, anyone can visit that Mill and get the special cloaks and map. Only your group, however, could have possibly received the information regarding Lady Tessa's quest."

"Got it. That all makes sense. Although it isn't the answer I wanted, it's at least a start for when we return."

"With Della's aid, it should make the undertaking easier, although there is certainly no reason to think it will be easy, seeing as it is the third in a very difficult quest chain."

"Oh, I don't think it will be easy at all. So far, we have been really lucky with the monasteries. I would be a fool to believe that will hold out. The first and second bosses almost killed us despite how easily we cleared the monasteries. If we encounter a set of mobs that prove to be truly challenging, I could easily see us having to return to leveling before finishing the quest."

"Indeed. That would be a waste of time for you, your teammates, and for our own mission."

"Exactly. Which is why I hoped you wouldn't be upset that I was continuing on the story arc and not immediately starting the next part of Lady Tessa's quest."

"No, Alex. I think the quest you have chosen is more beneficial to our goal, as it were. In the desert, you could search for quite some time, even with the aid of Della and the settlers, in order to find the nomads. As it is a desert, you would be less likely to encounter mobs and certainly less players and NPCs. The part you play now in the storyline will provide far more opportunities for discovery on the nature of the code."

"Those were my thoughts as well. Thank you, Wanderer."

"Think nothing of it, Alex."

I walked around the inside of the Wanderer's cave for a bit and looked at the tapestries hanging on the wall. They depicted ancient battles between knights and dragons. I knew it was all code and that the Wanderer could change it with a thought, but it felt like a part of the game. As far as that went, I felt like a part of the game as well.

I had spent far more time inside Resurgence than my teammates, and I had interacted with NPCs that I believed were driven by a far more powerful AI than the normal NPCs.

Stan, Waseem, and Sally were nothing like the normal NPCs we encountered. You could still have full blown conversations with the regular NPCs and they wouldn't repeat sayings or statements, but it felt a bit contrived. With my Rogue teachers, they seemed more... I don't know, alive.

"I know the ramifications of what we are doing are bigger than just a game, but I can't help but think about what's happening inside this world. I freely admit that I've grown attached to some of the NPCs."

"Naturally. The whole concept behind building a virtual world like this, with the addition of the RACs, was to get the players to feel a sense of ownership for the land. Robert always wanted the men and women who took part in the game to care about what happened to the people of Tholtos."

"Yeah. That's what I mean. I definitely feel that. So while I'm collecting information, trying to find the code, and getting better gear, I keep thinking about the game and the story line. I know these MMORPGs don't have true 'endings.' They can go on forever with the promise of never ending expansions and new gear."

The Wanderer nodded. "You will not see any of those things during the beta, but I am sure you are correct. AltCon will have an entire timeline set for introducing new content to expand their player base.

"As far as the beta is concerned, the one-year timeline provided for playing the game does provide enough time to the most advanced players to reach the final storyline quests."

"I'm sure it does. And I have no doubt it will be a multi-group event, because it is going to take one hell of a raid to finish off the Children of Loust. There is no way any single group could possibly beat Riff, not with everything Arthur and Kenyon were saying about him."

"I'm sorry, Alex. Of whom do you speak?"

I had been continuing my walk around the cave while I was exchanging dialogue with the Wanderer. I turned to look at him now.

"Riff. Supreme Overlord of the Children of Loust Army. Nine-foot-tall walking death. Riff Lifestealer."

The Wanderer continued to stare at me for several seconds before saying, "I'm sorry, Alex, but I have absolutely no data about anyone by that name in the game."

My memory is nothing like Dan's, but I have pretty good recall most of the time. And at that moment, several things were flitting across my mind.

> *"The unstoppable force that is Supreme Overlord Riff Lifestealer has been the cause of much heartache for His Majesty..."*
>
> *"...fighting the horde of Loust and their fiendish commander, Riff."*
>
> *"Overlord Riff has already brought the mood to an all-time low as our forces are repelled single-handedly by this brute..."*
>
> *"By the end of the day, all that was left around Supreme Overlord Riff was a puddle of blood extending meters out from his location. And it did not look like any of it was his."*

And just like that, I realized how screwed we were if destroying the code meant destroying the person or item it inhabited.

"Fuck me."

"Alex?"

"Well, I've got good news and bad news. I'm pretty sure I've figured out the code."

"And is that the good or the bad?"

"Both."

THE END OF RESTORATION
THE RISE OF RESURGENCE (BOOK II)

THE STORY WILL CONTINUE IN:

REDEMPTION

THE RISE OF RESURGENCE (BOOK THREE)

THANKS FOR READING!

I truly hope you had as much fun reading this book as I had writing it. While this book took longer to write than I had planned, I really felt that I found my voice and I wrote a better book for you, the reader. The byproduct of my enjoyment ended up being even more material to work with and a book longer than the first. I want to keep the story as a classic trilogy, so look forward to a short story or novella in the future as I put all this new material into the Resurgence universe.

PLEASE LEAVE A REVIEW!

I echo every other author out there, I know, but the reviews are so important to getting our stories noticed by Amazon. There has been a push to have LitRPG as its own genre, and the more stories with large numbers of reviews, the more likely Amazon will recognize our request. And I can tell you it was the feedback from the first book that made this second one a better story, both the positive and negative.

Finally, if you have enjoyed this book and want to interact with the authors of this genre and find more stories like this one, please check out these LitRPG groups, A LitRPG site and the LitRPG Society site.

ACKNOWLEDGEMENTS

I'd like to thank the great people who helped me along the way to making this second book. I wouldn't have been able to come out with a final product like this without all of their help. Thank you for all that you did!

- Dustin Frost (Editor)
- Rachael Johnston (Artist)
- Maureen Cutajar (Formatter)
- Terisa Rupp
- Stanley Justin
- Daniel Hamman
- Brenda B. Davis
- Cecilia Foust
- JD Williams
- Jason Wayne Wong
- Wayne Whitlock
- Jason David Geer
- Treb Padula

I HOPE YOU ENJOYED MY STORY!

I would like to introduce you to Aleron Kong, one of the founders of American LitRPG. He has written six best selling books in his best-selling series The Land. In his own words it's like "Warcraft, DnD and Sword Art Online had a sexy baby!" With over TEN THOUSAND positive reviews you can't go wrong!